MW01196459

HISTORY LESSONS

ZOE B. WALLBROOK

Published by Soho Press
Soho Press, Inc.
227 W 17th Street
New York, NY 10011
www.sohopress.com

Copyright © 2025 by Taumralyn, LLC.
All rights reserved.

Library of Congress Cataloging-in-Publication Data

Names: Wallbrook, Zoe B. author
Title: History lessons / Zoe B. Wallbrook.
Description: New York, NY : Soho Crime, 2025.
Identifiers: LCCN 2025005899

ISBN 978-1-64129-552-9
eISBN 978-1-64129-553-6

Subjects: LCGFT: Detective and mystery fiction | Campus fiction | Novels
Classification: LCC PS3623.A4445 H57 2025 | DDC 813/.6—dc23/
eng/20250305
LC record available at https://lccn.loc.gov/2025005899

Interior design by Janine Agro
Interior illustration: © Mlle Belamour

Printed in the United States

10 9 8 7 6 5 4 3 2 1

EU Responsible Person (for authorities only)
eucomply OÜ
Pärnu mnt 139b-14
11317 Tallinn, Estonia
hello@eucompliancepartner.com
www.eucompliancepartner.com

For Joel, who makes our life possible.

To Erica.
This is all your fault.

PROLOGUE

Sam Taylor had five minutes to decide how he wanted to die. In the living room, bleeding out on a rug, gazing into the cold, indifferent eyes of an enemy. Or on the run, making it no farther than the outer hedges of his backyard before being struck down like a hunted pheasant.

The doorknob jiggled louder this time, rattling the gold chain on the doorframe and whatever was left of Sam's nerves along with it. That gold chain was the only thing keeping Sam alive, and that one simple fact plunged his body into ice-cold fear, numbing the tips of his shaking fingers as they pressed against his temples.

Sam scoured the den's bookshelves and thick pillows, eyes wild, before landing on a poker leaning up against the fireplace. As if thin, hard metal could be the difference between life and death. As if he wouldn't get laughed at right in his face.

Will they bury my body when it's over?

No.

They'd cremate it. He'd heard the rumors. The facility was an arsonist's dream. Tracing would be impossible. Sure, there'd be human DNA inside those ovens, but whose? It would take a decade of subpoenas before the cops figured out if his body was among those vacuumed into the sky.

Boots shuffled behind the door.

Swallowing back the sour tang of bile stinging his throat,

he reached for his laptop and began the purge, blinking at the bright fluorescent screen as his data drained away along with what little time he had left on this planet. All of the evidence, gone. Untouchable. Untraceable. Unknowable. His life's work—for what? To prove what?

The scrape of metal on the doorknob jolted Sam away from his laptop. They were almost inside. Death was so close he could reach across the living room and touch it. There were no plays left to make. It was over. Wasn't it?

A voice, small and soft, offered a solution, however outrageous. *Call her.*

He grabbed his phone and dialed the memorized number before he could change his mind.

"Hello, you've reached the voicemail of—"

He hung up. Tried again.

"Hello, you've reached the—"

Another redial.

"Hello, you've—"

He hurled his phone into the couch with the velocity of a Yankees pitcher. "Fuck."

He plunged his head between his thighs, squeezing blond tufts of hair with tight fists, enjoying the pain stinging his eyes while he hiccupped out a few short breaths.

A thought struck his chest with the force of a baseball bat. *I can still tell her.*

He'd never wanted her to know. But if he phrased it right, he could lead her to the truth. Only she was smart enough to figure it out anyway. To take the data and run. To finish what he'd started. And then the world would finally know. There was little glory to be found in these last minutes of life but there might be honor in his death.

Sam grabbed his phone one last time. His thumbs flew across its screen. And just before the squeaking "pop" of a door hinging, before the rush of hard boots stormed his hallway, before rough hands groped his neck, before his bloodied face hit the rug, before the world went black forever, Sam hit send.

CHAPTER ONE

"Well, that went terribly."

Daphne Ouverture, assistant professor of European history, scholar of modern French imperialism, and semiprofessional rambler on the horrors of colonial medicine, slammed her car door shut.

"What are we talking about here on a scale of one to five?" The car's Bluetooth speakers took over, brightening Elise's light soprano. "One being that time you set your date's shirtsleeve on fire with a candle—"

"That was an accident," Daphne muttered. "We went on like two more dates after that."

"—and five being when you went out with that silver *fox* of a man who was super into you only for you to realize at dinner that he was the dad of one of your students?"

Daphne cringed while she maneuvered her car onto the road. No wonder she'd banned dating in Calliope.

"I wouldn't say that date was a complete bust, though." Elise's grin was audible. "That guy was hot. Like if George Clooney was a rugby coach?"

"Elise, you're one of my bestest friends on the planet but I beg you. Please stop. Remembering this is so horrifying I can't drive straight." Daphne's short, chunky braids tickled the nape of her neck as she shuddered. "That's what I get for thinking I could just casually flirt with somebody in the cereal aisle."

"You can totally flirt, babe." Elise, as always, chose to see sunshine, puppies, and free SZA tickets where there was scorched earth. "You just gotta do it with the right person. And your Bumble date tonight, Ricky—he wasn't it."

Daphne slowed her car at a red light. "Nope."

If only that DM hadn't pinged during an especially boring faculty meeting, a month after she'd finally given up on dating, Daphne wouldn't be driving back home on a Saturday night strapped into a dress so tight she'd need the jaws of life later to wrest herself free from it. But the Asianists had decided to wade into the department's Sisyphean struggle to determine whether the Modern Istanbul survey course counted toward the European or Middle Eastern history minor for undergraduate students, thus locking horns, yet again, with the director of undergraduate studies, whose task it was to assign this designation for the next academic year. Daphne was only a first-year professor at Harrison University—a Bambi in the eyes of her colleagues—but even she'd lost all hope that the meeting could be salvaged once her colleague began to explain in precise detail the long history of translocal mail runners on the Silk Road. Ten minutes into the diatribe, a giggling panic had bubbled up in her chest at the realization that she'd locked herself into this career for the next thirty years.

She'd reached for her phone as if it was a life raft on the Lusitania, desperate to prove that there was more to her future at Harrison University than fights over the Mongolian postal system. And there he was, this stud named Ricky who had promised her dinners and front-row seats to whatever her heart desired. Daphne found the thin, hard shell she'd built up for herself begin to melt like the chocolate flan he swore he'd make her from scratch. She didn't know what she hated more—wanting to feel wanted, or not being able to remember the last time someone had.

She'd been on enough dinner dates to know that the profile picture rarely matched the man. But lo and behold, the Ricky she'd met in the overstuffed restaurant appeared to be as dashing in person as he'd been on her phone screen. He'd swooped down to give her a peck on the cheek—and, she noticed, to check out her décolletage—oozing sex, adventure, and expensive aftershave. His scheming, twinkling brown eyes promised her a passionate night if she wanted it. And for the first time in a long time, she thought she might.

Not for the last time, Daphne cursed the Mongols.

"Did he like your story about Belgium, at least?" Elise asked.

"You mean how nineteenth-century Belgian colonial administrators in the Congo dismembered indigenous Africans for the purpose of scaring local villagers into creating profit for their newly emerging rubber industry?" Daphne gripped her steering wheel a bit too tight while changing lanes. "No, Elise, it turns out that explaining the evils of late-nineteenth-century European imperialism on a first date isn't exactly a seductive move."

After her lengthy side quest into tooth extraction practices in the French Caribbean, Ricky had, understandably, become engrossed in his steak. He'd only lifted his eyes from his plate once—at 6 P.M., to ask the waitress for the check.

Elise's voice softened. "You'll find somebody, Daph. I know you will."

"Will I?" Daphne asked, doubtfully.

"Absolutely, friend," Elise replied. "You're just going through those first-year blues."

That was one term for it.

Driving up the ramp onto the highway, Daphne could think

of a few others. Starting this tenure-track gig at Harrison University wasn't what she'd imagined. She had been elated when she got the phone call from the chair of the history department offering her the job. For the first semester, she'd floated around on campus in a daze, still not comprehending that *she'd done it*, damnit, *she'd really done it.* A job, fresh out of grad school—and at one of the most elite institutions in the United States, to boot? Barely a quarter of newly minted history PhD students landed any kind of tenure-track job at all. Eight months in and Daphne was a model of academic success, boasting a contract with a top university press to write her book on Black families in eighteenth-century France, a shiny new teaching award on her desk next to her favorite Josephine Baker coloring book, and a grant application to study in France that she was sure to win. Then the nagging feeling had set in like the gray clouds that loomed over campus the whole month of March.

Is this it?

Is this my life?

"You know," Daphne said, clearing the catch in her throat, "I generally don't mind my new life. I mean, I'm basically a crazy cat lady."

"That's not true," Elise corrected her. "You're a crazy *dog* lady."

Daphne's lips tugged into a smile. "Fine. But the same lesson applies. I'm either up to my eyeballs in course prep on campus or I'm at home with Chloe. My parents complain that I live like a hedgehog but they've accepted that my world is smaller than theirs. I thought I was fine with my life, too."

"And I'm sure most of the time you are," Elise said. "But let's face it, honey. You're smart, funny, beautiful—"

"Ha."

"—and bored."

"I'm pretty sure I'm too exhausted to be bored," Daphne said. "How about lonely?"

"That, too."

"Men don't have these problems," Daphne grumbled. "Wait, that's not true. At least none of the men *I* know have these problems."

As far as she could tell, men in academia fell into two categories: They either went for someone so closely aligned to their own research that the couple became the disciplinary equivalent of siblings, or they chose to marry women with the intellectual aspirations of a house cat. Daphne didn't want to date anyone at Harrison University—the thought of a colleague's lips on hers made her recoil—but she couldn't understand why most guys on dating apps were so put off by nerdy women like her. Most of the time, Daphne was so invisible she might as well have slapped a window decal on her forehead to prevent birds from smacking into her.

"We have become the men we wanted to marry," Gloria Steinem once said, but guess what? Men kept getting married anyway. And Daphne was just out here collecting books and bubble pens and coffee mugs that said "Best Dog Mom" on them and dodging Harrison University's awkward singles mixers for professors—which, let's face it, usually meant drinking pinot grigio at a sad, makeshift bar in a dining hall and gossiping university politics with some unpartnered queer folks while a few straight women circled around the one eligible bachelor like hammerhead sharks.

Daphne pulled off the highway, snapping out of her gloom in time to hear Elise say, "You'll find someone who loves you exactly for who you are, Daphne. I know it."

"Thanks, Mom."

"I mean it!"

Daphne said goodbye to Elise as she entered downtown Calliope, the university town that she'd chosen to call home. Off-tune carillon bells from the top of Harrison's bell tower clanged to life seven times, their chimes ignored by students lounging on tiny chairs and even tinier tables outside of Office Hours coffee shop, even though the last rays of the cold April sun weren't warm enough to justify such summery behavior. A barista was scrubbing off a fresh splash of graffiti from the café's panel window right as Daphne slowed her car to a stop at a red light. She squinted to read the fluorescent orange feminist prose—the Femmes Fatales, Calliope's renegade anonymous feminist flash mob, had struck again. A skateboarder whooshed past this week's visual attack against the patriarchy, holding some book on Heideggerian philosophy in one arm and his fluffy white cat in the other—which had been cause for consternation the first time Daphne'd encountered it. Now it had become daily life.

Feeling a bit more chipper, Daphne pulled into the tiny garage in front of her house, drawing instant comfort at the sight of her Victorian cottage. It was tucked away into the corner of a hundred-acre park like a secret—*her* secret—and as she jangled her keys in the door, she joyfully breathed in the sea of lilac, purple, and periwinkle flowers that she'd planted out front.

Daphne caught a mouthful of furry limbs and soft, kissable ears as soon as she opened the door. She buried her nose in Chloe's black velvet fur. Who needed shitty men when there were perfectly good rescue dogs?

While Chloe scampered outside to do her business, Daphne lifted her chin up to the darkening sky. She took her phone out to check for any calls she'd missed while on her plane crash of a date—and tilted her head at the bright notification on her screen.

Sam Taylor had called her? Four times?

That was weird.

She'd forgotten they'd swapped numbers. Or why. Sam was two years ahead of her on the tenure track at Harrison and in anthropology, a completely different department. She'd wisely chosen to avoid spending time with anthropologists in grad school after learning just what, exactly, ethnographic fieldwork entailed. Honestly it just seemed like a whole lot of grant writing and university-approved stalking.

Daphne looked up from her phone just in time to catch Chloe rolling and wiggling in the grass, paws extended in the cold night air. At least, she hoped it was grass. Chloe was an excellent dog who never jumped on people and never barked, but she sure loved to roll in smelly things. Anything at all, really. On one memorable walk, she had stopped, sniffed, and then rolled on an everything bagel.

Four times?

Maybe they were butt dials. Lord knows she'd done that before, the last time to the chair of her department while throwing her back out to Beyoncé's *Renaissance*.

Sam's text message put that hypothesis to rest.

Le chinois inventer l'eau sur la tête. Le Français inventer le silence.

"What in the shitty-ass French . . . ?"

She stared at the jumble of letters. Why was Sam texting her about Chinese people in barely passable French? That felt weirdly racist in a way she couldn't pinpoint yet.

The LCD screen of her cell phone went black in the time that Daphne's thumbs floated over it while she debated how to respond, if she even wanted to. If she was being honest with herself, all she really wanted was to put her bad date behind her and crawl into pajamas, not subject herself to an anthropology professor's whims.

You okay? Daphne texted in spite of herself.

Chloe bounded back into the house, eager for her dinner, her post-dinner snack, and a belly rub or three, and Daphne shoved her phone back into her coat pocket and followed behind, praying Sam wouldn't text her back. Obligation may have forced her to send that message but that didn't mean she wanted an answer.

ONLY AN hour later, when she and Chloe had begun to nod off in front of the muted tones of her television, did Daphne convince herself to let that text message go. Sam had probably texted the wrong person. And even if he hadn't, he obviously couldn't be bothered to tell her what he'd meant about the French and their supposedly soundless behavior anyway. That just showed her how few French people Sam had met.

Move on, Daph. "Don't go looking for drama where none exists," had been her mantra during those political days of graduate school. It had helped her sidestep ancient battles between even more ancient professors and avoid social situations that suggested even a hint of compromise. The only way to emerge unscathed from the "DEI-charity case" label white students had derisively slapped on her during those early years had been to become invisible except on the page. She liked to believe the purity of her dissertation, "Family Matters: Race, Gender, and the Making of Black Families in Eighteenth-Century France," had saved her from being gobbled up by the leviathan of malice that hunted for Black women in academia's hallways.

"Keep your head down," she mumbled, half asleep. There were classes to teach, papers to grade, another faculty meeting to endure. Swiping at her screen, Daphne deleted Sam's text message and dropped her phone back on her nightstand. She needed a clean slate tomorrow—that's what tomorrows were for, after all. And what was it that Elise was always telling her? "You're a history prof, hon, so you know better than anyone—life's for the living."

Ha. Daphne turned in her sleep. As a historian she preferred spending her time with the dead over the living. At least the dead never sassed her back or asked why she was still single. Her mood darkened. If only, she thought glumly, the dead could teach her how to live.

CHAPTER TWO

S even. She counted seven of them. Different sizes, different shapes, colors. If Detective Asma Ahmed cared enough about dogs she'd probably be able to tell them apart better. But instead she saw only short ones and fat ones, long ones and skinny ones, floppy ears or straight and taut, squat muzzles, long snouts.

Smoking.

Drinking beer.

Playing poker.

"God, what a strange painting," Asma muttered, staring at the canvas covered in dark velvety greens, muted grays, and teddy-bear browns. She must have seen the painting before, maybe on some poster advertisement slapped on a bus bench somewhere or at her husband's garage. Didn't make it less weird. She could feel herself frown, her lips pinching. Her mother's voice rang clear in her mind: *If you're not careful, this is how you'll ruin your face.*

"*A Friend in Need*," a quiet baritone offered. "By C. M. Coolidge, an American painter of the early twentieth century."

Asma turned away from the painting to find the world's skinniest giant peeling off his windbreaker. Standing a head above the army of crime scene techs dusting for prints around what usually must have been a very inviting living room, he folded the thin jacket, polite as ever, and dutifully turned it over to Kimmie, an intern tasked with supervising all storage.

Asma's eyebrows jumped so high they were practically crawling on the ceiling. "You showed."

Rowan Peterson covered his long brown shoes with the requisite blue disposable booties so he could finally step onto the carpet. His tousled black hair nearly touched the ceiling once he stood at full height. Hands on his bony hips, he peered at Asma through thin metal frames, his soft gray eyes curious, wary. "I did."

It had been fourteen months since Rowan had quit the police force to open a bookstore in Calliope. Fourteen months since he'd renounced policing as a public good altogether. And while he still came over weekly to eat her husband's grilled kebabs and read books to her three boys, his gentle, slow-moving walk was no longer recognizable to her within the context of a crime scene. Even though she was the one who'd asked him to come, seeing him now felt too peculiar, a little bit like running into your dentist at the grocery store.

Asma didn't move. Couldn't. "I thought you wouldn't come."

"Me, too," Rowan admitted. He slipped to the side to let a crime scene tech pass by cradling a tray of empty vials. "But you said that I'd find this case intriguing and that—more importantly—you required '*A Friend in Need*.'"

Asma stared at him.

Rowan's face fell. "The painting?"

"Oh, I get the joke," Asma replied, her shoulders loosening. "I just thought it was corny."

"There's no accounting for taste, I suppose," Rowan said.

"Whatever, Encyclopedia Brown," said Asma. "You wanna talk about the dead body on the floor or not?"

Rowan followed her eyes downward, his smile faltering. A

man lay on the scarlet and lapis oriental rug. His sleeping position would be so snug, Asma mused, if it didn't require breathing.

Scattered around him were books. In fact, everywhere Asma looked, she saw books. Some shoved into the floor-to-ceiling bookcases against a living room wall, their spines turned upside down, some laid open on the walnut-brown coffee table, others heaped up in piles on the floor.

Rowan pulled out a small black notebook—old habits died hard—and waved a hand for Asma to begin. "Details?"

Asma nodded. "The victim's a white male, thirty-two years old. His name is Samuel James Taylor."

Rowan's entire lithe frame froze. "The anthropology professor at Harrison?"

"Now you know why I called you," Asma said, damned if she could keep the pride out of her voice.

Whatever color his already pale face held disappeared. "He's famous, Asma. A rising star in academia, interviews on NPR, CNN, and the like. Did you read that profile on him in the *New York Times*?"

"The only thing I get to read for fun these days is Roald Dahl to the boys," Asma said.

"He researched the prison industrial complex and its perpetuations of violence and social inequality," Rowan said. "His writings were inspirational—transformative, even. They'd certainly buttressed my own developing beliefs."

Those beliefs, however much they'd caused a minor rift in the Calliope PD, were exactly why she'd asked Rowan to join this case. With her three boys, her husband, and her sprawling Iraqi family, Asma could barely keep her head above water as it was. She was excellent at her work but had little time for anything else outside of her job, at least until her kids were older. Back when Asma and Rowan had been partners, she'd relied on Rowan's passion for reading to expand her own thinking on cases. He'd see the facts differently, more sensitively, than any other detective on the force. His love of books had led him onto the force and out again.

Rowan tapped his pen against his little black notebook. "Medical report?"

"Jason Markham said the victim died between seven and eight o'clock," Asma replied. "No official cause of death yet but it sure looks like blunt force trauma to the head."

Asma knelt over the pool of sticky, almost opulent blood, gleaming in the light of a corner lamp. The victim's thick blond hair, carefully styled in lush waves, was matted in the back where the skull was cracked in.

She handed Rowan a pair of rubber gloves. "Time to see what's on the other side."

Together, they carefully rolled the victim onto his back. Even with the pallor of death settling into Sam Taylor's skin, his movie-star features were obvious: a strong jaw, slim nose, well-arched brows. Judging by his trim torso and bulging arm muscles, he lifted weights.

Rowan frowned. "His eyes."

Asma nodded. Purple, mottled bruising covered them both, swelling them shut. Under the eyebrows, thin skin had expanded to make room for burst vessels and puffed flesh.

Rowan carefully inspected the victim's right hand before following suit with the left. "No sign of bruises on the victim's knuckles or lacerations on his hands."

"Yup," Asma said. "And this dude was clearly strong enough to fight back. So why didn't he? Even if the fatal blow came from behind, whoever knocked him out like that attacked him in plain view."

"Bruises on his neck, too," Rowan said, tracing with his finger a deep blue path of rough skin on the victim's throat.

"But Jason doubts that strangulation is what killed him," Asma warned.

"Fair enough." Rowan pushed his glasses back up the bridge of his nose. "Wallet?"

"Back pocket," Asma said. "Driver's license intact, health insurance cards, a membership to the most expensive gym in town, cash."

"So this was no robbery," Rowan murmured. "Cell phone?"

Asma shrugged. "No one's found it yet."

Rowan stood up. He stared at the dead body in silence for several minutes, frowning. She knew what he was thinking. It rattled her, too, that missing phone. Nothing else taken but the phone?

Rowan shifted on his feet. "I wonder how he chose to organize his books."

"Really, Rowan? That's what's got you worked up right now?"

Rowan blinked at her. "I may happen to be a bookseller by profession but I assure you, my question is legitimate."

"Oh, I'm not dogging you because you left the police force to open a bookshop," Asma reassured him. "I'm making fun of you for being a townie. Only in Calliope would somebody ask that question at a crime scene."

It wasn't like the small research city of Calliope—home of the elite Harrison University—didn't attract crime. For every Harrison sophomore who decided to rebel against his parents, become a Silicon Valley tech bro, date an aspiring massage therapist named Jade, and smoke weed on the front lawn of an angry resident's recently renovated Victorian, there was another student crying to a 911 operator about a break-in. Heroin, meth, and other toxic concoctions occasionally popped by to say hello, irrespective of the town's attempts to stop them. Suicides, usually around final exams, also brought Asma out from her desk.

But murders? That wasn't Calliope's style. Especially not high-profile ones like this promised to be. With a population of just about 150,000 when school was in session, its status as an elite research hub stuffed with PhDs suggested a mecca of NPR listeners, bookstore lovers, hipster beer drinkers, and amateur beekeepers. Sometimes the shoe fit: Just last month Asma had leaned against the side of the Calliope Amphitheater, watching a bunch of dads whip out wads of cash from inside their windbreakers to buy bootleg Neil deGrasse Tyson tickets. But at this point in her career, she knew, like staring into a fun house mirror, that how you see yourself can be so different from reality. People were capable of anything, especially in a place where the veneer of good citizenship so easily masked their baser desires. It was Asma's job to take off the masks.

Sobs from the kitchen broke her concentration.

Rowan glanced at Asma. "Girlfriend?"

"Fiancée," Asma corrected. "Being consoled by a rookie."

"Who?"

"Evan Murton."

Rowan winced. "Good heavens."

"I know." Asma grinned. "I'll go check on him in a minute. The fiancée's name is Molly Henderson."

Rowan hesitated. "Of the Henderson family?"

"That one," Asma confirmed. The name alone was enough to get her boss, Captain Hamilton, breathing down her neck to solve the case at a breakneck speed. "She works at Harrison, too. Some kind of big shot there—vice president of community engagement at . . ." Asma checked her small black notebook. "The Benson Art Museum. She found the body."

Asma described what she'd learned since getting the phone call that had forced her out of her bed next to her snoring husband and dragged her in front of a modest-size Victorian home on the west side of Calliope that had belonged to Sam Taylor. Molly Henderson had just flown back from New York City for her last wedding dress fitting when she discovered the body. It had taken the junior cop on the scene—Amy Camper, a people pleaser if Asma had ever met one—about ten minutes to stop Molly's screaming.

Rowan seemed to mull that over. "Did she see anyone else?"

"Nope," Asma replied. "According to Amy's notes, Molly found him alone, front door open. Neighbors to the right were outta town, the others to the left at dinner downtown. Chain on the door was snipped."

"But only the phone taken," Rowan said. "Murder weapon?"

"Missing," Asma said.

"Hm." Rowan tapped at his notebook with a pen. "I still think his bookcases warrant further inspection. They appear hastily rearranged. Those piles on the floor also seem out of character, considering how tidy the rest of the living room appears."

"I'll put somebody on cataloging the library's inventory."

"Did Ms. Henderson proffer any reasons why someone might want to kill her betrothed?"

"None." Asma shrugged. "According to her, everyone loved him. Sounds like you did, too. You see why I called you in here, right?"

"Unfortunately, I do," Rowan murmured.

"So," Asma asked, whooshing out an intake of air she'd been holding. "What's your take?"

Rowan blew at a tuft of hair that had fallen onto his forehead. "No apparent theft. No witness. No weapon. No motive. Asma, we both know what you have on your hands."

Asma's throat burned as she swallowed back her own nagging worries.

"A shitshow," she finally said. "A real shitshow."

CHAPTER THREE

"You began with that story of Belgians chopping up body parts again, didn't you?"

Daphne bristled at the amusement in Sadie's voice on the phone. It had already been a rough afternoon, trapped as she was in her office wading through an endless sea of papers to grade while the clear sunshine beckoned her outdoors to freedom. She shouldn't have answered the phone at all, but it was impossible to resist picking up her friend's call whenever the ringtone blasted out Thot Squad's "Pound Cake" (Sadie's choice).

Daphne sighed. "Elise told you?"

Sadie cackled in response. "Only after I threatened to steal all of her Meg Thee Stallion merch."

"I'm honestly surprised you haven't purloined it yet anyway," Daphne said.

"Purloined?" said Sadie. "*Purloined?* You're really just going to drop that word in casual conversation and expect me not to make fun of you?"

"It's a perfectly good word," Daphne said.

"Jesus, you humanists are a trip," Sadie said.

"Whatever, spelling bee champ."

"One time," Sadie replied. "I got roped into that dog-and-pony show one time. And you won't let me forget it."

"Nope."

Daphne was fortunate to have two women in her life who had declared their undying love for her the moment they'd met. Elise Park was the human equivalent of spun sugar, the definition of sweetness and light, loyal and loving to an alarming degree, even if she was a professional toxicologist who studied deadly poisons for a living. Sadie—or Sadhika Pandaram if you were looking for a fight—shared the same unwavering commitment to Daphne that occasionally made her eyes water. But unlike Elise, Sadie's oath of friendship came with the glint of a steel knife, a promise of swift vengeance to anyone who might even blink wrong in Daphne's direction. Sadie's life motto was to keep a knife on the neck of your enemy and a foot on the neck of your friends.

"So what kind of dude doesn't appreciate a good dismemberment story or two?" Sadie asked.

"Most of them, Sadie," Daphne said, wincing at the memory of her date with Ricky. "It turns out most of them shrivel away at the first mention of bodily harm."

"Well, someone out there will enjoy learning about the history of French colonial violence within ten seconds of meeting you," Sadie replied with confidence. "One of these days, there's going to be a guy who's going to want to get all up in your West African-meets-Louisiana-Creole business the moment you bring up Charles de Gaulle or whatever the fuck."

"Awwwww." Daphne smirked. "You remembered his name. My history lessons are having a positive effect."

"It's literally an airport, Daph," Sadie replied. "The point here is that I got you, babe. And also maybe stop dating men. They're trash."

Daphne snorted.

"We still on for sangria this week?" Sadie asked.

"Just trying to get through my stack of papers first."

"You have like three days, you'll be fine," said Sadie. "Just give them all A's and be done with it."

"How are you allowed to teach undergraduates?" Daphne asked, not for the first time.

"I teach abstract algebra, that's different," Sadie retorted. "Everyone fails at that."

Daphne's bestie had explained her research in algebraic number theory more than once, but God help her if she'd retained any of it. All she knew was that whenever Sadie even mentioned the phrase "Diophantine equations," Daphne reached for a bottle of ibuprofen.

"Grade those papers, Daph," Sadie said. "That's an order."

Daphne hung up the phone.

Even in a town like Calliope, men weren't exactly beating down doors to date a French historian who rambled on for too long about archival storage practices. She could happily spend the rest of her days taking Chloe on walks and teaching students the horrible histories of imperialism and genocide. Too bad teaching came with grading, which was its own kind of torture. She was only two semesters into her job at Harrison but already, she'd rather hit her hand with a hammer than read thirty more papers on the global causes of World War I. It was wild how she could spend hours of her life trying to figure out how to help her students write and argue better only for them to ignore her. During her first semester, she'd agonized for an entire afternoon over one paper, only for her student to toss it in the trash on the way out of the classroom.

Daphne blew out a gust of air.

With the afternoon sun blazing across her office, she held up an essay with her thumb and forefinger, dangling it in front of her like a used tissue, longing for a trash can in which to drop it. Resentment tore through her chest, fierce and sharp. But facing a sea of passive voice–riddled papers was less terrifying than facing a perpetual state of grading purgatory where more papers came in than left Daphne's desk. Sadie was right. The goal was to beat the tides coming in.

Daphne flipped through her student Rohit's paper, "Constructing Empire: French Architecture in Colonial Vietnam." She found herself agreeing with his analysis of the Saigon Opera House as a symbol of French cultural power and was particularly enjoying his incorporation of scholarship on "Chinoiserie" on the European continent. *Chinoiserie*—she blinked at the word. Sam had texted her something about "Le Chinoise"? His deleted text floated at the edges of her consciousness, wisps of it tickling the back of her mind. She pushed on grading, hoping to get rid of that annoying pinging sensation in her brain, the radar that kept beeping its location to her from deep within the ocean.

"Le Chinoise" came back anyway, thrumming at a low note, and before she could correct herself she was twirling her cell phone in her hand in slow circles. It was surprising that Sam Taylor hadn't texted her back or at least bumped into her on campus already. She could see it, too. A knock on her office door, him running a hand through his thick blond hair again, scruffing it up, appearing sheepish when he actually wasn't.

"Grading?"

Daphne lifted her head. A scrappy white woman with chin-length silver hair leaned against her wooden doorframe. Miranda Nurse—professor of Japanese history, scholar of legal reform in seventeenth-century Kyoto, and chair of the history department, was examining Daphne with a puckered frown.

"How'd you know?"

"You have that hollowed-out look in your eyes. Like a veteran returning from war," Miranda replied. "I know it's a Monday morning, but do you have a minute?"

Daphne waved her in. "For my illustrious chair, I always have time."

The twinkle in Miranda's eyes was full of mischief. "Flattery really will get you places."

But Daphne meant it. Miranda was one of the only colleagues at Harrison to shield Daphne from being "volunteered" for every committee under the sun because she filled their diversity quotas. Miranda could take as much time as she liked.

Miranda softly closed the door behind her and sat down across from Daphne.

"I've got a case," she said after a moment's silence.

Daphne took in the mix of hardened grit and morbid amusement in Miranda's eyes. She could only be referring to one thing—plagiarism. "Who this time?"

Miranda's response was lightning quick. "That information's classified."

Daphne was about to crack a joke about the FBI swooping down on freshman dorms but then noticed the slight grimace to Miranda's smile. "So it's serious?"

"I already checked against our plagiarism software and got nothing."

"And Harrison's new AI detection program?" Daphne asked.

"Useless," Miranda said. "That program is as full of holes as an old sweater. You know it, I know it, and the *students* know it. No matter. My gut insists that this paper wasn't crafted by AI anyway."

Daphne pressed her lips together. "Hm."

"Look, I just want that brilliant mind of yours to read through a few lines of prose and see if any alarm bells go off, that's all."

Daphne hesitated. "Well, I—"

"The political scientists told me they roped you into one of theirs last week."

Daphne's nostrils flared. That was supposed to have been a secret between her, congressional scholar Andrew Slovak, and the junior in his class who'd lacked enough sense to know what Senate bylaws were supposed to look like. She should have known better than to trust anyone who made a career studying politics.

"Who told you?"

"Who do you think?" Miranda scoffed. "Christopher bragged about it at the chair's meeting. Said you were better than the Office of Academic Misconduct. Said those incompetent jackasses couldn't identify plagiarism to save their hides, even if he personally handed them a copy of *Harry Potter* with their own names scratched on it."

Daphne arched a brow. "So the bar is low, in other words."

Miranda's silver bob swayed as she shook her head. "No, Daphne. You're good at cracking these plagiarism cases. *Too* good. And word is spreading. We're going to have to figure out how to clamp down on the rumors before the art historians start getting ideas. They'd try to keep you in a locked vault where you're fed only soup and lifted passages from Wikipedia."

"They wouldn't—"

"Look me in the eyes, Daphne, and tell me Natalia wouldn't," Miranda said.

Daphne tried to find the good in Harrison's notorious chair

of art history. "Well, from what I understand, Natalia's had a difficult time of things lately."

Miranda snorted. "No, John the sociology chair is having a hard time. *You* try cajoling a department of raging Marxists into going along with the status quo. Natalia's just a sociopath with a gorgeous shawl collection. But that's what you get for studying medieval tapestries for a living."

Miranda reached into her bag and pulled out what appeared to be a twenty-page essay. She slid it across the desk.

Daphne loathed the pull in her chest to scour those pages for clues. Invisibility is what she wanted—*should* want. Except for on the page. There, she could be as charming or as witty as she wanted or stake a bold claim that promised to shake up decades of French historiography. All of the quirks of her personality, those odd bumpy spots that might cause someone to look at her twice—those she could express in her prose. But poring over academic work to catch a plagiarist? That veered too far away from the mantra she'd wrapped around herself like a thick down comforter through grad school.

"*Don't go looking for drama.*"

She stole a glance at the essay anyway. Looked up at a scheming Miranda, whose eyes twinkled once more with malintent.

"You know you want to."

"Oh, all right," Daphne huffed.

Holding the essay like it was a hand grenade with its pin pulled, Daphne leafed through its pages. Sized up its organization. Ruffled through its prose. Narrowed in on a paragraph. Circled back again to a sentence. Listened for its beat and swing.

After all this time, Daphne still didn't know how to name

her ability to recall statements verbatim—the aural equivalent to a photographic memory? All she knew was that lines would get stuck in her head like baby ducklings trapped under a storm grate, no matter the source. An academic article on the transformation of agricultural laws in eighteenth-century France? A gossip page claiming that Tyler, The Creator had eloped with some twink? Everything she'd ever read was lodged into her brain like melodies. Earworms. Each sentence had its own rhythm, its own fluctuation in tones. They were so easy to sing back.

For fear of getting looks, she chose not to explain this strange thing to people. Until last semester, when Ari Spinoza in Comparative Literature had met Daphne for cocktails one night and showed her a student essay on Senegalese poetry that he suspected of plagiarism but couldn't prove. That one had been easy enough. Daphne's mind had crackled the moment she hit page three: two paragraphs belonging to an obscure anthology on postcolonial literature. A month later, Wendy McAdams in Women's Studies knocked on her door with a writing sample on Simone de Beauvoir that looked "way too familiar." It took a few days before Daphne recalled the out-of-print issue of *Women's History Quarterly*.

The warning she gave to her colleagues was simple: In order to recall a text, she had to have already read it. There was a reason why her success rate in the Humanities and Social Sciences was significantly higher than in any other field. Laura Bolton in Biology was crestfallen at the news. Same with Sadie's colleague Mike Milovanovich in Math.

But occasionally she surprised everyone—including herself. She still had no idea when or where or *why* she'd read the NCAA's confidential plan to revise their contracts with ESPN but Gavin Lewis didn't care. The director of the Sports Management program was grateful that someone had figured out how Harrison University's star lacrosse player had managed to squeeze out a coherent paper for a class he never attended. She blushed at the memory of his muscular hug of thanks.

"Initial thoughts, dear?"

Daphne put the essay down. "A strong hook, really great close reading on nineteenth-century institutional policies, pretty good prose. The slight overreliance on Foucault suggests we're dealing with a grad student, though."

"We've already searched online."

"If I'm right, you wouldn't be able to find it on the internet anyway." Daphne stood up. "I know who wrote it. Just . . . give me a day or two to confirm it."

THE PROBLEM, Daphne supposed, walking across the chilly quad, was that she was in an unending two-front war between letting her instincts run wild and staying on the straight and narrow. Becoming a tenure-track professor at a hallowed institution like Harrison University was any scholar's dream. While defiant with her research and its challenges to French historiography, Daphne wasn't rebellious in her actions. Demanding that historians better account for the lives of Black people in European history might have been interpreted as boundary pushing in some circles of academia, but living a life that defied academic institutional norms courted disaster. Daphne wasn't interested in the latter. She didn't want to rock any boats. Frankly, the thought of being in a metaphorical boat at all was stressful enough as it was. Yet here she was, heading across the quad to do what could only be described as "snooping."

It wasn't difficult to spot the soaring cathedral that was

Harrison University's grand library in the distance. Its flying buttresses made of pale stone gleamed in the afternoon sun while the stained-glass windows twinkled out panoptic rainbows in bright light, as if the soaring structure of learning was sunning itself like a cat. A squabble had broken out among a pack of squirrels over a discarded donut. A skinny dude in shorts and a Harrison hoodie rushed over to break up the scuffle, imploring the squirrels to find a peaceful solution that involved sharing the maple-glazed concoction. A regular Gandhi, this kid.

Sailing past the library, Daphne made her way to Fischer Hall, home of the anthropology department, determined to follow her hunch about that paper. During Daphne's first semester at Harrison, Kiki Ilunga, a third-year PhD student in anthropology, had emailed her out of the blue searching for a cognate member for her dissertation committee. And while Daphne had been a bit surprised by the request, considering she'd been on campus for a total of two seconds, and that, as a rule, she didn't trust an anthropologist further than she could throw one, she'd changed her mind the second she'd read a seminar paper Kiki had written on gender and policing in psychiatric institutions in nineteenth-century Central Africa. The pair had hit it off immediately. A semester later, Kiki was now in the Democratic Republic of the Congo to conduct ethnographic research for her dissertation, having left behind an array of spiky succulent plants in her office on campus for Daphne to take care of. She probably should have said no when Kiki had placed her on plant-sitting duties, but Daphne knew what it was to be a PhD student whose research was located on another continent. The constant shuffling of belongings from apartment to apartment for the pursuit of truth created an inability to plant literal roots that would need long-term care.

Kiki's office was in Fischer Hall, where anthropologists wandered around in alpaca sweaters, waxing on about ethnographic fieldwork. Designed in the 1960s by architecture students on what Daphne could only assume was a particularly strong hallucinogen, the building's counter-intuitive twists and turns were a nightmare to navigate. Stairways led nowhere. The basement was only accessible by the second floor. Apparently it wasn't unusual in the first week of class to find at least one freshman crying and hugging her backpack in a corner, having given up on finding Anthro 101.

The first sign that alerted Daphne to unusual activity in Fischer Hall was, of course, the two policemen wandering around the lobby on the ground floor. Their relaxed stances told her that they didn't seem to be too pressed so she unfroze her limbs. After all, nothing in the vaulted atrium suggested that Fischer Hall was under some kind of threat but that didn't mean Daphne was willing to test drawing the attention of two cops, so off she went, seeking out the little-known staircase at the edge of the lobby and heading up the third floor. Now experiencing Fischer Hall's classic "two wrong turns make a right" for herself, Daphne opened what she thought was the entryway to Kiki's office—and managed to almost knock over a woman in a black leather jacket.

"Watch it," the woman growled after narrowly escaping Daphne's wide hip.

Daphne stammered out a "sorry"—right before realizing the woman was sealing off an office doorway with yellow police tape. She glanced at the nameplate.

Sam Taylor.

Daphne froze. Inside the sun-streamed room, the profile of a slender white man cast shadows against a bookcase. He was too tall to be Sam himself. Crouched low, lost in thought, he was swiping an empty bottom bookshelf for dust in a rubber glove. Strewn around him on the floor was crushed glass sparkling in the light.

Daphne blinked. Had . . . Had Sam's office been vandalized? Or—was Sam under investigation for something?

"How did you get up here?" the woman asked.

Daphne ripped her gaze away from the debris on Sam's office floor and back at the woman who was now glaring at her. Her shiny black hair was pulled back into a ponytail, and a frown seemed to be etched permanently on her face—which should have made her look like a grouchy troll but instead revealed all lush lips and high cheekbones that made Daphne feel about as beautiful as a pond frog. The woman was gorgeous and terrifying simultaneously, as if a Kardashian had been trained to become a ruthless assassin.

"Oh." Daphne offered what she hoped was an appeasing expression on her face. "I used a shortcut?" She pointed down the hall. "There's a back staircase that most people don't know about."

"Of course there fucking is," the woman muttered. "This building's a nightmare."

"By design," the tall man in Sam's office said. The amusement in his quiet voice rang loud. "The students behind Fischer Hall's design were deconstructivists. A few of them had allegedly taken inspiration from Sartre's play *No Exit*."

Had that man just spouted off French philosophy at random? To her surprise, Daphne wanted to open Sam's office door wider for a clearer view of him. But then her brain caught up to the fact that he was a detective, the woman was a detective, there were detectives in Sam's office, and so she took a step back instead.

"Rowan," the woman said, "can you call in for the building manager to lock this extra door down the hallway? I coulda sworn we got all of them." The woman turned back to Daphne. "You a professor?"

"Yup," Daphne replied, weirdly pleased by this assessment. Nothing about her encouraged anyone to consider that she could be a professor—let alone one at Harrison. She was always too young, too female, too Black. Even with her sparkling new plaque bearing the title "Dr. Ouverture" on her office door, she spent too much time correcting a whole lot of sophomores about her professional identity.

Dark brows furrowed. "Anthropology?"

"History," Daphne corrected.

"And you're here because . . . ?"

"I'm picking up a paper a PhD student wrote," Daphne replied, truthfully. "It's, uh, in her office down the hall."

The woman nodded. "Well, it was nice meeting you, Professor, but it's time for you to get that student's paper and go."

Inside Kiki's office, Daphne watered an array of stubby jade trees and ginseng plants, her mind reading in an infinite loop that strange text message from Sam in broken French. Had he gotten himself in trouble? She cooed over a few potted succulents sunning themselves on the window, willing her low murmurs to soothe her and the plants alike before shuffling through Kiki's file cabinets and searching empty drawers at Miranda's request. Thus far, her investigation, if she could call it that, had yielded nothing but a growing determination to keep going.

■　　■　　■

THE FRESH air outside Fischer Hall was a welcome relief, even if it did little to quell the restless zip in Daphne's steps. The stack of papers on her desk beckoned, but her feet took her in the direction of the Benson Art Museum. Whenever the job at Harrison overwhelmed her with its long, twelve-hour days, its unrelenting pace, the endless teaching prep, the countless meetings with students disputing a grade or faculty bickering over whether to overhaul the major, Daphne stepped into the quiet sanctuary of the museum to commune with their collection of French Impressionist paintings and time slowed down.

"Professor Ouverture!"

Thick auburn curls flounced across the quad. Branwen Rothkopf, a senior history major, was waving at Daphne with all the force of a floppy balloon Gumby advertising fifty percent off at the car dealership. Unnecessary. Daphne could have spotted the freckles smattered across Branwen's nose and cheeks from space.

Daphne pulled her student into a big hug. "Hi, Bran."

"I'm so glad I bumped into you," Bran said, her smile as bright as a princess-cut diamond. "Your feedback on my last chapter blew my mind. I knew there had to be more to say on interracial family networks than what I'd found. You are truly the best."

Daphne's cheeks grew warm. "I'm glad you're finding my reading suggestions useful. Honestly, supervising your senior thesis has been the highlight of my first year at Harrison."

Now it was Branwen's turn to blush.

It was the duty of junior professors to take on a senior

thesis at Harrison every year, a time-honored tradition that, faculty claimed, had birthed presidential candidates, a few late-night talk show hosts, some romance authors, and even a zoologist. When a shy and smiley Black girl with freckles and deep red hair in microbraids had popped in to introduce herself, Daphne decided on the spot it was a Harrison tradition she was more than pleased to support. Because goddamn, the kid could write. Better than Daphne could at that age, for sure.

"Actually, I'm glad I ran into you—do you know a PhD student named Kiki Ilunga? I'd love to introduce you to each other at some point, just so you can find an extra pair of eyes on your paper," she said quickly. Branwen didn't need to know exactly why Kiki was on Daphne's mind. "I just came from her office in Fischer Hall, and—why are you giving me a strange look, Bran?"

Branwen's freckled face had become quizzical. "You just came from Fischer?"

Daphne cocked her head to the side. "What's going on?"

"Professor Taylor died," Bran said. "You didn't hear?"

"He *died*?" Daphne repeated.

The lawn outside lost its bright green hue. If birds were chirping, Daphne could no longer hear them.

Sam had just texted her last night; he couldn't be dead. He was just delinquent, as usual. Someone like him could afford to be, as the universe had made clear to Daphne a long time ago.

"Not just that—murdered," said Branwen. "The news broke like an hour ago."

Yellow police tape outside Sam's door. Sparkly shards of glass on the carpet. A gloved finger sliding along a bookcase. Daphne's mind locked on to the facts.

Bran held out her phone. "Here, look."

Daphne read the same lines over again trying to make sense of them.

Found dead in his home . . .

Police are seeking anyone with information . . .

An uncomfortable, sticky feeling scraped across her chest. Did a text message in broken French count as information?

"Are you okay?" Branwen's dark brown eyes shone with concern. "Did you know him?"

"Not well," Daphne admitted.

The idea of being close to someone like Sam Taylor was about as realistic as the cafeteria lady befriending the local prom king. And knowing Sam, he probably had been the local prom king. And quarterback. And valedictorian.

"I've gotta run," Bran said, "but can I email you later with some questions?"

"Of course," Daphne replied.

After waving goodbye to Bran, Daphne stood frozen by an ancient oak tree. She hesitated to articulate to herself just what, exactly, her relationship to Sam was. He'd been at Harrison a few years already when Daphne had arrived, and he'd sauntered in and out of the campus's neo-gothic buildings and past the grumpy squirrels with a confidence that Daphne could never possess. The kind of confidence that gave him the audacity to negotiate to teach only one class a semester while she'd taught twice as many with the same heavy expectations to publish. The kind of confidence that inspired CNN anchors to bark at viewers to read his research. He was the golden boy, quite literally, with blond hair, sharp gray eyes, and an even sharper jaw line—only someone like him, with his growing celebrity, could get away with insisting that students call him by his first name when Daphne struggled to get hers to recognize that she even had a PhD.

Sam was, according to many people, brilliant. A future Pulitzer Prize winner, for sure. There was no doubt in Daphne's mind that he'd been arrogant, too. Occasionally, in line for beef Wellington or roast salmon at the buffet table at Harrison's faculty club, he'd try to pay attention to her long enough to remember to be kind to her. But somehow that had only made Daphne feel worse? His publicly courteous behavior toward Daphne felt like some icky performance of magnanimity that always left her feeling bad about herself. *See?* his behavior seemed to suggest. *I, too, can mingle with the brown mouses of the world.*

To be fair, places like Harrison were overstuffed with academics like him, convinced just as equally of their own genius as they were that Daphne must be lost on campus. While hires like Sam were celebrated as coup d'états rivaling the victorious battle of Waterloo, so far, many people at Harrison acted like she should be grateful to be allowed access to Harrison's grassy lawn at all. Like hiring a Black person was an act of charity.

Still, it was difficult to picture Sam as anything other than robustly alive, swaggering around campus while a bevy of students—usually pretty white girls—buzzed around him with the excited reverence of a K-pop fan club. He'd been murdered?

At home, Daphne greeted a wriggling Chloe, the shock of the day's events grinding away at her—Sam's death. Miranda's plagiarism case, too. She wanted to march up the stairs to her home office and rummage around until she found Kiki's paper, which she suspected was the original source. But when she returned from taking Chloe for a walk, exhaustion officially won out. Lord knew she had a full day of teaching ahead of her tomorrow, including an overdue book review for a French history journal that she still had to get off her desk. She wanted to shake off this growing unease, the hard pit in her stomach every time she thought of Sam's weird text message.

Later that night on the couch, eating some leftover peanut stew, Daphne sought to free her mind from what it couldn't control by turning on the TV and rummaging around for something watchable, eventually settling for half-following reruns of Oprah interviews.

"Were you silent?" Oprah asked Meghan Markle. "Or were you silenc*ed*?"

Daphne choked on her bite of chicken. Sam's text message came back, spinning, whirling, wheezing along her ears, a loud and angry carousel tune.

This time, in English.

"Les Chinois ont inventé la goutte d'eau qui vous tombe sur la tête."

"*The Chinese invented water torture.*"

"Les Français, eux, ont inventé le silence."

"*The French invented silence. They eliminated every form of distraction. No books, no paper, no pencil, the barred window completely sealed with planks of wood, though rays of soft light filter through a few small holes.*"

Henri Charrière's autobiographical novel *Papillon* from 1969, a tale of a prison break in French Guiana. Why had Sam whistled that tune to her? Daphne put her bowl down on her living room coffee table and walked over a grumbling Chloe to grab her copy off the bookshelf. But after a few moments of rummaging around, picking up and re-shelving books, she stopped.

Confused, she examined her books again. There was Maryse Condé's *Crossing the Mangrove*. She saw Aimé Césaire's collection of poetry. *Papillon* should be next, along with the other novels set in the French Caribbean that her auntie Emmanuelle had given her one summer in Paris. She pulled up her home-made library loan database. *Papillon* wasn't checked out, either. It was as if the book had just decided to walk itself off her shelf.

Daphne slid back onto the couch next to Chloe, shaking off the feathery feeling blooming in her chest. The book had to be on campus. Tomorrow morning, she'd probably find it on one of her shelves, snuck between texts like Sidney Mintz's *Sweetness and Power* or Lisa Lowe's *The Intimacies of Four Continents*.

Aside from Elise, there was only one person in all of Calliope that Daphne knew of who'd even heard of *Papillon*—and oh, how he'd carried on when she admitted that she had an original copy in French. She would ask him why he'd reached out to her about it, but she couldn't. Not anymore.

Because that person—Sam Taylor—was dead.

CHAPTER FOUR

Daphne rolled her head against her pillow, stretching out her back until she felt that familiar "click" in her neck. A cold, wet nose pushed her elbow across her face until she finally sat up in bed. She rubbed her hands across her dog's wriggly backside, accepting Chloe's well-meaning nudge to get up and supply her favorite peanut butter treat. Bleary eyed, Daphne stumbled down the stairs, going through her morning routine on autopilot.

Step One: Open the front door to let Chloe out to pee. Feel that glimmer of joy at Chloe frolicking through wildflowers in the meadow.

Step Two: Come back inside and grind coffee beans.

Step Three: Forget to drink water.

Step Four: Shake off a hangry Chloe while grabbing her bag of kibble from the top kitchen shelf.

Wait.

Chloe?

Damnit, she'd left her outside.

Wrapping her arms tight around her fuzzy eggplant house robe, Daphne swung open the door. Her pooch was waiting patiently on the front step, far too accustomed to Daphne's forgetfulness.

"Sorry, love," she mumbled.

A quick "mlem" of Daphne's bare leg, and all was forgiven.

It was a teaching day, which meant she had approximately twenty minutes of calm that morning before the panic of facing students set in, so while the pair munched on their breakfasts—Daphne may have slipped Chloe a fried egg on top of her kibble—she ignored her upcoming lecture on French colonial soldiers during WWI in favor of rummaging around on the internet for news of Sam Taylor. Social media lit up like a Christmas tree, the hashtag #justice4SamTaylor blazing across every platform. Local news shared a 1-800 number for a tip line in case anyone had information about his murder. Daphne pushed away her plate of eggs and toast.

Why had Sam texted her fragments from *Papillon* before he'd died? Had he needed help? If so, why hadn't he just asked his fiancée—or the police?

Even the thought of approaching Sam's fiancée, Molly Henderson, made Daphne's palms sweat. She was familiar—barely—with Molly, who was just as tall, blond, and conventionally beautiful as Sam, even if Daphne had found their engagement slightly perplexing. Where Sam had that dashing bravado that inspired teenage girls to write bad breakup poems, Molly was reserved to the point of appearing cold. Like other art historians that Daphne had met, Molly glided on and off campus wearing outfits that were impeccable, daunting, and frankly inaccessible. Vintage suits tailored to Molly's lithe frame. Scarves from a tiny market in the Tuscan countryside. Heels so high and slim that Barbie herself would topple over in them. And more recently, an engagement ring on her slim finger that boasted a diamond the size of a macaron.

Okay, sure, Molly was a bit standoffish, but maybe she had to hold everyone at arm's length. The Henderson family name was a powerful institution unto itself, birthing politicians, well-polished socialites, and at least one minor scandal involving a Kennedy once upon a time.

A soft cold nose nudged Daphne again.

"You know what?" Daphne said, looking down into Chloe's pleading eyes. "A walk would do us both some good."

After pouring a cup of coffee into a traveler's mug, Daphne slipped Chloe into her harness, having just enough time for a jaunt before Daphne dropped Chloe off at Aunt Linda's, a retired librarian who took in cash on the side for snuggling with Chloe and four other dogs while watching *The Price Is Right*. At seven in the morning, no one was out, except for the occasional jogger or random retiree laying down a fresh layer of mulch for the tulips. The sun was only just beginning to touch the corners of houses, to kiss the tails of bushy squirrels feuding with each other over peanuts that some resident had thrown out for them, to beat back the last of winter's cold. The bright promises of spring in the air kissed her cheeks as she wandered through neighborhood streets, past countless overpriced historical homes with organic vegetable gardens, white picket fences, and the occasional obligatory "Black Lives Matter" or "Love Is Love" sign splayed next to a bed of daffodils.

She turned a corner—

And spotted the wall of yellow police tape.

Bouquets of flowers drowned the lawn of a small white Victorian house, forming a shrine along the main path that led to Sam's front door. The harsh truth of death suddenly became inescapable, a physical reality just as much as it was an existential phenomenon that students debated in philosophy classes.

"Were you one of his students?"

Daphne whipped around. An elderly white lady wearing a wide-brimmed straw hat kneeled next to a raised garden bed, her gloved hands plunged deep into a soft mound of dirt. Chloe began wagging her tail to say hello, and when the neighbor greeted Chloe with kissing noises, her dog needed no further encouragement to bound into the woman's arms.

Daphne politely tugged Chloe back. "I'm sorry."

"Don't be," the lady in the hat said, patting her thighs for Chloe to come over. "I love dogs and yours is so shiny. And I was just asking you if you were one of Sam's students?"

"No," Daphne replied. "A colleague. In the history department."

"Oh, really?" The neighbor eyed Daphne while her dirt-covered hands massaged Chloe's neck. "You look too young to be a professor."

Daphne's smile tightened. She was used to hearing that refrain, but that didn't mean she enjoyed its tune.

"Well, I'm sorry for your loss," the woman said. "I'm Trudy Sandstone."

"Daphne," she replied. The less she revealed about herself, the better, if only to stop the curious questions about how someone like *her* could end up at a place like Harrison.

"It's been a shock to everyone. He was such a wonderful man," Trudy said. "Normally he comes over to take out my trash on Mondays, and when I woke up the other morning, I was wondering why it was still in the driveway. He's been helping me around the house, checking the plumbing or raking leaves on windy days since my husband died." Trudy's eyes welled up with tears. "Who's going to help me now?"

Daphne searched her brain for something neutral to say about Sam. "From what I knew about him, he was always eager to make a difference."

"Sam is—was. Can you believe I have to say that now? Was—very friendly with everyone."

Daphne nodded, distracted while she peered through Sam's living room windows. His dark blue curtains waved in the breeze, casting shadows against a framed poster of dogs playing poker. She could have sworn she'd seen it before but unfortunately, Daphne's gift—or curse, depending on her mood—was to recall texts and not images. Sam's walnut-brown bookshelves on the back wall were beautiful, though. Sturdy. Gleaming. Strong. Far nicer than the IKEA ones she had squeezed into every corner of her home. Too bad Sam's were messy.

"My goodness, he could be such a flirt—even with me!" Trudy's voice dropped. "I'm not one to gossip, but I'll admit that there used to be a bevy of women going in and out of his home."

Daphne stopped squinting at Sam's shelves and looked at Trudy, who took it as a sign to continue.

"I remember, I used to say to my Gerald—right before he died, that is—it would be easier for Sam if he just got a revolving door already. But then Molly came into his life and he calmed down. Isn't she just the loveliest? What a handsome couple. And you should have seen the ring on her finger, my God, somebody's a very hungry bunny."

Daphne searched Trudy's pale face. "Is Molly doing okay?"

"Heavens, no," Trudy said. "She found the body, poor thing. Right before the wedding."

DAPHNE PARKED in her usual spot on campus and began the trek to her office, pushing through the crackling nerves. Her gaze slid across the lawn. Hundreds of small white votive candles dotted the quad's wide lawn to memorialize Sam's death. Their presence angered the squirrels, who had to find new routes to their favorite trash cans to scrounge for pizza crusts while dodging the tiny flames.

Davis Hall soared above the gothic skyline, even higher than the library. As one of the oldest buildings on Harrison University's campus, it was a five-story fortress of erudition, known for its foreboding tower, sunny reading rooms, and gilded coffered ceilings so ornate they'd appear right at home in the Library of Congress. It was also home to the history department and Daphne's office, where Henri Charrière's book *Papillon had* to be in hiding. Taking the stairs to her office on the fourth floor where she and her historian colleagues resided, she had just enough time to check for it before class.

After trudging up four flights of stairs, she blinked around her office. Her broad desk and the thickly patterned rug that she'd found in a Turkish market years ago with her mother came into view as her eyes adjusted to the bright light, her gaze eventually landing on her bookshelves. Like those of most academics, her bookshelves appeared chaotic enough to provoke panic, but her system was actually organized well enough that most librarians would approve. She dutifully searched by subject, author, and title, running her fingers across beloved book spines that had expanded her thinking and changed her worldview over the course of many years. And got nothing. Her yellowed, aging copy of *Papillon* was nowhere to be found.

But she should have found it by now, right? There were only two locations where that crusty old thing could be—her library at home or the one in her office on campus. *Papillon* wasn't a book that she carried around with her in a tote bag, nor was it a novel she needed to teach anytime soon. Tote bags and purses were reserved for the latest Tia Williams novel or a new volume of essays on West African literature. So where was it? Why had Sam texted her about it?

It's at home, Daphne told herself. *I just missed it somehow.*

She glanced at the clock. And jolted herself out of her fog. Class—French Empire—started in ten minutes.

With a swift wiggle into her purple coat and her belongings ensconced in her backpack, she took off, shivering across the campus lawn and past those votive candles for Sam. Pushing the door open, Daphne wondered if she'd been the only one in attendance, anyway. In strange times like this, it was normal for students to scatter, and the eerie quad suggested that today might be one of those days.

Sure enough, the three people who were already seated were known die-hards and members of Daphne's growing cadre of favorites: Aspen, Rohit, and Tabitha. Aspen, a sophomore history major with a minor in gender studies, was in that adorable and frustrating era where they insisted on queering any fact that Daphne presented. Which was useful ninety percent of the time. The other ten percent, Aspen could derail the whole class.

Rohit, an electrical engineering major, cared far too deeply about the historical subjects they discussed to the point where Daphne was occasionally concerned for his welfare. Like many of her favorites, Rohit had been forced into a history class last semester—only to become more obsessed with the stories in it than a housewife watching a telenovela. When she had narrated the course of events leading to the Sepoy Rebellion of 1857, Rohit had literally gasped. He'd been trailing behind her like a puppy ever since.

Lastly, of course, there was Tabitha. Tabitha didn't give two shits about European history. But as a young Black woman at Harrison, she was eager to take classes with the few Black professors there were, so here she was, smashing the class with a 98 average and basically only paying attention to what Daphne said when she used the words "slavery" or "imperialism."

"I knew you three would be here," Daphne said, placing her backpack on the desk in front of the tiny auditorium. "I'm pretty sure the only thing that can keep any of you away from a classroom is a nuclear apocalypse."

Aspen crossed their arms at that. "I'd need to read a few articles verifying its existence first."

"There won't *be* any articles," Daphne replied. "You'd be dead already. That's the point of a nuclear catastrophe. Okay but seriously, guys—"

"Professor Ouverture, you should say 'folx,'" chimed in Aspen.

"—you think people are going to show? We've got like three minutes before class starts."

All three students shrugged.

"Professor Taylor got killed," Tabitha offered, "and the cops are everywhere interviewing students and now everyone's scared there's some kind of killer loose at Harrison."

"Which is preposterous," Aspen said. "He wasn't even killed on campus. And we all know that most murders are committed by someone the victim personally knows."

"Which would be someone at Harrison," Rohit said, pointedly. "Calliope can be dangerous."

"Are you kidding?" Tabitha said. "This town *just* held a teach-in on how to apply hormonal birth control to its deer population."

The #deerlivesmatter signs from protestors had caused Daphne's eyes to become temporarily glued to her brain, they had rolled so far back in her skull.

Tabitha snorted. "If Calliope were a person, it would basically be the Bubble Boy."

"I'm sure that we're safe on campus from whoever attacked Professor Taylor." Daphne leaned against her desk. "But how do you all know so much about murders?"

Aspen grinned. "I listen to true crime podcasts, like every other breathing human being in the twenty-first century, Professor Ouverture."

Tabitha made a face. "Don't bother, Professor. It's just a bunch of white people killing each other all the time. And yet they think *we're* the criminals."

"On that note," Daphne said, "I'm going to get my laptop set up and hope that students show."

It took a while—maybe longer than Daphne would have liked—for students to stream in toward their usual seats, unloading their backpacks and coats like ER nurses who'd just worked a double shift.

Daphne greeted every student individually, having memorized their names instantly before the first day of class. It flattered them that a professor could greet each student so quickly upon meeting them and Daphne didn't have the heart to tell them that she could memorize text faster than AI could generate a sonnet praising Trader Joe's in the style of Sylvia Plath. Plus, she really wanted her students to like her, so what was the harm in exerting a crumb of effort toward attaching faces to easily learned names?

With enough bodies in seats to run a class, she loaded her slides onto the screen and began with the usual housekeeping matters—their final exam, a reminder not to text in class, and an announcement that she planned to return their papers by the end of the week.

"When will we get our papers back?" asked a bro named Connor, dressed in sweatpants and an oversized Harrison sweatshirt.

There was always a Connor.

Every semester since Daphne had started out as a teaching assistant in grad school, she'd had Connors, Madisons, Ethans, Taylors, and Tylers, the last two of which were always a fun surprise to uncover on the first day of class, since their monikers guaranteed no gender affiliation. At least this Connor was sweeter than the Connor she'd taught last semester, even if he literally only cared about scoring higher than a C- on any given assignment.

"As I just said," Daphne replied, her voice low and slow as her patience began to thread, "you all will get your papers back by the end of the week. Any other questions?"

"Yeah," Connor replied. "Like, Professor Ouverture, why are we having class when, like, someone died, you know? Shouldn't class be canceled?"

"Canceled?" Rohit barked out in alarm.

"You know," Connor mumbled, "to like honor that professor or whatever."

"If we did that," Daphne said, "we'd push back our already tight schedule. Again."

Groans erupted from the students. Among them was Olivia Vail, a pretty brunette with pale skin and wide brown eyes who refused to wear anything but her Alpha Phi sorority gear. Olivia was her problem student this term, a graduating senior who was so checked out she could give an overdue library book a run for its money. The fact that she showed up at all was a miracle of such extreme rarity that Daphne felt compelled to register it with the Vatican. Normally Olivia's makeup was as flawless as her matching jumpsuits but today her mascara had blurred her eyes, which were unusually red and puffy.

"Or how about we take like ten minutes to reflect on Professor Taylor and get our conversation marked for extra participation points?" Aspen suggested.

"Yeah," said Connor, far too happy to endorse Aspen's proposal. "Let's do that."

Perhaps he meant his request to appear sincere but Daphne suspected it was because he hadn't done the reading. Connor(s) rarely did the reading.

But Daphne tried her best to take her students' concerns to heart, no matter how infinitesimal. And it honestly wasn't that bad of an idea. If students needed to take some time to process Sam's death, she could make space for that.

She stared down the crowd with her best poker face. "What do you have in mind?"

"Professor," Rohit begged, visibly distraught. "Can we *please* talk about French colonial soldiers' experiences of WWI and get into why they fought for an empire that denigrated them?"

"I'll start," said Connor. "I mean, I never met Professor Taylor but he seemed like a good guy, you know? He supported students on campus and stuff."

"Mmm," Daphne replied. That statement was emptier than a political campaign promise but she'd rather get a splinter under a fingernail than push Connor to articulate himself further. "Anyone else want to share?"

Tabitha's cute button nose twitched as if she'd stepped in something nasty. "I stayed as far away from him as possible. Y'all know my policy on learning about racism from white teachers."

"Duly noted," Daphne said before a white kid could voice their disagreement. "Anyone else?"

Daphne's ears pricked up at the gulp Olivia made in the ensuing silence. Olivia suddenly became far too engrossed in scrawling in her notebook.

"Olivia?" Daphne pried. "Did you want to say anything?"

Olivia kept scrawling. "Nope."

"Did you know him, Professor Ouverture?" Connor asked. "Professor Taylor?"

"Yeah," Aspen said, sarcasm oozing from their voice. "Because maybe Professor Ouverture's the killer."

"That's not what I meant." Connor's face crumpled. "Professor Ouverture, I would *never* accuse you of murder without just cause."

"I knew him a little bit. Not well, though." Sam's weird text message about *Papillon* flashed in her mind again but she pushed it away. She'd search for that book at home again later.

"What was he like?" Connor really was stalling for time, wasn't he? "Was he nice?"

Nice?

That wasn't exactly the word she'd use for Sam.

Cocky.

Arrogant.

She settled on saying, "Professor Taylor was someone who was committed to making a difference in this world."

Tabitha snorted. "Isn't everyone here?"

"Perhaps," Daphne said. "Some argue that the pursuit of truth in its own right is enough of a goal, regardless of outcome. Others think that production and dissemination of knowledge is always transformational. What do *you* think is the point of higher education?"

Imaginary crickets chirped in the silence that followed her question.

Connor shrugged. "I thought it was to get us jobs?"

Daphne opened her laptop with a sigh. "And with those words of inspiration to motivate us to new heights, let's get back to the violence of WWI."

Rohit's smile could have powered Calliope's electric grid.

BACK IN her office, Daphne considered the half-truth she'd just repeated about Sam, the same one she'd said to Trudy. She'd meant it, actually—Sam really had been eager to make a difference. Rumor had it he'd been talking to the dining staff about unionizing for better pay during his off hours, having found an attorney to represent them. She'd even seen him step between two students about to throw hands on the quad, his palms raised and CNN anchor voice low and calm. His plan to change society was practically the first thing that had come out of his mouth when she met him, which had annoyed her because who actually admits that what you're hoping to do is change the world? Most academics didn't think in those terms. To many high-minded scholars, the pursuit of knowledge—or even, dare they say it, Truth—was an end unto itself.

Or, rather, most academics professed not to think like that because they were probably too ashamed to admit their nagging suspicions: It wasn't easy to gauge if their work mattered.

Not Sam, though.

He *knew.*

At faculty orientation two summers ago, he'd swaggered in his fashionable blazer into the banquet hall, where baby faculty had been milling about, waiting for the dean to bark at them to get to work, and said loudly to everyone that his research on the carceral state was going to set the world on fire. Daphne had smothered her laugh. Because who said stuff like that with a straight face?

Another idea bubbled up, tickling that spot between her eyes. What if it was true? What if Sam's research really was going to change the world?

Daphne glanced up at the clock on her wall, gleaming bright in orange, white, and green—the colors of Ivory Coast's flag. It was such a tiny, silly thing, but her parents had gifted it to her years ago when, hiding in her Parisian apartment in the throes of dissertation writing, she'd let go of the entire concept of time. Deep into writing, having lived in her pajamas for days, she'd called her dad to share some archival document that she'd finished transcribing, only to be told that it was two o'clock in the morning and maybe she should go to sleep. The ticking clock told her that she had about an hour before a student was likely to knock on her door. She should spend that hour outlining the second chapter of her manuscript, which was about as coherent as a sorority girl waiting for an Uber at three in the morning. But maybe she could just casually peek around at Sam's research first.

Daphne scrolled through the library's database to see what Sam had published already—which was a lot by academic standards. Getting a scholarly article through the pipelines usually took at least eighteen months but Sam already had an article out in the flagship anthropology journal, which was a huge feather in the cap of any junior professor.

You have a big article, too, Daph, she reminded herself. Her piece on Black women's social networks in eighteenth-century France had won a prize from the French Historical Society last month.

Daphne continued to scroll through the never-ending list of publications in academic journals and newspapers alike. It became clear that Sam's work mostly stemmed from his secondary career as a really successful media pundit. She clicked on some headline title about "American Prisons" and jumped when a CNN video loaded up instead.

"Returning live to CNN, we have Professor Sam Taylor from Harrison University . . ."

Goosebumps prickled across Daphne's skin. There he was. Sam Taylor, alive, beaming sharp white teeth and unending confidence.

". . . and I'll say it again: It is absolutely shameful that the United States' prison population is bigger than the entire state of New Mexico, it's shameful that African Americans and Latinos make up over fifty percent of that population, and it's shameful that the United States government has no interest in reducing any of these numbers."

"But Professor Taylor, how do you actually propose to change what you describe in your research as a 'crisis'?"

"The solution I offer is the same that Black activists like Angela Davis have been shouting down for decades: The time has long come to abolish prisons."

Well, that take probably hadn't made Sam many friends. The comments alone on YouTube stoked admiration and hatred in equal measure and it was quite likely that the worst ones had already been flagged and removed. But maybe someone had decided to take their comments offline. Maybe some-one had decided to tell Sam to his face exactly what they thought of his work. Maybe one of them had blood on their hands.

After a while, Daphne angled her laptop screen downward and rubbed her face, conscious not to smear her already smudged eyeliner any further.

Guilt had started eating away at her. When had she started tuning Sam out? When had she decided that it was easier to ignore him while he droned on about his research rather than to pay attention to it? It wasn't entirely Sam's fault that she hadn't listened to him. It had always annoyed her how Americanists believed in the urgency of their work at the expense of others'. As if the lives of Africans, Asians, and other people from the Global South weren't just as important.

"*Prisons do not rehabilitate*," Sam was saying from her partially closed computer, "*they break people, they enslave people, they exist to further a racial capitalist regime that depends on the bodies of people of color in order to sustain inequity.*"

The spark flickered between her eyes again. A tune came calling back. Daphne knew that line.

It took a solid twenty minutes of rummaging through Sam's writings before she found the quote in a *New York Times* article from a few days ago. Sam had written another op-ed pontificating about the injustices of imprisonment but also claiming that he was on the cusp of exposing the violent and illegal operations of a local prison right near . . . Calliope?

Only a short drive from an elite university, Livington Prison is the dire opposite of enlightenment, Sam had written. *Inside the bare prison walls, inmates are denied access to clean water, and those who survive face a lifetime of physical disabilities from which they will never recover.*

The pulse in Daphne's throat quickened.

In Henri Charrière's novel Papillon *he writes that "The Chinese invented water torture. The French invented silence." But as I will show you in these next several columns, Livington mastered pain.*

This must be a dream, Daphne told herself, shoving herself away from her desk. A very weird dream in which a seventies novel and a murdered anthropologist equated . . . just what, exactly, other than some surreal nightmare that impacted her ability to function at her job?

That night, as Daphne lay in her bed, too exhausted to get up, too antsy to succumb to sleep lest the images of Sam's messy bookshelves come back, she clenched her fingers tight and released them slowly, just as her meditation podcast advised her to do, hoping to purge her thoughts. A soothing voice told her to breathe in and out while Chloe snortled and wheezed on her pillow next to her and she willed herself to follow the mantras being chanted into her ears.

And failed.

Opening her eyes wide into the dark, she almost choked on the tension and grief seizing her throat, slithering across her chest and down each and every one of her limbs. A voice hissed, quiet and true, for her to *pay attention*, for she could no longer avoid connecting the dots falling before her.

Sam had apparently been investigating some kind of danger-ous crime at a prison nearby. But what did that have to do with her? Why did he text her a line from *that* book? Why text her at all? Maybe it meant nothing? But what if it *did* mean some-thing? How the hell was she supposed to know? And what was she supposed to do about any of this?

The shards of glass strewn across Sam's office floor flashed in her mind.

And Daphne still didn't know how to pick up the pieces and make them fit.

Pay attention, the voice said again. And for the life of her, Daphne couldn't discern if that phrase was meant to be a sug-gestion or a warning.

CHAPTER FIVE

"The musicologists are mutinying."

Daphne yawned so hard her nose rattled. Another night of tossing and turning so wildly in her sleep had wreaked havoc with her mind. She'd accidentally kicked a sleepy Chloe off the bed. A vat of coffee this morning on her drive to campus had barely made a dent. Even Miranda's abrupt arrival into her office and shouty declaration couldn't lift Daphne out of her fog.

All because Daphne had rummaged through her bookcases and come up short. All because she couldn't get the shards of glass on Sam's office floor out of her mind.

Shit, she just needed to finish grading her papers.

"Did you hear what I just said?" Miranda was peering at her curiously. "The musicologists are mutinying—and Film Studies is joining them."

"But don't the musicologists always threaten to mutiny?" Daphne asked, biting into a piece of baklava from Greek Life Bakery.

"But this time they actually are."

"Whatever for?"

Miranda paused, her thin arms crossed while she leaned against Daphne's office doorway. "Did you solve the plagiarism case?"

Daphne's lips twisted into a tiny frown at Miranda's redirection. But she yanked the paper out of her bag and handed it to

Miranda. In the haze of last night's fit of sleeplessness, she'd finally overturned enough books and papers on her desk to find Kiki's paper.

"I did," Daphne said. "Do you know Kiki Ilunga, the graduate student in anthropology working on institutional confinement in Central Africa? I'm taking care of her succulents while she's in the Democratic Republic of the Congo doing fieldwork. Anyway, she asked me to be on her dissertation committee last semester and to get to know her work, I read this fabulous paper she wrote on changing definitions of madness and confinement in mid-twentieth-century Zimbabwe."

"I'll take your word for it." Miranda sat down across from Daphne's desk. "And you're sure the paper I gave you borrows from Ms. Ilunga's?"

"Well, yes, but—" Daphne squiggled in her seat. "Kiki's essay hasn't been published anywhere. And as far as I know I'm one of the only people who's read it. I'd ask her what's going on but she's across an ocean with spotty internet service."

Miranda's wiry, slender fingers twisted around while she assessed Daphne's bookshelves, stuffed to the brim with the usual volumes on histories of empire, France, race, and gender. When she turned to Daphne again, her taut frown had hardened. "I think it's time I tell you why the musicologists are vowing to overthrow the first estate."

Daphne jerked a shoulder. "Okay."

"However much it pains me to admit it," Miranda said, "they're enraged for legitimate reasons. Ken Miller."

The small hairs on Daphne's neck and forearms prickled.

"Yes, him, Daphne. I know."

Few people at Harrison made Miranda want to burn everything down to the ground quite like Ken Miller, the interim dean of the College of Arts and Sciences. It was easy to be so taken in by Ken Miller's Patagonia sweaters and tales of kayaking in the Alaskan wilderness that you didn't see the bus coming for your back.

"The only place Ken is fit to rule is Mordor, and even they'd want to file an OSHA complaint. I know I should stop yelling about this, but seriously, Daphne, what kind of a human refuses to work with his own grad student upon discovering that she's pregnant?"

Women on campus had raised hell after Ken's egregious violation of faculty-student relations but the damage had already been done and the promising doctoral student dropped out.

Ken Miller's most recent ascension as the temporary leader of the College of Arts and Sciences had cast a chill among faculty ranks. The College of Arts and Sciences was the largest college within Harrison University, housing the most foundational majors and drawing in the most undergraduate students per credit hour. While the College of Engineering or the School of Public Health were prestigious in their own right, it was the College of Arts and Sciences that kept the university coffers flowing.

Judging from faculty grumblings, the politics behind Ken's new appointment from anthropology chair to dean of Harrison's largest college had been shady as hell. The way Daphne understood it, one moment the previous dean had been cutting ribbons to celebrate the opening of a new technologically enhanced classroom and the next he was gone, having tendered his sudden resignation and appointed Ken Miller as his replacement. Faculty had had no say in the choosing of their new leader.

Granted, Ken Miller's appointment was only for a semester until Harrison University's board found a permanent hire, but rumor had it that Ken had already greased up members of the board so much that FEMA should have been notified of an oil spill. The faculty on campus were bracing themselves for the announcement of his tenure any day now.

"What did he do this time?"

Miranda leaned back in her seat. "He told the musicologists that they don't need to hire a second medievalist."

"But they don't."

Miranda wagged a finger at Daphne. "That's beside the point. Miller said that what the music department needs is an ethnomusicologist with a specialist in non-Western music."

Daphne paused. "I loathe him as much as the next person, Miranda, and I never thought I'd say this out loud, but I think I agree with Ken Miller."

"Of course you do. I do, too. But the fact of the matter is that the department should be able to hire whomever they want."

"Hence the mutiny," Daphne said.

Miranda laughed. "No, the mutiny comes from Ken Miller having the audacity to propose a short list of candidates—all of whom are his former students."

Daphne gaped at Miranda. "He can do that?"

"He shouldn't be able to. But who can say no to the interim dean?"

"There must be a way to stop him."

"Oh, there is." Miranda's gaze became inscrutable. "But it requires the same investigator who just told me that Miller had plagiarized from a graduate student."

"That was *him*?" Daphne's eyes widened. "He stole from Kiki?"

"Yup."

Daphne's jaw was underneath the basement of Davis Hall. "But—"

"Daphne," Miranda said, leaning forward in her chair, "I have it on good authority that Ken Miller believes that we've hired too many faculty who work on race and gender. He used the language of 'overcorrected' with the board last week."

Daphne's stomach dropped into her shoes. Her heart began to pound. "But he's an anthropologist who works on Africa."

"Exactly," Miranda said. "That's how he justifies his position to the board. He's an expert on 'those natives.' Who better to critique the transformation of American higher education and its supposed overreliance on race and gender theory than an old white man who studies 'primitive' Africans for a living?"

The world lurched. Daphne pinched her nose. "This just doesn't make any sense."

"It's bad enough that he's been a pestilence inflicted upon this campus for twenty-five years," Miranda said, "but the megalomaniac will be absolutely destructive if he's allowed to assume the deanship. Daphne, he'll sink your tenure case."

For a moment Daphne became weightless. She stared ahead at the six years of hard work before her, her push to prove she belonged at an institution like Harrison—destroyed in minutes by a vainglorious overlord with a penchant for Alaskan fly-fishing.

She swallowed. "Is there a way to stop him?"

"I believe so, yes." Miranda's look shimmered with cunning. "A small cadre's formed to ensure his permanent demise. Step one was finding out who was behind that essay you read the other day, which Miller submitted in his portfolio for the position. That paper was far too lively and intellectually rigorous for it to have been written by him, so I put you on the case."

Outrage and grief mingled together in Daphne's chest at Ken's theft. Research was the only real currency that any academic possessed. It not only transformed knowledge but it changed the author's career. To have it so blatantly stolen was beyond a tragedy. It was a crime. And unfortunately, Ken's misdeeds could cost Kiki her entire career if and when he denied any wrongdoing—her entire future, her livelihood snuffed out by a powerful man Kiki couldn't stop.

But Miranda wasn't done yet. "Are you ready for your assignment?"

Daphne choked on her tea. "Miranda—"

Her boss raised up a thin, veined hand. "Just hear me out. We're pretty sure Miller has something on the previous dean. How else can one explain that quick resignation? That man had the stubbornness of an old goat. Now, we don't know what's going on with Ken but the chairs and I knocked our heads together and we thought you might be able to find out."

It took several seconds before Daphne could squeak out her reply. "Me?"

"Oh, come off it, Daphne. You've been putting your unusual gifts to use for some time, haven't you? Isn't anything preferable to helping out Vicky in Archaeology, who I know for a fact is just too wrapped up in her own drama—literally drama—with Jay over in Theater to manage her own classes?"

Daphne bit her lip. "And what, exactly, am I supposed to do?"

"Oh, I don't actually *know*, Daphne," Miranda said. "None of us do. Maybe a visit to his office might turn up some hard evidence that we can present to the university president? Don't do anything illegal, of course. Just . . . see if you spot anything suspicious."

Daphne sat rigid in her chair inside her lovely office while the morning sun streamed inside, unable to move, unable to do anything but stare at her Josephine Baker coloring book. She resented it. This war in her mind, an ongoing conflict between coloring in the lines and ripping up the paper altogether to find out how it was made. She was just supposed to teach her classes, grade her papers, and be a good colleague, not . . . whatever this was. She certainly wasn't supposed to feed this Thing that occasionally whispered to her like some glamorous misbehaving cat.

Why did she even want to sneak into Miller's office and glean what had never been meant for her eyes? That was a question she couldn't yet face because she suspected she knew the answer. But with the fate of her own tenure case resting on her shoulders, and a welcome distraction from Sam Taylor's weird text message, her resistance to Miranda's charge collapsed like a house of cards.

Daphne fortified herself with one last sip of tea. "What was the name of the previous dean again?"

"Granbee." Miranda lifted her chin. "Kirk Granbee."

THE DEAN of the College of Arts and Sciences resided in Gordon Hall, a decadent eyesore that everyone at Harrison fondly called "The Dragon's Lair." Harrison University's administration and alumni usually refused to approve the construction of buildings that weren't designed by either Thomas Jefferson or an architect from the sixties on an acid trip but Gordon Hall was one of the few exceptions. The cream-colored castle wrapped in ivy was a testament to one moneyed alum's devotion to fulfilling a medievalist professor's basest fantasies. The Disneyfied monstrosity was as whimsical as it was nonsensical, and it took little to imagine a dragon sauntering up to the fortress's bailey, plopping its thick belly down, and wrapping its tail around the building's spire.

While the top floor of Gordon Hall was reserved for the president's office, the east wing hosted the dean's official suite—if you could survive the climb to get there. Only recently made accessible by elevator, the winding stairs that took you to the dean's office spilled out onto a soaring solarium with opulent emerald and sapphire tapestries draped across its thick stone walls. It was impossible to mistake the dean's office for anything other than what it was: one of the highest seats of power at a university used to birthing senators and Wall Street bankers.

Inside the waiting room, Daphne stared at a framed Italian Baroque painting next to the bay window. In it, a young white woman sat on a ledge, naked except for a small towel draped over one thigh, her graceful neck twisted painfully as she turned away from the leering men who whispered to her, disturbing her bath. *Susanna and the Elders*, read the card next to it, *by Artemisia Gentileschi.*

"May I help you?"

At the front desk, a white woman nearing retirement age gave Daphne a polite smile. Her small name plate beamed out IRINA SAMSANOFF.

Daphne waved awkwardly. "Ms. Samsanoff?"

The secretary's smile widened. "Please call me Irina."

Daphne took that as an invitation to smile back. "Hi, my name is Daphne Ouverture, and I was hoping to see Ken Miller? It's his office hours right now."

At that, the woman typed something at her desk. "You're a student?"

"No," said Daphne. "Faculty. In the history department."

"My, but you look so young!" Irina said. "When did you start?"

"Just this past fall," Daphne replied, proud of herself for keeping the irritation out of her voice.

"If it helps," Irina said, still typing some note on her computer, "I think everyone looks young these days. I used to be in the anthropology department before moving here with Ken, and I swear every year the new cohort of junior professors keeps aging down like Benjamin Button."

"Anthropology?" Daphne hesitated a beat before pushing on. "Did you, ah, know Sam Taylor?"

"He was a wonderful member of our community." Irina gave her a sad smile. "It's still such a shock, isn't it?"

Daphne grasped for a polite reply, settling for, "I'm sorry for your loss."

"It's awful," Irina agreed. "To be robbed and murdered, to have his life stolen from him. It's a tragedy for everyone."

It took all her strength to keep her gaze relaxed. Innocent, even. "Robbed?"

Irina nodded. "The police came in to talk to us about it this morning. His laptop and his phone are missing."

"That's terrible," Daphne said. "I was just reading one of his op-eds the other day. About a nearby prison?"

"Was it the *Washington Post* one?" Irina asked. "Or that article in the *LA Times*? He was so prolific."

"I don't remember," Daphne said. "But if his laptop is gone, hopefully his work is backed up on Dropbox or something like that."

"It sounds like it's all been deleted," Irina replied. "The detectives asked if I knew other ways to access his information, which I sadly don't. Anyway, you didn't come here to ask about that. What is it that you'd like?"

Daphne had no clue what to make of that. No academic in their right mind would go anywhere without a laptop, a backup hard drive, or at least all of their files in the cloud.

"You said you wanted to see Ken?" Irina asked, and so Daphne had to collect herself.

"Yes," she replied. "I had a few questions about—" What *did* she have questions about? "—Congolese history and I, ah, remembered that he was an expert. On the Congo."

"Sure," Irina said. "Go right on in."

The soft gentle lines around Ken Miller's eyes, formed from years of hiking in summer, crinkled as he rose up to greet her. Bright white teeth flashed against the light tan on his narrow face, giving him the cheery appearance of a silver fox on the cover of an REI catalogue clasping a fishing rod and a string of fresh trout.

"Tiffany!" Ken Miller reached over to give her hand a vigorous shake.

Daphne's cheeks burned hot.

"Nope, not Tiffany," she corrected him through a gritted smile. "Daphne."

Which meant she owed yet another old-fashioned to Tiffany LaFleur, Harrison's resident sociologist of medicine. Even though Tiffany had the waif-like gait of a ballerina and Daphne could simply think of a piece of bread and gain five pounds, the two of them were mistaken for each other so much on campus that Daphne had proposed, in a snarky kinda way, that they buy each other a drink whenever a white person on campus made that gaffe. They were different heights, different sizes, different skin tones—Tiffany's being a particularly freckly ginger snap cookie color that Daphne envied—but that apparently wasn't going to prevent either of them from joining Alcoholics Anonymous.

Daphne didn't really mind putting another on her tab at the Thirsty Scholar if it meant that she could hang out with Tiffany again. She just hated winning a contest that shouldn't exist.

Miller didn't even have the wherewithal to appear embarrassed by his mix-up. "That's right. Daphne! As Irina probably told you, things are a bit hectic here with Sam's passing but I can spare a few minutes to chat. You had a question about the Congo?"

Daphne gave him the most softball question she could think of, knowing he'd pontificate for a while, which he of course did. She tried her best to appear deeply engaged while impatience whirled around inside her: She had to get a moment alone in his office.

"But what about the theory that paternalistic definitions of chiefdom omit matriarchal forms of power?" Daphne tossed out in the hopes that she could buy another five minutes of bloviation.

Ken snorted. "A typical question from scholars of your generation. I actually think that we've overplayed the importance of matrilineal influence in the public sphere," and he was off again, chewing over her question like a hound with a bone. Good heavens, the man was eager to hear his own voice.

"If you can give me just a moment," Ken said, "I can email a few articles to you."

Inspiration flashed. "Actually, would you mind printing them for me?"

Ken's smile nauseated her. "Not at all, Daphne. Anything for a young colleague like yourself."

He hopped out of his chair and practically skipped down the hallway.

Before she could chicken out, Daphne yanked a hand across

Ken's desk, grabbed his laptop, and typed "Kirk Granbee" into his email's search bar. She prayed to Saint Josephine Bakhita for protection under her breath while she scrolled through a litany of messages, Kiki very much on her mind—until she found what Miranda was searching for. She read through the message twice, just to be sure, and hovered her finger above the mouse of Ken's laptop. Did she have time to search for Kiki Ilunga, too?

Ken's voice grew louder outside the doorway.

Daphne clicked out of the screen, swiveling the laptop back to its former position right as Ken sailed back in.

"Thank you so much for your help, Dr. Miller," Daphne said, taking a stack of papers from him.

"Ken." He grinned too wide. "Just keep me in mind the next time you want to chat about Congolese rituals. Maybe you could let me buy you lunch sometime."

Daphne tried to hide the panic in her eyes as she smiled back. Then she shot up and mumbled some sort of goodbye, grasping for the chair's front door like a life raft before flinging herself out of the office.

Perhaps that's why she didn't see the man coming.

She thudded right into a thin chest.

Large hands gripped her forearms to steady her—too late. Daphne still managed to topple them both to the ground.

"I am *so* sorry," Daphne squeaked.

"My sincerest apologies," a pleasantly deep voice murmured at the same time. It sounded warm. Inviting. Daphne strained her neck to peer up the long length of a male torso splayed out on top of hers. A pair of gray eyes inspected hers behind thin metal frames. They were curious and elegant—pretty, even.

She must have been holding her breath because she gasped out, "It's okay, I'm fine."

"Rowan?" came a familiar scratchy voice from down the hall.

Recognition sliced into Daphne's frazzled mind. The woman she'd met yesterday outside of Sam's office. The man who had been dusting the bookshelves and avoiding glass shards on the floor.

The warmth of his body was gone a moment later. From the ground she was surprised to see him—Rowan—at full height, his now tousled brown hair practically touching the ceiling. He stretched out a spindly arm to offer his hand. Delicate, long fingers that would make a pianist weep in envy joined with hers, pulling her upright with surprising strength. She wasn't sure who let go first but at the loss of his touch, she stammered out some kind of apologetic hello and goodbye while the pair made their way into Ken's office.

A minute earlier and they would have caught her. Daphne placed her cool palms against her very hot cheeks, blushing all over again.

"Professor Ouverture, are you okay?"

Daphne started. She whirled around to find Irina peering at her curiously.

"Oh, um, sorry," Daphne stammered. "I'm fine, I just—right. I'm gonna . . . I'm gonna go . . ."

But Daphne's feet refused to obey her words. "Who was—I mean, are those the detectives looking into Sam's murder?"

"You mean Detective Ahmed and Mr. Peterson?" Irina beamed. "They've been great to work with so far."

"That's lovely." Daphne was nodding too much. "Really lovely. Great. Lovely."

Irina's eyebrows lifted a hair.

"Uh, I'll see myself out," said Daphne. "Thanks again for your help."

Her smile was definitely too bright. Detective Ahmed and Mr. Rowan Peterson. Detectives here to investigate Sam's death. The circumstances surrounding that man's arrival were somber and dead serious, and Daphne should have been ashamed by how excited she was to finally put a name to that pretty face.

That she wasn't made her blush even harder.

"ISN'T IT a bit ungracious of you to be complaining, Kirk? Your Vanessa Waters situation didn't just handle itself. I did that. It's called a tit for tat. Surely you can see the irony in that, considering your predilection."

Back inside Daphne's sunny office, Miranda's frail form trembled. "Oh my God."

Daphne exhaled slowly, letting the evidence she'd uncovered take up necessary space in her room. "I take it you know who Vanessa Waters is?"

Her boss's lips formed into a thin, hard line. "Unfortunately, I do. She was a former psychology major here. A junior. She dropped out last year after having some kind of public meltdown in front of Granbee's office, if the rumors are true."

Daphne flinched. "Good lord."

Miranda bit her thumbnail saying nothing.

Daphne sank into silence. Exhaustion was beginning to nibble away at her insides, its sleepy fog sliding across her skin like silk. As a historian she was used to evidence being lost. Archives collected what they wished, leaving other traces of the past to fall to ruin—and that was if archives had survived bombings from wars to begin with. People destroyed records of their own activities during their lifetimes. Claude Monet had burned some of his own paintings toward the end of his life. Hell, even Sam Taylor's data appeared to be lost. Being a historian was to search for the truth with one hand tied behind your back. But Daphne forgot that finding the truth didn't always make you feel better.

Eventually she asked, "What are you going to do?"

"I don't know what I *can* do." Miranda met Daphne's eyes. "But whatever happens next, I'll make sure you're protected from the fallout."

"Ken can't get away with this, can he?"

Miranda cocked her head to the side, regarding Daphne with pity. "I'd like to say that's true. But if we've learned anything from our historical research, dear, it's that men can get away with anything."

CHAPTER SIX

In a university town like Calliope, there were certain items that poured onto the tree-lined streets in overabundance: artisanal vegan cheese makers, microbiologists who made mead out of their garages, yoga studios offering hot vinyasa classes, bike stores, coffee shops for writing the Next Great American Novel, and, of course, bars. Lots of bars. Most junior professors loved the Thirsty Scholar, a pub offering burgers, truffle fries, and Belgian ales under dim lighting, but since Sadie was barely allowed on the premises anymore after making good on her promise to a patron that he was "gonna catch these hands," Daphne, Elise, and Sadie had settled for Valencia as the location for their weekly outings, a Spanish restaurant with an extensive tapas menu, satellite dish–sized pans of paella, and sangria in jars the size of Paul Bunyan's head, and how could anyone resist that?

Seizing her favorite spot at the bar, a wide slab of white marble that was perfect for people-watching, Daphne placed her usual order for sangria and cheese croquettes and finally, against the backdrop of Baroque blue and white Spanish porcelain tiles, relaxed for the first time in an eternity while she waited for her friends to arrive. Her involvement in Miranda's quest to topple a kingmaker at Harrison no longer pinched at the corners of her eyes. Sure, she'd rather be invisible than take on a powerful monster, but it turned out that rage over Kiki's injustice was a fuel strong enough to override her career anxieties, at least temporarily. Even Sam's text message didn't grate that much against her skin anymore, with Daphne choosing to toss it off as a minor inconvenience. Waves of relief washed over her while she sipped her sangria. She'd kept waiting for some other shoe to drop—but it had never come. Sam's text had scrambled her brain for a few days but that's all it was: a fluke. *Papillon* would turn up. It was only a matter of time.

To that, Daphne took another swig.

She was still queasy about Sam's death, of course. Students had sworn to host nightly candlelit vigils until the killer was caught. Who knew if they'd ever find anyone? How many murders went unsolved, anyway? Judging by news articles and social media posts, no one had any idea why a beloved professor on campus had been bludgeoned to death in his own home.

"Hey girl hey!" Sadie swagged over to Daphne with a sangria the size of Los Angeles.

Elise trailed behind. "Girl, you look like a pirate with that bucket of sangria you're holding."

"Yeah, but a sexy pirate, am I right?" Sadie wrapped her sparkly lips around her straw and winked. Daphne burst out laughing.

Daphne, Sadie, and Elise became best friends after finding one another at some university-sponsored mixer for faculty of color last term. Daphne thought she had been making do just fine with her white colleagues—until Elise and Sadie had barged into her life. They all had different variations on how they met, on who first recognized the other, spoke to each other. Daphne mostly remembered trying to work up the courage to speak to Elise, who was more pristine than a newly unveiled Prada bag, with side-swept bangs that fell elegantly across her pale, slim face. Daphne'd managed to put two sentences together in front of her anyway, and in the process had learned that Elise was also a junior professor.

The conversation took off the moment Daphne and Elise realized they'd been raised by tough, immigrant mothers. At some point when swapping strategies for surviving varying punishment methods, a tall Brown Amazonian goddess in the most outrageous buttercup-yellow blouse had leaned across the bar and asked if she could compare notes.

By the third margarita, they were screaming with laughter about the perils of surviving middle school with a mother who refused to pack sandwiches like the white moms. By one in the morning, the trio was dancing to Lil Wayne at a bar downtown and making plans to meet for brunch the next day.

Brunch had lasted approximately ten minutes. Wearing sunglasses and croaking in pleading tones for coffee, they sat in silence, enduring the painful sounds of the bustling café—until Sadie pointed out that she lived around the corner and had a large sectional couch. They'd napped away the rest of the day in Sadie's living room like toddlers at preschool until their hunger woke them up.

One of Daphne's favorite memories to this day was waking up to the smell of spicy chicken curry—a pot of leftovers that Sadie had slowly warmed up—its potent combination of spices and herbs pleasantly torturing her nostrils. She and Elise had cried while they ate it, laughing and choking, drinking mango lassis to try to dull the pain so that they could keep going. For the rest of the day, the gang had watched old *Living Single* episodes and consumed an inordinate amount of Sri Lankan black tea, a tangle of legs and socked feet on the couch.

Something had clicked for Daphne that day—an actual

physical feeling of her brain making sense of herself. Sadie and Elise had gifted her with the greatest freedom through their friendship. The freedom to be her most honest, messiest self.

Elise eyed her up and down. "You doing okay, Daphne? You need another glass of wine? More charcuterie?"

"You're always so thoughtful," Daphne said. "Too thoughtful. It's why you're my mother's favorite."

"That's not true."

Daphne arched a brow. "You're slim and a scientist, Elise. You're every immigrant mom's favorite daughter."

"Amen to that," Sadie said.

"And I'm doing fine, I promise," Daphne said. "I just had a weird day at work. You?"

Elise's smile was too bright. "Good!"

Sadie put down her trough of sangria. "This bitch is a liar. What, Elise? You have a mug full of the hottest tea known to humankind and you haven't spilled any of it."

"Oh?" Daphne turned to Elise. "You'd deny your very best friend some gossip?"

"Of course I wouldn't!" Elise protested. "But you're looking a little tired, and I want to be respectful of—"

"Whatever, nobody cares," Sadie interjected, cutting through the air with her bejeweled and tattooed hand. As always, her razor-sharp fingernails matched her glittering lips. "Spill."

Elise stared deadpan at Daphne, her shiny, black hair swaying lightly as she cocked her head. "John is dating Ashley Durham."

"What?" Daphne yelped. "Ashley? The one who told us she thought that alopecia was a flower?"

Sadie snapped her fingers at that read.

"The very same," Elise solemnly replied.

Daphne was dumbfounded. "The girl who—honest to God—thought that five quarters made a dollar?"

"She also asked me once why I spoke such good English," Elise reminded them.

Even Daphne had to resist the urge to take out her earrings and fight.

"Men are trash," said Elise.

"Garbage," said Daphne.

"*Trash*," Sadie agreed.

Daphne had never cared for John, an economics professor at Harrison. Elise had been devastated when he had called it off a few weeks back after three months of dating. Daphne was, frankly, perplexed by Elise's grief. Elise was a goddess. Before earning her PhD in toxicology and becoming one of the world's leading experts in broad-spectrum antidote delivery, she had traveled the world for years working with women in local villages to create sanitation systems in water-precarious zones, all while fending off proposals from minor princes she'd met during her travels. John was, well, a guy who liked football?

"How?" Daphne asked in between bites of patatas bravas. "How did they even meet?"

"How do you think?" Elise popped an olive in her mouth, somehow managing to look even more elegant. "He came by to visit me one day at work. And then he bumped into Ashley later at the gym. So he says, anyway."

"'Later?' Waitaminute—" Daphne slowly put two and two together. "You don't think . . ."

"Yes, bitch," Sadie confirmed.

Elise just shook her head. "I'd rather not presume."

"Well I certainly will," Sadie said, her gallon of sangria

swaying in her hands. "And how nasty is that? John and Trashley Simpson were totally having eye sex in *your lab* with you right there. And then hooking up later at the gym! It's enough to make *me* want to *Lemonade* his car, Elise."

Daphne glanced sideways at Sadie. Most people wouldn't smash in the windows of a former lover's car with a baseball bat but Sadie wasn't most people. As the former bassist in an anarchist punk band, Sadie had cultivated a small but impressive rap sheet that included, among other things, punching out security at a live show, setting fire to an ex's car, and wrestling a televangelist to the ground.

"I'm going to change the subject in order to avoid becoming implicated in any violent acts." Elise grinned at Daphne. "Perhaps you have more uplifting news to share?"

Daphne took a long sip of her drink to erase the memory of Ken Miller attempting to pick her up in his office. "Nope. I'm just going to give more examples of why we need to shuttle men off to another planet."

Quietly, Daphne filled her besties in on Miranda's quest for vengeance. They dutifully gasped when Daphne revealed that Ken had stolen Kiki's paper and oohed at Daphne's investigative work inside Ken's office. Of course in that moment her mind played back her collision with that detective with the beautiful gray eyes.

"Are you blushing?" Elise asked.

"What? No."

Sadie's squint at Daphne was menacing. "I think she's trying to pull a fast one on us, Elise. Like we can't see her perfectly moisturized chocolatey-brown goddess skin glowing."

"No, it's not."

"Don't even try it," Sadie hooted. "I've sampled your Fenty

Beauty products from your tiny-ass bathroom before—don't give me that surprised look—and so I can one hundred percent verify that we have the same skin tone. I know what blushing looks like."

"Sadie's right, Daphne." Elise's eyebrows waggled suggestively. "Just because my love life may lie in shambles doesn't mean we can't discuss yours."

"Who'd you meet?" Sadie demanded.

"Nobody," Daphne muttered, not fooling anyone.

Sadie said as much. "You've always been a shit liar, Daph. Who is he?"

Daphne threw her hands in the air. "Okay, fine. I bumped into this guy outside the dean's office today. But I don't even know anything about him."

Just that I want to climb him like a tree, she added silently.

"I think he's a detective?" Daphne said instead.

Elise took a sip of her mojito. "Ooooh he must be on campus because of Sam's murder."

"Well, yes," Daphne said, taking in the deepening frowns of her friends. "We sort of crashed into each other and fell and he helped me up and he was just . . . he was very polite."

"Is it usual for detectives to stop beautiful ladies in hallways?" Elise teased.

Sadie was much more blunt. "Cops don't do shit for anyone. What? They don't."

Elise ignored them both. "So you bumped into him in the hallway and sparks started flying?"

"Maybe?" Daphne replied. "It's just . . . I mean . . . We didn't talk or anything but we exchanged this look, you know? And I—I don't know. I hadn't been seen like that in a long time." She'd felt almost naked under his gaze. Invincible. Powerful.

She was shocked by it—how instantaneous it was, how comfortable she'd been, how much she'd enjoyed it.

Perhaps the problem was that her friends couldn't understand because they were both gorgeous. Elise had the beautiful elegance of a Jane Austen heroine—like Jane Bennet or Elinor Dashwood. And for better or worse, Sadie possessed her own animal magnetism that drew mates to her like lambs to their slaughter. Daphne didn't feel plain next to them—not exactly, no—but she did feel less noticeable. The curse of her size, she'd long suspected. "Curvy" was usually a euphemism for "larger than acceptable by society's standards." Instead of standing out, at some point she'd just been rendered invisible instead.

Until those gray eyes had noticed her anyway. The detective's look of surprise—his blushing glances away—had made her feel more glamorous than Zendaya on the red carpet.

"That doesn't sound like most cops I know," Sadie grudgingly admitted. "But I'm not gonna be okay with this until we check him out first. If you're going to insist on having some cis dude rummaging around down there between your legs, the least we could do is make sure you share the same ideological position on imperialism."

"*Sadie.*"

Elise poured more water for Daphne. "What did the detectives find out about Sam, anyway?"

"I don't know." Daphne's mood dimmed. "It sounds like Sam's laptop and phone are missing. And that fact coupled with that weird-ass text message he sent me has—"

"Wait, what?" Sadie cut her off. "What text message?"

Daphne took another sip of her drink. She hadn't meant to bring it up. It wasn't that she couldn't trust Sadie and Elise with Sam's message from beyond the veil, but Daphne had only just come around to accepting that her missing copy of *Papillon* wasn't a big deal. And she wasn't too ashamed to admit that she worried about sounding like a conspiracy theorist about it, even if it was in front of two women who'd refused to go apple picking with her last semester because Mercury had been in retrograde.

"It's nothing," Daphne promised, drawing a narrowed glare from Sadie. "Actually, Elise, I was going to ask you this anyway. You know that book *Papillon*? Have you seen it lately? You gave it back to me last semester, right?"

"Correct," Elise replied. "Why?"

Daphne chewed her lip. "You promise not to freak out?"

"Of course, hon," Elise said at the same time that Sadie replied, "Absolutely the fuck not."

Daphne's eyes darted back and forth between the two women who had gotten so drunk with her at her birthday party they'd slept on her front lawn. "Sam texted me a line from that book."

Elise and Sadie glanced at each other in confusion.

Daphne sighed. "The night he died."

"What in the actual—"

"He did what?" Elise said, her voice low.

Daphne dodged Sadie's hands. "You said you wouldn't freak out!"

"Why?" Elise asked. "What did the line even say?"

"It's some random quote about how the French invented silence," Daphne replied. "And I wouldn't think much of it but I . . . I can't find my book anywhere. That's kinda weird, right?"

"Quite," Elise replied.

Daphne didn't like the darkening look to Elise's usually cheery face. "Well, whatever," Daphne said. "Five bucks says

I'm overreacting to his text message. It's probably just some weird coincidence. I'm fine."

Her best friends looked at her doubtfully.

"I'm *fine*," she insisted.

Later she'd laugh at how wrong she'd been. Daphne wasn't fine. Because when she waved goodbye to her friends that night and headed for her house, Chloe was barking. Her dog's angry shouts should have been Daphne's first clue to run. But she just fumbled with her keys at the door and ignored the strange odor in the air. She wrenched the door open, bracing herself for furry wiggles—and met sharp pain. Searing heat throbbed against her head. And for an instant, Daphne saw stars.

CHAPTER SEVEN

"**M**om!"
Tiny hands wrapped around her leg and squeezed.
"Well, look who the cat dragged in." Asma bent down to swoop up her youngest son, Mohsin, and smother him with kisses on his neck. His yelps of delight across the Calliope PD parking lot were pure music to her ears. "How was Dr. Sharif today?"

"Fine," Mo said. He dangled in her arms with a dopey grin. "My flu shot didn't hurt at all! She said I handled it like a champ."

"Then why'd you cry?" Omar, her eldest, asked.

"Why'd *you* cry?" Mo shot back, withering as always, earning a "whoop" from her middle kid Bassem.

A deep bass voice, usually warm, sent out a weary warning. "Boys."

Above the fray, the walnut-brown eyes of Hasan Ahmed, her husband of sixteen years, locked with hers in tired amusement. Asma added the slight weight of exhaustion taxing his strong shoulders to the tally of debts she owed him for being the primary parent to their three children. In between running two auto repair shops in town, Hasan was the one who took the boys to their doctor visits, met with teachers when she couldn't, and played the role of chauffeur by driving them to soccer practice. It overwhelmed her, Hasan's love, as it had when they'd first met as teenagers, peering at each other in between shelves stocked with bags of rice at Ameer's market.

While all three boys nattered her ears off at once, Hasan handed her the lukewarm burrito bowl that was meant to be her dinner—brown rice, extra cheese.

"But we're still getting Wendy's for dinner, right, baba?" Mo asked, batting those long eyelashes up at his father like Bambi.

"With fries and a frosty?" Bassem chimed in.

Omar hushed them. "Baba told us not to say anything in front of Mom."

"Oh, did he now?" Asma said, raising an eyebrow at her panicked husband.

"Well, uh . . ." Hasan's eyes widened when Asma took two steps closer. "You know . . . I was going to give them a treat—for doing so well. At Dr. Sharif's office."

"Right." Asma wrapped her arms around her husband's waist. "For being so good."

"Right."

"Not because there's no food in the fridge," Asma murmured against Hasan's mouth. "And you all would rather starve than eat my cooking."

The way his lips split into a wide grin. The clean, sharp row of teeth. The cackle in reply that scratched his throat. It was a damn shame that all that Asma could do about it was nuzzle his neck until the boys complained.

"Can we go yet?" one of them whined.

"What's the rush?" Hasan replied, not letting Asma go just yet. "Bedtime can wait."

But Asma walked them back to the van anyway. She snapped each kid into their seat belt. Planted noisy kisses on their cheeks.

"See you soon?" Hasan asked, and she nestled up to him

against the side of the car, warmed by the spring sun. His thumb lingered on her bottom lip, rubbing it slowly. Those brown eyes gleamed, calm and confident in tonight's outcome.

She gently shoved him away, and he laughed again.

BACK INSIDE her office, she munched on her meal while sorting through files and typing up her notes on the case of Sam Taylor's murder. The lack of a murder weapon and any noticeable motives for murder were frustrating, sure, but it was the absence of Sam's technological devices that intrigued Asma the most. What had Sam Taylor been working on when he died? Could it have gotten him killed? But why would someone kill for the contents of a laptop? All of her questions felt too premature, too rushed, too linked together in her mind. The best way to test their veracity was to detangle each from the other.

Asma turned to the whiteboard nailed to a yellowed wall, where an unending sea of scribble in blues and reds awaited her, needing clarity. Pinned against her too-sparse timeline of events—a neighbor's last spotting of Sam the afternoon he died, another neighbor's complaint about a pizza delivery driver that night, Molly's Uber drive home, that awful phone call to 911— were photos of Sam that Asma had grabbed from his office on campus, held up by magnets. In one of them, Sam stood dead center among a group of twenty, oozing charisma, his well-crafted smile aimed right at the camera. But that wasn't what interested Asma. It was the pretty Black woman behind him— belted purple coat, a fancy shawl draped around her neck—squinting in the wrong direction

The woman managed to be just as awkward in the photo as when she'd bumped into Rowan and Asma yesterday. Who was she again? Some history professor?

"Amy," Asma called out as the junior cop walked by, her arms stuffed with files. "You were the one who catalogued items from the victim's office, right?"

Amy froze at Asma's question, her swaying brown hair in a tight ponytail the only thing moving. "Yes. Did I do something wrong?"

"You know anything about this photo right here?" Asma asked.

Amy came inside Asma's office, said a quick "May I?" before placing her files on Asma's desk and peeling the photo away from it.

"Who's this woman?" Asma asked.

Amy Camper shook her head, frowning. "No idea, boss."

She shirked off the bad omen snaking up her legs.

Maybe it's just a coincidence.

As if there was such a thing in her line of work.

A knock at the door brought Asma out of the suspicion fogging around her.

Jason Markham, the county's chief medical examiner, waved a file in the air. "Ready for the report?"

Asma waved Amy out and beckoned Jason inside, her mind a jumble of conflicting thoughts while Jason made himself at home, taking over her desk to set up the display on her monitor. An image appeared on the screen—Sam Taylor, his body lying face-up, pale, on the cold metal table.

As always, Jason rattled off his notes faster than most people could process them. "The victim was a healthy, thirty-two-year-old white male, approximately six feet tall, one hundred and seventy-five pounds. Blood alcohol level tested slightly above the legal limit, his stomach contents yielded some kind of Asian dish: noodles, beef, soy sauce, and vegetables. No toxins in his system."

"Cause of death?" Asma asked. "DNA samples?"

"Impatient, as ever," Jason replied. "We don't have results back from the lab yet."

"Fine. Cause of death?" Asma repeated.

"Good things come to those who wait, my friend," Markham said, wagging his finger. "The bruises on his eyes and lower jaw occurred approximately three to four hours before his death."

"Defensive wounds?" Asma asked.

"Not a scratch. There's no indication that he put up a fight."

Jason was only repeating what she and Rowan had deduced already at Sam's house but it still bothered her, that fact. The lack of wounds. The lack of sores. Who didn't fight back? Unless, of course, your hands were tied behind your back. But either she or Rowan would have spotted that on his wrists at the crime scene.

"Any ligature marks?" Asma asked anyway.

"None."

"Maybe he was held at knife point," Asma said to herself. How else to explain the clean hands and bruised face?

"That question very much belongs in your department and not mine. May I please continue?" Jason asked. "The official cause of death is blunt force trauma to the head."

"Which we guessed already," Asma pointed out.

"Yes, but the devil is in the details." Markham crossed his arms. "The victim was struck on the right side of the skull by something like a meat hammer—textured, flat, and square. Heavy. Two by two inches. Based on the angle of impact, the assailant who used this instrument was most likely right-handed but I'm not betting my Florida condo on that."

Asma frowned at that. "Height?"

"Unclear," Markham replied. "I'm quite confident that the

victim was already kneeling on the ground when he was struck. But this means that the height variation for the assailant is quite extreme."

"So it could be anyone," Asma concluded.

Markham nodded. "Anyone over four-foot-eight and shorter than six-foot-three, that is correct. At least that means your ex-partner is out of the running."

Asma rolled her eyes. She'd never met someone more sensitive over his height. Rowan was constantly apologizing for it. If she had that kind of height she'd already be king.

"What *is* clear from our autopsy, however, is that the victim had been sexually active quite recently—as evidenced by the semen that we found on the victim's underwear and what I've determined to be a vaginocervical smear on the victim's body—and yes, I've already submitted a sample to get tested."

"Define 'recent' for me."

"For starters, he had sex on the day he died."

Only later, when she was back home, sitting on the floor, her back against the hallway going through the routine of convincing her boys to go to sleep, did the right question find its way to her.

Her arms were sudsed up to the elbows and Mo was shrieking some silly song about boogers in the bathtub when she froze at what had finally pierced through the din of her thoughts.

Molly Henderson hadn't arrived home until after Sam Taylor died.

So who'd had sex with the victim?

CHAPTER EIGHT

Shouting. So much shouting. Who was barking? Why? The throbbing of Daphne's head tasted metallic on her tongue. Her skin rustled against a sheet. Heat spread from the crown of her skull to her pinky toes. Try as she might to open them, her eyelids remained stuck together as if by magnetic force.

"What do you mean that a doctor has not visited her in over three hours? She has been here since last night! Do you not know who she is? Do you not . . ."

The noises around her began to recede into the dark but not before one last realization struck her.

That voice.

Its sound.

Determined.

Sharp.

Accusing.

Heavily accented.

Oh God.

What was her mother doing here?

DAPHNE PRIED her eyelids open sometime later and instantly regretted it. A painful throb heated the back of her neck and her temples pulsed. She squinted at the rays of morning sunshine peeping through the blinds and tried to concentrate on the thin, reedy voices bleeping through the hospital PA system. Her eyes watered while three blurry figures in front of her gradually came into focus.

On the left, looking like Barack Obama's jollier older brother, was her father, his blue polo shirt neatly tucked into his khakis like the retired senior citizen he was. In front of Daphne was a brunette woman wearing a white doctor's coat and a professional smile. She held up a manila folder almost like a shield—which, Daphne guessed, the doctor probably needed. Because next to her in rich jewel tones that danced brilliantly against the gleaming darkness of her flawless skin stood the most formidable woman Daphne had ever known. Her mother was as majestic as she was fearsome, and Daphne suspected that the doctor had already learned that the hard way.

Daphne blinked at her parents again. Weren't they supposed to be visiting her brother, Guy, in Philly? His wife, Jessie, was due any day now.

"Hi, sweetheart." Jim Ouverture's baritone was unusually quiet. Fresh tears made his eyes twinkle when he smiled at her. "You gave us quite the scare."

"You fool!" her mother said. "I warned you that where you lived was not safe. It was only a matter of time before a criminal would strike."

Fabiola Ouverture would say that. The most loving and least forgiving of Daphne's sleepy life between book covers, Fabiola had had plenty to say over the years about Daphne's non-spicy career choice. Convinced, as always, that death would befall each and every one of her children if not vigorously thwarted by prayer and daily admonitions to stay vigilant, Fabiola was the least assured by Daphne's replies that Calliope, as a college town, was the urban equivalent of Teletubbyland.

The doctor leaned against Daphne's thin hospital bed. "Hi,

Daphne. I'm Dr. Azari. You're probably wondering what's going on, huh?"

Daphne nodded—and instantly regretted it. Everything throbbed. She struggled to breathe, feeling underwater, close to drowning. It took several seconds before she could concentrate on the physician before her.

"You were brought in last night after someone knocked you on the head," Dr. Azari said.

"A knock?" Her mother sucked her teeth. "Why is this doctor saying 'knock'? Daphne, someone attacked you!"

"We placed you on a heavy sedative and treated your bruises and scrapes, although I'm pleased to report that by some miracle you don't have a concussion." She gave Daphne a reassuring smile. "You've got a bump on your head where the injury occurred, but you should have no permanent damage. We'll confirm that with an MRI later today. Take it easy for the next day or two and then you'll be just fine. Don't overdo it. No running or strenuous activity."

Daphne moved her neck, wincing at the pain. "I guess I still don't understand. What happened? I was attacked?"

Her father's reply was gentle. "That's what everyone wants to know, kiddo."

A few images began to sharpen. It had been just a regular happy hour with her besties. They'd talked trash about men. Elise had tucked away an exorbitant amount of paella considering her small size. Sadie had only threatened the bartender to take things out to the parking lot once. And then Elise had driven her home and . . .

And she remembered the throbbing. A stretcher. Chloe's frantic licks on her face.

Her parents looked ashen, sick and sad, older than she'd

remembered, older than she liked. She fought back the panicky feeling stinging through the fog.

"With your permission," said Dr. Azari while Daphne's mother glowered at her like a lioness protecting her cub, "the police would like to ask you a few questions. But only if you're feeling up for it," she hastened to add before Fabiola could interject. "Since we'd like to observe you a little bit longer here, I'm going to suggest that they meet you at your house later this afternoon when we discharge you."

"Do I have to stay here for the day?" Daphne asked.

"We would advise—"

"But of course you are staying!" Fabiola interrupted. "Why would you even ask such a silly thing? You must rest and gather your strength. The hospital may not have enough doctors here to adequately support you"—she shot Dr. Azari a withering glare—"but the nurses have been very helpful. I will make sure that they take care of you and help you get better, my baby."

Dr. Azari had met enough ferocious immigrant mothers in her day to know when to step out, even if her patient was a professor in her late twenties. The moment the door closed, Fabiola sat down and sucked her teeth, giving her daughter the death stare.

"Out of all of my children," she began, "I expected the least amount of drama from you. You are stable. You are unmarried and you do not go to Mass. But you are stable."

Daphne's nostrils flared. Of course her mother had managed to turn Daphne's pursuit of the quiet life into something undignified. "If everything didn't hurt right now, I'd be rolling my eyes so hard at you, Mother. How on earth is any of this my fault? I don't even know what happened."

"You live in that ridiculous cottage in the woods," her mother said.

"It's not in the woods," Daphne corrected her. "It's on a park adjacent to the woods."

"As if there is a difference! And what do you have to protect you from harm? That silly dog. Who is very sweet"—Fabiola quickly admitted—"but is too kind to strangers."

Chloe. Daphne looked around her hospital room. "Where is she?"

"Snuggled up with that friend of yours, Elise," Jim replied with a proud grin. "She didn't want to leave your side when you got hurt. So Elise volunteered to keep her until you could take her back. You say the word, and she'll bring Chloe on over."

Daphne's eyes watered again, and with the corner of her hospital blanket she swiped at her face, ignoring Fabiola's small eye roll of affection. "She's such a good girl."

"She cannot protect you, my darling, she is not a guard dog."

"That's because I don't want her to be. I got her precisely because she was so sweet."

A Black woman in scrubs knocked on the door before Fabiola could respond with a withering comment. "My sister's downstairs. She brought everything."

Fabiola rose up. "Even the scotch bonnet peppers?"

The nurse nodded. "And jute leaves."

Daphne pressed her palms into her eyes. "I'm sorry, what's going on here?"

"You feeling okay, Daphne?" the nurse asked. "You look a lot better than when you came in last night."

"I'm fine, thanks," Daphne said. Fabiola barked at Jim for cash from his wallet. "Just confused."

Her mother pecked Daphne on the cheek. "Miss Femi is an excellent nurse at this hospital who is also Nigerian. We were speaking of West African ingredients that are difficult to find in America and she told me of her sister's garden. Femi's sister grows egusi melons—here in Calliope! Can you imagine that? So. I will go speak to the police downstairs and tell them to see you at your home. And then I am going downstairs to purchase some of her seeds for your pantry."

You don't even like Nigerians, Daphne wanted to retort, but the possibility of eating fresh West African goodies kept her mouth shut.

"Jim," Fabiola said, sliding into her canary-yellow coat. "You must watch her while I am away. Close the curtains and make sure she lies still. She needs to rest but she won't—not unless you force her."

Jim broke out into a wide grin. "I'll watch her like I'm your Uncle Guillaume at our wedding, honey. She won't be able to pull nothing. No tricks, not a one."

Daphne waved at her parents. "I'm right here, guys."

Fabiola tossed one last suspicious glare at her daughter before chasing Femi down the hallway, abandoning Daphne to her father.

Daphne gave him her most hopeful smile. She loved Jim. Who didn't?

The living embodiment of a golden retriever, that one uncle who got everyone at the wedding on the dance floor for the electric slide, the equivalent of everyone's favorite mailman, Jim Ouverture had the personality of a suburban soccer dad handing out fist bumps after a game. Daphne was lucky—*so lucky*—to have grown up an Ouverture, a clan full of squabbling Creoles who made gumbo, feisty Ivorian women who haggled over wax print fabrics in Abidjan, and cousins who took all your money in vicious games of Bourré.

It was just that Jim's picture belonged in an encyclopedia under the definition of "snoop." And Daphne was lying in a hospital gown in Calliope when last night she'd been drinking sangria with friends. There were only so many questions from her father she could take, when her tiny world was spinning off its axis. Her family loved her, no doubt, but in the way that a pride of lions might purr at their adopted baby turtle. Like, sure, they could relate to Daphne's trials and tribulations, but her world was much smaller than theirs, and Daphne couldn't help but feel like her bookish life wasn't quite the adventure that the Ouverture family had signed up for.

"So, honey, you wanna tell me what's going on?" Jim asked gently. Prying. Not prying. "Anything I should know about?"

Daphne's heart skipped a beat.

"Do you know if anybody would want to hurt you?" Jim asked. The pain in his voice was unmistakable, and it caused Daphne's lungs to squeeze out air. "Is my baby daughter safe in this new town? I'm concerned, is all. Was this random?"

"I . . ." Daphne gulped. "I don't know."

Jim offered her a plastic cup of water and she gratefully sipped from it, rather than having to share her thoughts. What if her attack was just some random frat guy initiation gone wrong? During her first week in Calliope a beer trolley had crashed outside her park during Rush Week, spewing business majors and premed students across her meadow. Chloe had dutifully walked over with her to inspect the fallen heroes and make sure no bones were broken, patiently accepting their drunken pats on her head.

What was more alarming to believe—that she was the

victim of a random assault or that someone had struck her deliberately? And even if someone had wanted to attack her, why? Over Sam's weird text message? A book from the seventies? Something else? Every semester there was at least one student who thought they could try it with a professor but Daphne didn't think any of hers would resort to violence. And sure, Ken Miller was a bridge troll, but even he wouldn't resort to violence just because Daphne had searched his laptop—not if a potential donor could hear about it. Would he? The fact that Daphne could even name more than one antagonist was making her eye twitch.

Jim's voice remained mild. "Nothing?"

"Nope." Daphne's lie was so bold it stung her teeth. Not wanting this line of questioning to go any further, she changed the subject. "How much cash did you give Mother to spend on West African food? Did you give her everything in your wallet?"

Jim snorted. "Of course I did. Sweetheart, I'm just glad that your mother got along so good with the nurses. We both know that if they'd done anything other than treat you perfectly, she wouldn't have had any of it."

"And probably would have gotten us banned from this hospital for life," said Daphne, grinning.

It always caught her off guard to see her eyes in his face. Or really, she supposed, it was the other way around. She'd inherited much of her mother's bone structure and curves but her eyes—almond shaped and almost a glittery pitch-black—were an Ouverture trait going back generations. There was no denying that she was his daughter. And she was proud of that, most days, but feared it, too. What else might they share, beyond their Ouverture eyes and a fondness for bad jokes?

"Why is my daughter still awake?" Fabiola said, barging into the room with two cups of hot tea. "And why are the curtains still open? Who has lost their mind?"

Daphne reached for her mother's hand. "It's okay, we were just chatting."

Fabiola sucked her teeth again. "Did I ask you to speak?"

"Well, no, but—"

"Are you supposed to be awake?"

"*Maman*—"

"You will rest. *Now.*"

"But—"

Fabiola waggled her finger. "No more talking. Close your eyes. We are under Saint Camillus's guidance now, so no more whining from you, daughter. Everything will be fine."

Daphne knew better than to protest when her mother invoked a saint.

So did Jim. He leaned over and kissed Daphne on the forehead again. "We've got you, baby. You'll be okay, you know that."

Sleep whispered to Daphne's tender brain, tickling at the edges of her consciousness. And while the nurses wheeled her out to get her MRI scan, she couldn't tell if the tightening in her chest at her father's words was dread or excitement.

CHAPTER NINE

Daphne's mother pinched her from the front seat of the rental car. "Stop moving."

"Maman!"

"I told you already to stop touching your head like that," said Fabiola, her aristocratic eyebrows drawn tight with concern. "Just because your MRI scan came back clear and the hospital set you free does not mean that you can wiggle around like a worm."

Daphne rubbed her arm. "I'm not going to recover if my mother pinches me every time I move a muscle."

Fabiola scowled at her. "You were so sweet in your youth. Obedient. Other mothers were jealous of me because of my children's polite behavior."

"And they're not jealous of you now? I'm pretty sure all four of your kids have turned out okay."

Fabiola scowled. "I blame your father for this."

"What did I do?" Jim asked as he parked the car outside Daphne's house.

Fabiola pointed a finger at him. "You babied her."

"Fab, honey, she *is* the baby."

"Which is why she should be listening to her parents! When did she start refusing to accept our guidance? Who taught her to use her tongue against us as she now does?" Fabiola touched her clasped hands to her forehead in prayer and Daphne rolled her eyes. "*Saint Marie* give me strength."

"As much as I'd love for the two of you to continue enumerating my many faults," Daphne said, "I'd like to get some rest, please."

Daphne shut her eyes. Anything to stop her mother from complaining that Daphne's life was somehow both too small and too audacious. A quiet life might have been what Daphne craved but she sure hadn't been getting it lately.

A stray band of yellow police tape fluttered outside her door, no longer needed. A wet stain seeped into the doorstep from where someone had cleaned. More alarming were the feet planted by her entryway. Daphne had been expecting police, but standing just outside her front door in the afternoon sun were the same detectives she'd run across on campus.

The woman still terrified her. With sleek, black hair, crystalline amber eyes, and cheekbones so high they'd make Naomi Campbell throw at least two more phones, she could give suburban beauty queens a run for their money, a truth which Daphne instinctively knew to never divulge if she wished to remain alive. *He* was something else. Inordinately tall, almost inappropriately so. Daphne's cheeks warmed as she remembered his long torso pressed against hers on the floor of the anthropology department. His smile had been slightly crooked when his gray eyes had roved over her, splayed out underneath him.

"Who are you?" Fabiola demanded of the pair.

Detective Ahmed stood silent for a moment, ignoring Fabiola's scowl, her gaze zeroed in on Daphne, who squirmed in discomfort. "I'm Detective Asma Ahmed." She flicked up a badge. "This is Rowan Peterson, a consultant to the police. We heard about an assault yesterday from our colleagues," she said. "Can we come inside to talk?"

"No, you cannot," Fabiola said before Daphne even had the chance to open her mouth.

Daphne gritted her teeth. "*Maman.*"

"I understand your concern," Detective Ahmed said, "but in light of recent occurrences at Harrison, it's essential that we investigate—"

"What my wife is trying to say," Jim interjected, "is that we've had a really trying day. We appreciate you coming by but we think it might be best if we could just go inside and take care of our daughter, who's—hey, Daphne, honey, you okay? Daphne?"

She hadn't realized that she'd started sinking until she heard her mother's cry and the shuffling of feet. The same large, thin hands she'd collided with on campus grabbed her again and pulled her up before she collapsed on the pavement.

"Thank you," she said, glancing up again into Rowan's face. His pale cheeks flushed ever so slightly.

"Of course," he said, and for a while Daphne almost forgot how light-headed she felt because she was noticing for the first time ever the dark blue, almost purple flecks in his eyes. His voice was more golden than she remembered.

"Daphne Aminata Ouverture, you are coming inside this instant," barked out Fabiola.

"Right." Rowan gently but quickly placed her in her father's arms. "Here you are."

"Professor Ouverture," Asma said again, her dark scratchy voice strained, "we would really appreciate it if we could speak to you now rather than later."

"If we could all take a moment to relax, y'all would see that Daphne is in no condition to—" Jim began.

"Enough!" came her mother's cry of outrage, and like that,

Fabiola was off on a rampage while Jim and the two detectives tried in vain to reign her in.

Daphne shoved her arm into her bag, surfing through its contents until she found her key. She ignored her mother's war cries and walked up to her front door, jutting her key into the keyhole. She had just enough time to register the door was already unlocked before it swung open. She froze when she took in the sight of her living room.

Goosebumps traveled up her arms, turning her legs into jelly. The keys dropped from her hand.

Daphne turned. Fabiola, Jim, and Asma were staring over her shoulder, shocked into silence. Rowan stared directly at her.

"My books," Daphne quietly gasped.

She was the first to step inside. Books were everywhere. On her mahogany wood coffee table that she'd found with her mother at her favorite flea market in New Orleans, on her brightly colored floral rug, in Chloe's doggie bed by the bay window. Someone had strewn them about, ripped through their pages, slashed through their prose. Her bookshelves stood empty and the covers of her books torn, some of them she'd kept since high school like favorite pets. And for the first time since her attack, since her parents had rushed in to help her, since her world had been tipped sideways, Daphne collapsed to the ground and cried.

DAPHNE DIDN'T know how she ended up on her living room couch with her legs propped up but there she was, weeping into a pillow and apologizing to the detectives while her parents fussed over her, bringing her hibiscus tea and taking turns holding her hand.

In a spare moment of reprieve from being lovingly

smothered, she blinked up to find Rowan perched next to her on her ottoman while Detective Ahmed examined the site of her attack outside the door. He folded his considerably long legs around the base of the ottoman and crossed his arms. He was trying, Daphne suspected, to be ever so gentle with her, which only caused her to feel more . . . what, she didn't know. Flattered? Aware of the fact that she'd just been hiccup-crying in front of a grown-ass man?

"Daphne, forgive me for asking but you're a professor at Harrison, correct?" Rowan asked.

Daphne nodded, unsure what else to say or what he wanted from her, exactly. This was the third time the police and Daphne had met since Sam was murdered. From their perspective, that couldn't be a coincidence.

"Which department?"

"History." Daphne swallowed. "French history."

"What's your area of research?"

"I study Black families in eighteenth-century France," Daphne offered.

"Hm." A wisp of a smile, slightly crooked, tugged at Rowan's lips. "Before or after the Revolution?"

Daphne's heart skipped. She wasn't used to laymen knowing much about her area of study, let alone a detective.

"Kinda both?" Daphne found herself saying. "I mean, my project begins in the 1750s and goes for a while . . . ."

A new expression arose, somewhere on the spectrum between curiosity and confusion. "Are you new to Calliope?"

"I started in the fall."

Rowan's voice was barely audible when he said, "So that's why I haven't seen you before."

"I . . ." Daphne bit her lips, unable to tell if Rowan had been talking to her or himself. She willed her pulse to calm down. It was nothing. He'd meant nothing. He was just making conversation, and wasn't that what detectives did anyway when they were trying to set a victim at ease?

"You have a marvelous collection of Toni Morrison novels," Rowan said, abrupt. "Is it her complete catalog?"

"Not anymore," Daphne replied. "I gave *The Bluest Eye* to a friend in grad school and never got it back."

Footsteps marching down the hallway interrupted Rowan's reply.

"We're back, sweetie," Jim called out. "Can you tell those two friends of yours to stop calling your phone? That tiny one with the black hair who makes Korean food and the other one who scowls at everybody all the time?"

Daphne's brain eventually caught up to her ears. "Elise and Sadie?"

"Yeah, them two," Jim said. He handed over Daphne's phone. "They've been calling since you got to the hospital. They're worried sick about you, pancake, and somehow the scary one got my number and won't leave me alone."

Daphne blinked at the torrential downpour of text messages on her phone. "Okay."

"But first," Jim said, "Detective Ahmed's gonna ask you a few questions, if you're up for it."

"And then she will leave our house," Fabiola said with confident finality.

Detective Ahmed ignored that jab. Her frown was trained on her ex-partner. "Rowan, what are you doing talking to the vic without me?"

A spot of red bloomed on Rowan's cheeks. "Apologies."

Rowan rose from the ottoman, and the bright strokes of

color splashed across Daphne's living room suddenly dulled. *Come back*, she wanted to whisper. *Tell me what you know about Toni Morrison*. But he had slipped on a pair of blue rubber gloves and began sorting through her scattered books across the floor, his mousy brown hair shielding his gaze.

"So." Detective Ahmed plopped herself down on the same ottoman Rowan had just been sitting on, gripping a small black notebook. "Do you have any idea who'd want to do this to you? Any students who are mad at you, maybe?"

"What?" Daphne blinked. "God, no. I mean, sure I've got some students who want their A-minus to be an A but that's usual at Harrison, from what I've been told. It's only my first year here, but I can't see any student going so far as to figure out where I live and then knocking me out and tossing my books."

But then Daphne caught a flash of something. Olivia Vail: her sorority hoodie shielding half her face, an evasive glance that still itched under Daphne's skin days later.

"How about faculty?" Detective Ahmed asked.

The word "no" died on Daphne's lips. She'd told herself that Sam's text message and her missing book didn't belong to the story of her life, that each component was some surreal coincidence that didn't form a whole. But her damaged novels scattered across the living room rug had sliced through the web of soothing comforts she'd spun for herself. She had no choice but to clear the air and insist, however she could, that she wasn't involved in Sam Taylor's murder, even if, for some unknown reason, she was embroiled in his life.

But at the thought of telling the police about *Papillon* she slammed her lips shut again. Who'd care about some rando book? What if she sounded like the kind of nutter who was convinced that mermaids are real or that Destiny's Child was finally reuniting?

And oh God, Daphne was *so* not ready to spill any of this in front of her parents, who were pretending to keep to themselves in the kitchen. She could make them leave the house, she supposed. But that would only draw their suspicion. Given what she knew about her parents, they'd hunt down the information on their own anyway.

Daphne rubbed her palms against her face and sighed. "You're going to think I'm nuts, okay?"

"We'll keep an open mind," Asma assured her.

But Daphne could already hear the skepticism in the detective's voice. She pushed air out of her lungs again and spoke anyway. "A few days ago, someone texted me about a line from a book—it's called *Papillon*."

Rowan glanced up from a row of books he'd been studying. "By Henri Charrière?"

"You've read it?" Daphne asked, gaping at him, and then gaping some more when he nodded.

"It's about a prison heist in Latin America, correct?"

"In French Guiana, yeah." Rowan's face lit up and Daphne's own confidence swelled under his wide grin. "It was popular in the seventies. My Auntie Emmanuelle gave me a copy in French when I visited her in Paris after college. I noticed a couple of days ago that it was missing," she said, then paused.

Detective Ahmed remained doubtful. "That's a bit strange, but—"

"No, detective," Daphne insisted. "It's very strange. I'm the kind of nerd who keeps track of my books. It wasn't loaned out. There's only one person I know in all of Calliope who expressed any interest in this particular book." She swallowed. "And now he's dead."

Detective Ahmed froze at that admission, and Daphne wanted more than anything to disappear. She didn't enjoy being the center of attention. She didn't want to stand out for anything other than her teaching and research—and certainly not for something as confusing and, frankly, *scary* as this situation she found herself in. It wasn't lost on her that she was on a trial run at Harrison University, where she sure as hell planned to work hard to stay. Her life was quiet, studious, and manageable, which is what she wanted—no, *needed*—to feel safe in an overwhelming world. Others could be boat rockers. But Daphne intended to get her book done and teach her classes and enjoy her chosen profession as a French historian. Damn Sam Taylor for throwing a monkey wrench into her plans.

Detective Ahmed frowned. "Are you certain you didn't lend it to him?"

Daphne nodded.

"And no one else you know has it?" Ahmed asked.

"No," Daphne replied. "Did you find the book in Sam's possessions?"

Detective Ahmed grunted. "No idea." She shot a look at Rowan who, Daphne noticed, had partially opened his mouth to speak. "Are you saying that you think he borrowed it without your knowledge?"

Stole, Daphne silently corrected. Rowan's gray eyes slid to hers. She hoped her face didn't look as hot as she felt under his gaze.

"Yes. Yes, I do."

"Hm. Okay. So let's say that Professor Taylor did take your book," Detective Ahmed said. "How is this potential theft related to this incident? You believe it's connected to his murder?"

Daphne squirmed before finally admitting, "I don't know."

Rowan cleared his throat. "Is it a rare edition?"

"Well, no," Daphne said, feeling more foolish with each passing second. "It's not. You can find it in any Parisian used bookstore for like a euro. But that wouldn't explain why he texted me a line from it, would it? Or why my book is missing at all."

Nor, Daphne realized, could it explain why her bookshelves had been trashed.

Ahmed shifted in her seat but her gaze remained fixed on Daphne. "How well did you know Professor Taylor?"

"Sam?" Daphne's scalp throbbed. "Not that well."

Detective Ahmed asked, "Did you ever date?"

"*Sam?*" Daphne barked out a startled laugh. "No, we never dated." Out of the corner of her eye, Daphne caught Fabiola's suspicious scowl from the kitchen. "I swear it, *maman*. He's with Molly Henderson. Or, I mean, he was."

Fabiola sucked her teeth. "Hmpf."

Detective Ahmed hovered for a second. Daphne could have sworn that the detective wanted to push her on the topic of dating Sam.

After a beat she asked instead, "How did you meet?"

Daphne would have bet money that that wasn't the question Detective Ahmed wanted to ask.

"The first university-wide faculty meeting," she said anyway, "which is pretty much how all professors make their friends at Harrison. It always takes place the first week of September. We were both junior professors, although he started a few years ahead of me. I thought he was flirty and funny but also a bit cocky. He knew he was a rock star. He could be really fake-chummy with everyone, definitely a dude-bro. But then he'd buy everyone a round of drinks just because." She shrugged. "I don't know, we were just really different. He talked football and politics. He drank beer and scotch. Do I look like someone who's into stuff like that?"

Detective Ahmed didn't reply right away. "So you two never talked shop?"

Daphne snorted. "No, we never talked about work. Or, rather, he'd tell me about how he'd just appeared on Fox News and gotten into a fight with someone and I was supposed to smile and say, 'Wow, that's great!'"

Detective Ahmed peered at Daphne curiously. "That sounds frustrating."

"Kind of," Daphne mumbled, shrinking back from the anger in her voice.

"He ever ask you about what you research?"

"Yeah, did he ever get to see how smart you are?" Jim called out from the kitchen.

Daphne stared up at her ceiling. Was it too late to kick her parents out of the house? "*Dad.*"

"My daughter is a brilliant French historian," Jim shouted at no one in particular. "She's a former Fulbright fellow, she just won Teacher of the Year, she's won Lord knows how many grants for her research on the French Empire—*and* she speaks three languages fluently and knows another two still better than most Americans know English."

Of all the times for her parents to demonstrate that they had, in fact, been paying attention to her career, it had to be now?

Detective Ahmed quickly changed the topic. "You said he texted you about the book the night he died?"

"Yeah, but I deleted it," replied Daphne.

"I'd like to take a look at your phone, please."

Of course that came out more as a demand than a question. But Daphne rummaged through her purse to unlock her iPhone for Detective Ahmed anyway.

"Rowan?" Ahmed called out, and a moment later the pair of them had their heads pressed together in front of her glowing screen while Daphne tried not to panic at the thought of them reading her most recent text exchange with Elise over *Love Is Blind: Habibi.*

"He texted you a line from that book in French?" Detective Ahmed said a beat later.

"You found it?" Daphne was impressed. "And yeah. It's bad French, but French. He really butchered it."

Rowan returned to examining her bookshelves while the detective scrolled through Daphne's messages on her phone. "I take it you two didn't text often?"

"No," Daphne insisted. "We didn't text at all. I honest to God forgot we'd swapped numbers. Or maybe he got it from a group chat? There are a bunch of those for junior professors."

Detective Ahmed handed her the phone back. "And where were you when he texted you?"

"Oh, you mean on"—she started, until her stomach sank at the detective's insinuation—"the night Sam died?"

Fabiola marched from the kitchen to the living room to hover over Daphne again. "If you are suggesting for one second that my daughter had anything to do with that man's death—"

Detective Ahmed raised her hands. "Not at all, Mrs. Ouverture. I'm just trying to understand how everything fits together."

Daphne froze again. She didn't really want to have to spell out her love life to the detectives in front of her parents. Especially not in front of *him*—not like Daphne knew anything about Rowan other than that he had legs she could climb and the sweet, gentle constitution of a Dickensian orphan that made her want to shield him from life's harms. But Ahmed's hard stare was becoming difficult to ignore.

"I was coming back from a bad date," Daphne said.

Ahmed's amber gaze didn't waver. "Who with?"

"A man I met online—oh, hush, Mother, it's not a big deal. Everyone does it, and I checked him out before I met him in person. Anyway, his name is Ricky. I can give you his information if you want." Though she really, really hoped Detective Ahmed did *not* want it.

Of course the detective said, "Yes, please," and Daphne had to eat her words. She scrolled through her contacts to scribble down the number on a Post-it, which she handed over with a sigh.

"Where was the date?"

"The Butcher's Steakhouse."

The detective's gorgeously shaped eyebrows rose a centimeter. "In Livington? Why'd you go all the way out there?"

"If I put my dating profile in Calliope," Daphne explained, feeling itchy, "my students would be able to see it. Can you imagine getting a swipe right from a student? I've literally had nightmares about it. So I keep my personal and professional lives separate."

Detective Ahmed grunted, which Daphne took to be some form of approval. "Time?"

"The date started at six. I was home by seven-thirty."

The only sounds Daphne could concentrate on for a moment were the furious scribbles Detective Ahmed was etching into her notebook. Daphne's head swam. "Is everything okay? Do you think my attack's connected to Sam's death somehow?"

"To be honest," Detective Ahmed said, closing her notebook, "I don't."

Daphne blinked. "Oh."

An empty silence filled up her small living room. Only Rowan moved, swiveling away from a bookcase he was sorting and in the direction of his partner, his frown so slight and quick Daphne almost missed it. His lips parted, as if to interject, and just as quickly snapped shut again. He turned his back to Daphne and returned to shelving a Beverly Jenkins novel.

"It's a strange coincidence, sure," Detective Ahmed said. "But it's still too early in our investigation of Professor Taylor's murder to operate on an assumption like this. We're going to keep looking into who attacked you, Daphne. And like my colleague Rowan said, we'll check for your book in Sam's library. But I'm not sure what finding it—or not—will prove."

Daphne deflated faster than a birthday balloon. Her entire face was aflame again, this time from embarrassment. She worked so hard—*so* hard—to avoid placing herself in situations where she might look foolish, gullible, or anything other than a smart and studious scholar. Yet here she was, being verbally dismissed by a stranger.

Was it possible for an entire body to become weary in an instant? Daphne rubbed her palms against her eyes, hoping to also smoosh a tear or two from seeping out.

"We're almost done, Daphne, I promise," Detective Ahmed said, gentle. "Can you walk us through what happened to you last night? What we know for certain is that someone attacked you and vandalized your home. Let's start there."

Warm hands rubbed Daphne's back, and she looked up to find her mother wrapping an arm around her protectively.

"Sure," Daphne said. Exhaustion crashed ashore, mingling with defeat. "I was coming back from happy hour with my friends Sadie and Elise."

"Where?"

"Valencia," Daphne said. "The tapas restaurant."

"Good cheesy croquettes. What happened next?" Ahmed asked.

"My friends drove me home and I waved goodbye to them. I walked to my front door, same as always."

"Did you hear any cars driving by?"

Daphne shook her head. "No."

"Did you check your mail? Stop to check a text?" Detective Ahmed asked.

"No, I was pretty lost in thought and just wanted to let Chloe out."

"That's the dog?" Ahmed looked around. "Where is she?"

"My friend Elise took her. She's dropping her off later."

"Okay, so you didn't check your mail," Ahmed said. "Did you notice anyone in the park when you walked to the front door?"

Daphne shook her head. "No one in my line of vision, anyway."

Ahmed pressed on. "Any unusual sounds?"

"I don't . . . I don't think so."

"Smells?"

"Um . . ."

"Think, Professor."

Much to her surprise, tears of frustration sprang from Daphne's eyes. For heaven's sake, she could recite any passage of Homer's *Illiad* verbatim; you'd think she could remember what the man who attacked her had smelled like. But she couldn't and she feared she wouldn't ever be able to and all of her skills, all of her knowledge, her very existence, was useless, utterly pointless.

"I'm sorry," Daphne mumbled, dissolving into tears. "I know nothing. I don't know how to help you."

And at that, Fabiola had had enough. She marched to the front door and swung it open for the detectives to walk through.

"We thank you for your time, Detectives," Fabiola said, meaning nothing of the sort. "It was a pleasure for you to speak with us. We cannot say the same."

AS THE afternoon gave way to chilly night, Daphne dozed off waiting for Chloe's return. A whiskered muzzle of fur crashed into her chest sometime later, followed by instant tears streaming down her face. She roped a wriggling Chloe into a hug, Fabiola's own grumblings about "babying a dog" drowning out Daphne's joyful meeps and Elise's cooing noises.

She awoke again sometime later to the sharp scent of fried onions, garlic, and scotch bonnet peppers—fresh from that nurse's sister's garden—and smiled, bathing in the familiar sounds of Fabiola's humming in the kitchen and the sizzle of the hot pan cooking Kedjenou. In times of crisis, there was nothing that comforted her mother more than shoving Ivorian food down her children's throats like French farmers fattening up their geese for fois gras.

While Daphne lay on the couch rubbing a snoring Chloe, she puzzled over Detective Ahmed's startled glance at her final answer. But then Detective Ahmed had gone right back to insisting it made no sense to read too much into Daphne's missing book, and Daphne didn't know what to think anymore. Even hours later, the humiliation of Detective Ahmed's dismissal still jabbed like a bee sting. But Daphne's copy of *Papillon* wasn't special—even she had to admit that. The book's cover was in tatters, its pages coffee-stained and weathered.

A knock woke Daphne from her slumber. Footsteps from the guest bedroom upstairs followed, and Jim came marching down the stairs to the front door. She recognized the voice outside. Rich and round, like a cello. A minute later, Rowan Peterson appeared in front of her, his cheeks flushed from the cold springtime air. Their gazes touched. And for a moment, Daphne forgot how to breathe.

Jim ambled in past Rowan, his hands on his hips. "Sugar plum, Mr. Peterson—"

"Please," he said softly, "just call me Rowan."

"Rowan here wants to talk to you about your books for a minute," Jim said. "You okay with that?"

Daphne nodded, apparently having lost her ability to use words.

"Why don't I get you all some tea?" Jim said, heading out to the kitchen.

Leaving Daphne very much alone with Rowan.

He gave a half-smile and glanced around her living room, which was still in a state of disrepair. Daphne watched as his gaunt frame folded in on itself to inspect a copy of Roxane Gay's *Bad Feminist*. He didn't look at her, instead keeping his gaze on the piles of books still waiting to be returned to their shelves.

"Which one do you want to borrow?" she asked him after another moment's silence.

He carefully picked up a copy of Marie NDiaye's *Trois femmes puissantes*. Long fingers traced the black swirls of letters against the yellowed paper of an open page. "All of them."

Her stomach flipped. She let out a breath she hadn't known was trapped in her lungs. Unsure what to say, she said nothing. She would have swallowed but her mouth was even drier than that one time in high school she'd eaten a chocolate-covered cotton ball on a dare.

"Rowan!" Jim barged back into the living room again. "You take sugar or milk in your tea? Daphne, honey, I got you more of your mother's hibiscus miracle."

Jim handed her a small porcelain cup with a proud grin. Daphne could have pinched the man who taught her how to ride a bicycle at age four.

"Thanks, Dad," she said, keeping the irritation from her voice—barely.

Rowan took his cup with polite thanks, placing it on the coffee table as he took a seat across from her. Chloe had apparently decided to give up her entire life to this new stranger, judging by how quicky she rolled over for Rowan to rub her belly. He gladly obliged.

In fairness, her mother's hibiscus tea did help. After a couple of sips, Daphne found that she could exercise her voice and even form coherent sentences again. "You want to talk to me about Sam's library? Does that mean you might know where my book is?"

His eyes found hers again. "Not yet."

Those same feelings of disappointment and embarrassment rushed right back. It was one thing to get the cold shoulder from Detective Ahmed, but to be informed that her theory held no water by Rowan kind of made her want to fling herself into a cold lake. How quickly could she get him to leave so she could cry on her couch?

She let out a big sigh. "Well, thanks for trying. And thanks for coming by. That was really kind of—"

"Keep searching."

Daphne studied Rowan carefully. He was examining her right back, his gaze fixed on her, somber.

"You don't . . ." Daphne tried again. "You don't think I'm delusional?"

That same half-smile tugged upwards again, and Daphne wondered if wry expressions could cause dizziness. Surely a medical researcher had published a paper on the topic. "Quite the opposite, Daphne."

"But your partner—"

"Ex-partner."

Daphne didn't know how to finish her own sentence. There was something about Rowan's words, what he was trying to say and not say, that kept drawing Daphne closer to him, even as it puzzled her.

"Professor Taylor's library contained volumes on fitness regimens, an innumerable list of works on prison reform, and three paleo cookbooks," said Rowan. "But do you know what was absent among his possessions?"

Daphne's eyes widened. "Novels."

Rowan nodded. "Of any kind. Yet he quoted to you a passage from one."

Something flared to life inside her as she made sense of this new piece of information—hope, determination, maybe a mix of the two. "You think I should keep searching?"

"Of course," Rowan said simply, causing Daphne to smile down in her lap. "You're a historian, after all. I trust you to continue your pursuit of knowledge. My colleague will come around in time."

Daphne's skepticism must have blasted across her face because Rowan said, "Her situation is, ah, difficult."

"Detective Ahmed's?" Daphne asked.

"As you might imagine, there aren't that many women who reach her rank. As long as I've known her, she's found it imperative to close her cases as tightly as possible. She's under a great deal of pressure under normal circumstances, but a case involving Harrison University?"

The gilded ceilings of Davis Hall, imposing and powerful, soared high above in Daphne's mind. "Yikes."

"Agreed." Rowan pushed his glasses up the bridge of his nose. "That institution has enough lawyers on retainer to make her life miserable if she fails to solve the case well. It's one of the reasons why I agreed to lend myself to her cause. The CPD might have its . . . deficiencies but Detective Ahmed doesn't deserve to suffer for them." He set down his mug of tea. "I would have left the police force sooner," he continued softly, "if it weren't for her."

Daphne would have asked him why he'd left at all but Rowan had already decided to head to the coat closet to slip on his jacket, a wagging Chloe trailing behind him. He paused by her front door and gave Daphne one last look. "Be careful."

Daphne frowned. "What do you mean?"

"Let's call it a hunch." Rowan's long fingers gripped her doorknob tight. "But Daphne, if you're searching for this book, then so are others."

CHAPTER TEN

Daphne was propped up on the couch the next morning catching up on the latest *Real Housewives* drama while her mother scrubbed the kitchen counters—again—and sang along to Ivorian pop star Monique Séka—again, Chloe quietly crooning along with her.

Daphne pushed herself up on her elbows so she could sit upright—and regretted it. Her brain swished gently against her skull, like a jellyfish bumping into a buoy. She still moved around the world woozy, as if on a ship being tossed about by waves. She didn't need to touch that knot on her scalp to be reminded of her assault. The last few seconds of her attack kept appearing in fragments, screening across her eyes like a stilted film where the same images crashed into each other in an unending chaotic loop. Her mind had become a scratched vinyl record, skipping on the same track, unable to move ahead to the next song. She had no idea what could get it unstuck, to set her world back aright.

Keep searching.

Rowan's imploring still echoed. It was a relief to find someone who believed her on her own terms.

And now, a tiny part of Daphne wanted to prove Detective Ahmed wrong. Because Rowan had to be right: surely, *someone* was searching for this book. Why else would they have destroyed so many bookcases—on campus, at Sam's home, and now at hers? A killer was out there, hiding in plain sight. Someone was walking around the streets of downtown Calliope drinking a coffee or sitting down at a desk in the library to study. Who?

The chaotic whirlwind that was Sadie blew through her front door, clutching a flimsy plastic grocery bag sagging with goodies. "Guess who brought Sri Lankan snacks to the party?"

Daphne frowned. "Party?"

"Party," Sadie confirmed. "You, me, and Chloe. The *Love Is Blind: Habibi* reunion. A bucketful of Sri Lankan mangoes I smuggled in—don't ask. A large order of tacos incoming. All of this was your dad's idea."

On cue, Jim came clambering down the stairs knuckling a familiar suitcase. Chloe exploded into yet another furry round of wiggles, forming a half crescent moon while she twirled in circles between her favorite humans.

"I thought it would be a good idea to have someone come on by," Jim said in between croons to Chloe, "while I take your mother to the airport. You know she's been looking forward to terrorizing your brother."

At Fabiola's retirement party, Daphne and her brothers had joked that Fabiola could now devote her full energies to pursuing her heart's greatest passion: pestering her children for the rest of her life. They'd underestimated their mother's zeal. The woman spent her time bopping around from child to child, two weeks at a time, bullying them, feeding them, shouting at them, cleaning for them, correcting them, complaining to them, admonishing them, holding them, kissing them, loving them. It was supposed to have been Guy's turn to endure the brunt of Fabiola's love when Daphne was attacked.

"Thanks for the babysitter, Dad," Daphne said.

Jim shrugged. "I just thought you might like some company, is all."

At the sound of a taxi honking, her folks were off—but not before Fabiola pulled Sadie to the front door, demanding that she tell her where she got those mangoes because Calliope's produce offerings weren't cutting it.

"They pick the mangoes too soon," Fabiola hissed into Sadie's ear while Sadie patted her back. "And then they ship them to these organic stores for the white people because the shoppers do not know any better."

The trunk of a car slammed shut.

"Fab, honey!" Jim called out.

Sadie slid onto part of a sectional near Daphne, patting the couch cushion next to her for Chloe to join them. Soon, Chloe was snoozing away on Sadie's lap while Daphne and her bestie slurped away on mangoes so sweet and creamy they put the best Italian gelato to shame.

"Seriously," Daphne choked, "how are these actually legal for us to eat?"

"They're not," Sadie said. "Let's just say I got a Sri Lankan connect."

"Figures. Should we be worried about getting caught?"

"Not for what I paid for them. And any fallout would be worth it anyway because your mom's right about the mangoes in this town, Daph," Sadie said. "They suck ass."

DAPHNE JERKED her head up. Sadie and Chloe were a tangle of tattooed human arms and feathery soft spindly dog legs on the other side of the couch. She rubbed her face, tracing the thin corduroy lines that had become etched on her cheek.

Daphne smacked her lips. "How long have I been out?"

"Forty minutes," Sadie said, absent-mindedly rubbing Chloe's neck. "You need to sleep to let your brain heal."

"Right," Daphne replied, as something like embarrassment flushed at her throat. Was this her new reality, being known as an assault victim?

Sadie stopped canoodling with Chloe long enough to glower at Daphne. "What's going on? You're making that face."

"What face?" Daphne relaxed her lips into what she hoped was a serene, Mona Lisa smile.

See? I'm fine, Daphne tried to express with her eyes. *One hundred percent not freaking out at all.*

Sadie ignored her. "Are you feeling weird because of something that isn't your fault? Sam's weird-ass text message and your book disappearing. You getting knocked upside the head. It's not like you asked to be dragged into this shit."

Daphne blinked back tears. Sadie was, as always, right on target. And Daphne needed to hear that from someone she not only loved but also trusted. Enough to go road-tripping with through rural white spaces, even. But as much as Daphne's fists stopped clenching just a little bit upon hearing it, she still couldn't get over some deeper, nagging feeling pulling her down to the earth's core.

Fear.

Daphne's question came out as a low whisper. "How do I get out of it?"

Sadie peered at Daphne like a specimen in her lab. "What do you mean?"

"I mean . . ." Daphne turned her entire pajama-wrapped body to Sadie. "How do I pull myself out of this? What if I can't do it? And then I'm trapped like this forever, not knowing what's going on and why I'm involved in it."

"As if that's going to happen," Sadie said. Her dark brown eyes sparkled at Daphne. "What do I always tell you?"

"If you're at somebody's house and they don't rinse their rice before cooking it, get up and walk out," Daphne said.

"Run." Sadie pointed a finger at her. "Don't walk. Do not pass go. Do not collect two hundred dollars. That's some white people shit and we cannot abide by it. But also . . . ?"

Daphne sighed. "'You're smart, you'll figure it out.'"

"Precisely," Sadie said, ignoring the obvious mocking tone in Daphne's voice.

Jim Ouverture stomped back in from the airport. As usual, he cooed at his grandpuppy before heading over to the couch to coo at Daphne and then Sadie, never mind the fact that they were adult women with demanding professions. Sadie made some kind of joke and her father gave that same barrel-chested laugh that made everyone instantly fall in love with him—dogs, toddlers, divorcées who would think twice if Fabiola had anything to do about it.

And at the sight of his bright white teeth, his wide grin, and his twinkling Ouverture eyes, Daphne finally understood that she had someone to turn to about how to extricate herself from Sam Taylor's death.

ONLY ONCE Sadie had gone home from her babysitting duties, long after they'd let Chloe out to potty, did Daphne broach the question pressing against her chest. Jim had fixed himself a fresh cup of coffee and was lying on the couch next to her watching old highlights of the New Orleans Saints, the very portrait of a man content.

"Dad?" Daphne stretched out the syllable.

"Yes, sweetie?"

She hesitated. Once this Pandora's box was open, there might not ever be a way to close it again.

She took a step closer. "How do you find information that someone doesn't want you to know?"

James François-Dominique Toussaint Ouverture the Fifth looked over his mug of coffee at his daughter with a mixture of curiosity, amusement, and deep, hard-fought knowledge. "You sure you want to talk about this?"

Daphne wasn't. She nodded anyway.

Contrary to Fabiola's declamations, Saint Valentine wasn't responsible for bringing Jim and Fabiola together in Paris. Fabiola had come to France to study education so that she could eventually become a high school principal back home in Ivory Coast. What brought Jim to the City of Lights took each Ouverture child time to uncover. And each child, one by one, was sworn to never repeat it.

During a stay in Paris after high school graduation—a gift from her parents—Daphne finally learned the truth. Over breakfast one hot summer morning, eating apricots on her auntie Emmanuelle's miniscule balcony, Daphne had worked up the courage to ask her aunt what happened. Auntie Emmanuelle had said nothing for a few minutes, and Daphne saw Fabiola's own intense frown in hers, the mark of sisters from across an ocean.

"Your mother, she . . . she witnessed something," Emmanuelle had said, her tone and fluctuation more familiar to Daphne than the Baoulé songs of her youth.

"Witnessed what?" Daphne asked.

Emmanuelle shook her head. "She was always taking on extra work, you know how your mother is. She had come over from Abidjan to stay with me and within ten months—*pouf,*

Daphne. She was taking classes, she had two jobs, she was braiding hair at night to send some money to your mémé, God rest her soul. Your mother was on her morning shift cleaning hotel rooms in Le Meurice when she saw it."

Emmanuelle didn't know the specifics, but whatever Fabiola had uncovered was important enough on an international scale to require witness protection. In the spirit of cooperation, the CIA had coughed up a few extra hands to watch over this feisty West African woman who refused to cower before a powerful enemy.

Jim had been one of them.

"What do you want to know, daughter of my heart?" that same man asked her now.

"My book," Daphne blurted out. "I want to know where my book is."

Jim peered at her curiously. "*Papillon*? That's really what you want to know?"

Daphne fiddled with her hands. "Yes, of course it is. If I find it, maybe I can find out why I was attacked or why someone broke into my home."

Jim's silence filled every crevice of her cottage.

"I mean, what else would I be looking for?" Daphne asked.

His shrug was light, even if his gaze boring into hers wasn't. "I don't know, sugar bug. All I know is that your colleague's dead and the police don't know what's going on and it could be good for someone to look into it."

Daphne narrowed her eyes. "I'm not interested in solving Sam's murder, Dad."

"Really?"

"Really," Daphne said firmly. "I'm not."

Jim tilted his head. "Why not?"

"I don't do that." Daphne frowned. "I'm a professor. I teach about eighteenth-century France. I don't solve murders."

"You could do both, you know," Jim said.

Daphne rolled her eyes.

Her family's chosen profession was no secret, exactly, even if the nature of their work remained concealed by multiple international institutions. And while Daphne was happy enough for her father and brothers to splash about in a world of diplomats and kingmakers, she had long set out a separate path for herself. She held nothing against the family trade, personally, but the fact of the matter was that dead people had always interested her more than the living. Her parents had delighted in her path to a PhD program in French history, even if they spoke of her with the same kind of fondness for which someone speaks of the family parrot. She was the odd duck for wanting a quiet life among books, but everyone in her life had long accepted that fact. Hadn't they?

"I promise you, Dad, I'm just trying to find my book. So how do I do that?"

The stare between them lasted what must have been an eternity. "Your dead colleague. Was he married?"

"No, engaged."

Her father took a long sip of coffee. "Could you ask his fiancée?"

Daphne's neck tensed up just thinking about Molly Henderson. "Wouldn't it be terrible of me to just go over to her house and ask if her fiancée knew anything about a book? I mean, he just died."

Jim shrugged. "Bring a cake."

"What?"

"Bring a cake," he repeated. "Bring flowers. Bring something. Say you want to express your condolences."

"That feels insincere."

"That's because it is," he said to her, not unkind. He reached for her hand. "You always were the sensitive one of the kids— and no, that's not because you're a girl. I think you get it from me."

Only as an adult did Daphne recognize how Jim's sweet, sincere face had been such a disarming weapon throughout his career. "I sure don't get it from mother," Daphne joked.

"She's had a hard run. It makes her look tough sometimes. But you know she loves you more than anything."

Daphne looked away, furiously blinking back the tears in her eyes.

"Anyway, that's it. There's no secret way to get information, honey bun," Jim said. "It's pretty simple. There's talking and then there's cake. That's not so bad, is it?"

Daphne's shoulders relaxed a little. "So what do I say to Molly when I talk to her?"

"It sounds like the simplest question is probably the best one," Jim replied. "A book of yours is missing. You think her fiancé borrowed it. Has she seen it? When she answers you check her body language. Does she get stiff in the chest or shoulders? Does she look at you or look away?"

Daphne considered that. "What if I can't tell?"

Jim laughed. "Baby daughter—heart of my heart—you teach college kids for a living. How many dead grandmothers have suddenly turned up alive and well after a student's asked for an extension on their final exam?"

A smile tugged at her lips. "My student Jonah lost three grandmothers last semester."

"And how many extensions did that get him?"

"Two," Daphne replied. "I learned my lesson after that."

"Then there you go." Jim reached for his mug of coffee. "Some things you learn on the job. It's a skill you develop like any other. I see you with your research, though. This kinda detective work is a skill set you already have."

"How so?"

"Well—good sleuthing and good historical research aren't so different. You chase down leads, hunt down evidence. You're willing to be patient to find that one piece of documentation you were looking for to seal the case."

Miranda's commission to Daphne to find evidence on Ken Miller's misdeeds came back into view. She sat back in her chair and gripped her mug of coffee a little tighter than necessary. "Huh."

"You'll also reexamine what I'd call an eyewitness account until you've picked it apart and put it together again."

"Reading against the grain," Daphne said.

"I call that a classic investigative technique."

Daphne studied her coffee mug. As much as she resented admitting it, Jim was right. She relished the role of investigator. Finding fragile letters in French archives was a better high than any drug could provide. The difference between her and Jim, she supposed, was that Daphne preferred her subjects dead. What would it be like to follow the living?

"So I just . . . bring a cake?" she asked.

"Just bring a cake."

THAT EVENING, a steadiness returned to her hands as Daphne worked the batter, and the way her feet were planted firm on her kitchen tiles felt almost secure, even if sudden movements still made her stomach lurch. She beamed at her concoction a few hours later, a two-layer marvel of chocolate, sugar, and eggs baked to perfection. A thin ribbon of raspberry jam was tucked away inside, a delightful surprise to whoever bit into it.

The French invented silence.

It was wild how one text message, one line of prose could upend a life, spilling its contents out like an overturned laundry basket for everyone to see. But the only one who could put her life affairs in order again was the woman standing in her kitchen. And what scared Daphne most of all was that she didn't want anyone else to solve this for her, anyway. She craved invisibility. But she might just crave the hunt for the truth a little bit more.

The dark chocolate ganache on her cake gleamed bright and smooth under her kitchen lights.

A small sparkle, a tiny zip of electricity tickled up her right leg.

She quickly stomped it out.

"It's just a cake."

CHAPTER ELEVEN

That Sunday, Daphne gingerly nestled her freshly baked cake onto the passenger seat of her car and drove out deep into the west side of Calliope, where the stately homes became more opulent with each intersection. She pulled up to a mansion that made Monticello look like a chicken shack and found the security speaker next to a wrought-iron gate.

After a babbling introduction to security, the gate buzzed her in and she drove her hybrid sedan up the long driveway, past a line of well-trimmed fir trees that stood guard like a row of soldiers, and parked outside the main entrance. Tulips, hyacinths, and daffodils were just beginning to push up on the edges of the manicured lawn. The clipped-back bare rose bushes promised to turn the property into a perfumed paradise in a month.

Daphne pasted on a bright smile and rang the doorbell, cradling her chocolate cake.

The door opened to reveal an unknown woman with Molly's sky-blue eyes and blond hair cropped in a short pixie cut. She assessed Daphne coolly. "Catering goes to the back of the house."

Daphne's smile faltered. "Oh, no, sorry, I'm here to see Molly."

Skepticism remained scattered like freckles across the woman's petite face.

"I'm a colleague," Daphne insisted, stronger now. "Here to offer my condolences."

That got a slight eyebrow raise.

"Please forgive me," Daphne tried again. "What did you say your name was?"

"I didn't." She turned away. "Molly? You have company."

The mahogany door swung open fully. The woman walked away. Along her delicate neck a tattoo of a sword glistened, its grip forming a base by her shoulders, anchoring a sharp blade pointing to her skull.

Daphne clung to her chocolate cake and shifted her feet outside the door, feeling more embarrassed with each passing second. Coming over was a bad idea. She barely even knew Molly, but one conversation with Jim had given her the audacity to think she could squeeze her for information like a lemon for Poisson Braisé?

Daphne had already turned to bolt when Molly's low voice called out. "Daphne! No, don't leave!"

Sam's widow was slim and tall, adorned in a formfitting black dress, a gray wool shawl draped elegantly across her shoulders. Her long blond hair was swept up into an artfully messy bun that Daphne would never be able to recreate herself.

Molly looked stunning. Molly looked tired. Grief did strange things to a body.

Molly grabbed the cake and ushered Daphne inside with a jerk of her head. "That was my sister, Melanie. Sorry if she was difficult. She can be a bit protective."

Daphne's shoes sank into the expensive cream and silver Persian rug that covered most of the hardwood floor in the entryway. After gesturing to a closet for Daphne to hang up her coat, Molly led her past a formal living room and a high-ceilinged dining hall before taking her into a vintage kitchen with sparkling white tiles that was twice the size and three times as clean as Daphne's. Polished, impersonal, and beautiful—like Molly herself.

Molly leaned against the slick white marble countertop of her kitchen island and withdrew two gleaming spoons from a nearby drawer, then took a bite of chocolate cake. She moaned with pleasure. "Good heavens, this is good. This is so, so good, Daphne."

"Thanks."

"You didn't have to."

Daphne shrugged. "I know. I just wanted to come by and offer my condolences."

Molly looked away from Daphne and took her next bite. They both ate in a silence Daphne wasn't sure how to break. As the seconds ticked on, whatever courage she had drained away. She couldn't let it.

She decided to throw them both a bone. "Molly, can you remind me what you work on again? You're at the Benson Art Museum, right?"

"Mmm-hmmm." Molly put down her spoon. "I study Italian baroque art with a focus on women painters."

"Oh." Daphne rummaged in her mind. "Like . . . Artemisia Gentileschi? That's the only one I think I know."

"That's exactly who I study." Molly tilted her head to the side in thought. "How do you know her?"

"*My illustrious lordship, I'll show you what a woman can do,*" Daphne quoted, blushing at Molly's pleased look. "I read around. Plus, you just pick things up all the time if you're a historian. She painted at the same time as Caravaggio, right?"

"Yes," Molly said. "And at nineteen years old she was better than him. In fact, she'd already improved their styles and blended them together to make her own, all the while being suppressed from joining the academy by other male artists."

For a moment, however fleeting, Molly's blue eyes were shocking jolts of electricity. She was still formal if not distant, still a product of what Daphne could only assume was a finishing school but there was some genuine enthusiasm shining through her otherwise stiff poise.

"She sounds amazing," Daphne said. She meant it.

"She was," Molly replied. "It's been an honor to study her for a living. What do you do again, Daphne? Something with Africa?"

"French history," Daphne corrected. "Black families in eighteenth-century France in particular. Nothing that you work on—or Sam, for that matter."

That earned a gentle murmur of either approval or pity and Daphne was, once again, on the cusp of being swallowed up by the awkward silence of the moment.

Saying nothing, she watched, instead, as Molly gracefully cut another slice, fending off a polite invitation to join her in eating another piece. Molly's formfitting black dress could wrap around one of Daphne's thighs at best, but here she was, demolishing a chocolate cake with ease.

"You have a beautiful home," Daphne said quietly.

"Mmmm." Molly's pale cheeks were stuffed with cake. "Thank you. This house has been in my family for generations. I grew up here."

"Oh?" Daphne said. "That's kinda cool."

Molly lifted a thin shoulder. "My father was usually off

politicking all the time—he was a senator before he became governor—so this house was the family anchor. And then after my brothers left for boarding school, my mom, my sister, and I ruled the roost. You know how it is."

"Not really." Daphne shifted uncomfortably. "I didn't really grow up in one place. My family bounced around a lot. But I bet it was nice growing up in one house the whole time."

Something flickered across Molly's pale face. Hesitation? Skepticism? Just as quickly, it vanished. The woman was a smooth, polished gem, not a crack to be seen. Daphne wondered what it took for someone like her to break.

"When I moved back here a few years ago, the place had been empty for a while. It felt right to reclaim it. Sam and I were still trying to decide if we were going to live here or in his house when—"

Molly swallowed. She put down her plate, smoothing her palms against her skirt.

And it hit Daphne, then, that a life had been taken and that there were those grieving its absence. As a historian she was surrounded by grief, by death, by loss. Her entire job was to try to make sense of lives long gone. But she had the benefit of teleological distance on her side, of a two-hundred year gulf between her and those who had departed. Hindsight was a blessing and a curse in her profession, making it possible—difficult, but possible—to see the past for what it was but unable to talk to those who'd lived it themselves, who'd loved and lost and mourned.

In her own life, Daphne had escaped the anguishes of grief thus far. But now here she was, sitting across from it. Sadness, fresh and bright, overwhelmed Daphne, putting pressure on her eyes. "I'm so sorry."

"It's okay." Molly flashed an empty smile. "It actually helps to talk about Sam instead of pretending that everything's fine."

She wiggled in her seat again. "How'd you two meet?"

Molly's smile warmed, becoming real. "At a bar."

"Which one?"

"Pour Decisions." Molly's smile became small again. Wistful. "He was watching a football game and drinking a beer."

"Of course he was," Daphne muttered.

That earned a snicker from Molly. "And I'd just survived a long meeting with an administrator about God knows what and all I wanted was a glass of red wine. I'd seen Sam at a few functions before but we'd never talked before that night. Not really. Frankly, I thought he was an arrogant jerk. But then he made me laugh so hard I cried. It was supposed to just be a one-night stand, but then one night turned into two nights and then three and then . . . well. You get the drift."

Daphne honestly didn't. She'd never encountered Sam's soft mushy side nor did she think he had much of one.

Molly waved her dessert spoon in Daphne's direction. "I know what you're thinking."

Daphne startled. "I don't . . ."

"Look, to a lot of people Sam was this cocky guy." Molly's stare was pointed. "I thought he was like that, too, until I got to know him. He had a big heart, Daphne. He wanted to change the world. Which, yes, sounds ridiculous, but . . . he genuinely meant it. And he was also fun. We went camping, he'd randomly foster a litter of kittens, we'd sing karaoke together on like a Wednesday night at midnight. My family's so stiff and proper. But Sam wasn't like that all. He made my days light."

"Sam was fun to hang out with," Daphne eventually offered.

"It seems like he was always watching a new show or reading a new book. Even during the mid-semester craziness."

"That was Sam for you," Molly said.

"Speaking of books," Daphne began, "did Sam mention that he'd borrowed a book of mine called *Papillon*? It's a book on a prison escape in Latin America. He wanted to read it in French, the original language."

"He did?" Molly asked. "But I didn't think he spoke French that well?"

"Oh, Molly, his French was terrible," Daphne confessed—and Molly cracked up. "It was really, really bad. I mean I only heard it a handful of times but each one was more spectacular than the last. A bunch of us junior profs grabbed tacos one night, and at the end of the meal he patted his stomach and turned to me quite proud and said, 'Je suis plein.'"

"And what does that mean?" Molly asked in between giggles.

"I'm pregnant."

Daphne grinned when Molly doubled over in her seat from laughing so hard. Maybe underneath Molly's smooth polish was a bright crooked gem, after all, just as cracked as the rest of us.

"So then why did he want to read that book?" Molly asked, once she'd stopped giggling.

"I don't know," Daphne said. "I didn't actually know him that well."

Molly cocked her head to the side. "You didn't?"

"Not really, no," Daphne replied.

"But—" Something like suspicion flared to life in Molly's gaze. She bit back whatever she had planned to say next and took a spoonful of cake instead, swallowing and wiping her mouth before continuing. "What's the name again? *Papillon*?"

"Yes," Daphne said, relieved to no longer fall under that cold glare. "Have you seen it? Not like I need it back right now with everything you're dealing with."

Molly lifted a thin shoulder. "He didn't leave it here. But he didn't really leave anything here. I usually stayed at his place so I could give my sister a break from us."

"Oh, your sister lives here with you?"

"Off and on. It's complicated." Molly's lips twitched. "Anyway, the police have pretty much everything from his house, but maybe the book's in his office on campus?"

"I don't think so," replied Daphne. "I'll keep digging—don't trouble yourself on my account."

"So what was so special about that book, anyway?"

"I don't know," Daphne said carefully. "Maybe it was related to his research somehow? I know he was studying prisons. And he quoted from *Papillon* in one of his *New York Times* articles. Do you think what happened to him had something to do with his work?"

Molly grimaced. "It's definitely what got him killed. I see that look of surprise on your face, Daphne, but it's true. Sam was on the front lines of a war against injustice. And he paid for it with his life."

Daphne gave what she thought was a polite hum of acknowledgment, earning her a frown of disappointment from Molly.

"You don't believe me," Molly said, flat.

"It's not that, exactly."

"Then what?" Molly pushed.

Daphne took a few awkward seconds to probe her mind for the answer to her own discomfort. "I mean . . . we're academics, not CIA handlers, y'know?"

God, Daphne was really stepping in it, judging by the storm

cloud passing across Molly's face. Having just survived Detective Ahmed's interrogation herself, she could have phrased that better.

"It's just . . ." Daphne tried again. "Sam wasn't the first academic to write about prison reform initiatives in America, right? So I guess I still don't understand how what he was doing was so dangerous."

Molly's sigh was heavy. She stared out into the distance for a while.

"You're right that he wasn't the only academic studying the prison industry," she eventually said. "But that's not what I'm talking about. That's not what he was up to. This project Sam was involved in? It was different. It had nothing to do with academia."

"What do you mean?" Daphne asked.

"He was doing this . . . exposé of some kind," Molly said. "The *Times* was interested in running it. Sam was really close to wrapping it up and showing it to the editor. He was going to reveal the full extent of Livington's corruption with the help of a friend."

Daphne glanced at Molly again. "Who?"

"His friend from Nevada," Molly's pretty features twisted in concentration. "JP or JC or something like that. Even I didn't know his name. The point is that after JP's stint in prison in Reno, he moved out to Calliope following some girlfriend. But then he robbed a store or a bank or something out here and he was sentenced to Livington. JP began his sentence around the same time that Sam started grad school."

Sam's *New York Times* piece had promised to have more to the story. And even if his exposé wasn't purely academic, an insider accessing details others couldn't was every researcher's dream. Rarely did Daphne envy anthropologists but the ability to cross-examine and re-interrogate a witness was an aspect of their profession that she occasionally longed for.

"And Sam never told you this guy's name?" Daphne asked. "Or gave you his exposé?"

A wisp of blonde hair drifted over Molly's temple when she shook her head. "The detectives asked me that, too. I told them everything I know. I have no idea where it is. And Sam was always very secretive about it. He wanted to protect my family from any fallout. My brother's running for Congress, you know."

"Hm."

Molly stood up. "Well, I'm sorry I couldn't be more help with your book. Good luck searching for it."

Daphne knew an exit when she heard one. She stood up and winced. Dizziness took over.

"Daphne, are you all right?"

She would have responded but she was too busy willing the fiery throbs on her scalp to die down. Collapsing back into her seat, she pushed out several breaths and closed her eyes, hearing nothing but the pounding of her temples.

"I got attacked a couple of days ago," Daphne finally gasped out. "I haven't really told anybody about it."

Molly looked shaken. "Oh my God."

"I'm okay, I promise," Daphne said, hoping to quell Molly's disquiet.

"You don't have to be," Molly insisted.

Daphne shifted uncomfortably in her chair. "I guess I . . . I don't see what choice I have."

"See, this is what makes me so upset sometimes," Molly said. "As women we're used to pushing through, aren't we? Men can be such babies when they get a scrape but here you are, coming to visit me after your own assault. It's a good reminder of how much we have in us. I read this quote the other day that said, 'Women are powerful and dangerous.' It felt like a warning—in a good way."

Daphne croaked out, "You love Audre Lorde, too?"

Molly's eyebrows wrinkled. "Who?"

"Um, the quote?" said Daphne. "It's by Audre Lorde, the Black lesbian feminist poet. You know, the woman behind sayings like 'Your silence will not protect you,' and 'For the master's tools will never dismantle the master's house.' That kind of thing. Did—did you not know it already?"

"No, I just saw it somewhere downtown," Molly replied with an elegant lift of a shoulder. "Will I see you at Sam's memorial service?"

At the front door of Molly's estate Daphne blustered through a smile and stumbled to the car, with Molly waving behind her. One last question popped up, one last itch that Daphne couldn't resist scratching.

"Hey, Molly?" Daphne shouted. "Do you have any idea how I can get in touch with JP? I thought I could maybe dig around and ask him if he knows anything about *Papillon*."

"You can't," said Molly, visibly frustrated.

Daphne leaned over her car. "Why not?"

"Because he's dead, Daphne. He was stabbed in prison last month."

CHAPTER TWELVE

The Ivorian flag clock hanging from Daphne's wall in her office ticked by that Monday morning while Molly's last words swirled in front of her. Josephine Baker flashed her usual dazzling smile at Daphne from the front pages of her coloring book, all shimmering legs and slim hips twirling. The dancer's famous banana skirt offered little distraction to her growing alarm. She had been attacked, her bookshelves ransacked, and someone named JP had been murdered. Just what the hell had Sam Taylor gotten her mixed up in?

Whatever it was, it had gotten him killed. And now Sam's killer was out there on the streets of Calliope, tying up loose ends. Which might, it turned out, include Daphne. If only she knew why.

Daphne threw her pen to the ground. Kicked it for good measure, too. Maybe she should throw something heavier on the floor just to feel its weight smack the carpet. A copy of Michel Foucault's seminal text *Discipline and Punish* poked out from her stack of books, and Daphne yanked it out, twirling it around in her hands with a scowl. The slim volume was unfortunately too light.

She was just supposed to be finding *Papillon*. That's what she'd told her dad. She resented the implication that she wanted more than that. She resented even more the pulling in her chest—stronger now, after her conversation with Molly—that told her that she did.

What if she rummaged around a little bit beyond her book, just this one time?

It wouldn't be forever. Shoot, with only two more weeks until final exams, it probably wouldn't even be for the rest of the semester. And then she could return this part of herself back to its box.

Yeah, just like Pandora did.

Daphne squeezed her eyes shut. Sam had quoted *Papillon* in that *New York Times* article on Livington Prison—and which Molly had just confirmed was vital to Sam's exposé. The answer probably lay with JP, who'd just been killed. Who was he? How could she find out, now that he was dead?

You're a historian, Daphne told herself, *so think like one. How would you research a prisoner in eighteenth-century France?*

There had to be public records that documented the inmate population of Livington Prison. If Daphne could hunt down historical records of French convicts in Parisian archives, looking for someone who had been alive in the digital age had to be a breeze. If there was a skill set Daphne had developed over time, it was searching for the dead, even those—especially those—who society assumed had left behind no trace. Rarely was that the case. True, the archival holdings for a French monarch were denser than those of a peasant, but even the steadfast farmer's wife lived on in recipes, church pamphlets, folk tales, and the memories of those she'd left behind.

A few clacks on the keyboard and Daphne was on the gussied-up website for Livington Correctional Facility, which led her to the Department of Corrections site, which instructed its viewer on how to do everything from sending care packages to incarcerated individuals to locating someone's bond information. Some searching later, and Daphne had located a database of inmates through the state court's office where she could find JP's arrest record, felonies, warrants, and other documents, provided she could put in his name or a case number.

Daphne leaned back in her office chair, foggy. She was surprised at how the visit to Molly's house had taxed her. On the long descent down the driveway in her car, Daphne had checked out the rearview mirror in time to catch Molly on the steps of the front entrance, hugging herself. Daphne had been about to turn onto the street when she saw something through the mirror that had made her put on the brakes—Melanie's ghostly face, chalk white, its pale anger shining through an upstairs window.

Daphne shoved that last image aside. She stood up from her desk. Maybe a sojourn through the campus lawn would do her some good. Or, even better, a cup of tea at the faculty club? Usually Miranda popped her head in to fill her porcelain cup with some sencha tea—which she had somehow forced Harrison University to import yearly from Kyoto. Knowing the history department chair, she'd tied the high-end and locally sourced tea leaves to a study abroad initiative, three-day research colloquium, and some kind of award-winning scholarly publication. Daphne could sure use Miranda's strategic mind to sort through her fears of Ken's ascension. A cup of tea and a chat with her chair in the Faculty Club sounded like just the ticket. And shoot, if Daphne brought her stack of papers with her, maybe she could convince herself to grade some.

ESTABLISHED IN 1894, the Faculty Club towering over Harrison University's campus was, if rumor had it, responsible for the retention of ten MacArthur "genius" fellows, three Noble prize winners, and two presidents. Some might think its lure lay in its ornate, ivy-snaked columns guarding the entrance, forbidding all students from entering unless by invitation of a professor. Others suggested its popularity stemmed from its plush interiors, decorated by a society maven in the 1910s, who'd imported Italian marble, silk velvet curtains from India, and Art Nouveau stained-glass windows to establish the institution as the most prestigious on campus. Many pointed to its legendary banquet hall, which had hosted dignitaries and even a pope. But now, into her second semester at Harrison, Daphne knew otherwise.

It was about the food.

"The croissants are ready," shrieked Natalie Diaz, a classics professor and recent inductee into the American Academy of Arts and Sciences.

Daphne waved a friendly "hi" to Jamie the security guard and entered the high-domed lobby where award-winning professors were clamoring for the daily tea service.

Natalie bent over to read the chalkboard that some student-worker had just placed outside the doors to the main dining room. "They have an apricot glaze!"

The roar from the throngs threatened to topple the Chinese vases from their marble columns. It looked like she was going to have to engage in a sport more bloodthirsty than gladiators dueling a pride of lions in ancient Rome: competing for one of Chef Marcel's pastries.

The Institute for Advanced Study in Princeton had its legendary cafeteria, where astrophysicists and medievalists slid onto their plastic trays dishes such as roast salmon and asparagus, mushroom and fontina cheese pizzas, or schnitzel and potato salad, and searched for empty seats among the rows of tables at lunchtime. The American Academy in Rome delivered silky pastas slicked with tomato sauce, paninis stacked with mortadella, and roasted carrots in tahini and lemon.

Harrison had Chef Marcel. Stolen away from a Michelin-starred restaurant in New York City by the promises of an outrageous salary and an opportunity to finally coach his kids' soccer games, Chef Marcel and his culinary team were responsible for several successful hires and even marriages among the faculty. Unfortunately, competition to procure his meals had also led to a few divorces and even a lawsuit.

A queue formed across the lobby while the supposedly erudite and brilliant minds of this generation snipped at each other to watch their steps. Gradually, as required, the professors settled down enough to smother their mania and form a fuzzy shape that resembled a line. Chef Marcel's one rule was that the faculty quit acting like bickering kindergartners long enough to grab a tray and cash out.

Daphne had long become convinced that the only person on Harrison University's campus who could keep anyone in line—tenured professors, deans, shoot even the president herself—was a fifty-something bald Haitian man with a permanent scowl on his face. He held the fate of all faculty and staff in his gnarled hands, keeping a blacklist and checking it twice, sniffing at profuse genuflections of gratitude and silencing any protest with a haughty sneer.

At Daphne's turn to select a freshly baked croissant, she received one of his rare half-grins, being one of the few Black French speakers around.

His low bass grumbled out, "Comment va votre famille?"

Daphne basked in the silent death stares from her colleagues. They could stay jealous. "Bien, merci. Et votre fils, Patrice?"

She chatted just a second longer in French than necessary, inquiring into the status of his beloved team Paris Saint-Germain's quest to win the Champions League, before moving down the line. Behind her was a familiar forest green Patagonia sweater. Daphne frowned at Ken Miller, the memory of his blackmail threatening to ruin her teatime. At least she could take comfort in the fact that his schmooze had no effect on Chef Marcel, who growled at Ken's smile before moving on to the next professor desperate for his culinary benediction.

She settled down in her favorite spot: a sturdy chair next to the window overlooking Harrison's man-made lake. Staring out onto the large body of water—even if it had been crafted by millionaire donors trying to outdo Wellesley College's Lake Waban—always settled her down. A few sips of tea later and Daphne was mostly ready to confront her stack of ungraded papers again.

Tabitha had, of course, written a scathing indictment on European empires' shift from the transatlantic slave trade to indentured servanthood in the wake of the abolition movement of the early nineteenth century. Aspen had chosen to write a queer retelling of George Sand's romantic relationship with the stage actress Marie Dorval, which was no surprise. Connor's essay started, "The Merriam-Webster dictionary defines the term 'history,' as—"

Daphne would have to flip through that later. Sometimes it was just too painful to start with the weak ones. The repeated lack of originality often had Daphne screaming into the void. She'd spent hours and hours giving feedback to her students and for what? A few came to her in office hours to ask for help but plenty just took the papers and ran. They had no plans to improve their prose. They'd never wanted to. In becoming a professor, Daphne had apparently vowed to become Sisyphus, rolling that boulder of suggestions up the hill anyway. Maybe Sisyphus wasn't the right figure from Greek mythology. Maybe she was closer to Cassandra, shouting to her students to stop using the phrase "can be seen" in all of their papers, only to receive those canned lines in perpetuity.

Desperate to reassure herself that humankind wasn't entirely doomed to failure, she pushed through a few more papers. Her plan mostly worked until she got to Olivia's ill-conceived idea for an essay on the Paris Commune of 1871. Muddling through the usual descriptions of starving Parisians eating rats during the barricade, her wince at one particularly poorly written clause was irrepressible. Unfortunately, so was her yelp when she heard the whistling of a familiar tune, however faint, piping its melody back to her from the essay's pages.

Georges Clemenceau was such a good democrat that he didn't even try to resist the coup d'état during the Paris Commune of 1871. He categorically refused to allow French blood to spill in order to stay in power.

A sour tang warmed the back of her throat. It was Henri Charrière's *Papillon*, faint but unmistakable.

Georges Clemenceau—

"No." Daphne squeezed her eyes shut. "No, no, no, no, no. Nope. Nope."

Daphne counted out three deliriously long breaths and opened her eyes again.

. . . was such a good democrat that he—

Daphne groaned loud enough to startle a sleeping anthropologist in the corner.

Papillon again.

Olivia had altered the prose a little, but the melody was wailing.

Maybe it was a coincidence that Olivia's paper quoted directly from a French prison novel that most Americans had never heard of before. But Olivia's red eyes in class the other day, puffy from crying, said otherwise. And now, instead of drinking her tea and watching scholars in the hands of an angry Marcel beg for absolution while she waited around for Miranda, she was going to have to confront Olivia about a novel Daphne suspected was connected to the murder of a beloved professor.

Daphne's scalp throbbed. It was still so bruised, so tender. Willing her anxiety to quell, she let out a breath and considered her options. She could reach out to Detective Ahmed, but her chances of being taken seriously were about as high as Connor's GPA. Detective Ahmed had made it clear that whatever connection existed between Daphne and Sam was feeble at best and nothing more. And as for Rowan, he was . . . Oh, good lord, Daphne still had difficulties even thinking his name without blushing. He believed her, which was a lifeline she needed in the midst of this storm. There was, however, appearing thirsty and looking so parched you could cough up sand. Her mother had taught her to have at least *some* propriety and by God, Daphne would cling to those mannered lessons with every last finger.

Screw you, Sam Taylor. He was the one who'd got her into this mess by texting her a line from *Papillon.* Daphne was determined to get herself out of it.

Dear Olivia, Daphne typed. *We need to meet to discuss your most recent essay. I have some questions for you concerning its contents. Can you come to my office hours tomorrow afternoon?*

"Olivia Vail?"

Daphne turned to the sound of that unmistakably male voice—to find Ken Miller looming above her. When had he began to read over her shoulder?

His frown of disapproval was stark. "She's one of your students?"

"Hi, Ken." Miranda had made it clear that Ken was too

powerful to displease, so Daphne kept her smile bright while fleeing into her imagination. She was on a beach, drinking margaritas and tossing a ball into the ocean for Chloe to catch. "She's in my French Empire class this semester. Care to sit?"

"And you think she's done something wrong?" Ken asked, still looming over.

"Well, I don't know yet," Daphne replied carefully. "That's why I need to talk to her."

That frown kept growing. "Tiffany—"

"Daphne," she corrected.

"—Olivia Vail comes from a very prominent family with deep ties to Harrison," said Ken.

Deep pockets, Daphne heard.

"Her mother was class president and Olivia's father sits on the alumni advisory board. Olivia's grandparents still donate quite generously to the College of Arts and Sciences. I'd caution you against moving too swiftly to enact any kind of punitive measures," he interrupted, then paused as if considering his words. "It won't be the first time you might find yourself on the wrong side of a decision."

Daphne's smile peeled away as Ken's words struck her like a dissonant chord. "What do you mean?"

"Well, I know that Miranda's planning on bringing charges against me," Ken said. He stretched out in the seat Daphne had vacated. "All false, of course."

Daphne tried to keep her voice neutral while her stomach plummeted at Ken's news that he'd uncovered Miranda's plot. "Oh?"

Ken scoffed. "Claimed I'd copied from a student. The board's gonna see right through that, of course."

Blood pumped through her ears. She swallowed. "Of course."

Daphne couldn't bear the thought of Miranda being anything less than infallible—or even worse, getting caught in Ken's snare. She hadn't listened, hadn't *wanted* to listen, when Miranda had warned her that men could get away with anything. But what other interpretation was there for Ken's smile of triumph?

"And now, sadly, that student, Kiki Ilunga, is going to have to go before an academic misconduct board," Ken said. "You know, every year departments debate letting in students of color, knowing that they take more work than traditional students do, and every year I try to fight back and say that they're ready to meet Harrison's high standards. So it's a real shame seeing someone like Kiki struggle here after we've all put our faith in her. But what can you do?"

Rage, white and hot, lit up Daphne's insides.

"Which is why I'm thinking about your long-term successes here at Harrison." Ken inched his chair closer to Daphne, and Daphne longed to have the power to spit venom. "When I become dean permanently, I'll be paying attention to who has the university's best interests at heart. Especially in the history department. I'd hate to learn that Miranda pressured you into giving Kiki a passing grade when she should have failed the course."

It was fascinating how quickly a body could switch from extreme hot to extreme cold. How quickly the harsh and heavy weight of someone else's words could push against your chest. Daphne swallowed thickly, the blood in her veins turning to ice. Fear sunk into the marrow of her bones.

"The academic misconduct board is meeting in two weeks," Ken said. "I'd like for you to be present so that you can set the record straight about Kiki's plagiarized essay. Just . . . think about it, that's all." He stood up again. "At a place like Harrison, the clever ones figure out quickly which way the wind's blowing."

CHAPTER THIRTEEN

A cold wet nose shoved Daphne's dangling forearm. She propped herself up onto her elbows. Her shiny black dog was sitting patiently by her bedside, waiting to be let out.

"Good morning, baby," she mumbled.

They went through their usual morning routine, even if it was more subdued than usual on Daphne's part. After a second large cup of coffee, she somehow managed to drive to Aunt Linda's house, where Chloe bounded out of the car and into the retired librarian's arms without even once looking back.

God, she was sick of giving less than her best to Chloe in the mornings, and she was more than over the fog that clouded her mind until at least lunchtime every day. When had she become a walking zombie?

The day Sam texted you.

The day you got on Ken Miller's radar.

That man's threats were so thinly veiled they might as well have been tap-dancing naked in Times Square. And now, he had plans to bring Kiki before a plagiarism board once she returned from Central Africa at the end of the term. Miranda's plan of action had backfired, leaving Daphne to wonder how they could recoup their losses. What came next? Was there any way to protect Kiki from Ken's lies? Could Daphne fight the tides of inevitability sweeping Ken onto the throne? For a historian, nothing was inevitable and the future was always up for grabs. But occasionally it was difficult to find hope in the face of so much uncertainty.

Another question, barbed and nauseating, had also drifted into Daphne's dreams last night.

Had Olivia Vail known Sam Taylor?

Daphne couldn't figure out how to answer that question on her own without potentially committing a felony. Way on the bottom of the Harrison food chain, Daphne didn't have access to the main database that allowed professors to see student records. Only appointed faculty advisors had permission to see what courses were on a student's transcript, and even then, if they were caught searching for anyone who wasn't a student of theirs, they could face disciplinary action. FERPA (the Family Education Rights and Privacy Act of 1974) had enshrined student privacy into all educational records. Which meant that the only reliable way to uncover Olivia's relationship with Sam Taylor was the old-fashioned way: interviewing her.

The impending confrontation with Olivia circled her brain as she trudged over to the history department building, side-stepping a fresh slab of poured concrete right in front of the stairs. A printed sign, stapled to an oak tree, warned passersby to avoid the construction work, its white paper marred by thick scribbling in black permanent marker that Daphne struggled to interpret.

"PLEASE ~~ADHEAR TO~~ SIGNAGE"

It should say "adhere"

THAT'S CLASSIST

No it's not it's just spelling

CULTURAL THEORISTS ARGUE THAT OUR GRAMMAR AND SPELLING STANDARDIZATIONS (AND THE CULTURAL DISCIPLINING OF THEM) ARE MANIFESTATIONS OF IMPERIALISTIC HEGEMONIC NORMS THAT PERPETUATE INEQUALITY AND ENCOURAGE THE SUBALTERN TO SUBJECT THEMSELVES TO ASSIMILATIONIST IDEOLOGIES THAT ULTIMATELY HARM THEIR OWN COMMUNITIES

IT IS JUST A SIGN

POST-STRUCTURALIST HERE. THERE'S NO SUCH THING AS "JUST" A SIGN. ALL SIGNS ARE REFERENTS UNTO THEMSELVES.

Post-structuralists are the biggest cowards on the planet, FYI. All their arguments descend to moral relativism

AND WHAT'S THE ALTERNATIVE TO THAT, EXACTLY? RETURNING TO ENLIGHTENMENT-ERA UNIVERSALIST THINKING? THAT ROAD MARCHES US STRAIGHT TO AUTHORITARIANISM, YOU FASCIST

This whole thread is why people hate us

FOR THE LAST TIME IT IS JUST A SIGN

"Professor Ouverture?"

Olivia stood in front of the history building, biting her lip, a worried expression crushing her eyebrows together. At this moment, she looked every bit her age of twenty—too old to be entirely naive, too young to have fully reckoned with the consequences of her actions.

Daphne sighed. "Let's talk in my office."

It took surprisingly little prying for Daphne to get Olivia to confess to her misdeeds. Her brown eyes shimmered as soon as she sat down, the mascara beginning to seep onto her bottom lashes. "Yeah, I know what I did was wrong. I was tired and desperate. I haven't exactly been acing this semester."

Daphne crossed her arms. "I assumed that was the case. The students who plagiarize are usually the ones up against a wall."

Olivia's chin wobbled. "Harrison wasn't the right fit for me and I've known it since freshman year, but my parents went here and they kept pushing it on me and I was so afraid of disappointing them . . ."

Daphne opened the top drawer in her desk and grabbed Olivia a tissue—she'd started keeping a stash after a student meltdown her first week on campus—and listened while Olivia spoke. Unlike some of her peers, Daphne no longer took grave offence to a student's attempt to pull the wool over her eyes. Rarely did the plagiarized essay have anything to do with Daphne anyway, she'd discovered, and more to do with the student's hot mess of a life.

But a different question was beginning to bother Daphne, one that she feared she might have to push out of the weepy student before her. "Olivia, how do you know the novel *Papillon*?"

"Papi—what?" Olivia asked, blowing her nose.

"*Papillon*," Daphne repeated. "By Henri Charrière."

Olivia fiddled with the bracelet around her wrist. "Uh . . ."

"That's what I thought." Daphne paused. "Olivia, what's your major again?"

"Anthropology," Olivia replied. "Why?"

It was such an unassuming answer to anyone who lacked the context to go with it. Daphne applauded herself for not picking up her chair and throwing it. "Did you take any classes with Professor Taylor?"

Olivia's gaze grew wary. She gave the world's tiniest nod.

"Did he help you write this essay?" Daphne pushed.

Olivia squirmed in the seat, her face flushing to an unnatural shade of lavender. The lift of her chin was almost imperceptible to the naked eye.

"Why would he do that?" Daphne asked softly.

"Because he liked helping his students?" Olivia offered weakly.

Daphne's expression was stern enough that Fabiola would have applauded it. "Olivia."

The silence lingered. Olivia rubbed the back of her neck. "I know what this looks like. Would you believe me if I told you it wasn't like that?"

"Like what?" Daphne demanded, not caring any longer that her voice had risen.

"He was falling in love with me," Olivia blurted out. Her eyes held a mix of hope and defiance, and all Daphne could feel in that moment was pity.

"He couldn't help it," Olivia insisted. "I couldn't either."

Daphne resisted the retort to that delusion forming on her lips. "When did things develop between you two?"

"This term—but I started thinking there might be something between us last semester. He'd touch my arm in conversation, I'd go to his house for dinner, we'd end up so close on the couch. But then he'd get up and say it was getting late and that I should go home. I think he was afraid of something happening between us, honestly."

Daphne wanted to rub her face in exhaustion.

Olivia kept rambling. "But then he took me and a couple other students to the big anthro conference in January to present our undergrad posters, and I discovered that his hotel room was right next to mine and then late one night after dinner it was just the two of us standing in the hallway and one thing led to another . . ."

"And you kept seeing him after that?" Daphne asked.

"Yeah." Olivia spoke in a whisper. "We met up a few times. Always in secret. Usually at his place."

Disappointment and disgust rolled over Daphne in waves—not with Olivia, however. Sam Taylor had violated the most basic tenets of the professor–student relationship. Sam Taylor was the one who'd held the power over Olivia, which some young women maybe found attractive but Daphne only saw as a recipe for disaster.

"Olivia, did you know he was engaged?" Daphne asked.

Olivia winced. Then nodded. "I felt terrible about it. I really did. But Sam and Molly came from such different worlds, you know? Like Sam, I'm from this tiny rural place. I knew what he'd gone through to get where he was. Molly didn't."

Daphne was surprised by how smug Olivia sounded. "Did he tell you anything about the paper he helped you to write? About that book *Papillon*?"

"No," Olivia said, pleading. "I swear it. Honestly, we'd stopped talking much. He texted me like two weeks ago when I was in Miami for a girls getaway but that was the last time."

Olivia pulled out a bubblegum pink phone and unlocked it for Daphne to see.

Sam: **U turn in the paper?**

Here it was, Daphne thought, confirmation that Sam Taylor was a dirtbag. Oh, how she longed to call the Title IX office. "Why did you stop talking to him?"

A flash of irritation burned across Olivia's heart-shaped face. She bit her lip, holding back whatever anger and disappointment was rising to the surface.

Daphne tried again, gentle. "Something happen?"

She fiddled with her hands, refusing to look up. "I'd heard some rumors."

"Like what?"

Olivia picked at her nails. "That he'd been with some other girls, that kind of thing."

"Other girls?" Daphne asked. "Like who?"

Olivia's shrug made her look fifteen. "I was really upset. I thought we had something—and I still think we did. But now I'll never really know, will I?"

AFTER A day of teaching, Daphne stared at the plain white wall in her office, numb. Sam Taylor, darling anthropologist at Harrison, had been involved with a student. Sam had cited *Papillon* in a paper he'd written for Olivia. A paper that he knew would land on Daphne's desk. A paper submitted by a student he'd probably slept with.

Daphne shook herself off like a wet dog.

Usually, she could cheer herself up by spending an hour in the Benson Art Museum and basking in French Impressionist paintings but honestly right now she just wanted fresh air and some bubble tea to go along with it. She pushed herself away from her desk, slipped on her coat, and headed out, letting the bright April sun warm her. Drifting from campus and down the main street, she wandered by her favorite florist who was currently bent over, washing away a quote from bell hooks that the Femmes Fatales must have spray-painted on the door. A window across the street stopped her in her tracks, its gold embossed lettering sparkling across the glass.

Earthseed Bookstore.

Daphne loved Octavia Butler as much as the next nerd, but she'd always found that name a little cheesy, a little too crunchy granola for her taste. Earthseed had a reputation for being less of a bookstore and more of a maze, its narrow aisles stacked to the ceiling with old paperbacks and musty hardcovers. It had been the kind of bookstore that made it impossible to tell if the book you had fished out of the maw was worth ten thousand dollars or ten cents. At one point that might have been cute, but the threadbare carpets and stuffy air had just felt sad.

Daphne had missed Earthseed's reopening in January, and work had pummeled her for most of the spring semester to the point where she'd rarely left her house or campus. But the display of glossy book covers on a table inside beckoned her to join the buzzing customers mulling around. Earthseed had always specialized in rare editions. And while her conversation with Olivia about *Papillon* had gotten her nowhere closer to finding it, maybe Earthseed's new owner could tell her something about Auntie Emmanuelle's copy of the book. Maybe her seventies French edition of *Papillon* was rarer than Daphne gave it credit for.

A bell chimed its pleasant ring as she pushed open the front door. Large black and white tiles sparkled on the floor, and rows of bookshelves lined the exposed brick walls. The main floor was now shockingly wide and open, far removed from the claustrophobic cramped space that Daphne had first encountered as a new hire. Tables in the center offered even more books, stacked in neat piles, many with handwritten laminated recommendations. Two cashiers, both most likely Harrison students, giggled at the register near the main entrance, bagging up an elderly man's order of John le Carré novels. Wandering past a row of Colson Whitehead novels, Daphne took in the postcards and paper goods, the high-quality selection of Japanese pens, and her nose caught a whiff of coffee brewing upstairs from the café.

Earthseed was no longer musty or old. It had become the most intoxicating mix of erudition, comfort, and charm.

"That book is super-devastating, if you're looking for a good cry," a young woman said. She wore a thrift-store T-shirt meant for a five-year-old and a nametag that shouted AMBER in all caps. Her black hair was buzzed short on one side. "I can't recommend it enough."

Daphne blinked down at the book that had found its way into her hands. Tayari Jones's *An American Marriage* had made her ugly cry in a bathroom stall once. She hastily placed it back on a shelf.

Amber's pierced eyebrow lifted. "So something lighter then?"

"Um, no, I—" Daphne considered what she wanted to say next. "Is the owner of the store in today? I heard he collects first editions and I thought he might be able to help me out with an obscure book question."

"Of course," Amber said. "You're not claustrophobic, though, right?"

Daphne blinked. "I don't think so . . . ?"

Amber nodded. "Then come with me."

Following Amber, Daphne wandered into a small office near the back of the bookstore, where heavy cardboard boxes rose to the ceiling.

Amber knocked on the door. "Rowan? You've got company."

Behind a cardboard box, a pair of curious gray eyes popped up. They widened in surprise. "Daphne?"

Daphne's breath caught.

"Rowan?" she choked out. "You're the new owner?"

In spite of his tall size, he slid around a stack of cardboard boxes with catlike grace. He ran a hand through his mousy brown hair and leaned against his wooden desk, cheeks flushed. Daphne glanced around for Detective Ahmed, listening out for her usual grumbling. None came.

Rowan owned Earthseed. Rowan was the reason for the bookstore's gleaming, well-stocked bookcases, for its recent write-up in Lit Hub praising it for keeping the tradition of independent bookstores alive and thriving.

Daphne needed to sit down.

"Oh, so you guys know each other already?" Amber glanced back and forth between the pair. She popped a peek at Daphne's ring finger and promptly burst into a grin cheekier than the Cheshire cat's. "Davonté is gonna love—"

"Amber," Rowan said softly.

"You know what?" Amber kept grinning, walking backwards to the door. "I'll see myself out."

Trying to not shrivel up and die of embarrassment, Daphne took a seat at Rowan's desk and tried to remember the last time she'd checked her makeup.

When she looked up—and up—at Rowan again, he was staring at her, his gaze inscrutable.

He spoke quietly. "How are you feeling?"

"You own Earthseed?" Daphne asked at the same time. "You're now a bookseller?"

"Correct."

"By choice?" asked Daphne.

Rowan's nod was vigorous. "Very much so."

Daphne still had so many questions. "Because . . . ?"

"My mentor passed away, leaving me the store in his will. Not like that left me with no choice," Rowan said hastily. "Rather, his gift freed me to make this choice."

"I'm sorry for your loss," Daphne replied.

"Thank you," Rowan said, quiet. "May I again inquire as to your health?"

Daphne's neck and cheeks became warm. "I'm doing a lot better, I promise."

"And how is Chloe?"

"Great." Damnit, he knew just what to say to her. "Happy to be home."

"Good." Rowan's smile was small but warm. "Good, good. I suspect that you didn't enter my store to discuss my recent acquisition of Earthseed. How may I be of service?"

In that moment, Rowan's gray eyes had such a light to them, such clarity. Rare gemstones.

Earth to Daphne.

"My book," Daphne blurted out. "*Papillon.* I'm still looking for it. Earthseed specializes in first editions, right? I was going to ask if my copy of *Papillon* was rare. If that's maybe why Sam took it? If he took it, that is. Which I'm guessing you've already investigated."

Rowan swiveled his chair over to the computer monitor in the corner of his desk. "You're right that I have already located the answer to your question. Why don't I walk you through the results?"

He took a seat across from her and she went to peer over his shoulder. While he typed away, he blew a shaft of brown hair off his forehead, and Daphne willed herself to take a few steady breaths like a normal human. But he smelled nice and his skin looked soft and clear and he sat so comfortably at his seat in front of his computer as if he really was built to conduct archival queries online. Would it be weird if she told him he was a naturally good sitter?

Oh God, Daphne, what kind of a thought even is *that?*

"Here we are," Rowan said, briefly interrupting Daphne's shame spiral. He turned away from his screen and beamed at her—actually beamed at her—and Daphne wondered if she was having a heart attack.

"Well, Daphne," Rowan said, "the results remain the same: Your copy is as rare as the 2016 hardcover edition of *The Catcher in the Rye*."

"Ah," she said. "So, not at all?"

Rowan gave her an impish grin.

Daphne sighed. "Figured."

"Sorry I can't be of more help," he said.

"That's okay." Daphne bit her lip, wondering if she should share JP's name. Rowan wasn't a cop but it was clear that his opinion still mattered greatly to Detective Ahmed, or else he wouldn't be working Sam's case. What was even more embarrassing to Daphne was the fact that Rowan's opinion mattered to her, too. But thus far Rowan had just been so, well, *nice* to her and encouraging and she had to share her thoughts with someone who wasn't a nosy sixty-five-year-old CIA retiree or else she'd start climbing up walls.

"It's just—" Daphne stammered. "It's just that I was talking to Molly Henderson the other day—"

A flash of something lit up Rowan's delicate face. Recognition? Distrust?

"—and she mentioned that Sam had a friend who was killed in prison, JP or something like that, and so I was also maybe hoping that he'd know about the book, or the police would know about the book, or . . . I don't know. But I take it the police still have no idea what Sam was up to . . . ?"

Rowan paused at that.

"I mean, you don't have to—"

Rowan's look was pointed.

Daphne twisted away, clapping eyes on a framed autographed poster of Octavia Butler. It must have been from the seventies, judging by that *Star Wars*–era font lit up in neon yellow. She'd pushed too far. Guilt flooded her torso, flushing up her neck. Invisibility was her preferred cloak while she moved through the world, yet here she was, shirking it off shamelessly for knowledge. *For the truth*, she reminded herself, hoping it would give her collapsing bridge of courage a modicum of support.

"His name was Joey Camden."

Daphne's spine went ramrod straight. "Is that so?"

He shook his head and turned away from Daphne. The way Rowan's lips pursed together reminded Daphne of a stern math teacher she'd had a crush on once in Paris.

"What else do you wish to know?"

Daphne gaped at Rowan. Is this how Aladdin felt when the genie had granted three wishes?

"Is his murder related to Sam's?" Daphne was breathless.

"We don't know."

Another question floated up, one that she spat out against her own attempts to repress it. "Why are you telling me this?"

Again, a mix of amusement, defeat, and something else flushed Rowan's cheeks. "I—I don't know. I find myself wanting to share things with you, Daphne, which—anyway, if you come across any information that could be relevant . . ."

"I'll tell you," Daphne replied. "I know the deal."

At that Rowan pushed himself off his desk, giving Daphne a glimpse of slim, roped forearms. "Is there anything else I can help you with?"

Daphne would have given up a sabbatical for that to be the case. "No."

A corner of his lips tugged upward. "Then perhaps Amber or Davonté can interest you in the latest Ada Limón collection."

Daphne emitted the world's tiniest gasp. "How did you know that I liked her poetry?"

Rowan's smile was confident when he shrugged. "Lucky guess."

CHAPTER FOURTEEN

Daphne stood in front of her bedroom mirror and placed a braceleted hand on her wide hip, a gift from her West African ancestors. She twisted her back to check out her profile while Chloe nosed around her laundry basket for clothes to roll on. Her black dress was all proper and professional, skimming her curves without clinging to them. A lipsticked frown formed anyway.

She'd debated all week whether to go to Sam's memorial at all, considering what a human dumpster fire he'd turned out to be. Sam probably thought it was his God-given right to violate university rules of any kind if they didn't serve him. But seriously, dude, sleeping with an undergrad?

"Trash," she muttered. "Utter garbage."

At least she now knew his friend's name. Armed with it, she'd put her research skills to good use to find him. She'd pulled up court records detailing evidence of Joey's arrest for armed robbery here in Calliope. No one had been hurt when he'd tried—and failed—to rob a local credit union, but the damage was done, and off he'd gone to prison. Daphne had found the transcript from his trial easy enough, including character witness testimony from the jerkface himself, Sam Taylor. They'd grown up together in Nevada, before Joey's life had turned upside down at the death of his father and his mother's descent into drugs. Sam's testimony described Joey as a sweet, kind guy suffering from grief and addiction. Witnessing his best friend flit in and out of the prison system had radicalized him.

He'd fought hard for an early release for Joey based on good behavior, and when that had failed he'd started working pro bono for Joey's fellow inmates. It must have been from these cases that he'd devised his now-immensely popular seminar in which graduating seniors worked with those incarcerated to produce a weekly podcast documenting life in prison. That class had of course led to glowing write-ups in Harrison's alumni magazine, encouraging its star-studded graduates to donate money to fund more initiatives such as Sam's.

No wonder so many people on campus thought of Sam as a hero.

Daphne knew better.

The only reason—the *only* reason—why Daphne was still willing to go was because her life had become more entangled in Sam's death than a cat's claws in a ball of yarn. She needed to prove to herself that Sam *had* stolen that book from her, the little shit. There was also the fact that every single chair and dean would be at the service, marking who was in attendance.

She stared at the Black woman in the mirror, her head tilted to the side. Maybe she could wear that pashmina scarf to liven things up a bit? That one she bought in Aix that one fall? Nudging Chloe aside, Daphne began to rummage through her pile of laundry until her fingers touched the silky smooth, deeply purple shawl she was looking for.

The fact that she was trying to look this good for Sam Taylor's memorial service should have shamed her down to her pinky toes. But they were too busy going numb to care anyway, crammed as they were into a pair of high heels she'd worn precisely once, for a date.

The problem was that every time Rowan smiled at her, Daphne could just about run a marathon and then hit up a Beyoncé show. She wondered what his favorite book was. If he liked all dogs or just Chloe. Where he went grocery shopping.

Good God, woman. Daphne placed her hands to her cheeks. *Get a hold of yourself.*

"You look pretty, sugar plum."

Daphne turned away from the mirror. Her dad was standing just outside her room, leaning against the doorway.

"I look old," Daphne replied.

Jim scoffed. "If you're old then what am I?"

Daphne crossed the room and wrapped her father in a tight hug. "You're eternal," she said into his neck. "You're not allowed to age, you know that. Those are the rules."

His cheeks widened into a smile against hers. "The rules, huh?"

GloRilla's latest bop rattled into the bedroom. She slipped out of her dad's arms and peeked out the window. Elise and Sadie were here.

"Why do your friends have to play that music so damn loud?" Jim grumbled while she wrapped her shawl around her shoulders.

Daphne pecked him on the cheek. "I'll be back after dinner."

Jim harrumphed. "Be safe."

"I will."

"I mean it."

"*Dad.*"

THE STAINED-GLASS windows inside the Halston-Menckelman Interfaith Chapel cast interconfessional stories of friendship and love in shades of turquoise, gold, and ruby.

Emerald and topaz gems twinkled in the chapel's rose window. The sight normally warmed Daphne's heart, but as she took her seat in the pew next to Sadie and Elise, glamorous in jet-black silks, she could only feel jumpy. Nervous.

And that damn bump on her scalp kept tingling. She reached up with her left hand to pick at it—

Sadie smacked her. "Stop that. You're not a fucking cat."

"We're in church," Daphne hissed.

Sadie rolled her eyes. "This isn't a church, Daph. It's a feelings playground for white people with emotional baggage."

"Sadie!" Daphne said, checking around nervously.

Sadie fixed her a curious look. "What's gotten into you anyway?"

"Nothing."

Sadie's black eyes grew comically wide. "Are you . . . are you looking for someone?"

Yes. "No."

"Then why are you wearing mascara?" Sadie's lipstick grin was smug. "And why are you twisting your back out like that?"

"Gals, what are we whispering about?" Elise asked, sliding into the pew. "Did somebody fart in church?"

"It's not a church," Sadie said again. "And Daph's looking for somebody."

Elise's eyes twinkled. "That detective?"

Daphne wanted to deck her. "You don't even know what he looks like."

"I don't have to, Daph, 'cause if you like him I know he's cute." Elise turned around to scan the faces in the crowd. "Ooooh is that him?"

"Elise you've never even laid eyes on the—" Daphne followed her friend's gaze. "Oh."

It *was* him.

"I told you I could pick him out," Elise said. "He's tall, isn't he?"

"Too tall," Sadie said, raising a perfect brow. "Almost freakish, Daph, hate to say it."

"Stop it," Daphne said between gritted teeth, twisting around to make sure no one heard them. "Both of you."

"I would," Sadie replied, "but he's coming this way—and who's that woman he's with? Goddamn, she's hot. Is she a cop?"

Daphne rubbed one of her temples. "Of course she's a cop, Sadie. She's the lead detective. And, by the way, your timing with these matters is—as always—terrible."

Sadie shrugged, indifferent, and kept her eyes on the prize. A wolfish grin appeared on her face. "You know, I'm normally not one to fuck a cop—"

"Language!"

"—but she's a stone cold fox."

Daphne garbled out a small cry. "I swear to God I am running away from you both if you don't zip your flapping lips this instant."

The guitarist at the altar began strumming a polite, muted arrangement of Bob Dylan's "Knockin' on Heaven's Door" and Daphne groaned. Tunes by Tom Waits, Leonard Cohen, and Tom Petty followed, echoing gently through the chapel in soft waves. Sam's favorites. But of course. Daphne would never understand why some folks loved listening to white men who couldn't sing.

Though it took all the self-restraint she possessed, Daphne took in the latecomers streaming into the service instead, many of whom looked like her former students, instead of Rowan's long neck and his graceful, almost elfish ears. A few Jacobs, an

Abbie or two, plus several Emilys in her sightline had Daphne reaching for a whiteboard and breaking out into a small panic, wondering if her PowerPoint slides would load.

A familiar forest green Patagonia sweater caught Daphne's eye. Ken Miller had felt no compunction to change his uniform for his colleague's memorial service. He stepped up to the podium. No longer able to think of him as anything but a toad, Daphne listened to his words of welcome and immediately wanted to rip her ears off. Anything to stop his schmaltz from needling into her brain.

He finally stepped down to let a few undergraduate students share some words. But the longer they talked, the more a different sensation spread across Daphne's skin like film.

She couldn't shake off the feeling that someone was staring at her. But when she searched her peripheral vision for any familiar faces, she found none staring back. She fidgeted and waited for that tingliness to ebb.

It didn't.

She glanced over her shoulder again—there he was: a tall, trim statesman in his fifties in an expensive blue button-down shirt and shiny brown derby shoes. Everything about him whispered polish. Silvery blond hair—almost but not quite white—could only have been touched by the most expensive and loyal stylist. His face, weathered by sun and time, assumed a passive frown while he looked her over, as if inspecting an ant that had ventured onto his picnic cloth. He removed his cold blue eyes from her face, having lost interest, and Daphne suddenly felt so, so small.

With the ceremony starting, the Henderson sisters stood up from the front row of their pew. Their matching polished exteriors gave away little underneath. An uneasiness whispered across Daphne again at the sight of Melanie, remembering her angry face in Molly's window. An elderly white man followed them—their father—his arm cradled to support their mother, a woman in classic pearls and a black dress ripped from Audrey Hepburn's playbook.

Olivia Vail flashed to mind. Daphne felt pity for the woman who'd chosen to love Sam. Had Molly known? Approved, even? Daphne doubted it. Someone like Molly didn't seem receptive to the concept of open relationships.

But the memory of Molly giggling in her kitchen came back. To a lot of people Molly may appear like a well-dressed Vulcan but if you got her talking about Artemisia Gentileschi and Italian Baroque art, those tall barriers she'd erected came tumbling down. Daphne supposed that constructing walls was simply what pretty white women like Molly had to do to keep from being hunted all the time. Being a Black woman in white spaces most of her adult life, Daphne had never known that particular fear. The fear of being ignored? Check. The fear of not being taken seriously as an intellectual? A big, hearty check. But she never worried about her safety on the streets of Calliope in the way that some of these white women did. For every frosty barrier Molly built, Daphne was confident that there were at least twice as many men who'd do anything to knock it down, if given the chance.

Sam hadn't deserved her.

But good luck telling that to the eulogizers in the chapel. Their hagiographic speeches were nothing less than what Daphne expected for someone who had mesmerized Harrison's campus with his charismatic presence. To hear Ken Miller tell it, the man was a literal saint, educating young minds and fighting for the oppressed, all while producing field-defining scholarship at alarming rates.

A Unitarian minister took over from Miller and droned on

for a while about loving thy neighbor and Daphne smothered her frown of distaste, choosing instead to pluck a small tube of grapefruit lotion from her purse and squeeze a drop into her palms, twisting her fingers to rub in the cream.

Maybe Daphne wanted to knock Sam off his hallowed pillar a smidge. Maybe she wanted to make him less of a god and prove him to be a mere mortal. Maybe she wanted to show people that he was actually sneaky. A cheat. A thief.

Holy crap.

Daphne's hand flew to her lips. Out of the corner of her vision, Rowan snapped his neck around at that—like he could sense her mind computing, she thought with a shiver—his attention fixed on her. He raised his brows in concern, posing a silent question to her that she quickly grasped.

You discovered something?

Daphne's face was aflame all over again. But she nodded in the affirmative.

Bright light flared in Rowan's gaze. *Go.*

Elise spun around. "You okay, Daph?"

Daphne tapped a forefinger to her bottom lip. "I, uh—I gotta go."

Elise stared at her. "*Now?*"

Daphne nodded. "Can you cover for me? Just for twenty minutes, give or take."

Daphne stood up and squeezed her way past the other guests, apologizing profusely under her breath, embarrassed to her core to have her generous backside shoved prominently in mourners' faces. That older man that Daphne had found staring at her earlier was giving his best impression of a venomous snake while she walked by, and that only made her want to get out faster.

She hurried out of the chapel, cursing her heels as she broke into a run.

Once free, she rushed along the grassy path toward the main quad and past two squirrels engaged in a turf war between thick oak trees shading freshman dorms nearby. Neo-Romanesque and Gothic buildings replete with spirals and cupolas towered over her while she limped across a wide swath of lawn behind unassuming students in Harrison hoodies.

Her toes were on fire by the time she made it to the library, an otherwise imposing fortress surrounded by yellow tulips. The building's old, thick sandstone walls were designed to absorb sound, but her heels didn't get the message, loudly clacking while she hobbled down the hallway. She headed for the curving flight of stairs to the left of the circulation desk and climbed up to the faculty reading room.

Daphne stepped on plush carpet and released a sigh. She could breathe again. Bookshelves reached for the skies, surrounding her from nearly every angle, smelling faintly of leather and old paper. The morning sun broke through the ceiling windows, bright and cold. If it was any other day, the tidy columns of wide desks in the banquet-sized hall would be dotted with faculty, who usually sat in silence while examining everything from sixteenth-century manuscripts to eighties-era VHS tapes.

But today was not any other day, and the emptiness of the faculty reading room reminded Daphne to be quick about her task. She scanned the back wall for the row of gleaming lockers. Spotted the names emblazoned on each locker door.

Remington. Jones. Durham. Kerry. Martin.

Her lips pinched into a frown.

No Taylor.

She leaned against a locker. She'd been so certain that she was right. But if it wasn't in the faculty library lockers, where else could it—

A groan bubbled out of her.

Of course that's where it is.

She sent a prayer to Saint Josephine Bakhita to shield her from stares as she slipped off her shoes. Relieved, she hobbled back down the curving staircase—and then down one level more, until she reached the cramped hallway that led her to yet another staircase. She continued her dusty, dingy descent until she reached what everyone jokingly called "The Bunker."

Daphne pushed open a door made of dark ebony wood, and stepped into a surprisingly bright and cheery room that could comfortably seat about eight people, tastefully decorated with four cherry wood desks and paisley rugs. At the back was a set of shiny metal lockers that belonged in Silicon Valley more than a centuries-old library.

It figured that Sam had somehow managed to get one of the few lockers to the basement's secret silent reading room. It had taken her weeks to work up the courage to ask Miranda for one herself—only to be told there was a years-long waitlist. A locker in "The Bunker" was supposed to be as rare as one of Willy Wonka's golden tickets. Not for Sam.

The lockers didn't have names on them, so she smoothed her palms against each one, punching in the pin code she believed—*had* to believe—could lead her to what she was looking for.

She was on the third one when a tap landed on her shoulder.

She whirled around and—

Rowan's long, slim fingers wrapped around her waist, stabilizing her.

Daphne took a step back, her backside pressed against the lockers she'd just tried to break open. "You're here."

The corner of Rowan's soft lips turned up. "Excellent deduction, Professor Plum."

"Professor Plum?" she squeaked.

Somehow her hand was splayed against Rowan's warm chest. Funny, Daphne realized. His heart was pounding, too.

"Your purple coat," he murmured, his chin hovering above her forehead. "You're always wearing it."

Daphne took two deep breaths, waiting for her vision to clear and for the blood to stop rushing to her cheeks—only for her heart to skip a beat when he placed a hand on either side of her head, flat against the wall.

It would be so easy for him to lean down to kiss her if he wanted.

If she wanted.

She lifted her chin. "I . . . uh . . ."

Rowan went very still. Maybe she shouldn't have tilted her lips up like that.

And she *definitely* shouldn't have pushed her hips up like that—but damnit, he smelled like Ivory soap and laundry detergent and something else, something sharp and fresh and surely he wouldn't mind if she pressed her nose against his chest to better identify it—

"Rowan?" a scratchy alto voice called out.

Rowan gave Daphne one last look—knowing and wry and wanting—before stepping back. He straightened the sleeves at his wrists. "Asma, I'm in here."

Daphne almost reached out, hating the cold absence of where his body had been, but her good sense reasserted itself. By the time Detective Ahmed walked into the room, Daphne had restored her appearance to something she hoped didn't look quite as haphazard as she felt.

"Well, this is a creepy room, isn't it?" Detective Ahmed said, taking in the small space. "And why aren't you wearing shoes?"

In the haze of Rowan's touch, Daphne had blanked out on that fact. "Um, I—"

"Don't bother." Detective Ahmed examined the locker against which Daphne had very nearly engaged in indecent behavior. "What would make you leave your colleague's memorial service and come to the library, of all places?"

Daphne swirled her foot in large circles on the floor while the detective stared her down. She hoped she wasn't about to drive away the one man who seemed to find her nerdiness cute instead of a liability. "I figured out where my book is."

Rowan's eyes instantly darkened. Daphne's heart skipped another beat.

"Sam told me where it was all along." Daphne swallowed. "He texted it to me. 'The French invented silence'? A silent reading room. And that's when I up and left the chapel."

"Why this one?" Rowan asked. His long limbs propelled his body in Daphne's direction and she willed her knees not to buckle like a fainting Victorian heiress. "There are plenty of reading rooms on campus."

"That's true," Daphne said. "But the library's also a former prison—Quaker missionaries built it in the early nineteenth century."

"Preaching the gospel of rehabilitation and confinement, I take it."

His smile almost took her out. Daphne tried to remember how humans breathed air—inhale, exhale?

"Exactly," she managed. "This room in particular was

originally designed for solitary confinement. Everything in Sam's life revolved around his prison activism, so where better to store something secret than here?"

Rowan's eyebrows wrinkled in the most delightful way. Daphne would have given up her mother's closely guarded peanut stew recipe just to trace her fingers along them. She wouldn't mind feeling out his cheekbones, too—they were sharper than she'd first assumed—and testing out the plumpness of his lips while she was at it.

Good heavens, Daphne, stop.

"So which locker is it?" Detective Ahmed asked.

"I . . ." Daphne cleared her throat. "I don't know yet. Each one has a pin pad on it. I was going to start entering in numbers and see."

"At random?" Detective Ahmed's tightly drawn frown told Daphne what she thought of that idea.

"Well, I thought of the numbers, too . . ." Daphne trailed off.

Even in this chilly room Rowan's proud smile emanated heat.

"Of course you did." Rowan went to the first locker against the wall. "Asma, I take this one and you take the next. What's the number, Daphne?"

"1969," Daphne mumbled.

Rowan whirled around at her. "Not 1970?"

"No, that's when the English translation appeared," Daphne said, far too pleased that Rowan understood what she was talking about.

Detective Ahmed waved a hand in Daphne's face, breaking up their gaze. "Earth to you two aliens. What are you talking about?"

Rowan grinned on. "1969 is the year *Papillon* was first published."

Daphne's whole damn body tingled while the pair went from locker to locker, punching numbers into each keypad to no avail. Doubt, however small, whispered in her ear that she'd gotten everything wrong, that her search for evidence of Sam's theft was baseless, that she had no right to claim anything resembling victimhood at the hands of a man she didn't even know.

The "click" was soft, but unmistakable. Detective Ahmed flipped a locker door open and plunged her arm into its darkness.

Daphne watched Ahmed withdraw her hand. The corners of her vision became fuzzy when she took in what the detective had retrieved: a thick paperback, yellowed with age.

Daphne inched closer. "Check the inside cover," she said. "You should find my mother's maiden name—Dembelé."

Ahmed flipped through the weathered book, and when she didn't immediately respond Daphne couldn't help but wonder if maybe she'd gotten everything wrong. Maybe Sam had stashed some random library book in there, and so Daphne had created a fuss over nothing and just wasted everyone's time and Detective Ahmed was going to hate her until her grave, which was inevitable anyway, so she might as well accept the fact that—

"Well, I'll be," Ahmed's voice slipped out, and she flipped the book around.

There, slipped inside the pages of her childhood paperback, was a small silver key twinkling in the soft light.

"Gloves?" Detective Ahmed asked.

"Quite." Rowan whipped out two thin robin's egg blue rubber gloves and handed them to the detective. She put them on and carefully lifted the silver key out of the book.

"Professor Ouverture?" Detective Ahmed said, twirling the key in the light.

"Y-yes?" Daphne said.

"Thank you for helping us identify your missing book." She tilted her head back over to Daphne's direction. "We'll notify you with further information if we come across it."

Daphne shifted her already achy feet. "What does that mean?"

"It means—" Detective Ahmed said, closing the book. She gently led Daphne to the front door. "—that you're done here. We are no longer in need of your help. So please return to the memorial service and have a good day."

The heavy vault door closed on Daphne right as she opened her mouth to protest.

CHAPTER FIFTEEN

By the time Daphne returned to the service, the crowds had begun to spill out onto the front lawn and a line had formed where people mulled about in their black ties, saying their condolences to Molly and her family. She spotted Elise in the distance and joined her in the queue, surprised by the levity that had returned to her shoulders. Some Wall Street bro in a slim suit was trying to talk up Elise, making the kind of googly eyes that would have sent even Cupid running for a trash can to vomit in and Daphne wasn't even all that irritated by his refusal to acknowledge the Black woman in box braids hovering by her bestie. She was too busy celebrating the hard-won knowledge that she'd been right—Sam *had* taken her book, the weirdo.

Maybe, just as importantly, Daphne had proven to the detective that she wasn't just some incompetent academic who was booksmart and street stupid. Sure, she might know more about the Second Industrial Revolution than the average person—or that there'd even been a Second Industrial Revolution to begin with—but that didn't mean that she couldn't work a case. That didn't mean she couldn't shine a light into the darkness to find the monsters hidden under the bed. Historians were the ultimate truth tellers, after all, the party poopers and the Debbie Downers who held up the mirror to humanity and reminded everyone what we were capable of as a species.

Daphne was used to proving herself on the page as a professional necromancer of sorts, but now she'd done the same with the living. That alone was worth celebrating with a long walk in the woods with Chloe and a glass of wine with friends. Because Daphne Ouverture, assistant professor of History at Harrison University, was an excellent sleuth. And, for the first time since Sam died, Daphne Ouverture was finally free.

Daphne took a dutiful step forward in line and stared out across the lawn at three squirrels sunning themselves in the distance.

She *was* free. Wasn't she?

It was just that there was something about *Papillon*—and the key wedged between its pages—that wouldn't leave her alone. It didn't matter how often she inspected it or from which angle, as if she were a gemologist holding a rare black opal under a microscope. Sam hadn't just stolen anyone's book—he'd taken *hers*.

And she still didn't know why.

A sob broke out from somewhere ahead in line and Daphne tuned in to it. Olivia Vail, pale and beautiful in black, mourned a man who'd never loved her. Daphne searched around, seeking more faces to identify.

There'd been that man—the one with the cold blue eyes and haughty sneer who'd seen right through Daphne like glass. Where'd he gone?

Meanwhile, Elise kept chattering away at Pompous Bro, who turned out to be a state senator, her voice breathless while discussing her favorite subject: poisons.

"So many people mistakenly believe that cyanide or arsenic are the deadliest toxins," Elise said while the senator nodded along, and Daphne clocked the exact moment when a faint look of panic encroached into his adoring gaze. "Why do we keep forgetting the power of anthrax?"

The senator stopped nodding long enough to pause. "Uh ..."

"Or what's wrong with good old-fashioned ricin, or—ooh! Daphne, don't you have that story about a French maid who drugged a newspaper magnate in the early twentieth century using hyoscine?"

"Uh-huh," Daphne grunted while Olivia pulled out a crumpled tissue and dabbed it to her black-rimmed eyes.

"See, that's the kind of toxin that's really effective," Elise said, her smile sweeter than Easter candy. "It's fast-acting and can leave you in a coma for at least twenty-four hours if it doesn't kill you first. Isn't that so much more interesting?"

Daphne still had no luck finding that frigid man from the funeral. Someone else caught her attention: a young white woman, most likely an undergrad, with copper hair and cat-eye glasses who was far more devastated than she should have been at the passing of someone who had most likely graded her exams. And just past her, some other pretty white girl sobbed, her nose buried in a tissue.

Good grief. How many students had Sam been with?

Disgusted, Daphne ripped away from the line. And that's when she caught her. Melanie Henderson, Molly's younger sister and carbon copy with a short pixie cut. When an elderly man in a wispy hat at the front of the line suggested to Molly in some toothless way that Sam was in a better place, Melanie's lips twisted into something like a grimace. No, that wasn't quite right.

She was smirking.

T. S. Eliot once said that April was the cruelest month, but Daphne didn't see it. Not when the warmth of the afternoon sun was on her back while she sat on a park bench, soaking up the dense, verdant greens of the campus lawn. The crowds were gone, the Henderson family nowhere in sight, and Daphne could head to the junior faculty memorial for Sam Taylor knowing that she'd found the book he'd stolen from her. Which would be fine if she knew why he'd done it. Or how, come to think of it. She couldn't remember handing the book to him. Nor had she ever invited him over to her house. So then how had he taken it?

Daphne whooshed out a lungful of air, another question rising out of the chaos of finding her book. Had her attacker attended the same memorial as her? She honestly hadn't considered it. Now she couldn't think of anything else. Some shadowy figure dressed in black, trailing Daphne's every move in the chapel. There was that one older, colder man who'd assessed her with far too much knowledge and cunning for her liking, but she'd never met him before in her life, she'd swear by it. Otherwise, the whole notion of an academic inflicting violence on her felt preposterous. If someone had wanted to destroy her they'd begin by trying to taint her reputation. It's why she had been careful for so long. Polite. Cautious. Correct.

She squinted out into the distance—just in time to see Olivia marching across the chapel lawn. Trailing right behind her was Ken Miller, who called out to Olivia and pulled her aside by a bed of yellow tulips. Whatever he was demanding of Olivia was too quiet for Daphne's ears, but it was making the student look so deeply unhappy—which, to be fair, was the only correct emotional response to Ken's presence anyway. With each question Ken asked, Olivia's posture grew smaller. Under his shadow she shrank back into herself, rubbing her freckled arms and staring at the ground, her lips drawn tight, and a panicked urge to pluck Olivia out of Ken's claws to safety overwhelmed Daphne. A mix of fear and determination pushed her off that park bench and toward Olivia, only to catch Olivia's gaze. Her eyes widened. And, *oh God*, Ken turned around to see where Olivia's attention had landed—right on Daphne.

He turned his back on Daphne like a shot, his posture now rigid with outrage. He bent down to whisper something to Olivia, who winced and scurried away from the chapel. And before Daphne could bolt, Ken was on his way toward her, blocking the bright April sun from view.

Daphne's heart was somewhere in her stomach when he reached her. "Hi, Ken."

"Ms. Vail just told me that you've accused her of plagiarism." Ken fixed her a stern look. "Even after I explicitly told you to leave her alone."

Daphne could have bet a paid vacation to the French Riviera that Olivia's teared-up face had nothing to do with whatever grade Daphne had given her and everything to do with Ken being the human equivalent of a hissing scorpion.

"Ken." Daphne spoke slowly, keeping her tone firm, "Olivia violated academic policy."

"From your perspective," Ken's suntanned face darkened remarkably in anger. "Which, as a junior teacher, is far too green to be reliable. I see it time and time again—you rookies are too enthusiastic for your own good. To a hammer, everything looks like a nail."

"That's unfair," Daphne said. "I'm just trying to do my job."

"And I'm trying to do mine," Ken replied, shoving a finger in her face. "Whatever you think happened with Ms. Vail's paper, it didn't. Am I clear?"

Daphne labored to breathe under Ken's stubborn glare. Tears

formed at the corners of her eyes, promising to spill onto her cheeks. She shot her eyes down to the ground, taking in the gravel underneath her feet.

"All this snooping around on students and grading papers like some overzealous vigilante . . . it's got to stop," Ken said. "It's not proper behavior for a Harrison professor, and it sure won't get you tenure here. I'll make sure of that."

Daphne fought back a tide of nausea, her hands now clammy from sweat.

"You want to have a career here?" Ken began to walk away. "Be smart. Learn when to leave things alone."

CHAPTER SIXTEEN

"What do you want, Lacey?"

Asma squinted out onto the lawn, Rowan trailing behind her and Daphne Ouverture in the distance, talking to Sam Taylor's chair, Ken Miller. If she'd thought she'd find the woman Sam had slept with, she'd been mistaken. Based on the tears she'd seen at the memorial service, there were too many to count.

Two squirrels chased each other around thick tree trunks and up into the branches. Asma couldn't tell if they were enemies or friends.

"Actually," Pete Lacey said, "it's about what *you* want."

She sighed and squeezed the phone tight against her ear. Their computer forensic investigator was a brilliant hacker but putting up with his phone calls should come with a pay raise.

"What's this about?" Asma asked, hope buoying in her chest. "You got into Taylor's Dropbox account?"

"Yup." Lacey's smirk was audible on the phone. "But don't get too happy yet. It's been wiped clean. All his files are gone."

Asma's free hand formed a taut fist while the other gripped the phone so tight it might crumple. How was it possible that after all this time, she still hadn't caught a break on finding Sam's exposé? Her poor rookies had spent hours poring over inmate records at Livington, trying to find someone who matched the description Molly Henderson had provided in one of their interviews, finally landing on Joey Camden's name. Asma had blinked her way through Sam's scribbled handwriting on notepads, hoping to find a trail that could lead to his essay.

Asma exhaled one slow breath. "Do you know when those files were destroyed?"

"And where," Lacey replied. "Around six P.M. on Saturday. His own home in Calliope."

"So about an hour before he died?"

"Sure." Pete Lacey already sounded bored. "But that's not the reason why I'm calling you anyway."

"It's not?"

"I've got information."

Asma's grunted. "On what?"

"You know that professor you asked me to look into? That Black girl?" Pete Lacey said, his voice smug. "I know how she's connected to the vic."

She jerked upright in her seat. "You do?"

That photograph she'd found of Daphne and Sam had eaten away at her for far too long, demanding an explanation. More than that, her boss demanded one, too. *I like her for this*, he'd said just the other day. *That professor.* In the four years that she'd worked for him, Asma had learned that Captain Hamilton wasn't the trifling kind. When he caught on to a suspect, he was like a bulldog refusing to give up a bone.

"Give me about an hour or two to confirm a few things but if it's what I think it is? You're going to want to come down here."

CHAPTER SEVENTEEN

"Screw Ken," Daphne muttered into her third margarita. "Babe." Elise's light soprano rang crystal clear over the din of the Thirsty Scholar. Her sleek black hair swung gently like a metronome as she considered Daphne, head dangling to the side. "You okay?"

Daphne was too busy wallowing to dignify Elise's question with a reply. It was far more satisfying to fixate on the elaborate pity party she was throwing for herself. "Screw Ken, screw this job, screw *grading*, screw that key, screw that vault, screw Detective Ahmed, screw Sam, screw everything."

"Earth to Daphne Ouverture." Elise's decision to call Daphne something other than "babe" or "hon" would have normally alarmed her if she wasn't already preoccupied cursing out a dead man. "What's up? Your bottom lip is out and you look ridiculous, Daph. Cute and adorable, but ridiculous. But you know, I bet that tall detective you like would find it irresistible."

Daphne's pulse picked up at that. "You think?"

Elise rubbed her arm. "Of course, honey, you're so beautiful. But that's not the point. What's going on with you? You're moping more than you did when Latrice Royale got kicked off *Drag Race*."

Daphne's eyes narrowed. "Season Four or All Stars?"

"Does it matter?"

"I guess not." Daphne dutifully took a sip of water. "I just had a hard day."

She felt Elise's peck on her cheek and a gentle rub on her back. "Babe, you've had a hard *month*."

Detective Ahmed had creaked the heavy vault door shut on Daphne's adventure. She reminded herself that for as long as she could remember, she'd wanted an unadventurous life. The world had been too unwieldy from a young age so she had shrunk it down into the palm of her hand and made it legible, as readable as a book. Scaling her life down had saved her from feeling its sting.

Recently, however, with her blood pumping wild and her nose to the ground chasing a scent, she'd had to admit that there might be something to the family pastime of snooping. She'd even started thinking of herself as brave—until today. Ken Miller's threats were something much colder, much darker than anything a Calliope cop could say to her. Her career was on the line. Miranda's, too, possibly.

So that was that.

Back to her cozy life, to drinking tea on the couch and taking Chloe on walks and grading papers and poring over French documents from the eighteenth century, which she loved. That was enough. Right?

The memory of Rowan—his palms laid flat on either side of her head—warmed her already flushed cheeks. Would he reach out to her? Should she go to Earthseed to find him? She fiddled with her water again, her loneliness growing. The man had gawked at her bookshelves, seen straight through her like she was clingwrap, and he hadn't run away. He hadn't belittled her. He hadn't patronized her. All of it, he'd liked. Really and truly, all of it.

And Daphne no longer had a convenient excuse to spend time with him anymore.

She threw back the last few drops of her margarita.

Lisa Wickham, an assistant professor of archeology, slid over to Daphne. "Do you mind if I ask you a question?"

Daphne really did. There was nothing Lisa enjoyed more than getting into business in other departments that had nothing to do with her own research on ancient Greek foodways.

Lisa pushed her pert nose in Daphne's face anyway. "So . . . what was the deal with you and Sam?"

Daphne's margarita turned sour on her tongue. "Excuse me?"

"It's just . . ." Lisa tossed back a tuft of shiny blond hair. "People are talking. And I saw you with those detectives earlier. Are you helping them out with their investigation? And if so, no offense—"

"No offense?"

"—but how'd you get picked for that role?" Lisa's giggle was anything but cute. "Spill the tea already, was there something going on between you and Sam?"

Sadie smashed the half-dozen drinks she'd just returned onto the table, spilling their contents. "Lisa Wickham, you shut your busted-up face, you fucking snake."

The chatter dimmed.

Elise and Daphne clapped eyes on each other across the table, their shock, fear, and excitement bouncing between them.

Lisa's huff could have frosted over the entire pub. "Well."

As if Sadie gave a shit. "My friend has been going through one of the worst months in her lifetime and your skinny bitch ass decides that now—after a dead man's memorial—is the time to sink your poisoned fangs into her because, what, you need a distraction to keep you from having to face the fact that no one likes you?"

Daphne lifted her jaw off the floor, covering her mouth with her palm to smother her startled grin.

"I won't stand for this," Lisa snipped.

"That's right you won't." Sadie leaned forward, her bronze-rimmed eyes glittering black with rage. She pushed herself closer to Lisa, hovering a full pint of beer near Lisa's chin. "Because if you stay in here for one more minute, I'm going to throw my pilsner in your face and take this conversation to the parking lot. And I promise you that once I'm done with you, the only thing you'll be unearthing from the ground for the rest of your piss-poor career as an archeologist will be your missing teeth."

Whatever fight might have been left drained away from Lisa's body. She yanked her coat off the back of her chair.

"That's what I thought." Sadie jeered when Lisa stormed out. "Get fucked."

Emboldened by the round of applause from the table, Sadie shouted after her, "And don't ever talk to my friends again."

Daphne had to say something before security came over to toss Sadie out. "Sadie, you shouldn't have."

Sadie dragged a sip of beer. "Meh."

"No, seriously," Daphne said. "You just passed your trial-run basis here again."

"Whatever, they'll let me back in." Sadie cast her gaze around the table. "And since I'm about to get kicked out anyway, I'll go ahead and say it since no one else will. It's fine that we went to the memorial service to show our support, but let's be honest: None of us liked Sam."

No one protested. No one shouted words of defiance. No

eyes flared in outrage. In fact, Daphne noticed, no one made any eye contact at all. Over a dozen professors sat around the large round table packed with beers, fries, and empty margarita glasses, suddenly engrossed in studying its ancient dark wood. The only sound came from the laughter of a few librarians downing old-fashioneds on the leather couch nearby.

Daphne turned to one of the political scientists. "Not even you, Ben?"

Ben frowned down into his IPA. "I mean, we'd talk football and politics but that was basically it. I didn't really know the guy that well."

"Well, that settles it." Sadie knocked back a shot of whiskey. "The guy was an asshole."

"He once asked me if I was gay just because I was drinking a mojito," Chris, an art historian, offered.

"But honey," Sadie said, "you *are* gay."

"Yeah, but he didn't have to be such a dick about it. Or go on and on and on about how he'd donated to the Human Rights Campaign that one time—and how he'd tweeted in support when that one football player came out."

"Which one?" asked Sadie.

Chris's glance back could have shrunk a slug. "Do I look like I follow football? I don't know, some guy! Anyway, I was just over it. I was over his preacher charisma, I was over his self-righteousness, I was over his do-gooder Boy Scout bullshit. Straight people are the worst—no offense, everybody."

"None taken," Daphne said at the same time Sadie muttered, "Amen."

ESCHEWING ELISE'S offer to drive her home in favor of some solitude, Daphne sat in the back of an Uber, her mind and stomach sloshing with each bump and turn. She could blame some of her discomfort on the margaritas but the sickly feeling gurgling up to her esophagus had little to do with her inability to handle tequila. She could no longer keep at bay the queasy truth submerged just under the surface of her thoughts since Sam's death, now rushing up again in the wake of his memorial—in the wake of her colleagues' confessions that, apparently, they were wary of Sam, too. Her gut was telling her to listen, to face the real reason she disliked Sam so much: He had stared at her.

Staring probably wasn't the right word for it—but leering went too far. Still, there hadn't been anything innocent in that gaze. Once, at a university-wide faculty meeting, she'd shot him a quizzical response, and he'd at least had the decency to look away. He pretended for a while like the whole thing had never happened, just cutting in line in front of her again at the Faculty Club, making jokes about *Papillon*, bellowing out his throaty laughs.

Until the next time.

If she checked quickly, she'd catch his eyes roaming all over her body. It had been gross and unprofessional and Daphne had never known just what she was supposed to do about those unwanted stares, so she'd flung them to the far edges of her mind. Kept her focus on work. Then: murder, *Papillon*, tequila.

"Here is fine," she said when they reached the end of her street. The cottage was almost impossible to spot in the distance beyond the meadow, especially at night, reachable as it was only by what had to be the world's longest paved sidewalk.

After climbing out of her Uber ride, Daphne trudged down the moonlit path toward her door. Maybe an hour or so on her laptop googling cheap apartments in Paris could make her forget those looks again. Not like she could afford one on her professor's salary, but strolling online through her favorite neighborhoods sent her down soothing memory lanes that stretched back to childhood.

She'd start in Goutte d'Or, she decided—or maybe Château Rouge. Hell, any neighborhood that sold fresh cassava root and cheap bottles of Bordeaux would do.

The back of her neck prickled. Daphne halted in her tracks. She swayed back and forth.

Was that Chloe?

She stopped to listen—and realized her dog was howling in terror.

Daphne's heart exploded in her chest. Her fingers ripped off her high heels, tossing them to the side, and she broke out into a sprint for home. Her dog's frantic barking grew louder with each yard Daphne ran down her sidewalk, her feet pounding the pavement so hard she thought she would crack it.

She was about forty feet from her door—close enough to see her living room lamp's yellow glow—when an arm wrapped around her stomach and a hand seized her throat. Daphne's esophagus began to close. She pushed air in and out of her nostrils only for a sharp, burning scent to singe her nose. She drew an acrid breath in anyway and screa—

A hand clamped over her mouth.

"Where is it?" the man demanded.

The night sky spun around like its own twinkling Tilt-A-Whirl. Daphne blinked rapidly, choking. Her feet scrambled to find the earth below, while her fingers gripped the hairy forearm in front of her face so tight she heard her knuckles crack. Sweaty, meaty fingers gripped her cheeks and lips, indifferent to her scratches.

She gagged.

"Where is it?" he repeated.

Daphne took a few shallow breaths and willed herself to focus. *Think.* And then it came to her: her father's gift to her one sticky summer in New Orleans, a manual he'd commanded her to read as a young girl.

"Everyone has a moral right to defend themselves."

"That's right, baby," Jim had said, wrapping a napkin tight around her ice cream cone. "You know what that means? If somebody's trying to pull something on you, you gotta step to 'em. If you go into a fight knowing you're a hundred percent in the right, can't nobody take you down."

I'm in the right.

Her fingers became steadier in their grip, sharper, more piercing.

I'm in the right.

Anger came to her like hot lava, through her beating chest and behind her eyes, burning everything it touched. She planted her feet on the ground. Balled her fists. In the back of her mind, she memorized whatever she could about her attacker for when—not if—she survived. There was something soft on his left hand that muffled her cries—a bandage, maybe? Beneath the acrid scent of chlorine was the smell of tobacco and chocolate. And rammed up against her back was the angular, metallic feel of—

A pistol.

Daphne tensed—then squeezed her glutes, positioning herself into a crouch. She shot up and the back of her head cracked against his nose.

He's short.

She wrested an elbow free and drove it against his stomach—but it barely winded him at all.

And strong.

His left hand crushed her lips and jaw, the pain making her sputter.

Too strong.

"Where is it?" he asked again. "Last chance or you're coming with me."

But the only sound Daphne could force out of her lips was a cough. Then the man reached his free hand into his pocket for God only knows what. She formed a fist with the last reserves of her strength. She swung her arm back to punch the attacker right between the legs. A low "oof" escaped his lips. His hold loosened.

Daphne broke free and took off running.

She made it all of twenty feet before tripping on a jagged edge of sidewalk. She scrambled up as quickly as her trembling legs would allow—but not quick enough to escape her attacker. He seized her arm and yanked her back toward him. Daphne toppled into his chest. A soft piece of cloth smothered her eyes, nose, and mouth. She struggled against its sweet, cloying smell, but her lungs seized up before she could scream. Her throat closed. His grip tightened. And Daphne began to float into dark nothingness as her limbs grew numb and heavy, drifting off into the midnight sky. As her body crumpled to the ground, the last clear thought she had was that she thought she'd heard the crack of a gunshot.

CHAPTER EIGHTEEN

For all her life, Daphne had tuned her ears to the particular frequencies of different emergency sirens. In the States, the long wail of an ambulance was background noise on playgrounds in DC and New Orleans. The streets of Paris blasted out their usual mix of subway cars roaring and police cars bleeping out dual tones in short influxes. And once in Ivory Coast, Daphne had been lucky enough to hear the gunning of a local ambulance boat as it sailed across a lagoon.

Daphne may have been familiar with these noises but they brought her no comfort. Not when a couple of cops in uniform rushed over to where she was lying on the ground, cradled by her father. Not when a team of EMTs lifted her limp body off the dewy grass and onto a stretcher. Not when her father shouted for them to bring an IV bag. Grogginess dulled her protests as an EMT flashed a light into her eyes. Whatever instructions the medical team vocalized were lost in translation. Daphne followed the tangle of arms and hands above her head, slipping away, her consciousness itself a weak orb of light, fading in and out.

"Heart rate's at sixty BPM. Pupils?"

"Slight dilation but responding to light."

The knock on the door came hours later, after she had been medically cleared and everyone left, after a hot shower and a meal, after the morning's sun was just beginning to tint her meadow. Daphne was lying on her couch swaddled in blankets per Fabiola's barked-out instructions on a video call. Her mother had walked Jim through the process of making her version of an herbal tea popular among Fabiola's many aunties and cousins, refusing to get off the phone until Daphne had swallowed at least half of it. Daphne loathed to admit it, but its bitter flavor distracted her from the iron-rich smell of blood that lingered in her nostrils. That far-too-familiar mix of hibiscus, dandelion root, wormwood, and God knows what else hounded away its scent.

"Daphne?"

Chloe jumped up from Daphne's lap to give her customary greeting of visitors, her body a blur of wriggles and tail wags while she welcomed Detective Ahmed and Rowan. Jim chattered away to Detective Ahmed at the front door while Rowan slipped off his jacket and walked over to Daphne and God help her, she couldn't take her eyes off him. He stood just out of reach before her, as if another step closer might cause a planetary explosion. The anguish on his face was plainly written: Usually bright and gentle, his expression stormed from where he stood.

Eventually, he said, "I can't stay."

Daphne shoved down her disappointment with a watery smile. "Oh, okay. I understand."

"I just had to see you for myself. You and your books."

If she'd had an incoming thought in her brain, Rowan had wiped it out. Her smile became genuine. "You can come back for us anytime."

He ran a hand through that flop of mousy hair, his elbows almost touching the ceiling. "I—"

Detective Ahmed came in with Jim, and Rowan shrank

back, a feat Daphne would have thought impossible considering his height. She was learning that he never liked to make himself look the tallest one in the room.

"See you in an hour?" Detective Ahmed asked Rowan. At Daphne's puzzled expression she said, "I've gotta talk to you about something in private, Daphne. Your dad's allowed to stay for a while, too, but that's it. I'll fill everybody in later."

She waved a tiny goodbye to Rowan, winced at her own awkward gesture, and decided it was in her best interest to stare at her hands while he and Detective Ahmed murmured to each other to follow up on some leads. Detective Ahmed gripped the back of a wooden chair that Daphne kept in the corner for extra seating and dragged it in front of Daphne, her amber eyes glowing with sympathy when she sat down in front of her. "You up for talking?"

Detective Ahmed's gravelly voice was quiet. Not quite smooth but certainly much softer than Daphne had come to expect from her. The only thing Daphne wanted was to hide under her covers and sleep for a year, but she nodded anyway. The sooner she could share what happened, the sooner she might rest.

Detective Ahmed pulled out a black notebook and pen. "What happened?"

"I was coming home from drinks at the Thirsty Scholar after a junior faculty memorial for Sam," Daphne began, exhaling. "An Uber dropped me off and I was walking to the house when I heard Chloe barking like crazy. I ran over to find out what was wrong and that's when someone grabbed me in the park— probably about forty feet from my door. I fought back this time. At least I tried to. I headbutted him and punched him in the nuts."

That earned a small chin nod from Detective Ahmed. "Good job."

"But it didn't work, did it?" Fear was slipping into Daphne's voice. "He still managed to hold on to me."

Her dad reached over to squeeze her hand. "But you got in some good punches, baby girl."

Daphne shrugged. She rubbed her hand against the soft jersey knit of her blanket. "You can't fight back against chloroform." She looked up at Detective Ahmed. "It was chloroform, right?"

Jim's smile was oh so proud. "You've still got that good nose, daughter of mine. Just like your mother."

Daphne scoffed. "It's a pretty distinct smell, Dad."

Detective Ahmed's frown shifted between the two of them. "How do you know what chloroform smells like?"

Daphne fidgeted with a loose thread on her blanket. "Well— when I was growing up, my dad wanted my brothers and me to become familiar with scents that might signal danger. The smell of gasoline, chloroform, sulfur, that kind of thing. You know. Just in case."

Ahmed's face was too tightly pinned on hers. "In case of what?"

The doorbell ring rescued Daphne from answering that. Jim plucked himself off the couch to get it.

"A bouquet," he said, on his way back. "From Sadie and Elise."

Daphne pounced on the fresh-cut flowers. Her friends had given her just what she'd needed at the right time. They were always thinking of her.

"Anyway," Daphne said, "the guy who attacked me, he was slightly shorter than me. Maybe five four? He smelled like chlorine again and he was wearing an Ace bandage or something similar. Some kind of thick gauze wrapped around his wrist."

Detective Ahmed scratched away in that small black notebook of hers. "Mr. Ouverture, what did you see?"

"It's not what I saw so much as what I heard," Jim replied. "It was about twenty-hundred hours and I was on the couch with Chloe watching TV. The windows were open. It was dusk outside. Chloe must have smelled the guy, because she started barking like mad. When I looked outside, I saw a white man in the park. Dark brown hair, light blue jeans, denim jacket, Timberland boots. I couldn't make out his face. I saw Daphne coming toward the house from where the taxi driver had dropped her off. That's when he grabbed her. I heard her screaming and I—"

Jim struggled to breathe. Rarely did her dad lose his composure like this. He was someone who was confident in his actions and in their outcome. To know he'd been afraid rattled her more than anything else that had happened to her since Sam was killed. She reached over to touch him, to remind him that she was alive and breathing, her palms circling the warmth of his back.

"I'm okay," Jim said softly. "I'm okay."

Detective Ahmed's hard gaze softened.

After a moment, Jim patted Daphne's leg and went on. "I grabbed my gun and eased the front door open so I could get a shot at him. I didn't want him to know that I was there—I thought he'd kill Daphne on the spot if he suspected. But I couldn't tell if he had a weapon on him, so I waited. When Daphne fell, I took my shot. When he went down, I ran out. By the time I got there he'd picked himself up and run off—obviously I was more concerned about my daughter than chasing him down."

"Completely understandable," Detective Ahmed said. "I promise you we're on the hunt for him. All of the hospitals in the area have been notified to be on the lookout for a man needing to get a bullet removed. We're scouting local pharmacies and other places that have medical supplies. We *will* find him."

"For everybody's sake, I sure hope so."

Jim's voice was raw. Tired. And Daphne hated that she had put him through this. She was wired and tired, on the edge of tears or punching someone, she couldn't tell. "Detective Ahmed, do you know what's going on? Why did that man attack me?"

Detective Ahmed rubbed her palms against her jeans, and Daphne's growing pit of dread in her stomach deepened. Detective Ahmed did not strike Daphne as someone who let her nerves get the better of her. She seemed more the type to beat her own feelings into submission.

Daphne was about to repeat the question when Ahmed said, "Mr. Ouverture, I'd like you to take the dog for a walk."

Jim stiffened instantly. "Pardon me?"

Detective Ahmed didn't back down from Jim's glare. "Please."

There was enough sharpness in the detective's voice to cause Jim to bow out and head for the coat closet, a happy Chloe bounding behind him as soon as he grabbed her leash.

"You know," Detective Ahmed said once they'd left, grabbing her leather backpack and placing it on her lap, "you've caused conflict between me and my boss for some time."

Daphne didn't know what to say to that.

"From his perspective," Detective Ahmed went on, "you looked like a good fit for Sam's murder."

The blood in Daphne's ears pounded like a timpani. "But I have an alibi."

Detective Ahmed seemed to consider her words before she spoke. "Ever since Sam's death—even before it—you were everywhere. In Sam's text messages, in photographs, in the anthropology department hallways. Everywhere we looked, there you were."

Photographs? Daphne's fingers gripped her blanket so tight her knuckles yellowed. "That wasn't my fault."

Detective Ahmed appeared unmoved. "In my world, there is no such thing as a coincidence. And there were a lot of coincidences, Daphne."

"Why are you telling me this?" Daphne asked.

"Because I found something that may explain your coincidences," Detective Ahmed replied. "But I need your help to connect the dots."

"To prove my innocence?"

"Possibly," Detective Ahmed said, her tone irritatingly neutral. "But Daphne, I have to warn you: What I'm about to show you will be hard to see."

Detective Ahmed grabbed her bag, pulled out a set of photos printed in glossy color, and placed the first one on the coffee table in the center of the living room. Daphne picked it up, feeling its slippery shine.

"I don't get it," Daphne said in confusion. "It's a photo of me. On campus."

"Correct," Ahmed said.

"Who took it?" Daphne asked.

Detective Ahmed let out a long, slow breath. "Sam Taylor."

Daphne blinked. "Sam?"

Ahmed placed the next one down—Daphne inside the

Benson Art Museum, peering inside a sparkling glass case of treasures. She had been examining their collection of rare gemstones, which included a rough-cut jade stone that reminded her of a bracelet her mother had bought for her in Abidjan.

Ahmed said, "Our tech consultant was able to retrieve information from the victim's phone, even though its physical location is still unknown. We found the text message he sent you, for example. And we also found these."

Daphne kept nodding along, waiting for any of Ahmed's words to make sense, waiting for the discomfort to quit gnawing at her insides. "Okay, so Sam was taking photos of me. Why? I don't—was this for one of Harrison's media campaigns or something? Maybe he asked permission and I just don't—"

The next photo stole all words from Daphne's lips. In it, Daphne was brushing her teeth in her pajamas, getting ready for bed. Her heart plummeted into her stomach, beating louder than a drum.

Detective Ahmed's thick eyebrows formed a V. "Now, Daphne, these next photos aren't fun to look at, okay?" She laid them out across the table carefully, as if they were venomous snakes.

In all three images, Daphne's naked form was unmistakable—stepping out of the shower, dressing for work, changing into her pajamas after a long day. A teardrop splashed across a photo. It took her a second to realize that it was hers. Shame flooded through her in waves, promising to drown her.

"Why would he do this?" Daphne eventually whispered, wiping her hand across her cheek. "Was I some sort of joke to him? Did he think this was funny?"

"*No.*" Ahmed placed a hand on Daphne's arm. It was rough and warm. "And Daphne, you've done nothing wrong. Nothing."

Daphne hiccupped doubtfully, swiping a tear away at those photos puddled up on the table, mocking her.

Detective Ahmed leaned forward in the chair, clasping her hands shut. "Daphne, I think I already know the answer to this question but I still have to ask it. Did you know about these photos? Did you consent to them being taken?"

"No." Daphne held back a sob squeezing up her chest, her breathing uneven. "Of course not."

Detective Ahmed's amber eyes bored into hers. "Did he ever act untoward? Touch you or handle you at all?"

"He . . ." Daphne wiped the snot smearing on her upper lip. She needed to say it—why she'd never felt comfortable around Sam. Now was her chance. It was with relief that Daphne eventually whispered, "I used to catch him staring at me."

Detective Ahmed's expression softened.

"But I just thought . . . I don't know, I just ignored it. He was dating Molly Henderson. When I'm in white spaces I'm romantically invisible anyway. Most white dudes aren't exactly beating down my door to date me. So I shrugged it off. I didn't think it meant anything, other than that he was kind of—weird, sometimes."

"Daphne, was there any other indication that Sam was stalking you?"

Her jaw dropped so low it scraped her neck. "You think Sam was stalking me?"

"I do."

Panic raced through her heart at that simple, earth-shattering response.

"How often did he take these photos?" Daphne demanded. "For how long?"

"Often. Daily, maybe. We're not sure how far it goes back."

Those words were forty jolts of electricity. Daphne jerked her head back, trying to focus, trying to make sense of the nonsensical.

"But why?" she asked. "Why me?"

Ahmed sent Daphne a plain look. "I'm no psychologist but the few cases I've dealt with like this are usually about desire."

"That's impossible. He was with Molly." *And Olivia, among others.* "And I'm not his type. If I was, he would have asked me out on a date."

"Maybe," Ahmed said slowly, "Sam didn't want to date you."

The detective might as well have slapped her across the face. She stared down at the hands in her lap, waiting for the wave of revulsion to pass.

"Okay." Daphne swallowed. "Sam was stalking me. He's *dead.* What does that have to do with me getting attacked?"

Detective Ahmed rubbed her fingers along her ponytail, releasing a controlled exhale. It rattled Daphne to know how much this troubled the detective, too. "Remember how I said I have a theory? Well, Sam Taylor was collecting information on backdoor dealings and embezzlement at Livington Prison."

Daphne nodded along. Molly Henderson had told Daphne that much already.

"But what Sam also had was evidence of someone getting murdered—including the killer—on video. Perhaps on some kind of storage device that might have been more secure than the cloud."

The mountain of blankets around Daphne couldn't keep her from turning cold. It was rare for any academic to write something that could jeopardize their lives. But lo and behold, Sam Taylor had discovered the one thing worth killing for.

"And you've found the footage?" Daphne asked.

Detective Ahmed shook her head. "We haven't."

"But you know where it is?"

Detective Ahmed flicked her ponytail in a way that suggested otherwise. "Not quite."

Daphne shoved the blankets off. "Oh my God."

"Daphne—" Detective Ahmed held up her hands.

"Oh my God." Daphne's heart was a jackhammer, drilling pure fear up to her brain. "Oh my *God*."

It all came rushing to her at once: Sam's text message in French, her trip to the silent reading room in the library, the key that had been taped to her dog-eared copy of *Papillon*. The key that Sam had led her to—she was meant to find it. *She* was meant to open whatever it unlocked.

Ahmed's lips pressed into a grim line. "Did you two ever meet anywhere on or off campus?"

Daphne shot up like a rocket. "You think I have the video of Joey Camden's murder, don't you? You think I'm involved in this!"

"I don't," Detective Ahmed said. "Not directly."

"You just said your boss hates me and thought I was involved in Sam's murder."

"And I disagree," Detective Ahmed insisted. "But what if Sam told someone that you had this video? Or what if somebody caught Sam following you and put two and two together?"

"I don't have the video!" she shouted, her voice rising with each syllable. She paced around her living room, feeling like a caged rabbit. "I don't have it!"

"Of course you don't," Detective Ahmed said. "We know that. And I promise you that we're going to keep searching for it no matter what."

But the detective's reassurance couldn't quell the fire raging in Daphne's body, boiling her alive. A far more primal fear seized her throat, a new twisted reality that offered no way out. There was nowhere to run, there was nowhere to hide.

"And until then I'm just a sitting duck?" Daphne said.

The detective bowed her head.

"Because if you're right," Daphne said, "then whoever's out there looking for that video isn't going to stop until they get it."

The living room spun.

"They're not going to stop until they get *me*."

CHAPTER NINETEEN

"That mother*fucker*!"

Daphne would have offered up a hearty amen to Sadie's lengthy and highly specific vows of revenge if her besties' faces weren't smashed up right against hers, vying for the title of World's Most Intense Hugger. On her living room couch, smothered between the pair, she tried again to wrest herself free from their grips for a bite of fresh croissant that Elise had brought from her favorite bakery.

"Mmmmmpf," she squished out between smooshed lips.

Sadie wasn't done yelling. Her arms were squeezed around Daphne so tight she could give a python a run for its money. "The fucking *dirtbag*! I want to dig up his body and push it out onto a fucking pyre, Daph. Light that shit up right under the night sky."

"How about this?" Elise's usually light soprano had an obsidian glint to it. "Let's dig him up, sure. But before we set him on fire, we cut off his testes and feed them to a pack of wolves."

"Christ," Daphne whispered.

Sadie grinned against Daphne's cheek. "Elise, that's brilliant."

"That's if the wolves would eat them, mind you," Elise said.

"Fair point," said Sadie. "I wouldn't touch those things in a hazmat suit."

"And *then* we decapitate him—"

Sadie loosened her grip on Daphne to slap Elise a high five.

"—and then we place his rotting head in like, one of those old sports bag things that have the netting on them? You know the kind that are used to carry around volleyballs?"

Sadie's voice choked with pride. "I didn't know you had this in you, Elise."

"—and *then* we kick it into the ocean!"

"Okay, this is getting out of hand," Daphne said. "Also we don't live anywhere near the ocean."

"I can drive us!" Sadie shouted.

"Oooh, we've always wanted to go on a road trip together," Elise replied. "Isn't that such a lovely idea, Daphne?"

"Guys."

Elise wrapped her arms around both women again and sighed. "Sadie's going to be especially helpful when we feed Sam's rotting head to the sharks."

"Hammerheads," Sadie suggested. "Those assholes are fucking *mean*."

"*Guys*." Daphne gently pushed herself out of the hug. "I appreciate the warm sentiments but I'm not sure my next steps are going to be to dig up Sam's decaying body, dismember it, and feed it to different species in the animal kingdom."

Sadie shoved her hands in her pockets. "At least not *your* first step."

Daphne sent Sadie a pointed stare.

"*Any*way," Daphne said, feeling lighter, "I promise I'll get to the bottom of this."

"How?" Sadie asked, doubtful.

It was as much a surprise to Daphne as it was to her friends to learn that she had an answer. "I can't believe I'm saying this out loud but—I'm going to have to find Sam's killer."

They paused before erupting into outrage.

"Babe, have you lost your mind?" Elise screeched so loudly it threatened the glass. "What you have to do is get on the next flight out of Calliope and hide!"

"I can't do that," Daphne said. "Not when I'm who the killer wants. Not when I might be the only one who knows how to find him."

"That's what the police are for!" Elise practically shouted in her face.

"But they don't know how to find him, either," Daphne replied. "And I refuse to just sit inside my house with two policemen stationed outside for the rest of my life, waiting for the other shoe to drop. I have to at least try to find the killer. Don't you see?"

Sadie whipped out her phone and began dialing. "I'm calling your department and telling them to place you on emergency leave—no, better yet, I'm calling your mother. Someone has to talk sense into you."

"Put the phone down," Daphne said, reaching for Sadie's arm. "Listen, it's the only way. The killer thinks I have Sam's video. I just have to find it and see who's on it and then I'll know who the killer is."

"Oh, is that all?" Sadie replied. "Just find the video before the killer pulls a Jack the Ripper on you and strangles you?"

"First of all, Jack the Ripper knifed his victims, and second I'm guessing Sam's killer would prefer to use blunt force again based on his previous pattern of behavior—"

"Elise, I'm gonna smack her," Sadie said between gritted teeth.

"—but otherwise you have it right," Daphne said. "See? It'll be fine. I'm going to find the video. I'll take it to the police.

We'll see what's on it. And then I promise you both, I'm going to make Sam pay for what he's done to me."

It took longer than Daphne would have liked for Elise and Sadie to stop glowering at her but the pair returned to eating their croissants, leaving Daphne to ruminate on her new plan.

Where was that video? No matter how melodramatic Sam might have been, in this day and age it was unlikely to be a VHS tape. She pictured a USB flash drive, a slim piece of metal no bigger than her finger. She just had to find out where Sam had stashed it.

That small silver key taped to the back of her copy of *Papillon* came into view, Rowan's hands on either side of her head against the wall in the library's silent reading room. She let that memory linger before pushing it aside.

Seriously, Daph, what does that key open?

It was too small for an office door on campus but it might just unlock a small safe, a gym locker, or a bicycle lock.

The first of two policemen arrived to provide round-the-clock protection, interrupting her thoughts. They were a gift from Detective Ahmed—or rather, a stern command for Daphne to stay put inside her house until this whole business was wrapped up. The duo chatted up Jim, instantly fell in love with Elise, and recoiled at Sadie's snarl, which was for the best. Daphne supposed she felt grateful for their presence but the cold wet sensation of silent tears sliding down her cheek while she went to lie down told her that no, she was not.

Her home was supposed to be safe. It was supposed to be cozy and inviting, a den for Chloe and a hangout spot for Daphne and her friends. Usually it was. But a new, revolting truth settled like a fog onto her throw pillows, onto her chaise longue that she'd managed to ship from France, and onto the

Bedouin rugs her mother had haggled for in Rabat. Sam had, in fact, been inside her house without her permission. He'd grabbed *Papillon* right off her shelf, kickstarting this adventure hunt she had no choice but to join. He'd stained that which had once been pure.

Okay, so? Daphne told herself. *Expel him. Exorcise Sam from a place he had no business trying to claim as his own.*

Elise and Sadie gave her their goodbye kisses. Jim took Chloe on her evening walk, returning her to Daphne reeking of the woods and fresh dirt. In the silence of her living room that night, a sprawling Chloe on her lap, Daphne balled her fists. Sam didn't get a say in how she'd feel moving around in her own home. Neither would his murderer.

Only she could control that.

She started searching. She checked everything she could think of—her toolbox, a lockbox that she'd lugged around with her since grad school, the vault her dad had installed under her hardwood floors when she'd first moved in. Sweaty from heaving around storage boxes, Daphne plopped herself down in her living room and frowned at the conclusion that Sam hadn't smuggled it here. It was time to look elsewhere.

Gazing out the window and onto her green meadow, Daphne listened in her heart for the vow she'd made to her friends.

How do you make a dead man pay?

As a historian, she had multiple answers to that question, none of them immediately useful to her situation in life. The main and best form of revenge was to tell tales. History wasn't written by the victors so much as by those who held a grudge. History professors had made it their mission to feed those grudges, to nurture them, to flesh them out with historical documentation, and, ultimately, to write them down. The point

of historical writing was rarely to celebrate human achieve-
ments but to point out where the bodies were buried. But
historians wrote their books years after the fact, with the
advantage of teleological distance. Daphne didn't have that. She
had a selection of photos and a shitty text message. What was
she supposed to do with that?

She hated the photos that Detective Ahmed had shown her.
Thinking about them made her skin itch all over. She wanted
to rip them into pieces and feed them to a ceremonial bonfire
whose flames could purify her again. Sadie would know how
to do exactly that—how to get the pile of burning wood so hot
it'd scorch her eyebrows if she got within a foot of it. How to
channel her growing anger that Sam had taken what had never
been his to claim. Daphne didn't deserve this—this cruelty,
masked as obsession, marked as possession.

A thump and a grunt from above caused her to frown.
"Dad?"

What was going on upstairs?

Daphne abandoned her living room sofa and her view of
the meadow. At her bedroom doorway, she stopped—and
stared.

Her father was rummaging through her wardrobe like it was
a sales rack at Ross, tossing tops and dresses and tights across
her queen-size mattress. Chloe leapt inside to join him in the
fun, rolling around in Daphne's clothes and gently mouthing
one of her slippers.

Daphne crossed her arms and leaned against the doorframe.
"Had a good walk with Chloe?"

"Where do you keep your sweaters?" Jim asked from deep
inside her closet, dropping a pair of black leggings. "I can't find
them anywhere."

"I keep them in the guest bedroom." Daphne paused. "Why?"

"And your socks?" he demanded. He grabbed an armload of shirts and shoved them into Daphne's maroon suitcase—the one usually overstuffed with gifts going to or from Paris or Abidjan.

"Dad, what's going on?"

But she knew. It was one thing for Jim to face death and danger—hell, he'd been paid to do it for thirty years. But it was another for his baby daughter to go up against a killer he didn't know and couldn't name.

"Your socks, sweetheart, where are your socks?" he asked, opening cupboards and overturning drawers.

Daphne walked up to her father and gently placed her hand on his back. "Dad."

"I heard what your friends said earlier. About you getting out of town?" When he turned to her, his usually twinkling eyes were wild. "You've wanted to visit your cousin Bobbi in New Orleans for a while, right? You two used to run together like sisters. Your mother's already found you a cheap flight."

The tips of her fingers swirled circles on her dad's back. "And leave during the middle of a semester? Dad, I'm teaching."

He waved a hand. "Someone can cover."

Daphne raised an eyebrow. "On French colonialism? I'm pretty sure that's why Harrison hired me."

Jim inspected a leather belt. "And I'm so proud that they did—they absolutely made the best choice, baby girl. It's why they should be fine with you taking off for a while."

Daphne gently removed some of her skirts and tops from her dad's arms and placed them on her bed. She reached up to peck him on the cheek and give him her biggest hug, not letting go until he squeezed her back.

"I'll be fine, Dad."

His voice was thick with emotion. "You don't know that."

She put her nose to his neck, like she'd done since she was a toddler. "You're right, I don't—I can't. But I know I can't run. And Daddy, I don't want to. Chloe is here. My students are here. My friends are here. My *life* is here."

Miranda's cackles, Sadie's inappropriate ringtone, and Chloe's sweet tippy taps on her cottage floors—all of them were evidence of a life she'd built, one that she was proud to claim as her own. Harrison was worth fighting for—or, better yet, her life in Calliope was worth fighting for. Amidst Harrison's regal architecture jutting up into the sky and Calliope's downtown bookstores and coffee shops, she'd carved out something for herself. She dared anyone to try to rip that from her hands.

"And anyway, Dad," Daphne said, "leaving for a week or two won't solve the problem that somebody thinks I have something worth killing for."

Jim chuckled softly. "Now why you gotta use that smart PhD logic on your pops?"

He wrapped her in a hug again, tightly, and suddenly she was five years old again, running up and down neighborhood blocks after her brothers and eating fistfuls of fried plantains.

Daphne pulled away to face her father directly. "We're Ouvertures, right? That means we fight."

He tugged the sleeve of her sweater. "Always have, always will."

"And the good news is that I have a dad who taught me how."

The twinkle returned to his eyes. "Not like you always listened."

Daphne considered that. She'd spent most of her adult life ignoring her training, her family secrets. The past lives of others had always interested her far more than her own. Maybe it wasn't such a tragedy if that changed.

"You're right, Dad," Daphne said. "I didn't always used to listen. But I'm listening now."

CHAPTER TWENTY

"A B-minus?"

It was ten o'clock on Monday morning, and Abbie Foreman was waving her paper in Daphne's face. Students had dispersed after her French history class had ended. As always, she had handed over their papers only at the end of class. If she gave them back before launching into discussion, they would spend their class time preparing arguments in their heads for why they deserved a better grade instead of concentrating on the material Daphne had spent hours preparing for them.

Abbie Foreman—today's main star of the show—was gearing up for a real performance, judging by her flushed cheeks. Tabitha lingered by the whiteboard, her hair pressed and makeup game on point, giving Abbie a healthy dose of side-eye while clearly also gobbling up this drama. She'd snuck her phone out already to record Abbie's messiness, would most likely upload it on social media with the hashtag #babykaren if Daphne didn't stop her.

"A B-minus?" Abbie repeated. Her pained expression suggested a minor in theater. "I really got a B-minus?"

"Yup." Daphne slid her laptop back into her backpack.

"But that's unacceptable," Abbie said. "I don't get B's."

"I don't know what to tell you, Abbie," Daphne said. "This paper earned one."

Abbie's tantrum was making Daphne reconsider that trip to New Orleans, after all. She had spent hours yesterday searching in her house for anything that might require a small key, even sneaking into her neighbors' garden sheds and those "free libraries" to find anything that had a tiny lock attached to it. At least Chloe enjoyed the late-night break-ins, which involved sniffing out two different possums and a racoon, and chasing down several rabbits.

Abbie bunched the ink-stained sheets in her fist. "Professor Ouverture, I'd like a regrade."

Daphne sighed. She should have seen this coming. Abbie was an enthusiastic student, sure. She talked—loudly—in class about anything that Daphne threw out there for students to chew on, whether she had anything intelligible to say about the topic or not. But unfortunately for Abbie, she was one of those students who mistook passion for intellectual acuity. Being angry that the French Empire had caused violence didn't necessarily make anybody a sophisticated thinker on the topic.

Not that Abbie could have handled that indictment at the moment.

"Abbie," Daphne began, "you know my rule. How long do you have to wait before you file a petition for a grade reassessment?"

"Forty-eight hours," Abbie admitted, her breathing alarmingly labored.

"Forty-eight hours," Daphne repeated. "And you need to submit your petition to me in writing. Using my grading rubric to explain where you think you earned more points. And—"

Abbie blinked back tears. "But my parents—"

"It'll be all right," Daphne said. "Tabitha, stop filming this. Abbie, we'll talk about this later, okay? Everything will work out."

Fresh out of class, Daphne booked it over to the anthropology department in Fischer Hall in search of any signs of a storage unit that might require a small key. Cursing the architects for designing a building that could confuse M. C. Escher, Daphne did her best to be methodical while she opened janitor closets and roamed secretarial offices in the winding hallways. Being near Sam's mind was a cruel punishment from beyond the grave, but she tried to imagine what he would have done—she swiped her fingers across desks, pushed her palms against solid wood bookshelves, and sank her knees onto rough carpet to search underneath one podium that looked promising, only to find nothing. Upon opening one door, Daphne startled a classroom of fifteen students scrawling mathematical formulas on the whiteboard.

An hour later, Daphne limped out of Fischer Hall with nothing to show for her efforts except a now-dusty blouse and a headache that she was adamant to ignore for the sake of continuing. She was running out of ideas. Nothing had turned up at home. Her office on campus was barren. Fischer Hall was a bust. And to top it all off, she still had no idea if or how she'd run into Rowan again, making that fleeting relationship more extinct than a dodo bird. Not like she was going to stay alive long enough to date anyone anyway if she didn't find that video. While teaching. While trying to do her own research. While being a dog mom. And a responsible daughter—even if her mother might publicly repudiate that last claim.

Back at her own office, Daphne scowled at her Ivory Coast clock. She checked her inbox, hoping to find a "congratulations!" email from the French government awarding her a travel grant for the summer—only to scowl again at an email address in her inbox that she longed to block: Ken Miller's.

Dear Harrison community, the email began, *We have endured so much hardship in the wake of Professor Taylor's passing. In light of his death, we are honored to announce the establishment of a scholarship, funded in part by a generous contribution from the Henderson Foundation—*

Daphne deleted it.

She couldn't take one more tidbit from either Ken or Sam today. It was like the two of them were actively conspiring together across the veil to ruin her life. Daphne scrolled through her inbox some more, pecking away answers to a few students wanting to know if they could submit their assignment a little bit later than the deadline. She responded to a request for Black faculty to contribute to a panel on balancing their lives and careers here at Harrison (Surely that had to be a joke? The word "balance" was as recognizable to her as ancient Sanskrit), and scowled again.

A generous contribution from the Henderson Foundation.

Obviously the family had money. Daphne had seen it first-hand when she'd stepped inside Molly's mansion. But nosiness had Daphne scrolling through Molly's social media, anyway, searching for signs of wealth. It took all of two seconds for Daphne to find a recent post of Molly at what had to be the most expensive bridal boutique in New York. In half a dozen photos, Molly sat prim and erect as always, sipping champagne with her sister, Melanie, on a high-backed velvet couch under glittering lights, beaming a Mona Lisa smile.

Thirty minutes later and an inbox still not cleared, Daphne frowned at her reflection in her laptop screen. Something she'd huffed about earlier had dislodged a memory, an idea that she kept willing to come back. But it remained stubbornly out of sight, at the edges of her consciousness, its scent in the air, intimate and unfamiliar.

Conspiring.

Ken.

Two words that belonged together in the same sentence. At

Miranda's push, Daphne had caught him once. *Your Vanessa Waters situation didn't just handle itself. I did that. It's called a tit for tat* . . . Unfortunately, that refrain would be repeating in her head for life. Daphne hummed to herself, low and slow. Wouldn't it be a lovely gift to Miranda if Daphne could catch Ken again—this time for good?

SHE WAS packing up to go home that afternoon when a knock on the door snapped her out of her mental wanderings. Between Abbie's antics and Ken being a bag of rocks, her brain had decided it would be fun to mimic a jackhammer, which was proving to be as delightful as she'd suspected.

She'd finally slid her laptop into her backpack when the scent of rose perfume filled the room. Miranda popped her head through the doorway.

"What a week, huh?" Miranda asked.

"Miranda!" In all of the chaos of the past few days, Daphne hadn't had time to check in with her chair. She swept Miranda into a hug. "Ken said he'd uncovered your plot. Are you okay?"

"Down but not out, my dear. After thirty years of marriage to a wonderful man from Kyoto, I may have absorbed the Japanese trait for 'ganbaru,' after all."

Daphne tried the word out loud. "Ganbaru?"

Miranda gave a scheming wink. "Obstinacy. All of this is to say that I've been in secret meetings lately, the kinds involving chairs and provosts, if I'm being truthful, and only time will tell if they're paying off. But I don't want to bother you with this quite yet. Everyone's been asking how you're faring. Things on campus have been just so unsettling lately, with Sam's death and then your attack. Is it time to talk about taking a step back from teaching to focus on your mental health?"

"With only two weeks left before the term ends? Absolutely not." Daphne reached for her bag. "And not with Kiki's academic misconduct hearing coming up."

"As much as I wish to applaud your enthusiasm for pedagogy, Daphne, I still want you to be careful. You look like you could use some rest. Am I wrong?"

Daphne shrugged. "I probably do. But that's not what's on my mind."

"Hmpf." Miranda sniffed. "Fair enough. Then do share."

Daphne sat back down. Far too many problems floated up to the surface of her consciousness. Sam Taylor's shiny key. Ken Miller being a hobgoblin. Rowan's absence.

She chose to talk about the world's least affable administrator. "I think Ken's hiding something."

Miranda frowned. "Ken Miller is always hiding something."

"True," said Daphne.

"My dear," Miranda said, "if you want my help you're going to have to be a touch more specific, what with the pregnant TAs, affairs, plagiarism, and other scandals. What's he done this time?"

"I don't know," Daphne admitted. "I just . . . Sam Taylor wasn't the person everyone makes him out to be, Miranda. And Ken was his chair before becoming dean, right? Maybe he knows something."

"Of course he knows something," Miranda replied. "It's safe to assume that Ken has dirt on the devil himself. What's he covering up? You don't think—"

"I don't know," Daphne admitted, stopping Miranda before she could say *Sam's murder*. Was Ken somehow involved in Sam's exposé on Livington Prison? Did he know where Sam's research was located? Had Ken known that Sam was a creep?

Daphne sighed. The latter seemed likely.

She wasn't going to get anywhere with these questions right now. "How would you convince Abbie Foreman that a B-minus is a perfectly acceptable grade?"

Miranda gave Daphne a pointed look at that obvious change in conversation. But she must have been willing to let it go because she shrugged, strode on over, and shimmied into one of the chairs opposite Daphne's desk.

"Well, you're in for a treat," Miranda said, clasping her hands together. "She has *plans*, that one—a Rhodes Scholarship and then Princeton for her PhD. It's already been prophesied by her helicopter parents! So if you could kindly step aside and stop being the boulder in the way of progress, she can get on with becoming the youngest Supreme Court justice ever nominated."

"But the paper's not very good, Miranda."

"What does 'good' have to do with anything?" Miranda eyed her. "What's it on?"

"Baudelaire."

Miranda made a face. "The things you do to your students."

Now, it was well-known that Miranda made her students memorize all forty-seven Japanese provinces and their capital cities—and expected them to be able to identify the names even in Japanese script—but Daphne chose not to bring that up.

"It was a totally reasonable assignment," Daphne said good naturedly. "Abbie was supposed to write about how French men exoticized non-European women in art and poetry. Henri Matisse, Paul Gauguin, Eugène Delacroix, poems like Baudelaire's 'À une dame créole.'"

"You speak the most fabulously Parisian French, Daphne," Miranda said, smiling. "I hope Coco Chanel is screaming from the underworld."

Daphne grabbed the paper to show it to Miranda. "The whole point was to demonstrate how French society turned women of color into lustful, sexually deviant, insatiable monsters. They could be a concubine or a mistress but never a white man's wife. Abbie somehow failed to connect Baudelaire's exoticist writings to French colonialism, which was the purpose of the exercise."

Miranda tilted her head to the side. "You know what? Go take a walk. That'll clear your head a little bit. You could go over to the Benson—they just opened a new exhibit on European modernist portraiture that made me think of you. If you head over now, you'll get there right before they close and you'll have the whole floor to yourself, I'm sure of it. And even if you don't like the portraits, there's always that favorite painting of yours in the French wing to visit. What's it called again?"

"*Slave in Cairo.*" Daphne softened at Miranda's recollection. "By Jean-Léon Gérôme."

"Yes, that's the one," Miranda replied with a snap of her fingers. "You know, it . . ."

A thought louder than the carillon bells ringing in the distance drowned out the rest of Miranda's reply. Daphne's mouth clamped shut. Her nostrils flared. Her mind flashed on Sam's photos of her inside the Benson Art Museum. In one of them, Daphne was staring at her—an African woman in a portrait, her delicate nose shining in an unknown light, a simple salmon-pink carnation in her hair, mouth closed, eyebrows pulled together in brilliant thought.

Daphne's favorite painting. It hung in her favorite room in her favorite building on campus.

And she couldn't help but wonder if Sam Taylor had known that, too.

CHAPTER TWENTY-ONE

Alone in her office again, Daphne cradled her phone, thumb hovering over Detective Asma Ahmed's contact, and climbed, in her mind, her family's wide-bearing Francophone tree.

Jean-Léon Gérôme's painting of an enslaved Black woman in a market in Cairo was one of the many things that had convinced her to move to Harrison. With one peep at it a determined feeling had locked inside her tight: in Calliope she'd have a reminder of herself, of her homes both close and far away. Her Francophone world sprawled across time and space, living in contemporary markets in Ivory Coast or in nineteenth-century Parisian artworks. She bit into it when devouring Chef Marcel's croissants, she danced to it when Haitian kompa rumbled in her car. The French Empire was a history of violence and torn timelines, yes—but it was also all that Daphne really knew to be a "home" for her and her family. It was obviously against all museum policies and international norms to touch any pieces of art but part of her longed to reach out her fingers and trace the peach-toned flower in the subject's hair and ask the woman how to find one just like that for her own.

It was preposterous to believe that somewhere near *Slave in Cairo* lay a USB stick depicting a violent murder, that somewhere inside the Benson Art Museum was a device worth killing over, and that Daphne was the one person in the world who might have figured that last bit out.

But Sam Taylor had entwined his life—and inadvertently, his death—with her life. She couldn't ignore those photos that Detective Ahmed had placed on her lap. Sam had known every one of her movements, her teaching schedule, her daily walks with Chloe in the woods, her habit of wandering into the Benson Art Museum's French Impressionist wing when she needed cheering up. He had sought to own her with his camera lens, to mark her as his.

I'm glad he's dead.

Daphne stared at Detective Ahmed's number on her phone, waiting to feel regret or guilt for that sentiment. None came. She was too angry, too disgusted by his invasion into her life, too determined to banish him from it. Finding that USB drive was the only way to emancipate her from his coercion.

All of the air in her lungs compressed out.

But *where* inside the Benson could that video reside? The museum was a secret garden of tapestries, paintings, and books—endless books—but Daphne wasn't sure if anything inside required a tiny key to open it. It mortified her to even think that Sam had stashed the video in the Benson to begin with. His logic offended her, just as it offended her that she even had to consider Sam's depraved thinking as a kind of logic at all. But try as she might, she couldn't outmaneuver the fact that Daphne's life had been his secret, an inside joke for him and him alone. Except it wasn't anymore. He'd been forced to reveal it to her by texting her a quote of *Papillon* right before his death. He'd never meant for her to know about it.

Or at least not yet.

Daphne shook out that last thought like she were a wet dog.

Maybe Elise was right. Daphne should let the police handle the missing video. After all, Detective Ahmed was more than capable—eager, even—to take on villains, Batwoman style, and crush them to the ground. It was just that Daphne had this pesky habit of following her curiosity wherever it might lead her. Most of the time it was to an archive. Once, on a drive through the Provençal countryside bursting with lavender, her gut whispered to her to knock on the door of a thirteenth-century monastery. The nun who'd answered was puzzled but not hostile to Daphne's stammering request to see the list of women who had joined the religious order of Saint Clare in the 1780s. She'd found three more Black women for her dissertation that way. Denying herself the right to explore felt unbearable to her. It stood against everything she was as a professional searcher of the dead.

Nonetheless, entering the museum violated every rule Daphne had created to keep herself safe and her career intact. Searching inside could explode her small world. It could lead to her arrest or being fired. What other choice did she have?

She picked up the phone and dialed.

"Baby girl!" Jim shouted over the sizzles of a frying pan and a stereo blasting out Frankie Beverly's "Before I Let Go." Chloe's throaty howls crooned in the background.

"You ready to eat? I got the jambalaya on the stovetop and Luke and Noah have already given their blessing of it."

Daphne pressed the phone closer to her ear hoping to tune out the chaos. "Luke and Noah?"

"The boys stationed out in front of your house," Jim replied.

"Right," Daphne said. Her dad could befriend a hissing cat.

"I got to know 'em while you were out. One of them was a Marine, so you know I had to go ahead and do my thing."

"Did you now?" Daphne drawled.

"They've never had much Louisiana cooking before," Jim said, "so I thought I'd fix 'em a plate. If they stick around awhile, I might let them try gumbo next."

"In April?"

"It doesn't have to be winter to celebrate the Ouverture family's fine cooking," Jim replied. The Ouverture family's heavily guarded jambalaya recipe had been passed down since the mid-nineteenth century. "But that's not why you're calling, is it?"

At first Daphne couldn't identify the tension in her father's usually jolly voice or locate its cause of origin. Was it fear? Nerves?

Good grief. It was so much worse than that: excitement.

All of the Ouverture children had been, frankly, relieved when Jim had announced his retirement last year. Although Jim was in excellent health, crossing the threshold into his sixties had made his kids anxious. Retirement was supposed to have slowed him down, mellowed him out. He had always been a chipper man, quick and light on his feet. But the zippiness to his movements lately had a different tone to them, a freshness she hadn't seen since he'd been in the game.

"You found what that key belongs to, didn't you?" Jim asked.

Relieved and irritated to be so known, Daphne grunted by way of reply.

"And what are you gonna do about it?" challenged the man who'd taught her how to ski down the French Alps at age four. "That detective Ahmed lady wants to help. You gonna call her?"

"I don't know," Daphne replied, misery and fear creeping back in, tickling behind her nose. "What if I want to find it myself, first? Just to be sure."

"Okay, heard," Jim said, cheery as ever and undeterred. "Let's think about it for a second. Where does that key go?"

The Benson flared back to life again, all soaring white marble Grecian columns and ornate cornices surrounded by walls of glass, as if a minor god had placed a glass box over an ancient Greek temple. Some faculty still pooh-poohed the postmodernist architect who'd encased the art museum's original structure in glass but Daphne found its statement to be profound if unsettling. The museum's encasing evoked both the institution's fragility in an ever-changing world and also its complicity in hiding cultural treasures from public view.

"The art museum on campus."

"They had that exhibit on contemporary African painting, right? Your mother loved it."

Daphne snorted. "Because she was convinced one of the painters was the son of a woman she knows."

"I wouldn't put it past her," Jim replied. "So what's the harm in looking around?"

"I could get caught. Embarrass myself or lose my job," Daphne reminded him. Ken Miller was looking for a reason to set fire to the history department anyway, especially with Miranda on his tail. Daphne would gladly hand over her entire collection of French soaps not to be that reason.

"Impossible, that fancy boss lady of yours loves you too much," Jim replied. "Shoot, blueberry pancake, everybody does. What else has got you afraid?"

"What if I'm followed?" Daphne said, her voice catching. "Someone's still after me. And sure, there are police outside my house and there's lots of campus security but . . ."

They were both silent for a moment. Neither of them

wanted to be reminded of her recent assaults. Neither of them could forget.

"How about this?" Jim said. "Why don't I meet you at your office right now? Once I'm there you can head out to the museum first and I'll follow you from behind, just to make sure no one's trailing you."

Daphne checked her Ivory Flag clock, its short arm ticking close to 6 P.M.

"The museum closes in ten minutes, Dad," Daphne replied. "You can't make it to me in time."

"Oh."

In the silence that followed Daphne swallowed back the tears threatening to spill out. She needed her dad with her. She needed to find that video. She needed to catch Sam's killer and write the conclusion to this story.

Jim asked, "What's your gut telling you to do?"

Daphne sighed, resisting the urge to rub her face and smear her mascara everywhere. "Find that video. Now."

"Then that's what you're gonna do," Jim replied, firm.

"Really?"

"An Ouverture always trusts their instincts," Jim said. "It's how our ancestors survived the Middle Passage."

Daphne bit back a snort. "Sure, Dad. Our Ouverture ancestors are telling me to square up with a murderer."

"How about this?" Jim said. "You go on down to the museum and by the time you get there I'll have parked somewhere."

"Provided I don't get attacked in the meantime," Daphne said. It wasn't a joke, exactly, but she didn't know what else to call it. Sure, whoever'd jumped her hadn't been so brazen as to try it on campus, but what was stopping him now?

"Baby daughter, I won't let anything happen to you," said

Jim. "I've got an idea that'll work. Remember that game we used to play in Paris? By the Tuileries Garden?" Jim asked innocently enough. "You were about ten years old when we started—you used to love it."

The phone almost dropped out of Daphne's hands. She stared at it incredulously. "*The Crowds Game?*"

Jim's tone was mischievous and cheeky and loving. "Hope you've got some good walking shoes on your feet, baby girl. 'Cause you're about to tear up campus."

THE FIRST rule of the Crowds Game was simple enough: *Act Casual.*

If anything, it was a necessary reminder to Daphne to relax her shoulders, take deep breaths, and practice her mindfulness exercises while leaving Davis Hall for the quad. Anything else might alert her predator of her attention.

If, that was, anyone was even watching her. She found nothing out of the ordinary as she began her walk to the library. A couple was lying on the grass, the girl's head in her boyfriend's lap. A professor had chosen to hold class outside, barking out against the breeze some translation of Archimedes from the Greek while students huddled into their hoodies. And as always, a few squirrels were beefing by a trash can, this time over what looked like a slice of apple pie that had fallen to the ground.

The second rule was less pleasant but necessary.

Spot the Spotter.

Still jittery, Daphne passed by the tall water fountain where birds enjoyed bathing—an exact replica, she'd learned, of a *nasone*, designed in the late nineteenth century to give water to Roman citizens. Using its tall tower as cover, she finally checked her peripheral vision, finding nothing. The desire to glance behind her pulled at her chest with the force of a revved-up pickup truck, convincing her in that moment that Lot's wife had actually been a model of restraint. She kept her gaze ahead anyway because anything else went against the third rule:

Never.

Look.

Back.

The first time she'd played the game as a young girl, weaving through legs and strollers in the hot Parisian sun, she'd gotten lost and had almost wandered into a homeless community by the Seine River. When the police had found her wailing, her mother had been furious to discover what Jim had been up to. Beneath her mother's outrage had been fear. But Daphne had eventually come to love playing the game—and no one had played it better than tiny Daphne, the baby of the family, their only daughter, the parents' belated surprise.

She paused by the statue of some Founding Father figure long enough to whip out her cell phone and smile for the camera before trudging up the tulip-lined path that led to the Benson. The photo she took was worthy of an Instagram post, all smiles and bright colors on a spring evening—if not for the two men in the distance behind her, one short, one tall, both scrappy and lean, their scowling faces aimed right at her.

Two?

Her heart lurched into her throat.

On campus?

Surely they weren't—she was just paranoid.

They both wore rumpled jeans and faded T-shirts. Both could have been at home on campus as landscapers working the mulch on tulip beds. Her gut told her otherwise. It remembered the hand around her throat, the sweet smell of chloroform, the fuzzy feel of the grass against her face as she passed out in her lawn. She never wanted to be prey again.

Daphne hadn't realized she was dialing a number until she heard the quiet tone on the other end of her phone.

"Earthseed Books," Rowan said, and man, could Daphne get used to hearing Rowan greet her like that every day.

"Hi, Rowan."

"Daphne?" he asked, his tone both a hope and a question. "Is everything all right?"

"Nope!" Daphne said brightly. "I'm walking to the Benson Art Museum from my office on campus and I'm being followed by two men."

Across the din of customers and Amber's suggestion to give Brit Bennett a try, Rowan replied. "Pardon?"

"I figured it out," Daphne said quickly. "What Sam Taylor's key belongs to? At least I think I did. I'm like, ninety-five percent sure."

"Daphne—"

"I need to be sure, Rowan," Daphne said before he could persuade her otherwise. "Listen, I'm almost at the museum. I'm sending you a photo of the men following me. You can use that, right?"

"Daphne, please listen to me." Lining the authoritative tone in Rowan's voice was a tremor of fear. "Stay where you are. Remain among the crowds and Detective Ahmed and I will come and get you. We'll apprehend whoever is following you."

His voice didn't quite fade at the reminder, yet again, that someone was after her, but it certainly dimmed. She pushed down the panic bubbling up in her throat. Try as she might to tell herself otherwise, this wasn't a game. Sam's killer was still out there, seeking the very thing Daphne was hoping to find.

"Bring the key," Daphne said, firm. "And backup."

THE LAST call had just bleeped across the museum's speaker system right when Daphne rushed in through the sliding doors. In their reflection she caught the two men behind her slowing down at the museum's entrance, uncertainty freezing them in place. A young Asian American woman wearing that custom museum vest stood behind the front desk and smiled at Daphne through her braces. "I'm so sorry but we're not taking any more visitors."

"Ah." Daphne should have thought of that. She should have thought of any plan beyond showing up. But historians worked around the problem of time on a daily basis, so surely she could think of a convincing lie to keep her in the building. "I'm Professor Ouverture in the history department? My chair, Miranda Nurse, told me to meet her here, right by . . . Oh, shoot, I forget. Where do faculty store stuff here again?"

"Oh, you mean the lockers in the Schmetterling Library?"

Daphne did her best not to muffle out a yelp at what had been right before her very eyes. She didn't have to read much German to know that the Robert and Susan Schmetterling Library, dedicated to advancing scholarship in art history, translated into the Robert and Susan *Butterfly* Library in English. In French—*Papillon*.

"Y-yes," Daphne said. "The Schmetterling Library."

Of course at that moment Daphne's followers chose to enter the museum, the taller of the pair cradling a cell phone to his ear. In full view, they were more frightening than she'd let herself think about, all buzz cuts and mullets and tattoos and muscles meant for lifting chloroformed Black women professors off the ground and hauling them into car trunks. It took every muscle, tendon, and ligament in Daphne's body not to scream.

"Well, we don't want Professor Nurse waiting for you," the attendant was saying and Daphne barely registered it. "Just make sure to exit through the front doors when you're done."

It was time for Daphne to bolt. "Got it, tha—"

"Sirs," a security guard was saying. Daphne whipped her head around. "We're closed. Do you hear me? Closed. No, you can't—excuse me, sir!"

The man with the buzz cut and an elaborate neck tattoo shoved the security guard back, and the young girl with braces screamed. The guard slammed against a wall, stumbling, provoking a few other guests in the lobby to cry out—and recovered in time to pull out a taser. His assailant went down like a sack of potatoes. Daphne stood, frozen in place, her eyes locked on her other stalker—a reedy man with piercing black eyes, a cedar-brown mullet, and a sneer—as he stepped over his accomplice's body and began running straight to her.

Move, Daph.

But she was trapped like a mouse in front of a snake's hypnotic glare.

Daphne Aminata Ouverture, if he lays his hands on you he will kill you, do you hear me?

Run!

Daphne's mind floated above her body as she took off. She'd forgotten how ankles worked, how the balls of her feet touched the ground, that gravity existed and determined what she could do. She didn't know how she made it across the atrium and to the grand staircase, how she was leaping up the steps two at a time. She spotted a hiding spot in the distance. It wasn't much but it would buy her a few seconds to plan her own surprise.

Daphne dove behind a marble statue of Messalina, wife of the Roman emperor Claudius.

Silence fell. A pair of footsteps clacked against the polished stone floors, their echoes getting louder.

And louder.

The feet stopped on the other side of the statue.

It's now or never, Daph.

Biting her lip, she leapt out from behind the statue and threw her entire body weight against him. He whirled around, quick, whipping out a thick knife, its jagged blade made for skinning flesh and slicing through bone.

Daphne was faster. She stepped forward and kicked his hand like it was a soccer ball. He barked out a hoarse shout—and dropped the knife.

Daphne snatched it up and took off running again. She zipped up the smaller, adjacent flight of stairs like a Jamaican sprinter, knees high, hands cutting through the air. On the second floor she turned right and fled down a corridor, pausing briefly as she passed a room of Post-Impressionist paintings. To her alarm, a gaggle of students was straggling in front of Gauguin's Tahitian women, blocking the corridor.

"You have to get out of here," she gasped. She couldn't wait around to hear their complaints of a project deadline—she didn't have time.

She rushed down the hall, bursting through the doors that led to the Schmetterling Library Reading Room, where, as was to be expected, students and faculty alike were huddled over desks, uninterested in the passing of time. Her feet sank into the soft carpet. Daphne stared, panting, into the sunlight beaming through the room's floor-to-ceiling windows. Relief filled her lungs.

Long fingers curled around her shoulder.

She screamed.

The studious visitors looked up. At the sight of the knife in her hand, slashing the air in warning, and her attacker leaping out of the way, they gaped around in astonishment—and then bolted out of the room, sweeping notebooks and laptops to the floor in their wake.

"I know what you want," Daphne shouted, dodging the throngs of students rushing to the front door like a stampede of antelopes. An alarm blared through unseen speakers, and Daphne was dizzy, nauseous. "I'm not giving it to you."

The man's hatred for her radiated with each step he took in her direction while Daphne inched along a side wall, nearing the lockers she'd come here for—not like that mattered anymore, not with Sam's killer marching toward her. Her back scraped against the bookshelves while she searched for an exit, an escape, and her eyes began to water at the realization that there were none. She'd trapped herself in a corner with no way out. Her cold palm wiped away the tears pooling in her eyes.

While the man took slow, cautious steps toward her, angling for the best position to make his move, Daphne crawled along the sides of the wall, knees shaking, knife in hand, refusing to believe she might need to bleed someone with it, unable to see any alternatives. When her free hand touched the cold metal of a fire extinguisher, her heart soared.

He was two feet away, his glare pointed on the knife, hotter than hell's coals. "There's nothing you can say to get out of this. You're handing over that video."

He made a leap for her. Daphne dropped the knife and

curled all ten fingers around what she hoped was the handle of the extinguisher. She closed her eyes and swung.

Missed.

The extinguisher bounced off something hard.

Light droplets of water spattered on her shoulders.

Daphne cracked an eye open. Somehow she'd managed to smash the knob of a sprinkler system instead, activating all the room's sprinklers. Her attacker's face crinkled with confusion, then outrage, when the water began to soak through his shirt and jeans.

"That won't happen again," he assured her.

But the rage of Sam's betrayal rushed back to life, lighting the back of her eyes. She'd had enough of being at the center of a narrative that she hadn't written. She was determined to write the ending of her own damn story.

Daphne squeezed her fingers tight around the fire extinguisher. She crouched down and arched back her shoulders. "You bet your ass it won't."

He lunged.

She swung.

This time, the base of the extinguisher connected with his temple. The floor vibrated under his weight when he hit the ground, landing face down on the carpet.

Daphne gasped and dropped the extinguisher. She stood over the unconscious body of a man who'd wanted to hurt her—who'd wanted to *kill* her—feeling the cool water pelting her skin. The chaos outside became a distant hum. Her hands were shaking. She wanted to vomit. She wanted to roar.

A baritone voice reached her ears. "Daphne?"

Rowan. Rowan stood by the door. He stepped over the body and grabbed her shaking hands. She tipped her chin up. Her heart began to pound for a different reason at the look on his face—a mix of horror, curiosity, and naked desire.

It was the adrenaline, surely, that made her place her cold fingers on his flushed cheeks, that made her gaze into his eyes.

He leaned toward her, his expression a kaleidoscope of awe and need, and before she could second-guess herself, Daphne grabbed his collar, yanked him down, and crushed her lips against his, warm and sweet. She was pretty sure it was her idea to deepen the kiss; she was pretty sure it was his idea to push her up against the wall. His mouth dropped to the sensitive spot where her neck and shoulder met and Daphne groaned. She gazed up at the ceiling—apologizing to the painted fresco of erudite white men in togas scowling down at her from the heavens in disapproval—while Rowan pressed himself against her.

Daphne scooted her hips up. Rowan happily took on her weight, and her vision blurred. *On second thought*, Daphne said to herself, allowing her hands to roam Rowan's back while he planted more kisses on her neck, *Aristotle and his ilk can shove it*.

"What the hell?" came the scratchy sounds of a woman's voice.

"Daphne?" Jim called.

Rowan tore himself from her throat, and sadly, Daphne's feet touched the ground again. He stepped out in front of her to shield her from the onlookers gathering in the library doorway. *Ever the gentleman*. Daphne poked her head around his back to see a frowning Detective Ahmed. Only Jim's noisy cackles gave her a reprieve from the sounds of Ahmed's grumbles.

■　　■　　■

TWENTY MINUTES later, Daphne was wrapped in a towel, huddled up next to her father in the back of an ambulance, trying to stop her teeth from chattering. Detective Ahmed was still somewhere inside the Benson, most likely tagging and bagging the evidence Daphne had found for them. Daphne could hardly bear to look at Rowan, who had somehow become even more intoxicating to her, as he gave crisp replies to a young policeman. Every time he glanced in her direction they both blushed like teenagers at prom. A student snapped a photo of her from behind the line of police tape and Daphne scowled. Maybe it was just better to stare at her toes.

Only the confident march of Detective Ahmed could bring her upright again.

"Did you find the video? Was it in the Schmetterling Library?" Daphne asked.

"I'm not telling you shit, Ouverture," Ahmed snapped. "Do you know how foolishly you acted today? Do you know how completely dangerous that stunt was?"

Daphne's stomach landed somewhere down by her shoes. "I'm sorry, Detective."

Ahmed began ticking items off her fingers. "Endangering the lives of civilians around you—"

"The museum was closing—"

"—breaking into university property—"

"They *let* me in—"

"—obstructing a police investigation—"

"I was just trying to help!"

"—endangering the life of a police consultant."

Daphne was stunned. "Rowan?"

Ahmed raised an eyebrow. "Who else?"

"But he got here after I'd already knocked out that guy!"

"Are you going to be this feisty during the court case?"

"Yes!" Daphne found herself shouting. "Yes, I am!"

She shot back at the detective's gaze with her own defiant one. It lasted two seconds.

Jesus, it was like trying to stare into the eyes of a lion. Daphne inspected the dark laces of her shoes again.

"Well, good," Ahmed said. "Because we're gonna need it when we call you up to testify in court against your attacker."

Daphne whipped her head up to see a grin spreading on Ahmed's face.

"Do you mean—"

Ahmed pointed a finger at her. "I'm not telling you shit, Ouverture. But come down to the station after the medics have cleaned you up. We'll take your statement."

CHAPTER TWENTY-TWO

The interrogation room was wicked cold. Its fluorescent lighting, piercing and flat, did little to improve the six-by-eight space, nor did the thin metal chairs that everyone was subjected to sit on, Asma included. In fact, the only comfort from which Asma could draw was in the sight of the pair of disheveled, shabby men sitting across from her. Anthony Kenton's purplish face suggested he was still recuperating from the pounding the Benson Museum's marble floor had given him when he'd taken on the museum security guard and lost. To their own peril, people underestimated the sting tasers could deliver. Gavin Gray looked decidedly less wet and more vicious than when she'd found him lying in a heap on the plush carpet in the reading room, and she bit back a laugh at the realization that she had Daphne Ouverture, a teacher's pet's teacher's pet, to thank for his capture at all.

"Anthony Kenton and Gavin Gray, correct?" she asked.

There was nothing but the sound of the HVAC ticking away while it blew middling air across her perpetrators' necks.

"Kenton?" Asma repeated. "Gray? Both prison guards at Livingston Correctional Facility?"

Two faces sneered at her in silence.

She slid down in her chair. "I mean, you're right to just sit here and wait for your lawyer to show up. After all, what on earth is there that you could possibly say to us that we don't already know? We have you both down for multiple attempts on Daphne Ouverture's life. We got your buddy Jake Zimmerman in custody, too."

Anthony Kenton jerked away in alarm. Gavin Gray ground his teeth.

"You didn't know that, did you?" Asma said, her lips curving into a slow grin. "We tracked him down this afternoon. Poor guy's in rough shape, though, so we brought him to a hospital. With cops outside his room, of course."

Asma had combed through that week's police reports until she found what she'd been hunting for—a recent break-in at the East Calliope Animal Hospital, where a supply room had been ransacked. The security footage showed two men—one tall with a mullet, the other thick and beefy, wheezing in pain—razing the place before heading back to a blue pickup truck. A quick scan of the truck's license plate had revealed the truck belonged to one Mr. Jacob Zimmerman. They'd found him at home, lying in bed, sweating and delusional from the bullet wound in his shoulder, mumbling the kind of nonsense that only a fever could stoke. She'd been about to haul him in when Rowan had called her, frantic, and now here she was, her ass on a cold metal chair playing a new set of cards.

Asma tapped the spine of her notebook on the table. "So here's the deal. As much as it would please everyone to see you both serve time for your multiple attacks on Professor Ouverture's life, I'm actually here for something more important: the name of the person who hired you."

Anthony Kenton's gaze flickered to Gavin's for a split second, wary.

"Don't you fucking say anything," Gray spat.

Asma cocked her head to the side and turned down her lips

in mock disappointment. "Hm," she said. "Figured you'd say that. Look, it's not like I doubt that you're capable of master-minding this whole operation of abducting Professor Ouverture on your own but . . . actually, I do. A rotting houseplant's got more sense than either of you."

"Fuck you, bitch," Gray spat.

"Spare me. I've seen your records. For being prison guards, you've both got rap sheets longer than my arm—seriously, attacking your pregnant girlfriend, Gavin?—but all of your violent crimes have been personal up until now. I can't see either of you going after someone you don't know, let alone a profes-sor at a fancy place like Harrison. Which, again, leads me back to my original question: Who put you up to this?"

"Like we said earlier, we're saying nothing without our lawyer," Gray said, balling his fists tight. "Do you hear me? Nothing."

"'*We*'?" Asma said with a raised eyebrow. "'*Our*'? That's a lot of faith you have in each other. Well, whatever. Have it your way. You'll have plenty of time in your cells today to reconsider the nature of your relationship."

She smacked at the two-way glass with a flat palm and a rookie uniform came in to sweep them away.

ASMA GAVE it thirty minutes. That was enough time to run by a Chipotle, grab a burrito bowl with double meat, and grab Anthony Kenton from his holding cell again.

Kenton gave the greasy paper bag in Asma's hands a quiz-zical glance. "What's that for?"

Asma walked them back into the interview room again. "A thank-you present."

His wide face barely moved except for a brief lift of his forehead. "For what?"

"Your help."

His frown grew deep. "I haven't helped."

"Oh, you have," Asma replied, heading for the door. "More than you know."

Asma yanked a hissing Gavin Gray out of his cell down the hallway toward the booking station, making sure to glide him past the interview room where Anthony Kenton was gobbling up his burrito bowl under the looming shadow of a nervous junior cop.

Gray craned his neck around. "Why does he get food and I don't?"

"What does it look like?" Asma asked. "Your buddy ratted you out. Told us everything. The meal is our thank-you present to him for being such a thoughtful citizen."

"Bullshit," Gray scoffed.

But the twitch in his cheek betrayed him.

Asma sat him down and started the paperwork, taking her time scratching out in her unintelligible hand every detail she could think of. She stole a quick peek away from her stack of papers and smothered her smirk when she saw his face. Rats fleeing sinking ships looked less desperate.

Asma could have set her watch to his meltdown.

Gray cursed. "I knew that piece of shit wouldn't keep quiet. What do you want? I can tell you what you need to know."

Asma gave him a doubtful look. "We already have everything."

"Even Westmount's secret stash of cash? His bank statements? Tony doesn't know any of that. I have text messages. Emails. Proof."

Asma's pen paused in mid-air.

Andrew Westmount.

She'd needed him to say that name. Westmount was the man behind the embezzlement, Sam's murder, and harassing Daphne Ouverture. He'd sent those two after Sam and Daphne both, leading to Sam's death and Daphne's state of fear. And he'd pay for what he did, Asma would make sure of it. The thought sent a chill zipping down her spine. But she sure as shit wasn't going to let the man sitting across from her know that.

"Tony's talking about Sam's murder," she said. "Your part in it. How shit went down. What do you have to say about that?"

That puzzled Gray. "Murder? What the fuck is Tony talking about, the lying dickbag? I ain't got nothing to do with that shit." His face went ashen. "Sure, I beat him up, but what's that got do with him ending up dead? Look, what you want is to follow the money. Tony don't know nothing about the wads of cash that Westmount hid."

Once Gray started talking, it was impossible to shut him up. Between his testimony and their mountain of evidence, they had Westmount on so many charges his lawyer would be able to buy a second yacht on the legal fees from Westmount's case alone. That should have satisfied Asma. That it didn't was something she hoped to avoid thinking about until long after she'd gone home, kissed her boys goodnight, and crawled into bed. In the darkness, under covers, her husband's snores a comfort and a curse, the agony of truth would finally arrive. And then in the night's silence, she'd have no choice but to accept what her gut was telling her, to listen to the whispers of doubt feathering around her, telling her that she'd gotten Sam's murder very, very wrong.

CHAPTER TWENTY-THREE

Daphne drummed her fingers against her lips. Although she told herself that it was a sign of her deep concentration, it was, in actuality, because she wanted to feel if they were still warm from Rowan's lips. The taste of their mind-numbing kiss had faded from her tongue hours ago. But occasionally she thought she could still feel the ghost of it tingling against her lips.

Rowan needed to eat more. Daphne frowned at this revelation. His arms were too slender for any West African woman's comfort. Daphne's mother would be outraged by his bony chest, the too-trim waist. Fabiola would demand that he eat in front of her, suspiciously inspecting every bite. But would he like Ivorian food? What if he didn't eat fish? But everybody liked rice, right? And who could say no to perfectly fried plantains?

"And that's how I found myself transporting a dozen eagles in first class," Jim was saying to a few cops in uniform huddled around him by the front desk and they burst out laughing.

Her dad, an elbow propped up against the front desk, winked at the flustered receptionist and Daphne looked up to the heavens for help. Maybe a saint could heal her bruised back, too, while they were at it, since she'd injured it in the name of catching a killer and that had to count as good works, right? Honestly, Daphne just wanted to give her report and go home.

Relief, albeit exhausted relief, had finally crashed its waves through her body earlier, while she watched the men who'd wanted to abduct her get handcuffed.

She tried to gently coax Jim back to his seat.

A lost cause.

Jim launched into another tall tale—about that time when he met up with ▮▮▮▮▮ in ▮▮▮▮▮ and they ▮▮▮▮▮ and saved ▮▮▮▮ from ▮▮▮▮▮—and rather than stay planted in her seat to endure the same jokes she'd heard since she was a teenager, Daphne decided to poke around the building. *To better understand eighties architectural design*, she told herself, slipping past the front desk and softly padding down a long narrow hallway. *Yes, that's it. No other reason at all.*

A turn around the corner and—there Rowan stood, lost in thought, almost as if waiting for her. That familiar scent of ivory soap filled her nose. She pressed her palms against his chest and shoved. Into a dark storage closet the two of them tumbled.

"We may have to discuss how you developed such violent reflexes," Rowan murmured, wrapping her in his arms and pulling her close. Under his amused gray eyes, whatever defenses Daphne had erected were knocked down like a wobbly bookcase.

They took their time, hiding in the dim blue lighting among toilet paper rolls and antibacterial cleaner, exploring lips, teeth, tongues, smoothing hands over warm skin until she was drunk from his touch. He nipped his way down to the base of her throat before swooping up again to meet her lips. She groaned. It was so easy, too easy, to keep tasting him—like he was her favorite bottle of Bordeaux—until she was flushed, intoxicated. She was one nip away from unbuttoning his shirt when her last two remaining brain cells registered that there was movement outside the closet door.

"Rowan?"

He gasped for air. "Yes?"

He had the look of a starving wolf who had only just begun to feast on his prey. Daphne tried so hard not to succumb to the heat of his gaze. Not to sweep back that curl of hair that had fallen onto his forehead.

"Oh, screw it," she mumbled.

He broached the distance between them and crushed his lips to hers. Their hands were a flurry, frantic for each other's backs, caressing jaws, tickling napes of necks, and grasping waists, and Daphne felt something mend itself in her heart, a little crack that had appeared sometime after her fourteenth date, when she had started to give up on finding anything that might resemble what her parents shared.

Daphne had chosen an unadventurous life surrounded by books, old pieces of paper, actions that had taken place only on the page. And while she still loved much of that life, she just hadn't foreseen that stability and loneliness were sometimes best friends. Braided together, they had formed a dull ache in her chest that she'd never been able to shake, no matter how much time she'd spent pursuing her PhD or teaching classes. But the ache had disappeared. And older, hidden parts of herself had come tumbling out. She'd found them in her search for *Papillon*, and she had been astonished to discover how much she liked these shiny uncut gems. Daphne's heart swelled while she breathed in the scent of Rowan, and a vow formed in the darkness: to never let those pieces of herself get buried ever again.

"I want a do-over," Daphne said, pressing her palms against Rowan's stubbled cheeks. "Do you want to come over to my place later? For dinner with me and Chloe?"

He seized her hands mid-motion and kissed them. A crown of toilet paper rolls formed a halo around his head. "I would love that. When shall I stop by?"

Tonight, Daphne wanted to yell, but the realities of where she was and what her life had been like lately came crashing back. "Can I let you know? I should talk to Detective Ahmed first."

"Wise plan," Rowan said, a small grin forming that Daphne wanted to kiss away. "When the time is right, you know where to find me."

Daphne slipped out of the supply closet a few minutes later behind Rowan—clothes straightened, braids patted down.

"There you are, Strawberry Shortcake," said Jim, leaning on the wall right next to the storage closet. His beam was on the verge of becoming a smug grin. "Ready to give your statement?"

DETECTIVE AHMED'S office was surprisingly cheerful, considering that the woman was as comforting as a metal scouring pad. But the space she'd set up for herself was pleasant and even cozy, with framed photos on her desk of her with an absurdly handsome man and three young boys, a lovely Turkish carpet on the floor, and some steaming mint tea in tiny, ornate silver cups for pouring. On the wall was another framed picture, this time of a woman who Daphne instantly recognized as Asma's sister, bearing a sleek, black hijab, bright red lipstick, dancing hazel eyes, and a smile promising sass and collusion.

Daphne would have asked about her, but Detective Ahmed looked too tired to handle much else other than the investigation. The bags under her eyes were dark enough to frighten a racoon, and Daphne wondered when this woman had last slept.

Working a murder beat in a town like Calliope where everyone thought they knew better than you couldn't be easy.

"Time for my statement?" Daphne asked, taking a seat across from Ahmed's desk.

The detective nodded. "But before we get started, I wanted to show you something. Fair warning—it's hard to watch. You up for it?"

"I want to see it," Daphne said.

Detective Ahmed swirled the computer monitor around. Daphne watched the beginning frames of a video, quite shaky, its pixelation of poor quality. Daphne could make out some sort of locker room or set of showers, each one tiled in faded blue with a drain underneath where water was meant to flow. But Daphne saw only the deep red hue of blood from where Joey Camden lay, his fight against the two men who'd trailed Daphne to the art museum in vain. In the corner, a handsome face with cold blue eyes and silvery blond hair, blurred but familiar, stared at the scene impassively.

Daphne's heart stopped. "I recognize that man."

That got Detective Ahmed's attention. "You do?"

"He was at Sam's memorial," Daphne said. "He was staring at me. It gave me the creeps."

"His name is Andrew Westmount," Detective Ahmed said. "He's the director of Livington Prison. We think he had two prison guards at Livington—Gavin Gray and Anthony Kenton—kill Joey Camden for smuggling documents to Sam Taylor."

"Have they—" Daphne's voice hitched. "Have they said anything? About attacking me?"

"They admitted that Westmount hired them to follow you," Detective Ahmed said. "He's being arrested as we speak. And now we've got hard evidence against Westmount and the men who killed Sam. Thanks to you and the video you found."

Tears sprang up in Daphne's eyes. Relief flooded her body while she cried, sobbing harder while Detective Ahmed rubbed her arm and made soothing noises at her like Daphne was a kitten in distress. She hadn't known how much she'd needed to *know*. She hadn't known how starved she'd been for understanding, for empathy, for people to recognize that her truth *was* the truth.

Not for the last time, Daphne cursed out Sam in her mind. If only he had turned that video over to the police as soon as he'd received it, if only he'd done the right thing in the first place by making it public. Sam Taylor might have wanted justice for Joey Camden, sure, but he wanted that byline in the *New York Times* more.

The detective was a fast writer and sharp thinker while she peppered Daphne with questions about her trip to the Benson Art Museum, her search for the video, her attempts to thwart those prison guards who'd tried to take her down. By the end of it, the detective was still tired but a slight grin ghosted the corners of her lips.

"I think that's a wrap. But, Professor?" Detective Ahmed said. "You did good out there."

At Detective Ahmed's small smile, Daphne rubbed away the last few tears on her face with her sleeve. "Thanks."

Detective Ahmed grunted. "It's time for you to get some rest. Go home to your bed and to your dog and to your very suspicious father. You've earned a nap."

CHAPTER TWENTY-FOUR

"But we must *de*-scribe in order to *re*-inscribe the positionalities of the actors themselves to study the materialist affect that our metaphysical post-realities produce or even *re*-produce if we are ever to interrogate the post-social heterogenous constructs that manifest in what Habermas bravely called the 'Alltag.'"

Olaf the postdoc was speaking to a crowd of concerned academics and Daphne once again questioned her life choices.

It was the monthly history department-wide faculty meeting, where fifty professors with absolutely no training in running meetings came together to, well, run a meeting. That was a tough enough task under normal circumstances, but it was made worse whenever the critical theory contingent decided to weigh in on matters.

"For how else are we to counter the androcentric gaze if not by attacking the biopolitics under which and *for* which and *by* which it assumes and even *re*sumes that which cannot be nor *must* be understood as a resistance to . . ."

Daphne willed her eyes to stay open, a challenge made excruciatingly more complicated by whoever in the department had decided to dim the lights to a faint glow. At least she no longer yearned to pop open a dating app on her phone. Not like she knew what, exactly, her relationship with Rowan was, but that was what her future dinner with Rowan was for, whenever that happened. Daphne straightened out her spine and gave her most thoughtful expression to Olaf who was talking about . . . what was he talking about again?

"Such cataclysmic thinking speaks to both the commodification of our natural world and also to the *re*pressive tolerance and *op*pressive force of corporate structures under which the nearly rhizomatic discourse of environmental destruction appears ever-fluid and changing yet unstoppable," he said to his colleagues. Daphne nodded along with them in the hopes of appearing knowledgeable on whatever it was he was saying. Which was about . . . no, seriously, what *was* Olaf saying?

Miranda frowned. "Olaf, dear, does this mean you're against our switch to using recycled toilet paper in the bathrooms or not?"

And once again, Daphne thanked the gods of academia that Miranda had plucked her job application from the maw and insisted on interviewing her for the position of assistant professor of French history. With each meeting, Miranda held the center together, fielding questions and posing others right back, keeping the early modern Russianist from accidentally hijacking the conversation through her recollection of Moscow city council's procedural meetings in 1710 or reminding the critical theorists not to use "bricolage" as a colloquialism.

Honestly, Daphne didn't know how the history department had managed to survive before Miranda's ascension. While her reign was only two years old, in that time Miranda had managed to push through five hires, increase student enrollment in history classes, and balance out a budget that had drawn a deficit after the department had overshot their target admissions number for incoming PhD students.

Daphne longed for a world in which Miranda's political savvy and acute administrative skills could be unleashed upon the world. Because it was truly bizarre to her that in the course of one summer, most most academics were expected to evolve from students writing dissertations into management professionals who understood budgetary spreadsheets. To her mind it was irresponsible to have faculty—who'd spent their entire graduate careers learning how to read ancient Egyptian papyri or studying the gender politics of precolonial West African urban life—receive no training on book balancing, on Robert's Rules, on university policy yet be expected to somehow govern themselves in a responsible manner. Other than Miranda, Daphne had yet to see anyone accomplish this task with something akin to competency.

"Nonetheless," Olaf insisted, "what if our overreliance on and addiction to ecological imperialist methodologies was subject to a *de*-territorialization instead of a *re*-territorialization so that—"

"Anyone else have a question?" Miranda asked, her voice too bright and sharp. "Anyone?"

Daphne glanced at the clock and began to reach for her bag—only a few minutes were left before the meeting had to adjourn—wincing a little at the irony that her students did the same thing to her at the end of class every day. At least she wasn't the only one itching to leave, judging by the scratching of seats against carpet as people lifted themselves out of their chairs.

"One last thing before we go," Miranda called out to the unsettled crowd. "Not only are we a department of award-winning scholars and gifted teachers, it also turns out that we have a sleuth in our midst."

Heat flooded Daphne's wide cheeks as fifty pairs of eyes turned to her.

"Now I know that you all saw the news about the Benson Museum incident in today's *Harrisonian*, along with the article about the malfeasance at Livington Prison but please allow me to boast anyway." Miranda's beam was oh so proud. "Not only has our new assistant professor of French history almost completed her first year at Harrison to great success, she's also managed to locate the missing exposé of Sam Taylor, may he rest in peace."

A few colleagues murmured at that, and Daphne did her best not to frown at their reverence for Sam. It's not like they'd known he'd been a creepy leech.

"So here's to Daphne Ouverture," Miranda said, gesturing with her hand for Daphne to stand. "It's not every day that a historian exposes a conspiracy of theft and murder, but Daphne Ouverture did just that—all while grading, to boot!"

The room erupted into laughter while Daphne stood there, blushing furiously. All she wanted was to be buried six feet under like the people she studied. The sticky feeling of being dragged into his story without her consent clung to her skin.

Miranda grinned. "Congratulations to us all for having the good fortune to hire such an extraordinary colleague."

After the meeting, Daphne smiled tight while she packed up her bag and took a few pats on the back and handshakes from colleagues who'd interrogated her about the complexities of defining Blackness as a racial category in eighteenth century Europe during her job interview. She burst out of the conference room as soon as she could and headed out of Davis Hall, desperate to pick up Chloe and relax at home.

On the pathway to the campus parking deck, Daphne dodged bickering squirrels and a couple of curious stares from students and faculty alike, which she tried not to interpret. In the cool April air, hugging her thin coat tight, she tried not to resent how far and wide that *Harrisonian* article had spread already. It was only a matter of time before everyone found out that she'd stopped Sam's killer but it was still weird to be noticed for anything other than good teaching or excellent research.

After a long afternoon walk with Chloe, Daphne came home, pecked her dad on the cheek, then trudged up the stairs to her home office to fiddle with her PowerPoint slides for class the next day. Her French Empire class would be studying French tourism tomorrow, a topic that she usually enjoyed introducing to students, mostly to see them giggle at photos of vintage bikinis on the French Riviera. But she couldn't quite concentrate.

It took a little bit to uncover what she was really thinking about instead of vintage French suntanning advertisements. But then the memory of her colleagues applauding her for finding Sam's killer floated up again and she felt itchy.

Unhappy.

Dissatisfied.

Why?

She twirled a purple pen around at her desk. By all rights, she had every reason to feel something like peace, with the men of Livington Prison behind bars for attacking her and Detective Ahmed handling the rest. Her mind flicked over to Sam Taylor. The story of Sam's life and death—*how* it was being told—still grated against her skin.

The problem for Daphne was the same one that vexed all historians: context. Making sense of the past, contextualizing previous lives, was necessary and difficult work but satisfying if you could get it right. How you explained the origins and causes of the French Revolution came down to how you wove together the pieces of evidence left behind, how you threaded together the ideologies, social realities, material hardships, and cultural practices of a people, place, and time to reach some sort of deeper meaning. Shoot, even factors that some might find minor—how crops were faring, if the weather was rainy, if a dog had been let loose onto the duke's grounds—could have a domino effect on a historical moment if the conditions were right. History taught Daphne that there was a reason why most social protests occurred in sunny warmer months, for example, than in the cold dark days of winter. The past, Daphne believed, could occasionally be divined like tea leaves to bring revelations and even the truth.

Daphne firmly believed that most people died as they lived. And Sam Taylor had not led an honorable life. Sure, there were many instances of terrible deaths that could never be fully explained or avenged, no matter how much historians tried. So many faultless people had died in genocides, as victims of war or famine, their painful deaths exacerbated by the societies and states under which they had lived. But far more often than not, a French farmer died a French farmer. A mother died in child-birth. A French aristocrat died of gout.

A professor who was a creepy lurker had also died as one.

Sam's murder was about to be wrapped up in a tidy bow. But Sam Taylor's life was a palimpsest where violence gleamed through the praise people extolled.

It wasn't that Daphne believed that the police had locked up the wrong men in jail. They'd hunted down Daphne and deserved to be punished for it. She deserved to leave her house without worrying that someone was out to get her. She'd seen Westmount in that video. The image of his fixed stare, the very picture of an abuse of power, sent a cold drip down her spine. She just wondered if their actions alone could explain Sam's last hours on this planet. What if Sam had died as he'd *really* lived?

Daphne blew out a gust of air.

It was preposterous to believe that Sam's killer was still walking around campus or visiting a coffee shop in downtown Calliope. But even more intoxicating was the question Daphne wished to pose: What if Sam's death had nothing to do with his work as a prison abolitionist? What if he had been killed for some other, darker reason?

She didn't know the answer to that question. But, she realized, she needed to. Solving that question was becoming more important than accepting the mismatched and incomplete array of facts before her, because that was not only her chosen profession but also her calling. And one of the most glaring facts staring before her was his relationship with female students.

Daphne set down her pen. Years ago, when she had first applied for PhD programs, she'd become obsessed with Grad-Chat, a website where PhD hopefuls gossiped about admissions rates at Ivies and how to get into Berkeley or Michigan. While some of the information on the site was useful—admissions decisions, financial aid packages, which program was the better fit for French history—some tidbits out there were . . . well, it was hard to see them as anything other than gossip. "PhD student Daphne" avoided anything to do with gossip, slander, or rumor. But the Daphne who'd just survived an abduction no longer felt the same.

She opened her laptop.

A few clicks later, she was both relieved and disappointed

to see GradChat still going strong, if only because she'd hoped student anxieties about academia had abated. Fat chance. She typed "Sam Taylor" into the search engine and found a rainfall of gossip about his murder. A few prospective students asked around for other potential advisers for their PhD now that Sam was out of commission. With Sam's murder dominating the pages, Daphne was going to have to think more creatively to find evidence of his crimes.

The second time around, she typed in "Harrison" and "harassment." And got over two hundred results.

Her frown was taut by the time she'd finished reading the results, which ranged from queer students trying to find safe programs to study biology to another student professing to share a "mutual attraction" with a professor. She fiddled with the advanced search until she struck gold. Her stomach flipped.

THREAD: SERIAL HARASSER AT HARRISON

AnthroFemmeBot 101: Avoid the anthropology program if you want to have a career. Young hotshot prof kept sending me dick pics. I reported it to the chair and got stonewalled. Dropped out last year and I'm finally gaining my sanity back.

GinaContina02: I know exactly who you're talking about and I completely agree. Just got my acceptance letter to a different program. It's not as "good" but if it means I'll be safe then it's worth it to switch.

PollyPocketPhilosophy: I wish someone had told me that before I'd accepted the offer . . .

MimosasForBrunch: Why the fuck do these places keep letting shitty men stay in charge? If students are dropping like flies from a PhD program, that says more about the program than it does about the students! And I swear to Christ if one of you motherfuckers says "not all men" . . .

BioChem4Lyfe: "Not all men."

MimosasForBrunch: I'm going to find your home address and beat you to death with your own severed limb, BioChem.

BioChem4Lyfe: Not all men.

MimosasForBrunch: Fuck you and the horse you rode on.

[Moderators have closed the thread for violating civil discussion rules.]

Daphne pushed her laptop away, fighting back a lump in her throat. She needed a nap. She needed a hug. She needed a blanket. Reading what had been there in plain sight this whole time had crushed her spirit. Students had given up their dreams because of Sam Taylor. They'd come to Harrison with so much hope, only to watch their dreams dissolve to bitter ash.

How do you make a dead man pay?

She'd asked herself that question once, right after Detective Ahmed had handed her a set of photos that had burned Daphne's quiet life to the ground. Smothered between Sadie and Elise, the hurt of it all a sharp knife, she'd vowed to punish him for inserting himself in her life unasked. The question blossomed up again, acrid and sweet. There was no right answer to it, let alone a singular one.

So Daph, she asked herself again, *how do you want to make him pay?*

By uncovering each and every one of his secrets.

CHAPTER TWENTY-FIVE

"So you're telling me that the company that made the Michelin Man—who is quite literally that creepy over-sized marshmallow that the Ghostbusters blew up—is also the same company that tells us which fancy restaurants to eat at?"

Aspen sat in the front row of Daphne's classroom (because of course they did), viewing Daphne's painstakingly crafted PowerPoint slides with deep skepticism etched into their usually smooth pale face.

Daphne was running on exhaust fumes, having burned all of her energy searching for the names of women Sam had harassed at Harrison. She'd started first with the anthropology PhD program's website, scouring it for female students whose names she could cross-reference against GradChat, and coming up short. She didn't have much to work with but as a specialist of the eighteenth century, Daphne was used to working with less. Running on something like instinct was an unscientific approach to finding the women Sam had harassed but sketching out character portraits remained a necessary component of historical contextualization.

No wonder she no longer had any gas in the tank. She managed a smile in Aspen's direction, sleep weighing down her eyelids. "Yup."

"Because of capitalism?" Aspen's question was more of a statement.

"To sell car tires, yes," Daphne said.

Rohit raised a bony arm to interject. "And colonialism."

"That, too," Daphne agreed. Rohit puffed out his tiny chest with pride. "They'd introduced guides to North Africa by 1907 and were also very well known for their maps that charted colonial holdings for the metropole to explore."

Aspen appeared lost in thought. "History really is stranger than fiction."

"But how about we take a moment to consider other ways that colonialism and capitalism have historically been tied together," Daphne said. "With the last couple minutes of class, I want you to form small groups and brainstorm together a list of resources that only existed outside of Europe that Europeans relied on for everything from transportation and infrastructure to basic consumption. And how about one group googles around for popular products today like Palmolive soap and examines where their ingredients come from?"

Daphne was finally free to release her students when the long arm of the clock landed at 2:50 P.M. The familiar stragglers hung around to ask questions, as always, or simply linger in her presence, which she found adorable if alarming. She'd learned to be a little less afraid of her students and the pedestal they insisted on putting her on, even if she worried every day she'd do something or say something to get knocked off of it. It was just a matter of time, she figured, before one kid would decide flat out that they didn't like her and that there was nothing she could do about it.

Daphne waved goodbye, answered the usual questions, and slid her laptop in her bag. Usually, Rohit, Aspen, and Tabitha shifted impatiently in line while a Connor asked when the next paper was due but this time her trio formed a small semicircle around her, boxing her in to the podium where she lectured.

"Um, hi guys," Daphne said, taking a step back toward the whiteboard. "What's up?"

"Professor Ouverture, are you okay?" Rohit asked, his eyes wide. "We saw the news."

Heat flushed from Daphne's neck up to her cheeks at the three pairs of eyes pinned on her with concern. "Ah."

Tabitha surprised everyone by reaching over to rope Daphne into a tight hug. "The way this university tries to kill Black women on the daily. Professor Ouverture, I swear to God it's amazing you're still standing."

"Thanks for your concern," Daphne squeezed out between smooshed lips. "But I promise I'm okay."

Aspen patted Daphne on the back. "Good. Just don't go dying before we turn in our final papers. I'm going to need your feedback on my analysis of French soldiers seeking out gay sex in the colonies during WWI."

Fortified by her students' love and the bright blue April sky, Daphne arrived at her office, ready to resume her investigation into Sam's behavior. She chose to focus on university policies and faculty handbooks, sifting through hundreds of pages of legalese on sexual harassment and fraternization while blasting Afropop hits through her headphones. Each document was boring as hell and she sure wasn't going to find a student complaint in them, but she needed to familiarize herself with not only fraternization policies but also how Harrison University handled criminal offenses committed by faculty, if only to figure out how students who reported their attacks could have been ignored.

Because there was one middle-aged administrator who

Daphne suspected had known exactly who Sam had been and had refused to do anything about it: Ken Miller. That Patagonia sweater hid a multitude of sins. As the anthropology chair, Ken Miller had refused to do anything when the women Sam had abused had come to him, women who were most likely terrified and fearing that they wouldn't be heard.

Those women had been right.

Daphne wasn't sure if Ken's smothering of their claims was because of cowardice, pride, misogyny or all three wrapped up in an ugly bow but she no longer cared. He was never to be trusted.

Which meant that his reactions to Daphne's chat with Olivia Vail weren't to be trusted, either. He hadn't wanted Daphne to back off at the memorial because the Vail family was powerful. He wanted Daphne to stop talking to Olivia because she'd been sleeping with Sam, a known violation of university policy which neither Sam nor Ken had done anything about. Ken was covering his ass, plain and simple.

"Daphne, dear."

Miranda Nurse leaned against Daphne's doorway. Daphne's skin prickled in alarm. Miranda might normally appear like a frail older woman to outsiders, but one look at her in action and anyone could see that Miranda had enough energy to power a nuclear plant. An avid tennis player, swimmer, and a wrangler of three dogs herself, Miranda usually defined what it meant to age well.

But a light had been snuffed out of Miranda's eagle-sharp eyes. As she sat down across from Daphne, her shoulders drooped.

Daphne instantly reached over to grab Miranda's arm. "Are you okay?"

Miranda snorted. She croaked out a "no" and attempted something like a smile, exposing deep wrinkles around her eyes.

"Can I help with anything?" Daphne asked.

"As a matter of fact," Miranda said, sighing, "you can. Daphne, I'd like to write you a letter of recommendation for the job market."

Whatever it was that Daphne'd expected Miranda to say, it hadn't been that. "What?"

"You heard me," Miranda said. She turned to Daphne, her gaze sharp. "I've got an in at a few places and I'm setting up some interviews for you before the school year ends."

"But why would you—"

"It's the only way to save you," Miranda said.

"I don't under—"

"Ken's our new dean."

Daphne's office tilted on its axis. The air turned frigid. "But—"

"They're going to announce it by the end of the week," Miranda said. "And because he uncovered my plan to bring charges, he's already let me know that our department's going to pay the price for trying to prevent his ascension, beginning with my replacement."

Daphne's face went numb. "He can't do this. I'll talk to some of our senior colleagues. We'll fight this."

"Absolutely not." For a split second Daphne recognized the fiery woman who'd hired her. "That'll just give him more targets. We need to survive this deanship as a department as best as we can. Those of us who have tenure can weather this storm but you can't. I only have a few days left as chair, Daphne. Can you let me protect you while I still can?"

The tears in Daphne's eyes mirrored Miranda's own.

Together they used up the box of tissues that Daphne had bought for students, never realizing that she might need them for herself.

THE BORDEAUX in Daphne's hand was heavy. Its deep red hue, slick against the walls of her wine glass, usually brought Daphne comfort after a long day of teaching. There was something to sommeliers' claims that you could taste the soil, the region from which the grapes had been tended, and the notion that Daphne could be quickly transported to France just by one small sip of wine was a life raft that she clung to on dark days. It wasn't that Daphne wanted to live in France forever— after such a nomadic life she couldn't imagine living anywhere forever—but she needed to feel France on her fingertips at a moment's notice, if only to remind herself that she hadn't boxed herself in. It usually worked. Miranda's announcement had dulled her senses. It turned out that Daphne had found a fear worse than being trapped. Being kicked out.

"The taxi's here!" Jim called out.

"Dad, they're called Ubers these days," Daphne corrected as Jim lugged his suitcase down the stairs over Chloe's most vocal objections. Daphne took a sip of her Bordeaux to coat her clogging throat as Jim reached for his coat.

"You can call them Mr. Potato Heads for all I give a hoot," Jim said. "All I know is that a car and driver are outside ready to take me to the airport. You gonna give your old man a good-bye hug or what?"

Daphne shuffled up out of her seat in front of the TV and toward the front door and smothered him tight, enjoying for the last time that familiar scent of detergent and Old Spice that had existed since she was in the womb.

She didn't want him to go. Everyone who loved and protected her in Calliope would soon be gone—not only Jim but Miranda, too. She would be alone, something that she used to enjoy but was coming to resent. Alone with her thoughts, alone with the mess of Sam's life to contend with, alone without allies to steer her right. She might not even be employed at Harrison soon.

Her question came out muffled against Jim's neck. "Do you really have to leave for Philly to go see Mom and Antoine and everybody? Can't you just stay here forever?"

She felt his grin on her cheek. "Wish I could, pumpkin, but somebody's gotta make sure your mother doesn't kidnap her new grandson away from his parents."

"Antoine and Jessie can always make another."

"Your mother would just take that one, too."

"Hmpf."

Jim pulled away and patted her on the back. "I'm so proud of you."

"Dad." Daphne sniffled into the arm of her fuzzy house robe.

"I mean it, Daphne," Jim said. It was serious when Jim used a name for her that wasn't a baked good, a tiny animal, or some kind of sweetening agent. "You've got a good life here as a professor and you're gonna write that book on France that your mother will make everybody read."

"Hmpf," she repeated.

"And while you're flexing your scholarly muscles here at Harrison, you also got your other skills to get you through tough times. You can do *anything* you set your mind to, pancake."

Daphne considered her father's words. He might be leaving her but maybe she wasn't alone if she had herself to rely on. As an academic historian, Daphne might be the odd duck in her family but that wasn't a weakness. It was a strength. She was used to investigating whatever she wanted to on her own terms and in her own way. And shoot, she was good at it.

"You know what?" Daphne replied. "I think I really can do anything I set my mind to."

"Look at that!" Jim said, his smile so bright it competed against her living room floor lamp. "Never underestimate an Ouverture, baby, that's what I always say."

Daphne laughed. "Dad, that is a super-sinister saying. It's like the motto, 'A Lannister always pays his debts.'"

"A who?"

"Never mind."

A sliver of insecurity slipped into Daphne's consciousness.

"I can still be a little afraid sometimes, though," Daphne finally admitted.

"Afraid of what?" he asked.

She shrugged. "The usual: failure."

But Jim wasn't buying that. "You know, after all this time, I'm still surprised that you think I don't know you from your great aunt Hattie."

Confusion and amusement tugged at Daphne's lips. "Aren't you the one always going around telling everybody that we look alike?"

"You do—it's uncanny. Genes are a funny thing. But that's not what I meant. Being afraid to fail isn't your problem, candy cane. Never has been."

She glared at him. "Oh? If you know me so well, what *am* I afraid of, then?"

Jim's grin was cheeky. "Same thing you've been afraid of since you were old enough to finally beat your brothers at boules. You're not afraid to fail, honey. You're afraid to *win*."

As Daphne waved goodbye to her dad, the promise she'd made in the police station janitor's closet bloomed into a vow: she was ready to unleash all of those older, buried pieces of herself, to sharpen them to fine points so that they could pierce like sabers.

Miranda had said once that the past taught everyone that men could get away with anything. But the present was a state of constant change, where nothing was certain and anything was possible. That was the hope, the faith, the belief that Daphne instilled in her students. The past may have already been written, but the future?

Daphne balled her fingers into tight fists.

She was going to write that for herself.

CHAPTER TWENTY-SIX

The opulence of Gordon Hall's east wing grew dimmer the farther Daphne trudged her way up the winding staircase to the dean's office. She usually loved a good medieval tapestry or two, and *The Ogre of Fallacy*, an Art Deco stained-glass window depicting a gleaming, well-armored knight felling a three-armed monster, was wacky enough to make students giggle. The bright chandeliers that swung above might as well have been blackout bulbs for all they did to settle Daphne's nerves.

After a few deep breaths and a prayer to Saint Dymphna, Daphne blinked up at the domed gilded ceiling, waiting for her appointment with Ken Miller to begin.

She had a plan.

Everything would be fine.

She knew what she was doing.

It was just like riding a bike. Yup, like riding a napalm-covered bike speeding down a mine-studded highway at eighty miles an hour. In a hurricane. What could go wrong? Other than getting caught and losing her job and losing her friends and becoming a homeless outcast walking around downtown Calliope with a shopping cart full of chocolate lab puppies.

On second thought, was there any way out of this plan?

Of course Ken Miller had to come in just that moment and squash any good cheer she was trying to muster.

"Tiffan—Daphne!" Ken corrected himself just in time. He wagged a finger at her for it as if she'd caused the mix-up.

Yes, that was a very clever trick I played on you, keeping the same name I've had since birth. Daphne swallowed her snipe and beamed until her cheeks dimpled while she followed him into his office and took a seat across from him at his desk.

Ken leaned back in his throne, stretched out his arms, and snaked his fingers across the back of his head. "I take it you've heard that I've accepted the position as dean of the College."

It almost killed Daphne to choke the word out. "Congratulations."

"Why, thank you." Ken flashed bright teeth. "You here to talk about my proposition?"

"Yes," Daphne said, whooshing out a breath of air. "I've decided that I will testify on your behalf in Kiki's plagiarism case."

"Excellent move." That grin of his needed a good punching. "I knew you'd make the right decision. That makes you one of the rare good ones in your department."

Daphne harnessed her rage into a bright smile.

"Thank you," she said out loud, saying something far nastier to him in her mind. "But if I'm going to do this I'd like to get something out of it, too. Is it possible to receive a raise for next academic year? Is there a way to negotiate on salary and teaching? And on my research budget?"

"Uh . . ." Ken blinked. He lowered his arms. "We can certainly talk about that in the future."

"Could we please talk about it now?" Daphne replied.

Ken frowned. "I don't . . . I don't have that information on hand."

"Okay, but you do have boilerplate figures for junior

professors in the humanities, right?" Daphne pushed. "Could I see what one might look like?"

"Sure, I can email—"

"Can I have it printed?" Daphne asked.

For a second, however brief, irritation and suspicion flickered across Ken's face. But the excitement of having Daphne lie in front of the board on academic misconduct won him over. "Of course. My secretary will print it out for you right now. Anything else I can help you with?"

He slipped that last phrase in while standing up for her to leave.

"Actually," Daphne said, "I'm looking for this one chapter in an edited volume on local economic exchange in central African communities that formed around coffee. It's out of print. And the library's lost a copy, but I thought you might have it."

"By Fiona Viccenzi?" The light came back into Ken's eyes. "I was part of that book years ago. It started out as a conference in London. I haven't unpacked all of my books in here yet, so it's in a box down the hall. Can you give me a minute to go grab it?"

It's what I'm counting on, Daphne wanted to say while he shot out of his seat. As a backup solution, Daphne had looked up his publications and pinpointed the most obscure and inaccessible book just for the opportunity to get him lost in his own office suite and buy her a solid three minutes to search.

All she needed was his phone.

She yanked out Ken's messenger bag and rummaged through it, shoving aside pens, gloves, and a tube of chapstick.

No dice.

Sliding around his desk, she quietly pulled open drawers to peep inside, finding nothing. The bookcases were messy but searchable enough that she would have found Ken's phone if it was lying somewhere.

Footsteps from down the hallway grew louder—

Daphne dove back into her seat in time for the door to open again.

"Found it." Ken's head popped up over the doorway like a puppet. "The secretary's making a copy right now."

Daphne stood up. "Thank you so much."

"That's the last request, right?" Ken joked, not really joking at all.

The pocket of his Patagonia sweater had a distinct, rectangular-shaped swell to it and Daphne cursed herself for not spotting it earlier. Her stomach lurched knowing there was only one way to grab it. She smiled anyway. "Of course."

It's now or never, Daph.

Meeting him in the front door, Daphne grabbed Ken around his waist and pulled him in for a hug. "Thank you so much for protecting me."

At first Ken was too shocked to move much against her tight grip. Quickly—far too quickly, in Daphne's opinion—he loosened his shoulders and returned her embrace. "Anything for a pretty colleague like yourself."

The shudders kept rolling off Daphne's back as she marched down the hallway, desperate to get the hell away from him, wishing for Ken to be struck down with food poisoning, a rare and incurable virus, and debilitating insomnia—all at once. Leaping down a flight of stairs as soon as she was out of sight, she found the room she'd sought out in advance just for this mission: an enormous conference room dedicated to Harrison's board of trustees, who only met in it once a quarter. It was here where she planned to work.

In Daphne's first semester at Harrison she'd discovered a Reddit thread, of all things, that listed all of the rooms on campus where a student could escape to for anything from an online therapy session to casual hookups. While she chose not to think too deeply about students' usages, she'd nonetheless tucked away their recommendations for the future, grateful to whichever senior had proudly boasted of using the board of trustees conference hall to play *Fortnite*.

Sitting at the end of the oval conference table, Daphne yanked open her laptop. Heading straight to her university email account, she logged out of it and began typing in Ken Miller's username. In news that surprised nobody, Sadie had been the one to find his password last night. It had taken only a phone call and Sadie mumbling to "hang on I know a person" and voilà, thirty minutes later, no questions asked, Daphne had the information she'd needed.

"But what about dual authentication?" Sadie had warned. "As soon as you try to log in to a university account, it's gonna ding on Ken's phone and ask for permission to continue."

"Let me worry about that," Daphne had replied.

In the empty conference room, Daphne pulled out Ken's phone from her coat pocket. On the streets of Paris, Daphne had spent hours as a young girl mastering the basics of tradecraft—how to tail, where to find dead drops, when to dry-clean—and developing, of course, her sticky fingers. It turned out she had a real gift for picking pockets, and while her skills were rusty from years of neglect, nicking Ken's phone was satisfying confirmation that her own past was never too far away.

Once inside Ken's email account, Daphne took her time searching, browsing his inbox, typing in people's names, and double-checking dates. She rummaged through his "trash" folder, well aware that many people forgot to click "empty" on that thing more often than not.

Daphne had been hoping for a few nuggets of gold in the mine, some ammunition to add to her arsenal for her fight against Ken and for her ongoing quest to uncover Sam's misdeeds. How naïve she'd been. What Daphne had uncovered wasn't a few stray bullets. It was a nuclear bomb.

She collected everything she could with the time that she had. Keeping a tab of his email account open, she closed her laptop and slipped out of the hallway, dropping Ken's phone to the ground so that it appeared as if it had been in plain sight all along and must have simply fallen out of his pocket.

Outside, the afternoon sun baked the stone buildings, warming up the cold spring air, and Daphne bathed in it. For Ken Miller, the trouble of finding his phone would soon be the least of his problems. In his fight against the history department, Ken Miller had just lost. And Daphne Ouverture, descendant of Haitian generals and Ivorian farmers, had won.

A WHILE later, Daphne waited for Miranda on the side lawn outside Davis Hall. A metallic sculpture of some kind on the side lawn glinted at her, its pointed angles dancing maliciously when the sun pierced through the trees, an illusion of glass being shattered in real time. Or of knives being forged. Its jagged metal shards, the length of Daphne's legs, were sharp enough to be a hazard to some inebriated partier during Rush Week. The work was better suited for a battlefield than a museum, pointing directly at the viewer like canons aimed at a row of soldiers. Something about the shattered sabers picked at her brain, and Daphne wondered if their familiarity to her was simply because she'd studied enough eighteenth-century weaponry or because of something else—something she couldn't remember quite yet.

"It's an odd statue of sorts, isn't it?"

Miranda took a seat next to Daphne on the bench, her face half hidden in the leaves' shadows. "Funny you should ask to meet in front of one of the Henderson family pieces. Called *The Sword of Judith*, I believe."

Daphne took that in. "A Henderson family member donated it?"

"No, created it," Miranda replied. "Melanie—the youngest Henderson—she sculpted it. She was always a wild child."

Daphne peeked at Miranda, curious. "She was?"

"I mean, I'm not much of one to gossip—"

Daphne snorted at that.

"—but let's just say Melanie had a reputation in her youth. You must have heard some of the stories, no? No matter. I suspect that's not what you wanted to chat about."

"Right." Daphne shifted. "I've been thinking about Ken."

"Then of course you're wincing like that," Miranda said. "Not like we should give him any more of our gray matter, but is there anything in particular he's done that's caused you to wish for a swift death to release you from your agony?"

"Actually, yes." Daphne swiveled her entire body in Miranda's direction, greatly aware of how her plus-size frame overpowered Miranda's spindly one. "I think Ken's covering up some of Sam Taylor's bad behavior."

That got Miranda's attention. "Go on."

Daphne regaled the story of Sam Taylor sleeping with Olivia Vail, his stalking, and her growing conviction that Sam had not died a hero's death, after all.

"Good heavens," Miranda whispered.

Daphne swallowed. "Yeah."

Daphne stared out into the distance. A student in a Harrison hoodie and shorts kept patting his legs, trying to convince a squirrel to jump into his sweatshirt.

"And so you're trying to find the students Sam may have harassed?" Miranda asked, pulling out a sheath of paper from her bag, which she handed to Daphne. "That's why you've asked me for his student rosters from the last two years?"

"Yes." Daphne's heart swelled with gratitude. "Thanks, Miranda."

"That might get you a more narrowed list of women but you might not be able to winnow it down beyond that," Miranda warned. "And you still have to consider if there are women he harassed who never took a class with him. I hate to say it, but the only person who can contextualize your data is probably Ken."

Daphne's stomach churned. "That's what I thought."

She reached inside her coat to retrieve a small USB stick shaped like a dog bone and handed it to Miranda. Every piece of evidence against Ken Miller, every shell of ammunition, was on that device.

"I need you to hold on to this for a few days," Daphne said, ignoring the pounding of her own heart. "When the time comes, I'll tell you what to do with it. Trust me?"

Miranda grinned. "With my life."

Ken Miller was going to regret the day he'd ever heard Daphne or Miranda's name. Cold, dark excitement shivered down Daphne's neck at the confrontation coming, eager for her hours of preparation to pay off.

"On another note," Miranda said, patting Daphne's arm,

"I've found you a new position. Stanford. Assistant professor in the history department."

"Already?" Shock flooded Daphne's core. "Miranda."

"Yes, it's on the other coast but it's an excellent position and they'd take you immediately. In fact, the chair almost hollered into his phone when I told him about you. As he should, because you're a wonder, Daphne, you truly are." Miranda peered at Daphne, an unusual mix of insecurity and hope etched into the soft wrinkles around her eyes. "You'll consider it, won't you?"

A pit hardened in Daphne's gut, a conviction that flooded her senses and molded her lips into a stubborn frown.

"I don't plan on going to Stanford, Miranda." Daphne made sure to hold Miranda's displeased stare. "I'm happy here. And I plan to stay here a good long while."

"I just want you to be safe," Miranda said. "Your situation here is too precarious."

But Daphne no longer saw her present and future in those terms. Unlike Miranda, she was reading the facts of her life against the grain, seeing another outcome emerge from them altogether.

"It's not, actually," Daphne said. "Not if I can do anything about it."

Again Miranda was silent. "If you turn Stanford down, you most likely won't receive an invitation from them again. They'll move on to someone else."

Daphne lifted her chin. "Fine by me. I'm staying."

Miranda's expression was unreadable. "I hope you know what you're doing."

What a pleasant surprise it was for Daphne to reply with assurance. "I do."

CHAPTER TWENTY-SEVEN

Daphne woke up to a cold wet nose on her arm again. She rolled over onto her back to find her favorite pair of soft brown eyes staring down at her.

Your sleep habits are beginning to be a problem, Chloe's gaze said.

"I'm sorry, baby," Daphne mumbled.

Heaving herself out of bed, she let out Chloe to pee and scratched at her box braids through her satin hair bonnet. While Chloe bounded around to chase a bunny through the meadow, a blur of shiny black fur, Daphne smacked her lips, yearning for coffee.

Chloe was right. Daphne had to fix her sleeping habits.

Last night was no exception. She'd meant to go to bed at a reasonable time but of course it was when her mind had finally settled down that Miranda's note about Melanie sprang up. The thing was, once she'd begun looking up Melanie Henderson on the web last night, she couldn't stop.

Like Molly, Melanie was steeped in the world of art—as a practitioner, not an academic. Her website profiled a rising star artist of the canvas, marrying abstraction and feminist thought in oil paintings so large they could span the size of a small house. A profile in the *New York Times* called her latest gala showing "revelatory" and "visceral." *Hyperallergic* warned of the "brutality" of her art, which, as far as Daphne could tell by scrunching her face up to her laptop screen, involved slashing thick canvases with heavy lines of red paint. The stark white canvas against the iron-rich blood was strikingly familiar in a way that Daphne could not yet articulate.

There was something violent, almost lethal, about Melanie's work, even when encased in a feminine style—like her painting *Water Lilies*, which had to be some sort of critique of Monet that Daphne still didn't quite understand. The same lush lavenders, pinks, and yellows set against the deep blue of water had hardened, frozen into cold scowls set in intricate floral designs. But a jury had selected it for some sort of prize and with it, Melanie had won an artist residency and a small showing of her work at the Whitney.

It was when Daphne began reading through Calliope's old Reddit threads and gossip sites that her ears pricked to a delectable Siren song. Melanie Henderson, the last child and second daughter of the wealthy and elite Henderson family, had a record.

And not just any record.

The first time she'd been written up, Melanie had been a freshman in high school. Scrolling through old Facebook posts, Daphne uncovered an evolution in Melanie's behavior. It had started with vandalism and shoplifting. The owner of one jewelry shop complained online that he'd sought to press charges but a Henderson family attorney had come to his door and told him he'd regret it. A few months later, a fistfight at Ellsworth Academy for Girls led a teen to post the viral video online— which was eventually deleted. All Daphne could see was the trail of angry comments formed in its absence. By Melanie's sophomore year, she'd had more than her share of alcohol and drug possession charges, according to one old gossip blog, that also got wiped out by the Henderson family lawyer. She wondered how many other crimes Melanie had committed that some family member or an attorney had convinced a cop, a witness, or a victim to not bring to light.

Under the dim glow of her lamp last night, Daphne read through the last piece of state-filed evidence that she could access without needing a law degree or a police badge. Yet another arrest warrant—this time for "having sex in a public facility." The man she'd been caught with had also been arrested—for having sex with a minor. He'd been thirty-five years old to Melanie's fifteen.

Daphne'd bit the inside of her cheek so angrily she'd almost drawn blood. Everywhere Daphne looked, men were targeting young women.

A whizz of black fur came rushing back toward the house. Having successfully chased off the bunny, Chloe was ready for her breakfast.

Daphne yawned wide into the morning light. While Daphne shepherded Chloe through their morning rituals and eventually showered and dressed, one last nagging thought pierced through her morning fog. Melanie had been on a path to delinquency, for sure, appearing every other month in complaints on social media until the end of her sophomore year. But by April, the trail of Melanie's activities had gone cold, even on the most conspiratorial sites. Sipping her thermos of coffee, she dropped off a waggy Chloe to Aunt Linda, her mind sharpening under the caffeine's influence. It turned out that Daphne wasn't interested in the origins of Melanie's life of crime. A different question lingered on her drive to campus: What had made Melanie so abruptly stop?

■   ■   ■

Daphne's classes came and went. Her PowerPoint slides had worked out fine, the lessons she'd wanted to impart mostly reaching the correct audience, in spite of a few slumbering bodies in the back of the classroom—no doubt recuperating from partying the night before. Student questions always confounded her, going left where she thought they'd go right. Upon learning of the French origins of the Vietnam War, Amelia, a sophomore, had asked if Bob Dylan's music had ever been translated into Vietnamese and Daphne hadn't known how to reply.

Back in her office, she rolled around in her swivelly armchair and stared at the white walls, as smooth as the ridges on her brain at the moment. She was always drained after a long day of teaching, too tired to utter coherent sentences, too wired to focus on her own research. Like a deranged bumblebee, her gaze flitted from her laptop to her Josephine Baker coloring book, then back to her laptop. She checked for an email from the French government on the status of her grant application. Skimmed over the notes from the last faculty meeting, where Olaf had bravely stood in defiance or support of the university's new recycled toilet paper policy—the jury was still out. Went through her hard drive again to revisit some of Ken Miller's correspondence.

"Professor Ouverture?"

Branwen Rothkopf peered over the doorway. As always, Branwen appeared before her as a floating cloud, her thick auburn hair unleashed into glorious thick curls that blocked the view of anyone behind her.

Daphne shifted up in her seat. "Oh, hi, Bran."

"You have office hours now, right?" Branwen asked. Her freckled nose wrinkled in concern. "I'm not interrupting?"

Daphne pushed aside her small notebook of names. "Not at all. Come on in."

Branwen's smiley face was a stronger mood booster than serotonin, and while Bran flopped over into her usual seat, Daphne felt lighter in her chair. She wondered if any studies existed comparing teaching to a drug addiction. When a student you adored showered you with admiration, standing in the blast of their praise was a high far greater than any drug on the market could provide.

Branwen yanked her oversized backpack onto her lap and grinned at Daphne. "Thank God for office hours, right?"

Daphne grinned back. "Thank God for office hours."

During the early weeks of Daphne's first term, she'd sat jittery in her office, waiting for students to show up, disappointed when no one came. Had she alienated her students? Too nervous to ask them, too insecure to bring up her fears to any colleagues, Daphne had kept her neck down and typed away at her laptop each week with the door open, trying to beat down the feelings of failure curling around her throat like vines.

Bran had been the first one to step inside Daphne's office bearing a smile and a notebook filled with questions for her, telling her quite plainly that *of course* students didn't show up to office hours the first several weeks. From the perspective of many, there was nothing to talk about until the first assignment was due. Sure enough, a steady trickle of students had streamed in after that, and by the time midterm exams popped up Daphne had to figure out how to create more slots for students without jeopardizing her research schedule.

As a student, Daphne had been so grateful for the professors who had mentored her throughout college and grad school, who had delighted in her presence when she'd really done nothing more than ramble about the global impacts of the French Revolution. Now on the other side, Daphne understood that professors mentored students, true, but students also guided professors. Their observations of the world around them often surprised Daphne. Branwen's knock on Daphne's door guaranteed new epiphanies each time she ventured inside on her gangly fawn's legs and sat down.

"Okay, so here's the deal," Branwen said. "I've figured out the next portion of my thesis but can you help me find just a little more scholarship on Black familial networks in New Orleans in the early twentieth century? I have a case of someone who I think migrated up north during the Great Migration and maybe tried to pass as white, but I can't tell if his family knew or what they might have thought about it."

Daphne had too many recommendations, and probably babbled on about the prominent Dédé family for longer than necessary but Branwen's wide eyes and vigorous nods squashed Daphne's embarrassment. Feeling more comfortable as the conversation went on, and reminding herself that Branwen loved to be Daphne's guide, Daphne felt brave enough to turn to the question that pierced her own heart in two.

"Branwen," Daphne said when Branwen was beginning to pack up, "do you feel safe on campus?"

Branwen slid Daphne a look, her curly hair flopping over and bouncing down past her shoulder. "What do you mean?"

"I just . . ." Daphne twisted her fingers together. "Lately I've been reminded that not all professors are good to students— female students in particular."

Recognition flickered across Branwen's freckled face.

"Professor Taylor," Daphne said, displeased to even be saying his name aloud, "do you know any students who had run-ins with him?"

"Why?" Branwen asked. Her voice wasn't accusing, exactly, but neither was it inviting.

"Call it a hunch," Daphne replied. "I'm worried a student got mixed up with him and—"

Branwen's eyebrows rose. "You think a student killed him?"

"No, no," Daphne said. "Not at all."

Branwen's frown suggested Daphne's assurance hadn't worked. "They caught the guys who did it."

"True." Daphne worked quick to unbury herself from this hole. "Bran, I don't think a student killed him, or maybe I'd rather believe they didn't. But I do know that Professor Taylor was not the honorable man that Harrison's made him out to be. And that somewhere out there, a student might know that and need help."

Daphne swallowed, taking in Branwen's curious expression and willing her fingers to stop trembling.

"It's so weird what professors don't know," Branwen said, a frown molding her lips. "Students think that professors are like God, somehow omniscient and omnipresent."

"I promise you we're not," Daphne replied. "In fact, you've helped me out so much since I got here."

"Well then let me help you out again." Bran sighed. "Yes, I've heard things about Professor Taylor."

Daphne's heart lurched forward. "What kinds of things?"

"Not good ones," Branwen replied, her voice droll. "It's okay if I don't use names, right?"

Daphne nodded. What other choice did she have?

Branwen cast her eyes up to the ceiling, fighting some inner instinct to say the truth. Which suggested that the truth itself was harmful.

"Okay, so he was two-faced," Branwen said. "With white girls, he was flirty. He'd be polite to them, open the door, take them on dates, that kind of thing. Black girls? He'd either ignore or leer at us."

Daphne's eyes stung at her own recognition of Sam's pattern of behavior. "He did that with me, too."

"I'm so sorry," Bran said.

"I'm okay now," Daphne said, "but I understand what you mean about being two-faced. Can I ask how you know this?"

"Some of us talk." Bran sighed. "My old RA, for example? She was an Af-Am and anthro double major. Anyway, a bunch of the anthro students went to the annual conference last year and something happened to her. He went into her hotel room."

Daphne's heart skipped a beat. "Did she tell anyone about it?"

"No." Branwen bit her lip. "Too scared. Who would believe her anyway? That this hotshot white guy went after a Black girl on campus? She was about to graduate anyway, so she kept her head down and got out. She's in the JET program in rural Japan now."

The life drained from Daphne's body. "Oh my God."

Branwen nodded. She stared down at her lap. "Yeah."

Daphne didn't know what to say. She couldn't help feeling like she'd failed Branwen and all other students like her. Why hadn't she tried to investigate this sooner? How could she have made herself more available to her students earlier?

"Branwen, I'm so sorry," Daphne said. "I could have been there for you better. I should have asked if you were safe."

Branwen's shake of her curls was firm. "Professor Ouverture you literally just got here. How were you to know that the house was on fire?"

Daphne tried not to dissolve in a puddle of tears in gratitude toward Branwen's grace. It still felt undeserved but she'd do her best to live up to Branwen's view of her from now on.

"Was there anyone else who Sam had gone after? Someone recently?"

Branwen shook her head "no"—another look, one of apprehension, swept across her freckled face.

Blood pounded in Daphne's ears. She wanted to know. She didn't want to know. She wished again that none of this had ever happened in the first place.

"I heard . . ." Branwen frowned. "I don't know this girl, though. A freshman, maybe on a sports team? Something went down like two weeks ago."

Daphne's stomach fluttered. "Around the time Sam died?"

Branwen didn't like Daphne's question one bit. She crossed her arms. "Professor Ouverture, what are you implying?"

"Nothing," Daphne said. "But—"

"But what?" Branwen asked. "You think she had something to do with Sam's death?"

"No," Daphne said. It wasn't a lie but it wasn't the entire truth, either. She refused to believe that a student had killed Sam. But she couldn't underestimate the power of a young woman cornered, either.

"Good," Branwen said. "Professor Ouverture, being at Harrison isn't exactly easy. It's your first year here and something like this happens to you? If I were her I'd be trying to get out of here so fast I'd break a world record."

"But what if she did kill him? Or knows something about his murder?" Daphne asked.

Branwen shrugged. "Who cares? This might sound mean

but from the perspective of a lot of us, it's a blessing that Professor Taylor is dead. One less predator in the world."

DAPHNE'S LUNCH that day consisted of her father's jambalaya and a side of screaming anxiety while Branwen's words stabbed sharp needles into her brain. Being one of the "only ones" was an experience Daphne knew all too well—the only woman of color in a class, the only Black student taking a French literature seminar, let alone sailing through it with an easy A. She'd read through the dean's list at Harrison and all she saw were names like "Owen Smith" or "Rebecca Sandstone," and Daphne's loneliness from her own school days throbbed like a phantom limb. A unicorn—that's what a professor had called her once. Daphne was special, she was unique, and she was lonely, just so lonely sometimes. No one talked about herds of unicorns for a reason.

And here Daphne was hunting for one.

A new message pinged in her inbox. Daphne slid her mouse over to open it—

Harrison University is pleased to announce the creation of a new center dedicated to art and social justice. Led by inaugural director, Molly Henderson, The Institute for Women and the Arts is the first of its kind in the nation to focus exclusively on women artists, past and present, who . . .

Daphne skimmed through the email. She should be happy for Molly, and she kind of was. But annoyance crept into Daphne's countenance anyway like a pebble in her shoe at the memory of her mentioning Audre Lorde and Molly's lack of recognition at the name. So much for intersectional feminism.

Another ping had her clicking her mouse again and at the sender's notable email address her heart lurched. With shaking hands, she opened the message from the Rousseau Foundation.

Congratulations, Professor Ouverture!

Daphne skimmed the email and reminded herself to exhale, reading for the terms and agreements of the award while her smile grew with each second ticking by. She couldn't wait to share this news with Miranda and with her parents and friends. A whole summer in France! Getting back into her favorite archives was just what she needed after this surreal spring term. Chloe was already registered and vaccinated for overseas travel, and her old landlady in Marseille was eager to take the pair of them in. Her days would be filled with walks among lavender fields with Chloe, jaunts down to the Mediterranean for swimming on weekends, and reams of papers and court filings to read from the archive of the French colonial office for her final round of book research. Daphne grinned at an image of herself, Elise, and Sadie visiting her favorite shops and cafés and tree-lined streets while fending off the usual suitors who would take one look at Elise and propose marriage on the spot. Provençal men were nothing if not dramatic, and it turned out Daphne much preferred the quiet bookish type.

Rowan's shy smile and soft lips returned to her mind—and dizziness and nausea struck Daphne with blunt force.

In two weeks, she'd be in France—and away from Rowan all summer, killing whatever was blooming between them before it had even started.

CHAPTER TWENTY-EIGHT

"Hi, Ken."

The glossy cherry-wood door gleamed when it swung wide open. The newly minted dean of Harrison University held it at bay, boasting his usual shirt and khakis, beaming at her with far too much delight.

"Daphne!"

At least Ken got her name right this time. Daphne smiled in approval while he got her settled into his office, wiping his messy desk in some sort of gesture of chivalry and beckoning her to have a seat. She was more than happy to feign eagerness at the sight of his pale face. She needed Ken to think that he had the upper hand.

For now.

"So what brings you to my office on a Tuesday morning?" Ken asked, leaning back in his chair with his arms crossed behind his head. Dark rings of sweat colored his armpits. "We here to talk about Kiki's upcoming plagiarism case? Or would you like to learn more about Congolese cultures?"

Daphne blinked at him in confusion for a minute until she remembered that matriarchal Congolese social systems had indeed been what they'd talked about the first time she'd met him. Or, rather, what he'd last rambled on about for ten minutes before threatening to fire her.

"Actually, Ken, I'd like you to write down the list of women who complained to you about Sam's sexual harassment while under your chairship."

Ken's smile flickered. His pit-stained arms remained stuck behind his head. "Pardon?"

"Oh, I'm sorry." Daphne cocked her head to the side. "Did that come out weird? I'll try again. I'd like you to write down the list of women who had complained to you about Sam's sexual harassment while under your chairship. *Please.*"

Ken lowered his arms. "Even if I knew what you were talking about, I couldn't tell you. We both know that student data is confidential and protected under FERPA unless it's for official university business."

"Oh, I know," Daphne replied calmly. "But you're going to give me the list of names anyway."

Ken scoffed at that. "And have Harrison's legal team on my hide?"

"They don't have to find out," Daphne lied. Her text to Miranda was already drafted, commanding her to upload that USB stick of Ken's misdeeds and share it with Harrison's president the moment Daphne finished mauling Ken into bite-size chunks. "I doubt you're the first person at Harrison who's given away confidential information before. You won't be the last, either."

Something flashed across Ken's face—dawning, curiosity, fear. "And who exactly are these women who you claim said things about Sam?"

Oh, how interesting.

Ken wanted to fight her on this. And while Daphne was running on three percent battery life, she held steady anyway because Ken was about to discover that he was, in fact, bringing a proverbial knife to the metaphorical gun fight.

"That's what you're going to tell me," Daphne replied slowly, like she would to a temperamental toddler. "And before you try it, don't say Olivia. Yes, she was having an affair with Sam and yes, you were trying to cover that up. But that's not why I'm here."

Ken's nose twitched.

"Sam Taylor was taking advantage of young women on campus," Daphne said. "Women who felt too afraid to speak up about it. And when they finally worked up the guts to come to you in your capacity as chair, you swept his crimes under the rug. That's unacceptable."

Ken's scoff was well-rehearsed. "Listen, I don't know what Miranda's told you over in the history department, but I'd advise against besmirching the name of a recently deceased colleague whose publication record was heftier than what you weigh, Professor Ouverture. Which is saying something."

Daphne's chest burned with hot fire.

"This kind of behavior?" Ken jabbed his forefinger on his desk. "That's unacceptable. It's the kind of thing your chair would do—hell, Miranda could give Dick Cheney a few lessons in incivility—but I thought you'd learned since our last conversation."

Daphne snapped.

"*Listen, Sam,*" Daphne began, "*it's not the graduates who are the problem here (although they're unhappy, too), it's the under-grads. They don't know any better and no one will understand. Just because they're fresh bait doesn't mean you have to go for the kill every time.*"

With each sentence Ken's face sagged into a new decade.

"You know," Daphne said, studying Ken carefully while he grabbed a tissue to wipe the top of his lip, "to your credit, it took me a while to figure it all out. Your emails to Sam? They were careful. Coded."

"I'd heard . . ." he said, his voice low, "that you had this . . . ability. When did you—"

"The other day," Daphne replied. "I hacked into your account. I did a few targeted searches but my guess is that there are more emails out there?"

Ken shoved himself away from his desk and yanked a bottle of water from his mini-fridge.

"Ah. So there *are* more," Daphne confirmed. "All the more reason why I need that list of students who complained to you about Sam."

Ken chugged at the bottle and wiped his lips with the back of his hand. His stare at Daphne had turned to stone. "No."

"But—"

"So you learned that Sam was a bit of a Don Juan, so what? I'm supposed to let you drag down my department because a couple of girls had boundary issues? I'm supposed to just roll over and let you tarnish Sam's good name?"

"What if his murder is tied to something that happened to one of those girls?" Daphne asked.

"Oh, come off it, nothing happened," Ken said.

"You don't know that."

The glint in Ken's eyes was rock hard. "But you do?"

Daphne's rage came back hard and fast.

She squeezed her eyes shut and conjured the text from somewhere behind them. "*Everything's booked, Laura. Continental Hotel, Room 1156. Told Sharon our grad seminar's in Chicago doing ethnographic research. Friday at five o'clock?*"

When she opened them again, Ken's chest labored to breathe and oh, how it pleased Daphne to witness his pain.

"Like I said." Daphne clasped her hands in her lap. "Your messages were careful. It took me some time to decipher them. Do you think your wife will need more time or less?"

It took a while for the resignation to find a home in Ken's shoulders. When Daphne was certain that Ken could no longer worm his way out of her demand, she spoke again. "So here's what's going to happen next. You're going to compile a list of students who tried to lodge complaints against Sam. And then you're going to resign from the dean's office by the end of today."

"What?" Ken pushed out of his slump. "Why? No. I won't—"

"Ken, you've been a terrible leader," Daphne said. "All you do is lie, blackmail, bribe, and threaten people. Accusing Kiki of plagiarism? Forcing Miranda to step down?"

He sneered. "Miranda Nurse is—"

"*How does Vice-President of Educational Leadership sound? We'll push it through over the summer when the board's on leave,*" said Daphne, noting a new shade of red blooming up Ken's neck.

Ken sputtered. "This is illegal—"

Daphne ignored him. "*Just make sure your daughter's application goes through Peter at the admissions office. We'll get her a Harrison University sweatshirt in no time.*"

"You can't be—"

"Serious?" Daphne finished for him. "I absolutely am. Because not only have you been shielding a predator from justice and having your own affair with a student—both of which the Title IX office will love to sink their teeth into by the way—but it turns out you've also bribed half the board of trustees into voting for you."

"Emails can be deleted," Ken choked out.

"I know," said Daphne, her smile bright and vicious. "Which

is why I stored your messages on a flash drive. Wouldn't local media love to get ahold of it? Or better yet, your wife?"

If a look could burn skin Daphne would be a charred skeleton.

"So." Daphne's eyelashes would never be longer than a blade of mowed grass but she batted them anyway. "The list of names?"

CHAPTER TWENTY-NINE

Eight.

Eight women over two years.

Eight unprotected souls Ken Miller had ignored.

Eight students who now moved through life with a great deal more caution than they used to.

Daphne blinked at the lines of hand-scrawled text that Ken had provided for her and pushed away from her desk. Thirty minutes into googling them, one name stood out from the rest.

Cassidy Reid.

A pretty young thing gave a dimpled smile on Harrison's athletics website, at most maybe seventeen years old. She was a track and field star from Maryland who apparently could hurl shotputs with the force of a cannon. Her hobbies included eating jollof rice, cat-sitting, and watching reality television. She had just declared her major in anthropology and planned to study abroad in West Africa.

Nausea splashed over Daphne. She wanted nothing more than to pack up her bag and go home for a nap.

An inordinately tall man stood in front of her door and knocked. Whatever exhaustion was weighing her down evaporated under Rowan's bright smile in her direction.

He leaned against the door, his head almost knocking the top doorframe. "Hi."

Daphne smiled back. "Hi."

Heat flooded her cheeks, warming her palms. When was the last time she'd had anyone admire her like she was a rare first edition of a Jane Austen novel?

"May I come in?" Rowan asked.

The Rousseau Foundation's email popped back into her mind. Two weeks, that was all the time she had left before she caught a plane with Chloe to France. Two weeks until whatever burned between them would most likely be extinguished.

But how could Daphne say no to Rowan after the corners of his eyes had just crinkled adorably like that?

She ushered him in. "What brings you to campus?"

Daphne could have spent an entire lifetime basking in that stare of his as he ambled into her office. Sitting across from her, Rowan was about as tall as Daphne standing.

"Earthseed Books is partnering up with Harrison to host a symposium on Black science fiction," he said. "We were just meeting to discuss the logistics. How many books to be available for purchase, that sort of thing."

"And your conversation just so happened to take place in the history department?" Daphne teased.

"Uh, no." Rowan bent his head down, shy. "Not quite. But I thought that while I was here, I could bring you a small gift."

Rowan reached into his messenger bag and teased out a freshly printed book still wrapped in cellophane. His long, elegant fingers grazed hers when he handed it to her and Daphne could have blacked out on the spot.

"*Brown Girl in the Ring?*" Daphne flipped the book around to read the book summary on the back cover.

"By Nalo Hopkinson," Rowan offered. "It's one of the books that the English department will be discussing for the symposium, in part because a new edition was just released. The cover is less visceral than its original but the contents within should still appeal."

Daphne peered at him curiously. Oh, he wanted her to like it.

The tips of his ears burned red. "Hopefully," he said.

Daphne placed the book on her desk. "Well, thank you."

Rowan shrugged, a small smile beaming back at her. "Anytime."

"And I'm sorry I haven't reached out yet about dinner," Daphne said. "Things are still a bit chaotic over here. But I'd still like to—go to dinner, that is, if—"

"Yes," Rowan replied, breathless. "I mean, that is if—"

"Absolutely."

Apparently neither of them knew what to do next because they were just sitting there, hovering above her desk, smiling at each other like teens on a first date. The only thing missing was the braces.

Rowan slung his messenger bag across his thin, broad shoulders again. "I should get back to work."

"Oh." Disappointment deflated Daphne's smile. "Of course."

He turned to her again. "Unless you'd rather—"

"Sam Taylor wasn't the hero everyone thinks he was," Daphne blurted out.

That sent a puzzled expression scattering across Rowan's delicate face.

"I think that's already been established," Rowan replied. "But I take it your most recent claim derives from something other than his stalking you?"

Daphne nodded, desperate to share what she knew, desperate to keep the knowledge to herself for fear of hurting the women already tormented by Sam.

But good grief this was *Rowan* she was talking about, who'd renounced a career in policing for bookselling. He'd quite literally just handed her a Black feminist science fiction novel and could probably recite Emily Dickinson poems by heart. She could trust him with this.

"What if he was, um . . ." Daphne breathed. "What if Sam was responsible for assaulting young women on campus?"

Rowan's eyebrows shot up to the ceiling.

"Including a freshman from this semester," Daphne said. "I didn't introduce this topic very well, did I?"

"I think you introduced it wonderfully," Rowan said, gentle. "I take it you find the investigation of Sam's murder to be incomplete?"

"N-no," Daphne stuttered. "Or yes. I mean—I don't know."

Rowan nodded thoughtfully for a moment. He sat down at her desk again. "How can I help?"

The shock of those simple words jolted her upright. Rowan's support steadied her in her seat. "I just have this nagging feeling. On the surface Sam was this great hero but in reality he was awful, especially to Black women. He stalked me, he harassed grad students on campus, and I now have it on excellent authority that he assaulted a freshman this term. And I just wonder . . ."

"If she was involved in Sam's death?" Rowan asked, pushing his glasses up his nose in concentration.

"Yes," Daphne said. "Or no. Or rather, I don't *want* her to be involved in his death. Honestly just the thought of it is enough to smash my heart into tiny pieces. I don't want to get anyone in trouble and I certainly don't want to be responsible for a student going to jail. I don't think I'd be able to live with myself if that happened. It's my job to look after them, not tear them down. It's hard enough to be a Black kid at Harrison as it is. But . . ."

"But what?"

"But I also want to know the truth," Daphne admitted.

She let the words sit in the air for a minute.

"I mean, that's kind of my job," Daphne said. "As a historian. We're invested in uncovering the truth. It's what we do. And that truth has to always be contextualized and understood within its own world."

"The historian's pursuit," Rowan quipped. "To provide the necessary context so that the truth can be made legible."

"Exactly," Daphne said. God, this man got her. "And right now the context of Sam's life doesn't fit with what appears to be true about his death."

Daphne sat back, breathless and a little overwhelmed. With the threat of abduction no longer hovering above her, Daphne's brain had started to clear. Today was the first time she could recognize her own frustrations with Sam's murder, and her own desire to solve it, however vexing that desire might be. How had Rowan wrung this confession out of her?

"I see," Rowan said quietly.

Daphne nodded.

"Daphne, we may not have known each other very long," Rowan said, "but what I do know of you suggests that you make for an excellent detective on your own, in part because of how you see Sam's victims."

Daphne blinked. "Which is?"

"As innocent." Rowan crossed his arms. "In your heart of hearts, you believe that, if there is someone out there who has knowledge of Sam's death, they either acted in self-defense or can help you find the truth. Your gut has brought you this far, Daphne. I'm confident it can guide you to that truth."

She was about to speak but then closed her mouth. That invisible string plucked between them again and he leaned toward her.

Their lips parted.

"Yo, Daph!"

Daphne ripped her hand away from Rowan's to find Sadie and Elise at her doorway. Elise, as always, appeared demure and polished in some sleek pastel number that played beautifully against her pale skin and dark hair while Sadie's outfit was outrageous as ever—a bright almost neon green dress stung Daphne's eyes, subdued only slightly by the jet-black tights and punk-ass Doc Martens.

Sadie burst into Daphne's front door, breathless. "Girl, get ready to—oh, hey."

Rowan stood up, then immediately shrank back at Sadie's and Elise's open, unabashed staring. Except, of course, he still towered above them. He towered above everyone.

His voice was barely audible. "Um, hello."

"Hi, gang," Daphne replied, plastering a large smile on her face. "Um, Rowan, these are my friends Sadie and Elise."

Rowan offered a hand. "Lovely to meet you both. My name is Rowan Peterson. I work at Earthseed Books, if you're familiar with it?"

"Oh, we know who you are," drawled Sadie.

The earth could have swallowed Daphne whole.

"Rowan," Daphne said, sending her besties a death glare. "I forgot that my friends are here to take me to lunch. We try to keep a weekly standing lunch date."

"Chef Marcel made Jamaican curry chicken," Elise said. "With fried plantains."

Daphne whirled around at Elise. "He *what?*"

Rowan's smile cracked wide, showing white teeth that had recently nipped at her throat.

"Rowan," Elise said in a way that sounded innocent to outsiders who wouldn't know any better.

He reluctantly tore his gaze away from Daphne. "Yes—Elise, is it?"

"That's right. What a great memory you have!" Elise's expression was far too sweet for Daphne's comfort. "Out of curiosity, what do you know about the history of Belgian colonialism?"

Rowan pressed his lips together. "Pardon?"

Sadie lit up like the Rockefeller Christmas tree. "Yeah, Rowan. What *do* you make of the fact that Belgians used to dismember local Africans as a form of intimidation for their rubber industry?"

"Oh, so you've also read *King Leopold's Ghost*?" Rowan asked, his pretty gray eyes bright with interest.

Daphne would have given her entire salary to wipe the smug expressions off of her best friends' faces.

"OKAY, SO he's clearly read up a little bit on Belgian colonialism," Daphne snipped at lunch, jabbing a fork into her curry chicken. She sent her besties a hard stare. "That doesn't mean you two have the right to saunter around my office clucking like peacocks."

Elise waved a fork of plantain in Daphne's face. "Peacocks don't cluck, Daph."

"Yeah, Daph," Sadie said, chomping on a bite of rice and peas. "Peacocks don't cluck."

"Well, what kind of sound do they make?" Daphne snapped back. "Also, damn this curry is delicious."

"Isn't it?" Elise said. "And peacocks make this caw-cawing noise instead. Kind of like a crow?"

"Yeah, Daph," Sadie said, her smug mouth stuffed with chicken. "Like a crow."

"You two are ridiculous," Daphne said. "And I love you."

"We know," they both replied.

"Kick rocks," said Daphne.

"Oooooh." Elise held up her buzzing phone. "Leila keeps texting about the women of color gala. She's worried no one's going to show up."

Daphne frowned. Leila Gamal, a law professor, was usually a chatterbox with Daphne. "Why didn't she text me?"

"Because, like most people at Harrison, Leila knows that you've been going through a lot lately and need to rest," Elise said. "And also because Sadie threatened to burn down Leila's garage if she pestered you too much."

Daphne sighed. "Sadie."

Her bestie gave her a bear hug. "What can I say? That's what friends are for."

An idea floated up just in time for Daphne to snatch it. "Actually, what if I'd like to go?"

Elise peered at her skeptically. "To the party?"

Daphne nodded. "Yup."

Elise frowned. "Don't you deserve some peace?"

She did. But Cassidy Reid deserved more. Even if she would rather stay at home with Chloe and watch *Drag Race*, the fact of the matter was that the gala offered Daphne a chance to find her and speak to her from a position of safety and support.

"I need to go," Daphne said. "There's someone I'd like to meet up with there."

Sadie and Elise gave each other sideways glances. And then shrugged.

"Okay, fine," Sadie muttered. "But if Leila talks too much I'm still burning down her garage."

AFTER LUNCH, an afternoon slump fogged over Daphne's office, pressing her down in her seat while she blinked at her laptop screen. Three different thoughts, all protruding in three different directions, competed against each other for attention. First, that the men who Daphne had taken down had been hired by Andrew Westmount to attack her. Second, that Sam Taylor had preyed on young women on campus—Black women especially—including Cassidy. Third, that Melanie Henderson was a woman with a criminal past and an artistically violent present.

The problem was that Daphne still couldn't help shake the feeling that each individual piece of information was important, even necessary, to understand Sam's murder. She just couldn't figure out how or why.

"Daphne, darling?"

Miranda knocked on Daphne's door.

"I've just had a telephone call. With the President's Office. They've acknowledged receipt of the USB stick. And they've informed me that Ken Miller has just resigned."

"Thank Jesus." Daphne held her breath. "Does that mean that Kiki's hearing is—"

"Called off." Miranda marched over to her and wrapped her skinny arms around Daphne's much larger frame. "You are phenomenal, Daphne."

Daphne smiled into Miranda's cheek while they rocked together side to side. "I bet you say that to all of your junior French historians."

That earned Daphne a cackle and a firm pat on the back. "Well, this calls for a celebratory dinner. That Spanish restaurant you like? Before the term ends?"

"Of course," replied Daphne.

Miranda granted Daphne a proud smile and waggled her fingers goodbye.

A tiny panic caused Daphne to stop her chair from leaving. "Miranda wait—"

"Yes?" Miranda replied, one foot out the door.

Whatever Daphne wanted to say got caught in her throat, eventually coming out in a rushed garble. "You said you knew Melanie Henderson? That she was a wild child?"

The lines on Miranda's forehead shifted. "Yes . . . ?"

Daphne gestured for Miranda to have a seat. She gave a half-hearted shrug and the pair of them shifted over to Daphne's desk again, recently cleared of all bubble pens and graded papers.

Miranda crossed her legs. "What do you want to know?"

"An odd detail's been bothering me," Daphne said, remembering the acute finality of Melanie's criminal record. "Did something big happen to Melanie or her family when she was in high school? Something that made her change her behavior?"

"Like what?" Miranda asked.

"I don't know," Daphne said. "I just know that after her sophomore year, she stopped getting arrested. I was wondering if there was a reason why."

Miranda tilted her head to the side, causing her silver bob to wave gently in the air. "Heavens that was at least, what, ten years ago? Possibly even fifteen? I think you and Melanie are probably the same age, late twenties or thereabouts, correct? Good grief I must appear old to you."

"Not at all," Daphne replied.

"Well," Miranda's voice was dry. "I feel old. Too old to be recalling events that have faded into obscuri—oh."

A cold chill glazed over Daphne's entire body as Miranda's lips twisted in disgust.

"Oh, that's right," Miranda said softly to herself. "I remember now."

Miranda clapped eyes on Daphne that were hard and sharp.

"This isn't a pretty story, Daphne," Miranda warned.

"That's okay," Daphne replied.

Miranda wasn't satisfied. "Why do you need to know this?"

"I don't know," Daphne admitted. She'd been saying that a lot lately, and was starting to wonder if she was a demented parrot squawking the same line in a loop. "Call it a hunch."

Silence filled the room while Miranda bit her lip and considered Daphne's words. "I'm not doing this with the door open."

"I'll close it," Daphne offered.

"No, no." Miranda waved a finely wrinkled hand in the air. "Allow me. It'll give me time to think."

Daphne gulped in a few big breaths to calm herself down while Miranda went about securing Daphne's office, willing her heart to return to a light jog instead of its current sprinting speed.

"Okay," Miranda said after she'd perched herself back on the chair across from Daphne. "I can tell you what I know and what I heard but like any account, you'll need to take what I say with tablespoons of salt, understood?"

"Of course," Daphne replied. "That's what historians do. We read against the grain and interrogate every word."

"Our bread and butter." Miranda flashed a tiny grin. "It's why I hired you. You get it."

"Thanks."

"And it's remarkable what you are able to remember, Daphne. I had just mentioned Melanie in passing when we were in front of that statue of hers, yet here we are—"

"Miranda . . ." Daphne said, fearing her chair had lost the plot.

"Right." Miranda waved a hand. "Melanie. Daughter of Mark and Minerva Henderson—Mark being the senator turned governor, of course."

"Right."

"But the most important name you're looking for is Magnus Chaucer," Miranda replied. "He's most likely the real answer to why Melanie's behavior stopped, the odious man."

That had Daphne sitting up straight. "Who?"

"Magnus Chaucer, a local businessman here in Calliope—and Minerva's brother."

"Melanie's uncle?" Daphne asked.

Miranda nodded. "He lived with the family at their mansion in Calliope. He was there to help out Minnie and the girls while Mark was governor at the time. There were rumors about him."

Daphne swallowed. "What kind of rumors?"

Miranda's gaze sharpened. "This is hearsay, understood?"

"Understood."

"I was never close enough to the family to verify anything or go to the police," Miranda insisted.

A tiny knot of alarm flared up in Daphne's gut. "Police?"

"My daughter Umi was about thirteen at the time and had been invited over to some sort of function there to celebrate her recent ballet competition," Miranda said. "We were set to go until a mom friend at the time warned me to keep my eye on Umi at all times. The uncle wasn't to be trusted."

The tiny knot flared into a category five hurricane. "Magnus Chaucer was ..."

"That's what I heard," Miranda said. "I wouldn't testify this under oath. But it became this open secret that even extended to the Henderson girls themselves. A different mother swears she caught Magnus with one of them once."

Daphne gaped. "His own *niece*?"

"Again, I wouldn't swear to this." Miranda held up her hands in protest. "I just remember the mother saying she saw him in a window with Molly or Melanie late at night. But the Henderson family is powerful so everyone just kept their mouths shut."

"And he wasn't arrested?" Daphne asked, her voice shrieking.

"No, dear," Miranda drawled. "He died instead."

Daphne actually gasped.

"At the family home." Miranda was just warming up. "In fact, I remember because Molly had just graduated and Umi played flute in the marching band at the graduation ceremony."

"How did he die?" Daphne asked.

"Officially the word was heart failure, but I don't know. Everything happened lightning fast. One minute there was an ambulance outside his house and then the next his body was sent straight to cremation, apparently at the order of the attorney general's office. Which was under the direction of the governor, mind you. And the governor was ...?"

Daphne choked. "Melanie's dad."

Miranda pointed at Daphne. "Correct."

Another memory must have struck, because Miranda's shoulders tensed up. "Daphne, there's one more thing. If I remember this right, the whole family was there at the time, and a former neighbor of mine—a rather difficult woman with too many cats but that's a story for another time—she had stopped by that morning to drop off some cookies for Minnie or something like that. And she said the scene at the house was a mess. Minnie was weeping, Molly was whiter than a sheet and wouldn't say a word."

"And Melanie?" Daphne whispered.

"A 'strange little bird,' my neighbor said." Miranda paused. "She swears that when the coroner came to remove the body, Melanie was smiling."

CHAPTER THIRTY

The fabric of Daphne's wax print dress was too thin for the chilly Tuesday evening air. But she slipped it on over her head and spun around in front of her bedroom mirror anyway. It suited her, she thought. Cerulean blues as inviting as the ocean and a strong royal purple that enriched her skin tone bumped up against each other in vibrant circles ringed in white and gold, narrowing her waist, celebrating her curves. She adjusted a sleeve. If only Rowan could see her in it.

"*A scandal is coming to light at Harrison University,*" a soft alto crooned on Calliope public radio. "*Former dean of Harrison University, Ken Miller, has just resigned from his position less than one week after taking office. In a public letter explaining his decision, Miller states that he is choosing to 'spend time with his family,' but sources close to Harrison university's upper administration reveal that the university is investigating him for blackmail, bribery, and potentially covering up incidents of sexual harassment and assault.*"

Daphne might have puffed up her chest while she ran her palms along her thighs, smoothing out her dress.

"*While it is unclear whether these incidents could end up leading to a formal arrest,*" the reporter said, "*the police have nonetheless promised to investigate these allegations.*"

The phone blasted out a GloRilla anthem that Elise had made Daphne download for her ringtone and Daphne picked it up. "Hey, Elise, you outside?"

"We're pulling up right now," Elise said.

"Give me a few minutes and I'll meet you in the parking lot."

Daphne smooched Chloe's soft jammy jowls and headed for her kitchen. On the stovetop was a Le Creuset pot, bubbling away with peanut stew. Fabiola's insistence on stuffing her freezer to the hilt with Kedjenou, attiéké, and other Ivorian dishes generally drove Daphne up the wall but today her mother's famous peanut stew would be put to good use.

As bait.

Cradling the very hot pot in a cardboard box a few minutes later, Daphne walked up to Sadie's SUV and placed the food in the trunk.

"Nice dress," Elise said when Daphne climbed in. "You get it in Paris?"

"Abidjan."

Daphne palmed her fabric. No one could say that Ouvertures weren't clever.

LEILA GAMAL'S house was a painful reminder that not all professors lived the same lives. From a distance, ancient hickory trees studded the edges of her sprawling estate, making it impossible to see the towering greenhouse, swimming pool, and tennis court that Daphne could never have afforded. The minimalist villa perched atop the hill like a modern fortress watching for invaders.

Daphne felt like one of the marauding hordes herself when all three of them were buzzed in through the iron gates and zoomed up the driveway. Elise and Sadie dropped Daphne off at the entrance to look for parking, leaving her a tangled knot of nerves on the wide doorstep.

Until she rang the doorbell.

The Chicken Dance clucked out where carillon bells had once nobly chimed.

Daphne snorted. That must be Leila's doing. For being an acclaimed professor of international human rights and married to one of the biggest sports agents in the country, Leila was a complete goofball. Daphne was so busy laughing at the new doorbell that she missed who swung open the door for her.

Daphne froze. "Molly?"

Molly gave her usual polite smile. "It's lovely to see you again, Daphne. Do come in."

Daphne dutifully followed her inside and placed her peanut stew on a solid oak table already resplendent with dishes. "I didn't expect to find you here."

She wasn't unhappy to see Molly, exactly. But her presence gave her an uneasy feeling.

"At a gathering for women of color?" Molly whipped her long blond hair around and gave Daphne a playful wink. "Why ever not?"

Daphne blinked. Molly's teasing did nothing to dispel the feeling. "I, uh—"

Molly placed a hand on Daphne's arm. "I'm kidding. I'm not staying long. I just popped in to say hi to Leila. We're neighbors."

"That's right, you live around the corner."

"Just three houses down. I stop by sometimes after work and help her out if she needs it. Come on—I'll take you to her."

Daphne followed Molly down the hall, toward Leila's atrium. Boasting high ceilings, spacious windows, and intricately woven Persian rugs, the atrium was bursting with dozens of thick, lush tropical plants, some the size of small trees—a veritable hot greenhouse on a cold spring night. Leila had eschewed traditional sofas, instead scattering soft and vibrant cushions across the floor, each one begging to be touched, moved, shuffled, sat on. Sitting in Leila's atrium and breathing in fragrant orchids was like traveling to North Africa—just a plane ride away from Daphne's family in Abidjan.

A blur of raven hair and bangles raced in before Daphne could settle down on her favorite cushion. Daphne didn't know if it was possible for someone to be such a caricature of themselves but Leila was in the most Leila outfit ever—light, breezy harem pants and a crop top covered by a thick wool cardigan that reached down to her knees. Leila looked so warm she might catch fire if she didn't freeze to death first.

"Daphne!" As usual, Leila kissed her on each cheek, which was either a nod to Leila's Egyptian heritage or Daphne's Parisian childhood. Figuring out which was hopeless because Leila, like Daphne, was a mishmash of experiences and cultures. "I am so glad you're here! I wasn't sure you were going to make it because your life has been like one adventurous camel ride and Ken Miller has just resigned—did you hear about that?—which means that everyone is losing their minds in joy which I shouldn't even mention because you have not been feeling well since you got hurt—and by *who*? Some monster, Daphne, an absolute monster!"

"Oh, I'm doing oka—"

But Leila wasn't finished—not even close.

"Of course you're okay but we can't get around the fact that you were in the hospital and that a madman was after you because you look a little paler and thinner than usual, which is just so upsetting but Daphne dear, please have no worries about tonight because I have so much food already on the table, including those stuffed grape leaves you said you liked that I had last time and that cauliflower salad from the Syrian bakery, the one where I helped them sue that customer in court? Of course you remember, you're such a good friend. Anyway, you look terrific, don't you?"

Daphne glanced over to Molly, who was intently studying her shoes. "Oh, thanks, Leila, I—"

"That dress, Daphne, it is very flattering on you. It gives you the glamor of a Nubian queen, it really does—you would be the talk of all of the markets in Luxor, and Daphne, my God, how the men would fight over each other for a date with you! Oh—but I thought I saw you with a man at the memorial service. Tall and skinny, no? Like a tree? That's right, there is your smile because you liked him right back, I could tell. It's true! I think what you have is promising enough, and you could tell by the way he was looking at you that he was really into you and why shouldn't he be because you are a goddess, Daphne, a real goddess."

Molly gently placed a hand on her shoulder. "Leila."

Leila tossed her head back and forth to her two guests. "Oh, that's right, where are my manners? What would you like to drink? Wine? A cocktail? I have some gin and tonics ready to go, even though I still hate the British for—well, everything, really, even if they claim to have invented constitutional democracy which hasn't been too great for them lately anyway, now has it?"

The ringing bells of polka music echoed through her house again.

Leila's hand flew up to her forehead. "Oh, the guests! You two catch up. I know you must have lots to talk about—none of it good, of course, I am truly so sorry that you both have suffered so greatly this month—but I do hope you can bring comfort to each other in these dark times. What is the world coming to?"

She spun and rushed out of the room.

Daphne met Molly's eyes.

They both burst out laughing.

"Leila's always like that, isn't she?" Daphne said.

Molly grinned. "Running a mile a minute? Oh, yeah."

Daphne plopped down onto a stack of pillows with a soft thud, tucking her legs beneath her. Molly, meanwhile, swooped down gracefully on a pillow next to Daphne like an advanced yoga instructor and Daphne tried not to feel like a toad squatting next to a delicate crane.

Against the faint tinkling of piano keys somewhere in distance Daphne held her tight smile into the silence that stretched between them.

Unsure what to say next, Daphne blurted out, "Congratulations!"

Molly made a puzzled face and Daphne wouldn't have minded if a heavy object fell from the sky and took Daphne out, considering how gracefully she kept handling awkward encounters.

"Oh," Molly said. "You mean for my new position?"

"Director of that new institute for women and the arts, right?" Daphne said.

"We secured the funding a long time ago but I'm glad it's now coming to life," Molly said. "It's going to be terrific. All I've wanted for the longest time was to create a center for women supporting other women in their intellectual and artistic ambitions. And come to think of it, we might rope you into something."

Even in a world where that offer didn't involve intertwining herself with the fiancée of the man who had stalked her, Daphne would be wary—suspicious that she wanted Daphne wary of anything that suggested she was there to tick a diversity box. But then Miranda's gossip came back to her and she let the wave of pity for the Henderson girls override the "no" forming on her lips.

Molly continued, undeterred. "We're going to open our institute with an exhibit on Mary Cassatt and her relationship to French Impressionism, which you might enjoy," Molly said. "Cassatt was American but lived most of her life in France and it would be wonderful to have a French historian give a lecture on the history of Americans in Paris."

Daphne hated to admit it, but Molly's invitation had its appeal.

"You don't have to answer right away," Molly said quickly, reluctance apparently written all over Daphne's face. "Just a thought."

"Thanks," Daphne replied, relieved. "Talking to people about Americans in Paris is fun, actually. People often know the usual suspects like F. Scott Fitzgerald and Hemingway but you can bring in other artists, too, like Edmonia Lewis."

Molly hesitated. "Who?"

"Edmonia Lewis? Her face is on a postage stamp?" Daphne tried again, annoyed at having to explain to Molly, yet again, who a famous Black woman was. "She was a Black sculptor who worked in Rome before moving to France in the 1890s. Her family was Haitian so I got really sucked into her biography at one point. Anyway, she and Cassatt were born in the same year—1844—which I've always found interesting, and they lived in Paris at the same time. I've long wondered if they knew each other."

"I forget how much historians love numbers." Molly's laugh was forced. "I'll have to look into her. Anyway, I hear that I have you to thank for possibly catching Sam's killer?"

Daphne's face grew hot. "Uh . . . someone told you?"

Molly smiled. "The *Harrisonian* piece clued me in to your . . . participation."

Daphne plucked at the sleeve of her dress. "I didn't really do anything."

"I doubt that's true," Molly said kindly. "Did the police tell you where things stand with their case?"

"Not really," Daphne said.

"Well, Westmount is a big fish to fry. I don't like to throw my family name around, but I'm sure it will be much harder for him and Livington to escape prosecution now that we're involved." Molly spoke quickly with a slight edge in her voice. "It's bittersweet that Sam's work will be carried out with his death. Thank you for securing his legacy."

Daphne hoped her smile wasn't nearly as plastic as she imagined it to be. Because in truth, she was hell-bent on destroying Sam's legacy by finding the girls he'd sought to ruin. But it wasn't like she could say that to Molly. Nobody wanted to be the one to say to a grieving partner, *"Hey, your dead fiancé? He was kind of a predatory asshole who assaulted women on campus,"* did they?

"I promise you I didn't do much," Daphne settled for instead. "And the police still have to be thorough in their investigation. Maybe they'll talk to some of Sam's students about what happened."

Molly's slim jaw set. "What would his students know about anything?"

Daphne held up a hand. "I have no idea. I'm sure the police are just covering their bases, you know, talking to faculty and staff and anybody else who knew Sam."

"But—" Molly wouldn't finish her sentence. Peals of

laughter erupted from outside the atrium. "You know what? I'm going to see if Leila needs anything in the kitchen."

Before Daphne could speak, Molly'd swept herself up and walked out.

Heat blossomed on Daphne's cheeks. She shouldn't have pushed. Things were already confusing enough without Daphne pretending to be a historical reenactor of the Spanish inquisition. A sudden light panic prickled at Molly's disappearance—she needed to find Cassidy and get out of here. The women in Sam Taylor's life had already suffered enough.

When she got to her feet and moved to the door, her toe caught on something soft, and she nearly tripped.

Daphne bent down to apprehend the culprit, and her fingers curled around the soft, ostrich skin handle of a very expensive bag—Molly's purse. She must have forgotten it when she jetted out.

The purse swung gently in Daphne's hand while a feeling bubbled up in her chest. She tried to gulp it back down, but it kept expanding, sucking up the oxygen in her lungs, clamming up her throat.

There was nothing for it—those pesky Ouverture instincts her father always crowed on about would not be ignored.

She opened the bag and rummaged through the contents, nudging aside tubes of lipstick and concealer, a hairbrush, some skin cream, lifting out Molly's wallet. Inside one of its flaps was a driver's license bearing the same blond hair and blue eyes of all the Henderson women, a health insurance card, a few business cards. Other than the shimmering American Express Black Card screeching "money," nothing was out of the ordinary. She picked up Molly's cell phone and woke it up, willing the photo that Molly had chosen as her screensaver to give her the password. She was surprised to see neon pink graffiti blasting out against red brick from somewhere in downtown Calliope: WOMEN ARE POWERFUL AND DANGEROUS.

The Femmes Fatales were never not a good time, Daphne mused, returning the phone to its bag. Too bad the renegade art group couldn't give her the password to unlock Molly's phone.

She rummaged through Molly's purse one last time, hoping for something—anything—that could be . . . she didn't even know. Interesting? Useful? A piece of gum was lodged in a crumpled-up toll receipt. A limousine company's business card lay at the bottom of the bag, crinkled at the edges.

Footsteps echoed out in the hall.

Daphne shoved the wallet back into Molly's purse and dropped it to the ground like a sack of potatoes.

A head popped around the door. "Daphne?"

Daphne could have passed out with relief—it was Leila.

Leila waved her on over. "Are you the one who brought that peanut stew that everyone is talking about?"

Oh, *crap.*

Daphne rushed out of the atrium, trailed by a chattering Leila.

"It smells delicious, Daphne, like this dish I ate at a Sudanese restaurant in The Hague once, right after that knife attack that we talked about that one time but before that terrible bombing incident, did I ever tell you that story? It involves a chef and some firecrackers—"

Daphne hurried into the foyer, keeping her eyes and ears open for mentions of her stew.

Leila didn't need Daphne much to continue her conversation. "I put the stew out on the table but I haven't started serving it yet because I did not know what temperature would be best for such a simple yet elegant dish. I would have microwaved it for you, but our microwave just broke—and I told myself, Leila, what are microwaves, anyway? They are technologies of terror. Surely you know, Daphne, that they can be turned into bombs?"

"I—"

"Of course you do. I saw a microwave bomb go off years ago on the streets of Cairo once when I was a teenager and my mother said that's it! She would never in her lifetime buy one of those things so I didn't grow up with one, and my mother just cooked everything from scratch, which makes me a disappointment because I love my microwave, even though you can't tell right now because ours broke last Saturday, right when Molly came back and I was about to bake this delicious chocolate lava cake that you can put into teacups for dessert. Dante thinks we need a new one, of course, but these American men are soft babies—except for that one you were seeing, who was so promising, Daphne, right? When will you see him next? Are you blushing again? You look so beautiful when you blush, Daphne, really, I mean you look beautiful all the time, but you look like a rose along the Nile when you smile like that and I swear that if you weren't dating Mr. Giant, I would try to fix you up with one of my brothers, and yes, before you can object, Cairo is very far away but there is Skype and Zoom and WhatsApp and even our iPhones can communicate with each other so that the distance doesn't feel quite so long, and really, I think I could arrange things just so—"

"That's very kind of you, Leila, but I—"

That's when Daphne caught the phrase she'd been hoping her food would deliver.

A thin voice, young and strong, sang to Daphne across Leila's running commentary. "I bet this is just what the peanut stew in Ghana tastes like."

"Leila, if you'll excuse me—no, of course—I promise I'll find you later," Daphne insisted. Her wax dress rustled while she moved toward the buffet table, where two girls cradled bowls of steaming stew and spoke to each other over the din.

Cassidy Reid stood by the pot, dressed in marigolds and sunbeams, murmuring to a friend. "You've gotta try it."

If Daphne didn't know any better, she'd think Cassidy was just some happy-go-lucky freshman giggling with friends. Nothing about her sweet grin, those gleaming box braids, the tapping of her feet in a happy dance at Fabiola's stew suggested that darkness had marred her life. Nothing about Cassidy indicated that anything was wrong at all, which made Daphne angrier than anything else. How many women had to pretend in public to be perfectly fine, when their bodies had been snatched from them?

She silently seethed while she made her way over to Cassidy and the two girls next to her. But like Cassidy, she chose to portray to the world a much happier fiction. Daphne gave Cassidy a wide smile. "I'm glad you like the stew."

"Are you Professor Ouverture?" Cassidy's face lit up. "Did you make it?"

Daphne nodded. "A family recipe."

"It's delicious," Cassidy said. "And your dress is so pretty. Did you get it here?"

"No," Daphne said, "my auntie Emmanuelle sent it to me from Abidjan."

Cassidy spoke shyly. "You're from Ivory Coast?"

Daphne couldn't help grinning. "And France. And New Orleans."

"I've always wanted to go to Africa," Cassidy replied, almost breathless. "Next semester I'm studying abroad in Ghana."

And just like that the pair were on a couch in a far corner, away from the crowd, talking about Senegalese hair braiders and where to find decent black soap in Calliope (the answer: just order it online). When Cassidy stood up to get herself another helping of stew, Daphne's resolve wavered. She hated that she might break this young student's trust by prying into her life. What if Cassidy ran away, vowing never to speak to Daphne again?

Cassidy returned with her bowl filled to the brim. "Is something wrong?" she asked.

Daphne hesitated. She didn't want to go through with this anymore. But she was a razor's edge away from learning the truth. She needed that truth to live. Cassidy might, too.

"Cassidy," Daphne said with a sigh, "I've been looking into terrible things that a professor did on campus." She swallowed. "Sam Taylor."

The light left Cassidy's face. Daphne was miserable at the thought that she was responsible for snuffing it out.

"And somebody mentioned that he might have been after you. Before he died, that is. And I . . ." Daphne didn't know what to say next. "Did he . . . ?"

Cassidy trained her gaze on the bowl of food in her lap. Her nod was almost imperceptible.

"Are you okay?" Daphne asked weakly, loathing her own cliché question.

Cassidy shrugged. "I mean, is anyone okay after something like that?"

"No." Daphne curled her fingers into fists. "No they're not."

The women around them smiled, laughed, and chatted underneath glittering lights and to the sounds of a jazz trio performing live and it took all of Daphne's strength to quell the nausea rising in her throat.

"I'm so sorry, Cassidy," Daphne choked out. "Would you be willing to talk to me about what happened?"

Cassidy measured Daphne up with distance. "Why?"

Daphne paused at that.

"Why do you want to talk to me about it?" Cassidy asked quietly. "I mean, I hear you're a wonderful professor on campus and all but I don't—I guess I don't understand how this is any of your business?"

"That's fair," Daphne said, the heat coming to her cheeks. "And it's not my business."

"Then why—"

"Because I worry," Daphne blurted out. "I worry constantly about what it's like for you and other girls on campus. I worry that you're alone, I worry that you don't have anyone protecting you from harm, I . . . I worry. I know what it's like to be the 'only one' in your classes. To be honest, that's all I've ever really known. I just thought things would be better for the next generation of students. I was wrong."

Daphne's heart was thudding in her rib cage while Cassidy spooned her stew in silence. Maybe she'd said too much. Maybe she'd said the wrong thing. Maybe she'd overstepped her bounds and should apolog—

"During my first week at Harrison a student in my dorm told me to go clean his room," Cassidy said. "Like I was his maid."

Rage blinded Daphne's vision.

"Not like there's anything wrong with being a janitor," Cassidy said quickly, seeing Daphne's face twist in anger. "But it stung. I made my family so proud by getting into Harrison. And then this happened?"

"At a reception last month a professor handed me her used napkin," Daphne replied.

"She did what?" Cassidy shrieked.

"Yup," Daphne said, gratified to see Cassidy loosen up a little. "A tiny old white lady. I forget what field. Maybe Russian literature?"

"Good lord." Cassidy placed her hands on her cheeks. "Professor Ouverture, does it ever get better?"

Daphne couldn't help but hear the pleading in Cassidy's tone, however much she might have tried to smother it out.

But Daphne couldn't lie. "I don't think so."

Cassidy's unreadable expression didn't change. "Does it get easier?"

Daphne let out a sigh. "I think you just learn not to care so much what some people think. It's hard and I'm not the best at it. But lately I've been feeling a bit more confident in who I am. I just need to try really hard to make sure I don't let other people take that feeling away from me."

She soaked up the warm colors of Leila's living room. "But I also know there are people on this campus who wish us harm. When it came to Sam Taylor, I think I let my guard down too much. I, um . . . He . . ."

Daphne ripped her gaze away, choosing to focus on a ruffled pillow. Her breathing became shallow. Why, oh, *why* was her brain choosing now to actually process all that Sam had done? She yanked a tissue out of her purse and dabbed at her watery eyes. She didn't want to think about how close she'd come to having her life taken away from her.

"Sorry . . ." Daphne choked out, mortified, trying to stop the tears from straining down her cheeks.

Cassidy said nothing, and Daphne didn't know how to read Cassidy's silence through her tears.

"You're right," Cassidy eventually said in a low whisper.

Cassidy's eyes darted around Leila's living room, checking for listeners. "Something did happen to me."

Daphne's heart thudded in her chest.

"But . . . it's complicated." Cassidy bit her lip. "I don't want to talk about it here."

Daphne wiped away her cheeks with the hem of her dress. "Cassidy, would you be upset if I suggested we talk to the police?"

Cassidy gave a disparaging look. "What for? The man's dead."

"True," Daphne said. What was there to gain from dredging up pain?

While women murmured or laughed in glimmering lights around them, the pair sat in silence. Daphne wanted to find a way to climb this insurmountable barrier. She couldn't let Cassidy down. She couldn't let *herself* down.

"Here's the thing," Daphne said. "Right now, everybody thinks Sam was a hero. And that's not fair to you or to me or to any of the other women out there he hurt. I want the truth about his life to come out in the most accurate portrayal possible."

Cassidy's previously sunny demeanor remained closed off, unreachable.

"How about this?" Daphne tried again. "I know someone who can probably give us the best advice about what to do next. He used to be a detective but he isn't anymore. Now he runs Earthseed."

"The bookstore?" Cassidy said, doubtful.

"Yes." Daphne nudged herself closer to Cassidy. "It's closed now but what if we talked to him first thing tomorrow morning? I trust him with what you have to share. I really do."

And much to Daphne's comfort, she meant it.

CHAPTER THIRTY-ONE

Daphne was ready for the weather to begin warming up. The clouds lurking above Harrison's campus were too dark, threatening rain, ripping away any chance students had of wearing sunglasses and soaking in any sun. She'd wanted to bring Chloe with her, if only to provide some furry comfort to Cassidy for the unpleasant task ahead, but had changed her mind at the last minute, unsure if Cassidy was comfortable around dogs. Many West African families—hers included—believed pets were best left outside of the home, but Daphne treated Chloe like family. She wished everyone could experience the joys of pet companionship.

A breeze rippled across her shoulders.

Maybe Daphne was lying to herself. Maybe she'd selfishly wanted Chloe to come because she was worried about what was soon to unfold. She'd spent the first hour of her listless sleep convincing herself that Cassidy wouldn't show up at all. She might change her mind. Or worse. What if someone tried to silence Cassidy for knowing too much about Sam? Ken was probably in hiding from the fallout but would that prevent him from smothering Cassidy's voice?

Daphne wrapped her purple coat around her tight, willing her body to stop shivering. Or shuddering. She couldn't tell the difference anymore.

As promised, she marched herself to Ginsburg Dormitory

where Cassidy was living, where steep gable roofs over pale stone sheltered two hundred women on campus. The first women's dorm at Harrison, Ginsburg was an homage to the Tudor style and the dour moral protestant politics that came with it. Like most universities, Harrison had kept women from enrolling at their institution until the 1920s, and even then they could only study "practical" degrees such as home economics. To keep the women under strict security lest they tempt a Harrison man, the university had built and padlocked Ginsburg Dormitory for them, never accepting the fact that the women were not the cause in Harrison's moral status declining.

The men were.

"Hi, Professor Ouverture!" Cassidy said, and Daphne's doubts and fears of Cassidy being a no-show melted away.

Cassidy huddled into her buttercup-yellow spring jacket as she pushed through the heavy glass doors to her dorm building, appearing far happier than the storm clouds above. In fact, if Daphne could describe Cassidy's mood, she'd have used the word "serene." Maybe it was Cassidy's cup of coffee gripped in her soft gloved hands that was responsible for her optimism. Maybe it was simply finally being listened to by someone in authority that gave Cassidy a reason to offer a soft smile. Regardless, while Daphne walked Cassidy through downtown Calliope and chatted, she found her own mood improving with each step down the tree-lined sidewalk to Earthseed Bookstore.

The door chimed soft bell tones when Daphne pushed it open and Daphne spotted Amber's buzz cut and an all-too-knowing grin.

"Professor Ouverture," Amber said, welcoming the pair in while balancing a stack of books in her arms. "I see you've brought a friend. You here to see Rowan?"

Of course that name did unspeakable things to Daphne's insides, and she schooled herself to keep it together for when he inevitably showed up. She still had to appear professional, after all, even if she couldn't say, exactly, what she needed to be professional about.

"Is he available?" Daphne asked.

"He will be in a minute," Amber replied. "Can I interest either of you in a collection of poetry while you wait? Rowan loves this new edition of W. S. Merwin."

"Does he now?" Daphne said, raising an eyebrow at Amber and her not-so-subtle suggestion.

Rowan's delightfully low voice cut off Amber's reply. "Daphne?"

And there he was, walking toward them, that now-familiar gangly walk of his Daphne's favorite thing since the invention of the baguette. Too bad that trailing behind him was Detective Ahmed in her usual black leather jacket, tight ponytail, and wary frown.

Detective Ahmed marched right up to her. "What are you doing here? Who's that with you?"

"Oh." Daphne blinked. "Um, hi, Detective, this is my student Cassidy."

Cassidy dutifully waved a shy hello, earning a smile from Rowan and a grunt of recognition from the detective.

"We'd stopped by to see if Rowan was free for a consultation."

"On what?"

"Um . . ." Daphne stalled while Cassidy flung her a panicked look. "On Ghanaian literature. She's interested in writing about it for a class."

Rowan's expression was polite if puzzled. Detective Ahmed's thick eyebrows drew together tight with suspicion.

"Can it wait?" Detective Ahmed asked.

Daphne shifted her feet. "I'd rather it didn't."

"My apologies, Daphne," Detective Ahmed said. "Let me be clearer for you: It's going to have to wait. I've asked Rowan to come down to the station with me. Andrew Westmount's driving in. We're going to charge him with murdering Sam Taylor."

CHAPTER THIRTY-TWO

On the drive down to the station with Rowan, Asma peeked at her reflection in the mirror. And yet again, she frowned at what she saw. Her amber eyes were too light, her hair too dark. Her sister Dina used to complain that Asma was made up of extremes—features, emotions, expressions—and today she felt the sting of that remark. Asma took another glance in the mirror. A woman with jet-black eyebrows and sallow skin stared back. It didn't matter how she felt, the face told her. It only mattered that she keep swimming.

Asma parked her car, nudging at Rowan in the passenger seat next to her. He was leaning against her car window, staring out into nothingness. He shifted when she nudged him again, listless.

"You still gonna watch the interview?" Asma asked.

"Yes," Rowan said, but an uncertainty sang out through his reply.

Asma gathered her notebook. "But what?"

Rowan fiddled with the volume knob on her car stereo. "Daphne had come to me with something important. Some*one* important. She wouldn't say what it was but . . ."

"You could tell," Asma finished.

Rowan blushed. But he nodded.

"I'll talk to her," Asma said. "After we nail Westmount's head to the wall."

Asma had put in too many long hours searching through bank accounts and old HR personnel rosters to turn away this opportunity to put Westmount behind bars. He was a crook, plain and simple, and a violent man. For years Asma had heard rumors of beatings, brutalities, and even death at Livington and she'd been unable to do a damn thing about them. It was men like Westmount who'd driven Rowan to quit, who'd tainted the work that she did on a daily basis to bring those who committed violent deeds to justice.

Justice? Rowan had asked her once. *What justice is there in prison?*

Then why are you here? She'd shot right back. *Life isn't a fairy tale like in one of your books, Rowan.*

He'd spouted some philosopher to her, someone claiming that punishment and rehabilitation could not be achieved within the same institution and oh, how they'd fought. It had taken weeks to get them back in the same room together. Another week to apologize. A week after that for Rowan to get that phone call from Earthseed Books, saying the owner had left Rowan the store in his will.

Okay, so fine, maybe Asma was a little too eager to charge Westmount but she believed—she had to believe—that taking out men like him was part of the necessary work to make society better. As far as she could tell, academics loved to create theories for a better world but Asma was the one who was trying to actually build one, one case at a time. Asma was for all kinds of changes to policing, sure, but at the end of the day she still believed that innocent people needed to be protected from bad ones and that it was her job to do that. Which meant holding people responsible for the crimes they'd committed. Fancy Harrison professors would call her reasoning simple but so be it: She didn't want to live in a world where people got away with murder.

Rowan might no longer see the good in her work but she did. And she still needed him to be on her team. She needed him to help her eliminate Westmount's potential to harm anyone ever again.

In the cold interview room, Andrew Westmount sat back wearing a small grin on his face that Asma longed to wipe off. Next to him was a woman in an equally expensive suit, her thick auburn hair swept up in a tight bun, and Asma barely stifled a groan. Some might call Johanna Piesling, attorney-at-law, a shark but Asma knew better: That woman was a pack of piranhas stripping you of your skin in under ten seconds.

"Detective Ahmed," Johanna said, flashing her perfect white teeth. "I wish I could say it's good to see you but I promised my husband I'd cut back on lying. How are your boys?"

Asma gritted her teeth. "Fine."

"I think one of mine left his glow-in-the-dark rock kit at your place the other day," Johanna said. "Can Bryan swing by and pick it up?"

Damnit, it was like a splinter had wedged under her fingernail already.

"Can we just get started?" Asma asked. "I'm here to go over a few facts. You know the names Anthony Kenton, Gavin Gray, and Jake Zimmerman?"

"Not that I can recall," Westmount replied, smooth as stone. "They don't ring a bell."

"See?" Johanna said. She placed her hands on the table and pushed herself up. "Easy peasy. He answered your question. We're done."

"But these men all claim to know you," Asma said. "In fact, they said you hired them."

"So?" Westmount scoffed. "Livington Prison employs hundreds of people. You can't expect me to know everybody who works for me."

"That's not what they say," Asma countered, shaking her head. "I'm tempted to believe them. They've shared too much."

Those cold blue eyes became slits. "Too much of what?"

Johanna wrapped her fingers around Westmount's forearm. "Don't say another word."

Asma pressed her shoulders hard into the back of her cold metal chair, contemplating her next move. "Mr. Westmount," she said into the cold, dark silence, "I'm going to have to read you your Miranda rights."

While Asma recited the words she'd memorized in her police academy training, Johanna reached for her phone and murmured something into it, probably to some panicked lackey.

Westmount's laugh was hollow. "You can't be serious."

"I am," Asma replied. "We're charging you with embezzlement, the conspiracy to murder Joey Camden, the conspiracy to abduct and murder Daphne Ouverture, and the murder of Sam Taylor."

"What?" Westmount shouted.

Johanna crossed her arms, unimpressed. "On what grounds? With what evidence?"

Asma had been waiting for this moment. Everything that she'd been working for since finding Sam's lifeless body on his living room rug had come to this.

"Game," Asma said, holding up the USB stick that Daphne had found in the Benson Art Museum.

"Set."

Asma plugged the USB stick into her laptop, pulling up a video of Joey Camden getting stabbed in the showers. In the mirror's reflection, a weathered face with cold blue eyes and silvery blond hair stared at the scene, indifferent.

"Match."

With her hands flat against the table Asma spread out sheets of paper like money: spreadsheets detailing the embezzlement scheme at Livington, bank transfers, and sworn testaments from Gray, Kenton, and Zimmerman, testifying that Westmount had paid them to make Daphne Ouverture "disappear."

Asma waited while Westmount picked over the pieces of evidence in silence.

"You know," he softly said, "I'd heard there was a video. Tossed it off as prison gossip until Sam told me he had it."

"Keep your mouth shut," Johanna hissed.

Asma gave a half-hearted shrug. "Turns out it wasn't."

The silence in the room stretched into the night. Asma followed Westmount's mind while it calculated its next moves, groping for trapdoors, escape windows, secret chutes. She waited to see just how long it would take for him to accept that he was walled in, that all exits were sealed off, that there was nowhere to run.

Johanna cleared her throat. She could have sworn that the red on Johanna's flawless cheeks hadn't come from makeup. "Detective Ahmed, I need a moment to speak to my client."

Asma grabbed her belongings. "Sure."

Waiting in the hallway while the pair of them conferred was the longest five minutes of Asma's life. She was just about to wonder whether she should knock on the door when it opened next to her.

Johanna's red-lipsticked lips were drawn tight. "We're ready."

"So am I."

Back inside, Asma sat across from a man used to a life of wealth and prestige beyond anything she'd ever known as the sixth daughter of Iraqi refugees. She should have felt something akin to pity at the sight of Westmount shivering and dazed. But Westmount's callous disregard for Daphne's life had burned her from the inside out.

"We're willing to negotiate," Johanna said.

It was Asma's turn to scoff. "On what?"

"On the embezzlement and abduction charges, for starters," Johanna continued. "But we're not going to budge on the murder of Sam Taylor. You're going to drop that charge."

"What?" Asma almost shot out of her seat. "Are you kidding? He's guilty as sin."

Westmount snapped out of his fog, his blue eyes wild. "I didn't kill that man."

"No," Asma corrected, "you ordered your men to do it for you. We have motive and DNA from the crime scene."

Johanna was not impressed. "Do you have *my client's* DNA?"

"It's only a matter of time before we match it," Asma said, to which Johanna simply snorted again and crossed her arms. "We also have ample correspondence between you and your men to prove conspiracy."

Johanna cocked her head to the side with pity. "Detective Ahmed—"

"Enough of the bullshit," Asma snarled. "You knew that Sam Taylor was working on an exposé about your prison." She waved her manila folder of notes in his face. "You and your men went to his place two weeks ago, stole his laptop and phone, and then you murdered him in his living room."

"Detective Ahmed," Johanna warned.

"And then you attacked Daphne Ouverture a couple of days later when you found out that there was still evidence out there incriminating you, even after you'd wiped his laptop clean. Or did Sam tell you that Daphne had the USB stick? Did he tell you that right before you killed him?"

"No," Westmount snipped. "You're getting this wrong."

"Andrew, shut up." Johanna leaned forward. "Detective Ahmed, this is unacceptable. If you don't stop badgering him we're walking right out of here and any deal is off the table."

"I need answers, Johanna," Asma replied between gritted teeth. "He either gives them now or in front of a jury."

Johanna's gray eyes were pinned on Asma. Hard. "Fine. Andrew? Talk."

The pale skin stretching over Westmount's strong cheekbones was taut with frustration. He squeezed his jaw, fuming. But he then sighed and dropped his shoulders, swiping a hand through his silvery mane.

"You're right that I went to Sam's house last week," he said. "We went to . . . confront him about his research."

"What time was this?" Asma asked.

"Around six at night," Westmount said. "We asked him about what he'd been collecting. We grabbed his laptop and that cocky son of a bitch laughed at us."

Recognition sparked like a crack of electricity along Asma's spine. An uneasiness pooled in her gut. That sounded too much like Sam for her liking—confident enough in his fate to laugh in the face of others.

Westmount continued. "He'd deleted everything on it already. And he told us it didn't matter if we destroyed his laptop because he had a backup copy of that video that we'd never find. It was with someone we didn't know. But I scrolled through his phone, Detectives, and saw all those photos of that Black girl. I figured she had to have them."

Asma rapped out a steady beat with the manila folder on the table. "So what's your alibi for the night Sam died?"

Westmount wore frustration and self-pity like a second suit when he let out a chuckle. "I don't have one."

Asma shook her head. "That's not good enough."

He raised his hands. "I know you don't believe me but it's the truth. I was driving back to Livington from Sam's house. I came home around seven that night. I was alone. My wife and kids were all at a school play. I ordered pizza and probably have a receipt somewhere to prove it."

Asma listened for the lie, finding only a ghostly absence in the silence after Westmount spoke. The doubt that had come to her in the dark each night whispered again at her temples like tendrils, soft and faint but achingly present. What had she gotten wrong? What had she missed?

"I didn't kill Sam," Westmount repeated.

Asma parted her lips to contradict him but surprised everyone by snapping them shut.

Westmount's teeth were bared as he snarled. "It's the *truth*."

CHAPTER THIRTY-THREE

"Now what?"

Cassidy and Daphne were back on the sidewalk in downtown Calliope, trudging their way back to campus. While people ate lunch on restaurant patios in the sun, the two of them wandered slowly down the pavement.

"I don't know," Daphne admitted.

She couldn't quite meet Cassidy's eye. Daphne had so wanted to give Cassidy an opportunity to safely share her experience. After being tossed aside by Detective Ahmed, Cassidy probably wanted nothing to do with Daphne anymore. And Daphne couldn't blame her.

They'd reached a park bench overlooking the sprawling campus lawn, its vast acreage bright and densely green with spring's new grasses. Daphne couldn't help but feel like a failure. She'd failed to protect students on campus. She'd failed to protect even herself. And now she'd failed Cassidy, too. But maybe she could try, just one more time, to correct her past mistakes.

"Cassidy," Daphne began, "I'll understand if you don't want to talk to me about what Sam did to you, but if I can be someone in your life to hold space for your pain and to bear witness to it, I'd be honored to. No strings attached. Okay?"

Cassidy's plump lips formed a small *o*.

"I mean . . ." Daphne's cheeks were furnaces. "You don't have to talk. I just—"

"I'm a delivery driver," Cassidy said. "I was just meant to drop off the food and go home."

Daphne hovered for a few moments before ushering them both to sit down on the bench. "When?"

"That night," Cassidy said. She joined Daphne on the bench. "The night Professor Taylor died."

The Big Bang had exploded the universe and created whole planets and a million different species in the time it took for Cassidy's statement to make its way into Daphne's brain. Those words were exactly what Daphne had wanted to hear. They were exactly what she'd been afraid to hear.

"It's not your fault," Daphne said. She reached over to grip Cassidy's hand. "What he did to you, it's not your fault."

Cassidy seemed to toy around with that idea while she squinted out onto the lawn.

"I was in his class, you know," Cassidy said. "Intro to Anthro? I was doing okay, getting B's. I could have done better but every time I tried to talk to him about my progress he was . . . he was weird to me. Cold one day, nice the next. I couldn't figure it out. And then like a month ago he pulled me into his office and tried to kiss me."

The campus lawn ahead of them blurred.

Daphne spoke quietly. "He did what?"

Cassidy picked at the skin on her palms. "And he said I could get an A in his class if I was willing to put my back into it. I just had to give him what he wanted."

It was almost a relief to feel so much rage coursing through her body. "That is disgusting. I'm so sorry."

Cassidy shrugged, still squinting ahead. "I went to the chair about it—Professor Miller? He said it was my word against Professor Taylor's and told me to drop it. So I did. It was too late in the semester to drop the class so I tried to avoid him after that, I really did," Cassidy said, turning to Daphne. "I only showed up to lecture after class had started and I sat in the back. I didn't go to office hours. I didn't want anything to do with him."

Daphne made sure to hold her gaze. "I believe you."

"Thanks," Cassidy said thickly.

"Can I ask what happened?" Daphne asked tentatively. "The night Professor Taylor died? You said you were there?"

"I drop off food deliveries on the weekends to make extra money," Cassidy said. "I'm on a good scholarship at Harrison but I still need to eat and my parents don't have much. It was actually my last delivery—Chinese takeout—and I got the address wrong. If only I'd read the address correctly, I—"

"No," Daphne cut her off. "Absolutely not. None of this is your fault. Understood? Professor Taylor was supposed to be a responsible adult. He was your professor. And he attacked you."

Cassidy rubbed her palms against her jeans.

"You are never to blame for this, okay?" Daphne said.

Cassidy nodded. "Okay. I knocked on the door to drop off the meal. It must have been around seven in the eve—"

Cassidy's mouth snapped shut. She closed her eyes. Her nostrils flared.

Daphne's heart started to pound. She didn't want to hear what came next.

"I was shocked when he opened the door. I wasn't expecting to see somebody I knew. And he looked rough," Cassidy said. "Terrible. Like he'd just gotten into a fight? I—I felt *bad* for him." She scoffed. "He was angry, pent up about something. His eyes were swelling shut and he had these really red marks on his neck but he basically barked at me to come inside and to bring the food into his kitchen. It wasn't even *his food*. I normally wouldn't have done that with any customer but he was my professor and

I wasn't trying to get on his bad side, so I did it. Of course it was when I tried to leave the kitchen that he ... when he ..."

It was so strange, how bright the sun had become while Cassidy slowly unfurled the darkest memory of her time at Harrison.

"I pushed him away. He laughed at me." The flickering of leaves from the oak tree towering above them cast shadows on Cassidy's brown skin. "He just laughed. Can laughs be mean, Professor? His was just so mean. I ran for the door and he tackled me down in the living room. He ... he wouldn't stop. I started screaming and he wouldn't stop. At some point he covered my mouth with his hand so tight I worried I was going to choke and die so I just ... stopped screaming. When he was done, I ran out of there as fast as I could.

"Did you know that I decided to go to the hospital the next day to get tested for a rape kit? I was on my way to report it to the police when I found out he'd been killed. And then I got scared everybody would think it was me who'd killed him. That's a cruel twist of fate, right?" Cassidy's hands formed two bone-cracking fists. "It's hard to accept that I'm never going to be able to confront him for what he did to me. Some days I'm okay with it. The man got what was coming to him. But other days I'm just angry—so, so angry. How am I supposed to get closure?"

Daphne sat frozen to the bench while Cassidy began to cry, terrified by how close she was to succumbing to this same fate. Belatedly she remembered a packet of tissues languishing in the bottom of her purse and grabbed one out for her.

"You know what's strange about that night, though?" Cassidy said, wiping her eyes with a tissue Daphne gave her. "I'm convinced somebody else was there."

Daphne didn't breathe. "Oh?"

"I mean, I didn't see anybody in the house. I just got this feeling, you know?"

"Fair." Daphne touched her forefinger to her bottom lip and thought about what her dad might ask in this situation. "Any cars in the driveway when you got there?"

"Ummm . . ." Cassidy squeezed her lips tight. "Yes, one. An Audi. Blue."

"How do you know that?" Daphne asked.

"Because my family drives Fords," Cassidy replied. "My dad has this whole thing about supporting Detroit automakers and Audis are on the blacklist."

Daphne pressed on. "Was the TV on when you came in?"

"No."

"Any food cooking in the kitchen?"

"I didn't smell anything."

"How about the sound of running water?"

Cassidy seemed to try that out. "Yes, in the bathroom."

"Did you use the bathroom?"

"No."

"Did Sam?"

"No." Cassidy's eyes widened. "Wait, does that mean—"

"I don't know," Daphne admitted, even while the neurons in her brain fired off like a ping-pong machine. "What time did you say this happened again?"

"Around seven?"

"How can you be so sure?"

"Well, the bells on campus always chime on the hour, right? I could hear them ringing at Professor Taylor's house."

Something was nagging at Daphne's brain, desperate to come out but she couldn't quite reach it. "Did you see anything when you left later?"

Cassidy's tone became frustrated. "Well, no, not really. Students were out. The carillon bells were chiming. I mean, it was just the usual—"

"*You.*"

Daphne whirled around at that familiar male voice—and dread plunged deep and hot into her stomach at the sight of Ken Miller, ragged and unkept, his face mottled red with rage, charging straight at her.

Daphne shot up off the bench. "Cassidy, please go get campus security here."

Cassidy gave her a puzzled look. "But—"

Daphne swept Cassidy up off the bench. "*Now.*"

Ken was in front of Daphne before she could even say goodbye to Cassidy. "You've ruined my life," he said, breathless. He loomed over her, crowding her, overwhelming her. "You've taken everything away from me."

Daphne watched helplessly from over Ken's shoulder while Cassidy fled with her phone to her ear to call security. She took several steps back. Ken filled in the empty space. Panic hitched in her chest.

"You had no right," he hissed. A fleck of his spit landed on Daphne's left cheek. Pressed up against the bench, Daphne found herself too scared to wipe it off. "You had no right."

"Ken—" Daphne tried.

"Are you happy?" Ken leaned over to shout in her face. "Is this what you wanted? To ruin my life?"

And somewhere inside Daphne, that tight string of fear and dread snapped. What rushed out in its place was anger, hot and molten, boiling its way up Daphne's entire body. In that moment, the purity of her rage upon her, it came to Daphne to place her palms on Ken's chest. And shove.

Hard.

Ken stumbled back. He waved out his arms in circles to catch himself from falling but it was too late. His ass landed with a thud on the grass.

"Leave me alone!" Daphne roared. "You know who ruined your life? You did, asshole."

Ken rolled around on the lawn with all the grace of a beached walrus. Two campus security guards were sprinting across the lawn in her direction, and Daphne could have sobbed in relief.

It was comical, really, witnessing two middle-aged men in uniforms tackle another middle-aged man in the throes of a temper tantrum. Ken kept rolling around in his favorite Patagonia sweater, his arms writhing against their restraints, hollering in broken refrain that Daphne had destroyed him.

Jesus, and some people think women are hysterical, Daphne thought while Ken screamed for the guards to let him go at once.

One of the guards struggling with Ken tipped his chin at Daphne. "Ma'am, are you okay?"

"Yes," Daphne said over Ken's sobs. "I am now."

IT TOOK a while for campus security to take her statement, for Ken to stop crying long enough to give his, for Daphne to reassure a shaken Cassidy that she was fine and that Cassidy should go back to her dorm, for the crowd of students who'd witnessed Ken's meltdown to dissipate. But eventually Daphne was able to wrest herself free from yet another incident on campus and head for her car to pick up Chloe. While she made her way across the lawn and down the path to the faculty parking lot, she blinked away Ken's shouts in her face and tried to remember what Cassidy had told her. Cassidy hadn't killed Sam.

Someone had been in the bathroom when Sam had attacked Cassidy. Daphne grumbled to herself as the carillon bells chimed the time, trying to remember what else Cassidy had told her.

Only when a student collided into her shoulder did Daphne notice that her feet had stopped moving.

Popcorn crackled in her mind.

"Sorry, I—"

But Daphne couldn't even finish her usual apology. The two-tone clanging of the carillon bells was almost deafening. But even louder was the rush of dawning flooding through her. The solution had been in front of her all along, given to her by the Femmes Fatales.

Like a sharp pinprick, the fluorescent scrawl of graffiti seared the frontal lobe of her brain.

WOMEN ARE POWERFUL AND DANGEROUS

"Oh, my God, of course. It's the *timing*, Daph," she hissed to herself. "It's the *timing* that matters."

The screensaver on Molly's cell phone was so bright in her mind it felt like a searing pain. But it wasn't the graffiti on it that jarred her anymore. *When* the Femmes Fatales had sprayed their message in downtown Calliope was all that mattered.

Daphne dodged a freshman zipping along on a pink scooter and made for the grassy lawn, narrowly missing a fat red squirrel digging up treasures. She parked herself on the steps of the anthropology building, her mouth drier than after a second glass of red wine. She fought the urge to laugh, knowing how ridiculous she sounded when she spoke her revelation into the air. "I know who killed Sam."

CHAPTER THIRTY-FOUR

"Thank you so much for seeing me again on such short notice," Daphne said, taking her seat in one of the soft leather chairs in Molly Henderson's study. Her well-worn flats sank into an expensive cream and silver Persian rug that covered most of the hardwood floor.

"Well, your timing's not great, Daphne," Molly replied, gesturing to the chefs and waitstaff running through the hallway that led to the main kitchen. Three doors over in the Henderson family's regal banquet hall, a light jazz trio plucked out Cole Porter tunes for a crowd of nearly forty administrators gearing up for dinner that Wednesday night.

Molly closed the door softly behind her. She took a seat on a leather chair across from Daphne, her blue eyes wide and open. "You said you wanted to talk to me about Sam? How can I help?"

Daphne's stomach wasn't a pit of butterflies. It was more like a ravenous cavern of venom-spitting vipers who'd just spotted an innocent bunny wandering into its maw.

She didn't want to do this.

She desperately wanted to do this.

Daphne swallowed. "The painting of *Judith Slaying Holofernes* by Artemisia Gentileschi."

She was rewarded with a puzzled look from Molly. "Yes?"

Daphne spoke quickly, words tumbling out one after the other. "I read your dissertation on it."

Molly tilted her head. "Really?"

"Your introduction arguing for a feminist reading of Baroque symbolist portraiture?" Daphne stammered. "It was amazing."

"Thank you," Molly said, smiling politely—as always—and glancing impatiently once more down the bustling hallway.

Daphne nudged forward in her chair. "Is it true that the primary male figure—"

"Holofernes," Molly offered when Daphne reached for the word.

"Holofernes, yes," Daphne said. "Is it true that he's made to look like Artemisia Gentileschi's former teacher?"

Molly's smile stiffened, just a crack. "Well, yes."

Daphne waited. "And that her teacher was also her rapist?"

Molly evaluated Daphne again, her lips twitching. "Yes, he was. Gentileschi took him to court over his actions."

"Where he was tried and convicted," Daphne said.

"For two years." Molly's words were crisp. "His sentence lasted for two short, measly years. And then it was annulled. And just like that, he was put back out onto the streets."

"What a despicable form of justice," Daphne said.

Molly's voice hummed with disgust. "Wasn't it?"

"No wonder you wanted to write about her."

Any warmth that Molly had shown Daphne evaporated into thin air. She clapped eyes on Daphne with an icy stare. "Why would you think that her assault had anything to do with my interest in her art?"

"Because of your own," Daphne said.

It was a bomb she'd lobbed, one of many she hoped would land in the right spot at the right time. Time would tell its impact. Molly remained as poised as ever, confident in her

ability to feign ignorance, to charm and woo her sparring partner, even as Daphne saw right through her disguise.

Molly clasped her hands. "I'm afraid I don't understand."

"But I think you do," Daphne said, earning a look from
Molly. "It's why you had this unique ability to identify with
your historical subject. I mean, I have a connection to what I
study, too, I think, but it's more tied to French colonialism and
the transatlantic slave trade, so it's different. Not more or less
abstract, I should say, just . . . different."

"Daphne," Molly cut in, "is this going anywhere? Because I
really do have to—"

"I learned a little bit about your family the other day,"
Daphne said quietly. "It was so upsetting."

"Involving?" Molly said, almost mockingly.

"You and your uncle."

Rage exploded from Molly's eyes, darkening them to an
imperceptible shade of indigo.

"When did it start?" Daphne asked quietly. Molly didn't owe
her an answer. Molly didn't owe her anything. But any good
historian worth their salt would tell you that secrets didn't want
to be buried. It took too much energy, too much willpower to
fight off reality for too long.

So Daphne waited while Molly inspected her plush Persian
rug. She didn't mind that time slipped away while pots and pans
from the kitchen clanged softly in the distance. Time was the
historian's advantage, her curse, her gift.

"When I was nine," Molly said, her voice low. "Nine or ten.
I don't remember."

"When did it stop?"

Molly looked up, her question mocking. "When do you
think?"

"With his death," Daphne said, kindly. "Around the time of your high school graduation."

Molly's throat fluttered as she swallowed.

"My guess is," Daphne said, "that two things happened at the same time. First, that in spite of doing everything in your power to keep your uncle away from your sister, he'd begun to molest her, too, right?"

Molly's nod was barely noticeable to the naked eye.

"Second, you realized that once you went off to Yale for college, you'd no longer be able to protect her."

"I was already failing at it," Molly said, her voice thick and mottled. "She'd started acting out so much. Her behavior was only going to get worse."

"And you couldn't go to the police, could you?" Daphne asked.

Molly let out a bitter laugh. "Even in high school I knew the truth. The chances of my uncle ever getting prosecuted were always low, and the time he would have served—if he'd been found guilty—would have been just as short. But none of that mattered anyway, because he was connected to my family. Could you imagine the scandal if this had ever come to light? Have you *met* my father? Do you know who he is? He'd never allow this to become public knowledge. He never would have allowed this to go to trial."

"Definitely not," Daphne agreed.

"He still has a lot of influence," Molly warned.

"I'm sure." Daphne sighed, disappointed by Molly's threat. She really didn't want to have dispatch this next bomb. She had hoped, instead, that Molly would make the revelation of the truth easier for her. So much for hopes. "But Molly, if I figured out a murder from fifteen years ago—"

Molly raised her eyebrows. "Murder?"

"—then isn't it likely that I figured out what happened to Sam two weeks ago?"

Before Molly could interject, a woman in a tall chef's hat knocked on the door. "Ms. Henderson? Dinner's ready to be served."

It was like Molly had an off switch. Molly didn't so much as squint at Daphne when she recrossed her legs, tossing back her long blond hair over a shoulder, and straightened out her skirt. Sympathy oozed out of Molly's pores when she addressed the chef. "I'm so sorry, Leslie, but you're going to have to go along without me."

The chef frowned. "Are you sure, ma'am?"

"Positive." Molly's smile sparkled. "Let the guests know I'll be running late."

The door softly clicked shut and Daphne peered at Molly again. What an Emmy-winning performance. Her political family had turned Molly into a terrific actress.

But the Ouvertures knew how to turn themselves into knives.

Daphne pushed. Hard. "When did you discover that Sam was a rapist?"

Molly's mask slipped away, leaving only a pale face tortured by disgust and hatred.

"Two weeks ago?" Daphne offered. "That Saturday night when you murdered Sam?"

"I did no such thing," Molly hissed. "I was at my dress fitting in New York. I was flying back to Calliope when he was killed. I found his body, remember? An Uber dropped me off. I mean, really, Daphne, the police have confirmed all of this."

Daphne didn't dignify that with a response.

"*Women are powerful and dangerous*," Daphne said. "You quoted it. When I brought cake to your house?"

Molly was puzzled, impatient. "I don't under—"

"And I remember at the time finding it funny that you didn't know who Audre Lorde was—especially since you're opening up a center for women and the arts—but then you told me you'd seen it downtown. And then I saw the photo on your phone. And I don't know if you saw the Femmes Fatales' graffiti on the drive to or from Sam's place, but it was definitely gone by the time you told the police that you first landed back in town. The only way you could have known about that graffiti is if you'd been in Calliope."

"Well, maybe I didn't take that picture," Molly said. "Maybe someone else did and they sent it to me and I liked it so I saved it on my phone."

"I thought of that, too," Daphne said. "Really, I did. But then I started thinking about flight logs."

"And mine will show that I was on the flight," Molly said, as if speaking to a child. "Like I told the police, I caught my seven o'clock flight back to Calliope and got to Sam's house at eight-thirty, where I discovered him on the floor."

"It'll probably show that a 'Molly Henderson' boarded, true," Daphne replied. "But didn't you go to New York with your sister? And I wondered—what time did she fly back?"

Molly's skin turned alabaster.

"My guess is that your sister had boarded a flight right before yours," Daphne continued. "A last-minute standby upgrade to first class. She made it onto the plane just in time. Or, at least, someone with Melanie Henderson's ticket information did. Do you know how easy it is to switch tickets once you're through security? I mean, who's gonna check?"

There were venoms less toxic than Molly's glare.

"Which is why," Daphne said, "I'm going to suggest to Detective Ahmed to find video footage from JFK. I wonder what they're going to see? Or better yet, who they're going to see? Which Henderson sister will they find? You or Melanie?"

Molly jerked her head up at that. "You leave her out of this."

"Out of what?" Daphne demanded, calling Molly's bluff.

Molly flinched as if Daphne had slapped in the face.

No, secrets never wanted to be buried. And right now, the secret Molly was carrying burned through her like a freshly lit match to paper. Molly appeared brittle, sitting rigidly in her chair. It would take only one blink—one flap of her long pale lashes, heavily coated in mascara—for the fire to explode.

She clenched her teeth, almost baring them at Daphne.

"You want me to say it?" Molly asked, holding her head high. "Fine. I'll say it. I killed Sam. Not Melanie. Me."

Daphne's heart thundered in her chest. She should have felt victorious. She should have felt elated. But in the back of her mind, she knew she wasn't going to sleep tonight—not unless she was prepared for the nightmares to howl in her ears.

Daphne studied Molly—chin thrust out, blue eyes blazing. When Daphne's question left her lips, it was quiet, more of a resigned command. "How? What really happened that night?"

Molly dragged out a long breath from her lungs, biting her lips until Daphne worried she'd draw blood.

"We were having problems," Molly said. "Okay? I knew he could be such an outrageous flirt. I saw how he interacted with girls on campus. I wasn't blind. I tried to brush it off. He loved me. He'd asked me to marry him, at any rate—me. Nobody else. But then—" Molly's nostrils flared, as if smelling something pungent for the first time. "But then a sophomore named Olivia confronted me last month. I should have just left him then. I honestly should have."

"Why didn't you?"

Molly rubbed the armrest of her chair. "He promised he'd change. Isn't it always the same old story?"

"But he didn't."

"You're a historian, Daphne. You should know better than anyone," Molly said. "No. Men never change. In fact, he just got worse. Or maybe I realized he was worse than I thought. There I was in New York, trying on wedding gowns and sipping champagne and I was just so *angry*. At the airport on the way back Melanie suggested that I go home early and catch him in the act. So I took her flight and drove straight over to his place and let myself in. He must have been out for a walk. I went upstairs and got ready to shower. I was showering when he—"

Molly closed her eyes. "I heard that young girl's screams. And suddenly I was paralyzed. I was lying on the bathroom floor in a towel, just praying that this was all a nightmare that I'd wake up from soon."

She slumped back into her seat and rubbed her arms, her eyes vacant, trapped in her shower again.

"After that girl left, I was still in the bathroom. Shivering. I hadn't changed out of my towel. When Sam came in to relieve himself, he was startled to see me there. And I was shocked by his appearance. Disheveled, he had two bruised eyes, some marks on his throat. I didn't know what was going on or who had caused them.

"At first he tried to comfort me because he could tell I was freaked out. But once he realized what I'd witnessed, he told me I'd imagined the whole thing. Like I could be so easily duped. He put his clothes back on and headed downstairs. I followed him. I was just a blubbering mess. I asked what was going on with his face and why he'd raped that girl and that's when he turned on me. He got in my face, telling me I was just some stuck-up bitch who couldn't please him. That he'd *had* to do this—because of me. I think that's when I realized that the woman downstairs hadn't been his first—or wouldn't be his last. And that's when I also decided to do something about it."

Daphne nodded. "Just like with your uncle Magnus."

Molly's back was ramrod straight now. "I'd stopped a man once. I could do it again."

"A meat hammer?" Daphne asked.

The calm pallor of Molly's face didn't change. "It was in the kitchen. An engagement present from my parents. He'd been on the floor in the living room putting his scattered books back together on the shelves when I grabbed it and hit him on the head. It was all so easy, really."

"Where's the hammer now?" Daphne asked.

"Bleached and buried in my backyard." Molly shuddered. "To think that I let him kiss me, let him touch me."

"But you didn't know," Daphne said quietly.

"It doesn't matter, does it?" Molly's laugh scalded Daphne's skin. "All my life, I've fought against monsters like him. I've written about them, I've warned young women about them. And then to discover that I was engaged to one?"

Molly's laugh lengthened into deep sobs. Yanking out a spare tissue from a box nearby, Daphne handed it to Molly while tears continued to spill down. Rage and anguish shaking Molly's entire body. In that moment, Molly belonged in one of the very paintings she studied, where divine retribution and feminine sacrifice appear in brilliant brushstrokes against golden halos, bright white temples, and dark clouds of clapping thunder.

"But why kill him?" Daphne asked. "Why not just go to the police about him?"

Molly stared at Daphne, incredulous. "And have the world find out I was engaged to a rapist?"

Daphne jerked her head back and removed her hand.

"Daphne," Molly said, "I'm launching a new center for women and the arts at Harrison. Everything I've built up over the past decade, all of the work I've put into creating the kind of safe havens that Artemisia never had—that *I* never had—and I'm supposed to give that up because of him? Risk my new center and my new position because of him? Because of the gossip and the rumors that would follow my career for the rest of my life?"

Daphne blinked. She took a moment to formulate her quiet reply. "That doesn't give you the right to kill someone, Molly. It doesn't give you the right to throw me and all the other women that Sam hurt under the bus."

"Did you hear anything I said about my family?" Molly demanded, a haughtiness returning to her tone. "Going to the police means opening yourself up for scandal. We don't do that."

Daphne had to get through to Molly somehow. "Think about the girl he attacked. She's been terrified of telling anyone what happened to her. She was so scared that no one would believe her. How will she get closure if you cover this up?"

"I'm so sorry about that, Daphne," Molly said, wiping her cheek, "but that's not my concern. I hate that she's become a necessary sacrifice for the greater good but hopefully I can use my institute to fund students just like her one day."

It took a moment for Daphne's brain to catch up to her ears. "A scholarship?"

Molly cast her eyes down.

"Sam's assault is a trauma that Cassidy's going to live with for the rest of her life—which is something you know about," Daphne said, her voice rising. "And you're suggesting a *scholarship*?"

"What else should I do?" Molly asked.

"Apologize, for starters," Daphne said. "Do you know the hell she's been through—*I've* been through—because of Sam? And fine, you don't have to give a shit about me as one of your peers on campus—and I can well enough hold my own, Molly, I promise you that—but what about students like Cassidy? What's she supposed to do about what happened to her?"

"Keep quiet," Molly snapped. "That's what she *should* do if she's smart. It'll be my word against hers, anyway. And I promise you that mine carries more weight."

"It'll be my word against yours," Daphne repeated. "Where have we heard that before?"

Molly recoiled at Daphne's quip.

Daphne didn't care. She grabbed her phone and called Detective Ahmed's personal number. Tears spilled over for Cassidy, for girls like Branwen, for all of the young women on campus who had suffered from Sam and would face no protection or support from women like Molly.

"What—" Molly blinked. "What are you doing? Who are you calling?"

"It's too late," Daphne said. She stared at Sam's killer with a mix of disgust and pity, the ringtone bleeping into her ear. "The police already know that I'm here. Now I can tell them why."

CHAPTER THIRTY-FIVE

The news of Molly's arrest went as Daphne expected. The president of Harrison expressed her shock and dismay and promised to appoint a new director to the Institute for Women and the Arts that Molly had founded. A few colleagues promptly announced on social media that they "had never liked Molly" and had long been suspicious of her, and Daphne read their virtue signals with the eye roll they deserved. Harrison University's many graduate students, always the most unpredictable lot, were, from all accounts, divided over the question of Molly's innocence. To some, she was a feminist hero, a vigilante who'd sought justice in the face of such evil and should be honored with a plaque where Sam's office had once been. To others, she was a cold-blooded killer whose decision to bludgeon Sam to death with a meat hammer was evidence of privilege and its dangerous ability to shield wealthy white people from reality, thus calling for yet another teach-in on Robin DiAngelo's book *White Fragility*.

What gratified Daphne the most, however, was the shifting tide turning against Sam Taylor. So far, mercifully, the women he'd attacked remained anonymous to public view, shielded from stares or criticisms that they should have "just fought back" or accusations that they were liars. Sam's monstrous actions, on the other hand, were finally on full display.

Daphne couldn't undo the past, however much she wished.

She'd give anything to vacuum up the pain Sam had caused to each girl, as if removing a blood stain from white carpet. She'd settled instead for cards and flowers, sent quietly to each young woman's dorm room, with a note that if they ever wanted to talk she'd be waiting. In the remaining week, she'd reached out to trusted faculty to raise money for students of color on campus facing emergencies.

Somewhere in the chaos of Molly's confession, Melanie's subsequent arrest for withholding information, and the next wave of public reaction rippling across Calliope, Daphne learned that Andrew Westmount, former director of Livington Prison, had been stabbed in his isolated cell away from the general population and was in critical condition, and she'd had to take an entire afternoon to battle away the many emotions that kept roaring up to the surface. Guilt over the fact that she'd placed him there, anger that he'd tried to abduct her, and guilt over feeling angry that he'd tried to abduct her. Only a walk with Chloe through the woods brought Daphne back to herself, and closer to accepting the truth that she was not responsible for the cascade of events that Westmount, Sam, and Molly had caused. It didn't always help her to sleep at night but it made the mornings easier to face.

She was almost finished packing up her backpack in her office when the knock on her door came.

"Daphne?" Miranda came in. "Ah, good, there you are. You're dressed rather nicely, aren't you?

"Oh." Daphne reached for her laptop to shove it in her bag. "I'm, uh, seeing someone a little later."

Miranda sized her up quicker than Daphne could catch a freshman fibbing on a pop quiz. "Is it that exceptionally tall and well-mannered detective I saw you with the other day?"

Daphne sent her a look. "Miranda . . ."

Miranda held up her hands. "Fair enough. I've stopped by to share some good and bad news."

"Oh?"

"Good news," Miranda said. "Ken's banned on campus. And the two board members he'd been colluding with have been forced to step down."

Daphne snorted. "Good riddance."

"Agreed," Miranda said. "All the chairs signed a letter calling for their resignations."

Daphne's forehead wrinkled at that. "Even the math department?"

"Even the math department." Miranda's grin deepened the lines around her mouth. "It turns out that in his short time as Dean, Ken Miller had the audacity to remove Complex Analysis as a requirement for majors, which, from the mathematicians' perspectives, might as well have been a hate crime."

Daphne let out a low whistle. "If that's what gets them to mutiny."

"And turn on their brethren. It's been a beautiful past twenty-four hours, really." Miranda sighed. "It's like we're witnessing the fall of Rome. Or the Romanovs. Or the beheading of Louis XVI."

"You know that led to the Reign of Terror, right?" Daphne said.

"Oh, so Robespierre got a little carried away." Miranda swatted away Daphne's warning with a hand. "Anyway, that's not the only news I have to share. Daphne, dear, I'm leaving you."

Daphne's brain had difficulty taking on what her ears were telling it. "What?"

"I'm becoming the new dean of the College," Miranda said,

her smile proud and wide. "I mean, after all, *someone* has to set this desiccated husk of a ship back on course. And who better to do it than me? Sadly, this means I won't be your history chair anymore, but at least I'll still be around on campus. And needless to say, I'll be very involved in your tenure case."

Blinking back tears, Daphne wrapped Miranda into a tight hug, earning the same awkward pats that Miranda tended to give Chloe. Harrison University was going to be in good hands under Miranda's leadership. Daphne had been right to fight to stay here, where squirrels threw down over pizza slices and Chef Marcel's freshly baked pastries awaited and her students came to her fresh-faced and eager to envision a better world.

"See?" Miranda said, wiping away at Daphne's cheeks with her sleeve. "Occasionally we historians do get a say in how life turns out."

Daphne considered Miranda's beatitude of hope as she headed for the faculty parking lot, got into her car, and began her drive home. So many stories deserved to be written that were left out in the cold. It was the historian's job to correct society's gross errors, to point out the past in order to steer the present and the future. Her own future, however, remained uncertain.

Daphne began to itch on the drive. The more her car zoomed home, the more nerves played with her mind, clammed up her throat, quickened her heart.

What if this doesn't work?

She dialed her dad, eager to hear his comforting voice.

"Daphne Aminata Ouverture." Daphne's heart quickened at her mother's growl of displeasure through her car speakers. "You choose to call your father instead of answering my phone calls?"

"That's not true," Daphne protested. "I just . . . uh . . . I was busy."

"With what? You are no longer getting yourself killed by

sticking your nose into other people's business, so what could occupy your newfound time?"

"*Maman.*"

"Are you hoping to disgrace your family again by using my cooking that I made for you to spy on innocent strangers?" Fabiola demanded.

"Daddy told you?"

But Fabiola was just warming up. "After all that I have done for you, after the care I took to make sure you received a proper education—"

"Hi, honey." Jim's loving baritone voice came through the car and Daphne breathed a sigh of relief. "Sorry about that. Your mother's just a little upset, is all."

Daphne scowled. "She wasn't even here for any of this!"

Jim was silent for a brief moment. "Come to think of it, I think that's why she's upset. Next time we should make sure to include her."

Daphne almost dropped her phone. "*Next* time?"

"How's Calliope, honey?" Jim asked. "You doing okay?"

Her father's love for her rang through the phone and warmed her up on a chilly April day.

"I'm better now," she replied.

"What's up, pumpkin?"

"Oh," she sighed, "I just have to do something that I don't want to do, that's all."

"Grading?"

"No, something else."

"Ah." He must have figured it out from her tone. "Well, trust your Ouverture instincts. What are they telling you?"

She scowled. "That there's no getting around this."

"But what else are our Ouverture ancestors saying?"

"That's not how this works, Dad."

"Really? I'd say they've gotten you out of a couple of scrapes before. So come on, baby daughter. What's the Ouverture gut telling you?"

Hm. She thought for a moment until something clicked. "That this isn't the end."

"Well, then." His smile carried to her ears. "There's your answer, sugar plum. You want anything else? Your mother and I are about to walk up to Sacré Cœur. Shake off our jet lag."

"No, Dad," she said, smiling back. "We're good. Miss you."

"Miss you, too. But don't you worry, baby girl. I never stay gone for long."

DAPHNE WAITED.

Her butt felt like a solid block of ice frozen to the cold steps outside her front door. She stared out at the sun sinking down over the woods outside her home. A ways away, two squirrels got into it at the base of ancient oak tree, probably squabbling over some acorns or tulip bulbs that hadn't yet blossomed. She breathed in the fresh air, full of hope and promise, willing herself to feel the same.

When one of the squirrels ran down into the grass, its bushy tail shot up in surprise. Chloe was crouched low, ready to attack. The squirrel high-tailed it back. Triumphant in her ongoing war to terrorize woodland creatures, Chloe sprawled out underneath the tree's branches with a goofy grin on her face, her pink tongue dangling from one side. Chloe had no interest in chasing deer, possums, or skunks—she'd learned that one the hard way—but squirrels? They were her white whale, what she dreamed of at night when her paws trembled and jerked in the air and she woofed into the dark.

When her dog bounded across the meadow to the parking lot, Daphne leapt up off the cold ground. "Chloe! What has gotten into you?"

She followed Chloe's gaze to its destination and her pulse quickened.

A jumble of arms and legs ambled over to her, holding a flurry of something soft and black with patches of golden brown.

A shy half-smile greeted her. "Hi, Daphne."

Daphne stopped in her tracks. "Rowan, is that a puppy in your arms?"

"You know, I really like hearing you call me Rowan," he said, grinning. He stopped a foot away, his arms struggling to contain whatever was wriggling inside of them.

"Oh, what a sweet baby!" Daphne couldn't resist: She leaned into Rowan's chest and breathed in puppy smell. Her fingers cradled floppy ears and tiny teeth chomping on her fingers.

Rowan gently extricated Daphne's fingers from his puppy's mouth. "Charlie, stop that. We discussed this."

"Charlie?" She squinted up at Rowan. The sun and his eager smile almost blinded her.

His face was full of pride. "Yes, she came with that name."

"From where?"

"Happy Valley Rescue," he said. He hesitated for a second and then swooped down to give Daphne a peck on the cheek. "I met her last week. I think I like it. The name, that is. She reminds me of Charlie Chaplin and his slapstick comedy."

Daphne scooped up Charlie from his arms, and within half a second her face was covered with tiny puppy kisses. When she heard whining, she looked down to see Chloe circling in and out of their legs.

Daphne squinted at Rowan. "Do you have a leash? Do you want to see if Chloe and Charlie will get along?"

Rowan's soft lips parted in alarm. "Why wouldn't they?"

She reached out and rubbed his arm, in spite of herself, in spite of what she knew. "Don't worry," she said. "Chloe loves everyone. Charlie will be fine."

Sure enough, after just a few sniffs, Chloe took to Charlie, and the two of them bobbed off into the grass. Chloe kept her play light, perhaps recognizing from Charlie's awkward puppy romping that she was dealing with a newbie. She'd been a mother once, Daphne remembered. Perhaps some instincts never went away.

She stole a glance at Rowan's gray eyes, brilliant with light and laughter at their dogs playing in the meadow. She wanted so badly to have this. To have the two of them facing the sunset with their dogs every day, the minutes and hours passing by. It was within reach, too, depending on how the next five minutes went.

"Before I forget, I have a present for you." Rowan turned to his messenger bag and pulled out a weathered copy of a familiar book and handed it to her.

"*Papillon*!" Daphne twirled it around in her fingers. "The book that started it all."

"I suppose you never wish to see it again," Rowan replied.

"Correct."

"Extremely fair. I'm happy to help you burn it if you'd like."

That earned a giggle from her.

"You wanted to see me, Daphne?" He beamed at her with such adoration that she wanted to cup his face in her hands and kiss it.

"Let me get you a drink first. Water? Wine?"

"Water would be great. Charlie kept me up most of the night. Bathroom breaks, puppy energy, and the like. But that's all normal, isn't it?"

"Yeah, those first two weeks are a nightmare. But she'll settle into a routine soon enough."

Daphne ducked into the kitchen and emerged with two glasses of water and a plate with brie and crackers. She paused in the doorway, letting herself enjoy the sight of Rowan entertaining the two dogs. Charlie kept running back to Rowan for reassurance, which he gave her lovingly with long rubs down her back and soothing, quiet words.

Damnit, she was getting jittery again.

"Daphne, what's wrong?" he asked once she sat down, his eyes caressing her face.

Daphne's fingers reached up against her will to cradle his jaw, smoothed out his worried brows. "Rowan, I won't be able to see you for a while."

Rowan flinched, as if stung. The glass of water in his hands tipped to the side, spilling out. He corrected course but it was too late. The damage had been done. "But—"

Daphne leaned over and crushed her mouth to his in a furious embrace. When she pulled back, she gave him her widest smile. "It's not because I don't like you. Of course I do. I want to spend every second with you. But I just got a research grant to go to France. I'm going to be away until August."

Shock widened those pretty gray eyes of his. "When do you leave?"

"Next week," she replied.

She thought she'd be able to tell Rowan these words without destroying her own soul. Until Rowan had ambled over to her with a puppy in his arms and a smile that made her feel like she was the rarest prize of them all.

"Congratulations," he said, but disappointment had already seeped into his spine and bent his rail-thin frame. Loneliness took over him like a second skin, making Daphne want to break all of the promises she'd made to her fragile future.

Rowan stared ahead. "Would you, uh, could we still—I mean if you—"

Daphne kissed him again for so long that he was blinking when she finally pulled away.

"I came up with an idea," Daphne said, her own lips bruised and warm. She inhaled a quick breath, letting it out through her nose.

"You did?" Rowan said, catching his breath.

Daphne grinned. "If you're up for it."

"I should hope that you would know by now that I'd try anything for you," Rowan replied with a tiny frown.

Daphne's eyes watered. "Right. Um . . ." She inhaled a quick breath, letting it out through her nose. "How would you feel about starting our own library?"

A spark of hope lit inside him. "How would this work?"

"I don't really know," Daphne replied. She wrapped her arms around his thin chest to snuggle into his warmth. "I just thought we might send each other books to read while I'm away. I'd send you a book and vice versa. Could I interest you in French editions of Octavia Butler, perhaps?"

Daphne's stomach flipped at his devilish grin. He swooped her into a hug that quickly dissolved into a kiss and suddenly Daphne was drowning, just drowning in his arms, and vowing to cancel her plane ticket to France.

She gasped as he pulled away and held her at arm's length.

"What would you like?" His eyes searched hers. "Toni Morrison's *The Bluest Eye*? You said that you're still missing a copy."

"Oh, no pressure," Daphne said. "I can get one some other time. But I should probably read more Octavia Butler if we're going to keep seeing each other. Maybe her book *Kindred*?"

Rowan frowned. "I find the Xenogenesis trilogy a more generative entryway into Butler's oeuvre."

"Of course you do," Daphne said. "And I'm sure you have all kinds of thoughts to share about Butler's indictment of humanity's self-destructive nature." She leaned forward to kiss him on the lips to stop him from speaking. "You can pontificate on the topic later. Slip me a note in the book?"

A shy grin parted his soft lips.

Daphne groaned. "Man, I'm going to absolutely hate waiting these next couple of months. But if we can pass the time by reading together, it'll be worth it."

"And if it isn't?" Rowan's eyes shone with worry. "Worth it, that is. What if you change your mind?"

"What if you change yours?"

Rowan's lips twitched. "I'd rather you didn't ask such absurd questions, Daphne."

"Well, that settles it then, doesn't it?" She slipped him a piece of paper with her French address on it. She let the softness of his lips warm hers. "Figure out what you want me to read soon. I'll be waiting."

CHAPTER THIRTY-SIX

Hot sun baked the warm grayed stones in the path that led Daphne through a sturdy pair of wrought iron gates and into a small park, where she passed by families out for an afternoon stroll and old men playing boules in the sand. Children screamed in the playground, packed as ever, and even in this heat a grandmother roused up the energy to tut her displeasure. Under the dappled shade of towering cypress trees on one of Marseille's many town squares, Daphne swung past her favorite fruit and vegetable market, sellers shouting out offerings of lavender honey, bunches of thyme, and strawberries ripe to bursting. She'd come back to it in a moment, after she'd fetched Chloe for their own evening walk. Then, she'd allow vendors to sweet talk her into buying some fresh carrots for Chloe ("c'est sain!") and white asparagus for herself ("c'est bon!") and visit an overstuffed bookstore where she'd struck up a friendship with the owner over Patrick Chamoiseau's 1992 novel, *Texaco*, both having an affinity, it turned out, for Martinican literary fiction that questioned what it meant to be creole.

June was Daphne's favorite month in Provence, when whatever was left of the bitter cold Provençal wind known as the mistral had been evaporated by a summer heat that, while innocent enough in the early months, sent people scurrying for shaded alleyways and covered side streets by July. While the

French colonial archives might not have air-conditioning, its modernist, cubic design kept the interior cool and dark, away from the blanching sun, and Daphne had adjusted, as always, to life away from AC, where shutters and cool evenings kept the heat away.

Chloe's adjustment to the French coast was seamless, smothered as she was by the landlady's affection and her grandhumans' occasional visits to check in on her when they weren't harassing a different Ouverture child. Her dog was happiest sniffing around local city squares for scraps, receiving pets from children and grumpy old men alike, and, above all, going for long swims in the Mediterranean, just as Daphne suspected she would. In just ten minutes, Chloe could leave the cool first floor of Daphne's apartment building and dive into clear blue water that rivaled Jamaica's beaches. The look of pure glee that spread across Chloe's face when she splashed into the waves was reason enough for Daphne to vow to bring her back next summer.

Daphne's phone rang on the beach, right when she'd decided to tell Chloe it was time to go home. "Hi, Sadie."

Sadie didn't bother with the usual niceties. "Bitch, guess what?"

"It's nice to hear from you, too," Daphne said, willing her sarcasm to echo across the Atlantic. "I'm doing great, thanks for asking."

"Stop talking," Sadie replied, "Elise is engaged."

"She's *what*?" Daphne shrieked. "When did this happen?"

"Last night," Sadie replied. "You were dead asleep because you were in France but check your phone log. Elise whined that you weren't picking up her phone calls today."

"That's because I spent it in the archive, as usual," Daphne replied.

"Did you figure out who that letter belonged to?"

Occasionally Daphne solved vexing cases at the French colonial archive in exchange for free photocopying and a peek at an unprocessed box or two.

"A countess from the Loire Valley who'd run away with a mere banker," Daphne replied. "It was quite the scandal at the time. You see, she'd donated money to the British antislavery movement and he—that's not the point. Sadie, Elise is engaged? To who? She wasn't even dating anyone."

"It's 'to whom,' Daph," Sadie replied. "And I dunno, one of those minor princes that she collects like baseball cards proposed to her, who else?"

Daphne didn't even know what to say. "Which one is it? The guy from Thailand?"

"No."

"Switzerland?"

"No."

"Canary Islands?"

"No."

"Luxembourg?"

That earned a scoff. "As if she'd ever call him back again."

Daphne stared out in concentration. She was quickly running out of princes. "Good God not that Brunei one, I hope."

"Jesus, no, Daph, get a grip," Sadie said, impatient. "It's the Moroccan one."

"Oh." Daphne considered that. "Well, out of all of the princes, he sounded the least bad."

"I guess," Sadie said, doubtfully. "But he's a man and he's rich, so by nature that makes him awful."

"I just hope she knows what she's doing," Daphne said.

"Of course she doesn't," Sadie replied. "Elise lives in a world where people accidentally hand her Super Bowl tickets, what do you think is gonna happen?"

At least the trio had enjoyed their trip to Los Angeles, even if none of them knew how the game of American football worked.

"Anyway, you okay?" Sadie's voice was hesitant, and Daphne stopped trying to call Chloe over. "You, ah, haven't had any nightmares about fuck-face?"

"Your new moniker for Sam is inappropriate to say the absolute least, but no," Daphne promised. "I haven't. I'm okay."

She meant, it, too. Upon stepping foot in France, Daphne had vowed to exorcise him from her mind. She was done letting Sam live in it rent-free. She'd had enough of the dead. She'd much rather spend time with the living.

"Good," Sadie replied. "And how's the giant? Any books come in this week?"

"Not yet," Daphne admitted, ignoring the mix of disappointment and impatience tap-dancing on her chest.

It was Daphne's turn to receive a book from Rowan, and she'd been up late almost every night the week before trying to guess what he might pick. As the mistral in May had given way to the warm summer days of June, they'd exchanged Ralph Ellison's *Invisible Man* (his choice) and Alexandre Dumas's *The Count of Monte Cristo* (hers), a volume of Tracy K. Smith poetry that she hadn't enjoyed and a Leïla Slimani novel that he had. Last week she'd come to her mailbox only to find it empty. She doubted he'd lost interest but had no explanation for his delay.

"Text me when you get one," Sadie said.

"Not if?" Daphne asked, annoyed at her own whining.

"Not with that nerd," Sadie replied. "Honestly, Daph, I'm

surprised he hasn't just shipped the Library of Alexandria to your apartment yet."

An hour and a scoop of vanilla ice cream later, Daphne had finally convinced a soaking wet Chloe to walk back to her apartment when she twisted her key into her squeaky mailbox, quelling her feelings of hope. She peeled open her eyes to find a package bearing US postage. Inside was a gift wrapped carefully in paper, the lines of which were measured out with scientific accuracy to meet at the right creases. Mindful not to tear anything, she cut through the pieces of tape until the wrapping paper folded out like clockwork and a thin book with a robin's egg blue cover lay in her hands.

It was a first edition of Toni Morrison's *The Bluest Eye*.

She flipped it open. Her hand flew to her mouth when she spotted the delicate loops and swirls of Toni Morrison's autograph on the title page.

A small note was wedged in between pages like a bookmark and Daphne tugged it out to read it.

> *To complete your set.*
> *—Rowan*

Daphne closed the book. Placed it in her bag. And slunk into her apartment grinning like a sly cat. How lucky she was, Daphne thought, while Chloe shook herself off in the hallway, to have a life back in Calliope that she was looking forward to living.

ACKNOWLEDGMENTS

WRITING IS not, cannot, and will never be a solo endeavor. I have benefitted immensely from the advice, wisdom, and critical feedback of many, and without their care this book wouldn't exist.

Above all, I want to thank/complain about my sister, Erica, who, upon reading the first few pages of my ramblings, told me that my writing was great and that I should "keep going." That was, in fact, a lie. Those early pages were shit, Erica. But your leap of faith in my newly developing abilities was a lifeline in a dark time. (Un)fortunately, your unfounded optimism also persuaded me to write further, which led to years of joy and agony as I pushed out this novel, a traumatic intellectual process from which I have yet to recover. I curse you and I thank you, eebs.

At a key moment, Kellye Garrett scooped me up from the gibbering chaos of social media and plucked me into a supportive environment where I met fellow crime writers of color and learned about a world much larger than my own. Her intervention in my writing journey and her advice on navigating the publishing world have had a lasting impact and I am eternally grateful for it.

Elizabeth Little is a sneaky witch who changed my life and taught me how to push my prose and develop an ear for dialogue and did I mention that she changed my life???? I am so proud to call myself one of her mentees, even if I'm a bit terrified by her powers of perception. It is a wonderful and frightening thing to be so well-known. Honestly, I should file a lawsuit.

Michelle Richter took my book on during the early days of the pandemic and saw it through many drafts before bringing it to Soho and I thank her for showing me what it took to get a book ready for an editor's eye. Taj McCoy has been the most wonderful agent, sage, and guide through the publishing process since I signed on the dotted line. Her wisdom has been such a gift.

Everyone at Soho has been a joy to work with. Alexa Wejko has been a fearless editor and visionary and I demand that the world supply her with an unending stream of puppy videos henceforth and forthwith. I thank Rachel Kowal, Mia Manns, Sarah George, Lily DeTaeye, and Taz Urnov, for their endeavors, and I will never forget Juliet Grames insisting on Zoom that what matters above all is the prose. She's right.

Along the way, I've had the good luck to make writer friends who read through drafts and pitches of my work and celebrated small victories with me. Thank you, Elizabeth Brookbank, Joseph Crawford, Gigi Griffis, JL Lycette, Joe Passanisi, Delia Pitts, Irene Reed, and Manju Soni.

Friends have been my first readers. I thank Allison Alexy, Anne-Marie Angelo, Asma Baban, Rachel Barber, Kerstin Barndt, Domenic DeSocio, Jessi Grieser, Caroline Kita, Michelle Kuo, Emily Levin, Jennifer Lynn, Michelle Moyd, Tiffany Ng, Sarah Quinn, Renee Randall, Janum Sethi, Alex Stefaniak, Nafeesa Syeed, Lauren Stokes, Kim Teal, Priyanka Teeluck, Kristen Turner, and Clare Zuraw.

Adi Bharat and Annette Joseph-Gabriel graciously put up with my French queries. Sara-Jane Vigneault answered my questions about Aix and Marseille with patience and even joviality. Over bites of Honduran food, Avery Williamson made sense of a world I was struggling to understand. Hilary Bown constantly rescues me from myself.

Family has gotten me through the writing ups and downs. I'd be a puddle on the floor without Joel. I don't exactly know what I'd be without him, which probably smacks of codependency but after nearly twenty years of being together I might as well be truthful about it. Jonathan, thanks for all the "wellness checks" and for reminding me that Wendy's makes frosties. Malika and Rufus have been wonderful additions to my life. Sophie has been shining that "world's greatest manager" award on her desk since she was a puppy. I thank her for keeping me honest.